"THERE IS SO MUCH I DON'T KNOW ABOUT MEN."

"I don't know what to do when they pay me all those flowery compliments . . ." She ran her hand over his arm lightly. ". . . Or what to do when a man does that."

The raw desire she saw on his face made her pulse race out of control. "Do you think all those men were paying me those compliments because they want to get my fortune?" she asked in a raspy whisper.

He was very still. "No, you are absolutely wrong. It is because they all wanted to do this."

A thrill ran through her as he lowered his head and brought his lips to hers.

ALMOST A LADY

SONYA BIRMINGHAM

AVON BOOKS ◆ NEW YORK

ALMOST A LADY is an original publication of Avon Books. This work has never before appeared in book form. This work is a novel. Any similarity to actual persons or events is purely coincidental.

AVON BOOKS
A division of
The Hearst Corporation
1350 Avenue of the Americas
New York, New York 10019

Copyright © 1993 by Sonya Birmingham
Published by arrangement with the author
Library of Congress Catalog Card Number: 92-97463
ISBN: 0-380-76766-X

First Avon Books Printing: July 1993

AVON TRADEMARK REG. U.S. PAT. OFF. AND IN OTHER COUNTRIES, MARCA REGISTRADA, HECHO EN U.S.A.

Printed in the U.S.A.

RA   10   9   8   7   6   5   4   3   2   1

Almost a Lady is dedicated to my son and good friend, Tom Birmingham, a big Texan who loves to laugh and likes the old tales best. Like Alex, the hero of this book, he lives life by his own terms, and has a great yearning for the exotic lands. A true Renaissance man, he is equally at home discussing fine art or his special passion, the American wilderness. When he was just a boy, I told him to listen to his heart and he would be his own man. He did . . . and he is.

Tom . . . may your fields be green, your streams clear, and may the sun always warm your back.

With gratitude to George Bernard Shaw, who created the first Cockney Cinderella and believed in the spark of fire that can turn the lowliest of us into "wondrous creatures."

Chapter 1

London, 1880

"**S**ee these teeth marks on me 'and? The 'ellcat bit me, she did. A proper little devil is whot she is!" whined the chief matron of Holloway House of Detention as she tried to keep up with the tall well-built man striding in front of her.

But Alexander Chancery-Brown acted as if he hadn't heard her. The earl's face and keen gray eyes reflected an unyielding will and a steely strength of character. When they rounded the next corner, the matron noted the firm set of his handsome jaw and his aura of calm but potent masculinity.

Even at the ridiculous hour of five in the morning he was dressed in elegant evening attire—a black wool jacket that emphasized the width of his shoulders and close-fitting breeches which outlined his flat stomach and heavily muscled thighs. He wore a top hat and kid gloves, purchased from a shop much favored by the Prince of Wales himself.

"She fought with the prisoners in the common ward so much I 'ad to put 'er in with ole Sally," the matron went on, about to burst with frustration. "Why is the judge releasin' 'er to your custody, sir? And why 'ave you come to fetch 'er at *this* 'our of the mornin'?"

Alex disregarded her questions. He had no intention of explaining that he had made arrangements about the girl

1

the previous afternoon, but hadn't been able to face the task of taking responsibility for a scruffy street urchin then and there. Nor was it any of her concern that he had just left a late-night party and the warmth of a Cyprian's arms.

They arrived at a barred door and the matron reached for a jangling ring swinging from a cord at her waist. Alex casually leaned against the wall and slid her a weary gaze as she clicked a large key into the lock, then opened the creaking partition.

Before moving on, the matron sniffed and drew herself up importantly. "I tried placin' 'er in the kitchen, but she always causes trouble. Yesterday I went into 'er cell to break up a fight and she dashed a bleedin' chamber pot on me!"

Ignoring her again, Alex scanned the dim cells, looking for the girl. One cubicle housed an old harridan; the next, a heavily painted soiled dove, gowned in scarlet satin.

A sense of frustration filled his chest as he thought of what lay ahead of him. He had felt the same way six months ago when a band of Indian zealots stormed his compound in Delhi. At the time he had simply been Colonel Alexander Chancery-Brown of the Royal Indian Army instead of Lord Tavistock. During the lengthy battle his friend Major Hempstead had been at his side and they had shared a flask of fine Irish whiskey. Now Tom was discharged from the army and living in India while *he* was saddled with this preposterous responsibility only three weeks after setting foot on British soil.

He turned to the blowsy, heavyset matron, who wore a cheap blue uniform with frayed cuffs. "Would you be so kind as to show me where she is?" he asked, reining in his aggravation.

The woman brushed back a lock of gray hair. "She's jest to the left, milord, but like I said, you don't want 'er!"

Suddenly Alex heard screeching voices, clattering furniture, and ominous thuds. He and the matron rushed toward the shadowy cell and found a middle-aged woman and a slender girl rolling on the floor, kicking and pulling at each other's hair. At first the older woman seemed to have the best of the fight, then the filthy girl shrieked and heaved her aside. Quickly falling on top of her, the spitfire lit into the woman, all the time spilling out a string of abuse that blistered the air.

The matron ran to the cell and rattled a key into the lock. "Stop that!" she ordered, swinging open the door. "You'll kill 'er, you little devil!" She hurried to the girl and clasped her about the waist, then, tearing her away from the woman, she shoved the hoyden against the wall, where she crumpled to the floor. With a determined grimace, the matron picked up a bucket of water and splashed it into the girl's face.

The filthy creature shook her long silvery-blonde hair, splattering water droplets over the cell. Her eyes flashing, she rose to her feet.

Alex flicked a critical gaze over the minx. She was a willowy girl with a pale face, doe eyes, and wild, disheveled hair. Dripping locks brushed her rosy cheeks. Her expressive eyes seemed enormous in her dainty face—intense and arresting, they danced with defiance and a hint of sensuality. At first he thought they were brown, then he realized they were a deep blue, almost violet. Wet from the drenching, a pink bodice and a black skirt clung to her body. Even in rags, she projected an air of confidence that belied her delicate, childlike appearance.

Clearly the challenge would be even greater than he had expected. The general had called her lovely but poor, intelligent but uneducated. In truth, she was an unruly guttersnipe, a regular Whitechapel hellion.

And she was his alone for the next six months.

As he studied the girl, the matron snapped, "Well, 'ere she be, milord. The meanest li'l tart I ever knowed an' I'm right 'appy to be 'andin' 'er over to you!" She moved away to help up the other prisoner, who had raised herself to a sitting position.

Alex stripped off his gloves and tucked them away in

his waistcoat pocket. "Are you Pell Davis?" he asked sharply.

The girl straightened her rumpled clothes and ran a hand through her hair. "That's right. That's my name," she answered, giving him a cheeky grin that brought out a dimple in each cheek. "Whot's yours, guv'ner?"

Annoyance wrinkled his brow. Fresh from the military, he expected those below him in rank and social station to obey him swiftly and without questions. This bit of a girl was as pert and spicy as an Indian curry. "You impudent chit. I'm asking the questions here."

"That don't mean you can't answer a few, too!"

He arched a brow and parried, "You, miss, have a saucy tongue for someone in your predicament."

Looking somewhat abashed, she lowered her gaze.

He walked toward her, observing that even in the chilly April weather the child wore no shoes. As he stopped near her side, he caught a whiff of her dirty clothing and fixed her with a hard stare. "You were jailed for picking pockets, weren't you?"

She tossed back her tangled hair. "Maybe I was and maybe I wasn't. I'll admit I've picked a few pockets in my time, but nobody's proved nothin' concernin' this latest situation. I'm waitin' for a trail."

"I was told you were a homeless waif, but instead, it seems you're a second-rate criminal."

"I ain't no criminal," she came back hotly. "I obeys all the duly convoluted laws, I does. I never swipes nothin'— unless it's absolutely necessary. You knows, if the police spent as much time in the streets as they do in the pubs, the crime rate would fall by a shockin' rate."

Alex bit off a smile. "I see you're a philosopher as well as a thief."

"I ain't no thief, and I feels highly indigent that you would call me one!"

"The word is *indignant.*"

"That's whot I said." She pulled herself up to her full five feet, two inches, and raised her chin. "Sometimes I

cleans fish at Billingsgate, but my real profession is sellin'
fruit," she added, her voice shot with pride.

He walked about her, studying her delicate body, large
eyes, and almost childish mouth. "Indeed?" he said absently.

"*Yeah.* I always 'ave the best fruit in London . . . the
juiciest berries, the ripest plums, the sweetest apples. But
with all the rainy weather the strawberries 'ave been
mushy this spring. Things 'ave been shockin' bad lately."

"Really?" he said as he neared her side once more.

She widened her eyes as if his response might have
been an insult. "You ever try to sell five pecks of mushy
berries with 'em goin' more rotten on you every day? Bet
you ain't!"

Amusement momentarily softened Alex's mouth. "Why
were you fighting the other prisoner?" he asked casually.

Pell squared her shoulders and pulled a bit of cloth from
her bodice. "She stole my 'andkerchief, she did." She
brandished the tattered cloth and threw a contemptuous
look at the other prisoner. "I never could stand a blinkin'
thief!" she added, tucking the handkerchief away again.

Alex moved forward to better study her features. He
was now so close he could hear her raspy breath and feel
the warmth of her body. When he impulsively wiped a
smudge of dirt from her high cheekbone, she raised her
hand to slap him.

He swiftly caught her wrist, then pulled her face toward
him. "If you ever try that again, you'll regret it deeply."

His tone made a shiver run up her spine; she moved
away and nodded. "I understands you, guv'ner, but who's
to say you're man enough to back up your words?" Hands
on hips, she walked in a circle, raking him with a fiery
gaze. "I don't like gents touchin' me. Who the 'ell are you
anyway? Look at you, dressed up as cocky as the ace of
spades. You look so proud you wouldn't call the queen
your mum!"

He inclined his head for a moment as if she were a great
lady, then caught her troubled gaze. "My name is Alexan-

der Chancery-Brown—Lord Tavistock to you. I've come to take you out of Holloway."

"Come to take me out?" Laughing merrily, she threw back her head and light flickered over her white throat. "Quit snappin' my garter," she said, clasping her small hands over her bosom. "You wants to put me in one of those fancy 'ouses where men come to do whot they shouldn't. A bloke whot I knows does the same thing regular-like. 'E's always bailin' out bits of muslin and 'e's a bloody rum customer when 'e's drunk." She shook her finger at him. "You've got a good line, but the clothespin fell off. I'll 'ave you know I ain't 'avin' none of that business. I may 'ave picked a few pockets, but it was always from those who could lose a penny. I've been shockin' 'ard up, but I've always kept my legs together, I 'ave!"

"I don't want to put you in a house of prostitution, you little baggage." He cleared his throat, struggling to say the words he dreaded. "I'm going to take you home with me."

A confused look passed over her face, and for a moment she looked like a stunned child. "Go along, Bob," she breathed in hushed tones. "You're the strangest gent I ever knowed. There you stand, a fine figure of a man, and you wants to take 'ome the likes of *me*? You ain't 'alf doin' yourself proud, you know. I bet there's plenty of tidy-lookin' girls that would be glad to pig in with you and give you some of whot you fancy." Gradually her expression changed and she looked at him suspiciously. "Say, you ain't one of those queer blokes whot likes to get whipped on their bum, are you?"

In one swift movement, Alex clasped her arm, pulling her toward him. Lord, the obstinate child had almost tried him to the limits of his patience. It looked as if he'd have to drag her kicking and screaming into a world of wealth and position that most people would barter their souls to possess.

As she shrieked and struggled against him, the matron and the other prisoner watched with open mouths. At last the girl broke away and fell against the marred wall, her eyes wild with panic. "I said I ain't goin' with you! You could smack me on the 'ead with a bleedin' poker and I wouldn't go with you. Why should I? I 'as my standards, you know!"

Alex sighed heavily, mentally cursing the day he had promised the general to care for her. "Because, my lovely hellcat," he drawled blandly, "you are now a very wealthy young woman."

She stared at him with skeptical eyes. "Whot are you talkin' about?"

He gave her a faint smile and quietly said, "Your natural father, General Fairchild, has left you half of his fortune."

Pell blinked several times, trying to digest his words.

Alex took out his gloves and yanked them on, amused at the stunned look on her face. For a moment he thought he might have to present her with a bulging sack of gold coins before she would take him at his word. "All right, get your things together," he told her matter-of-factly. "We must leave right away."

She stood stock-still for a moment, then moistened her lips and ventured, "I . . . I still don't understand. If I'm the one whot's filthy rich, 'ow do you fit into all this, guv'ner?"

Alex smiled to himself. "Don't you understand, girl?" he said smoothly, extending his hand toward the open cell door. "You have just inherited a fabulous fortune, and fate, being the unpredictable female she is, has chosen me to teach you how to spend it."

Pell stared at Alex with puzzled eyes as their hired carriage clattered along Victoria Embankment, making its way toward the West End. The hackney had already passed King's College and Sommerset House, and on the other side of the dirty windowpane the sky was changing from black to silvery-pink. "Wait a minute," she said, slowly leaning forward. "Let me get this right. You wants to make me into a laidy?"

"It was your father's last request."

She sat back and straightened up. "Blimey, you've lost your mind! I could never be a laidy. Anyway, I ain't clapped eyes on the gent since I was seven years old." She shoved out her open hand. "But if money is the root of all evil, I wants to be evil to the root. Jest give me the cash and I'll be gettin' out at the next corner, thank you very much."

Alex gave a dry laugh. "I can't give you the money. It's not in my pocket, it's tied up in your father's investments. You'll receive it when you've met your obligations."

Pell met his gaze and drew in a shaky breath, noticing a warm sensation in the pit of her stomach. A feeling of delicious expectation that she did not understand glowed within her bosom as she studied his striking face. With his dark hair, rakish features, and heavily muscled body he was the best-looking man she had ever seen. Then she sighed. Good-looking or not, he was just another high-falutin' nob. "Whot gives you the right to tell me whot to do?" she retorted.

He pulled a paper from his vest and tapped it against his gloved hand, thinking she looked like a petulant child. "This does. It's an agreement between the general and myself. In simple terms it says I'm your guardian for six months. You will not be of age for several months anyway, so you need someone to see to your affairs. Until my guardianship is over, you will live on an allowance issued by your father's solicitor, Mr. Peebles ... and you will obey me."

She put her hand on the door lever and made a face. "And whot if I won't do it? Whot if I just jumps out of this carriage right now?"

He raised a brow and put away the paper. "Go ahead, but you won't get your money," he replied evenly.

Her eyes flashed. " 'Ow did you get me out of the detention 'ouse, anyway?" She chuckled. "Bribe the judge?"

Alex grinned, recognizing the irony of the situation. "No, I bribed the man you robbed. With the help of the police, I located him, and after I paid him a princely sum, he agreed to drop all charges against you."

A slow smile broke over her face. "You mean I don't 'ave to go to no trial?"

Alex gazed out the carriage window. "No, you don't have to stand trial or serve any time. Yesterday afternoon I presented papers to the judge saying you are now my ward, and he released you into my custody."

She laughed merrily, showing her dimples. "Ding dong bell and bloody 'ell. That was a tidy piece of work!"

"It was more than a *tidy piece of work*. It means that I'm responsible for you." Regarding her again, he scanned her graceful form, surprised to notice a surge of protectiveness welling within him. She was so small and ragged. Indeed, he had to fight the urge to smile every time he looked at her. Scrunched back in the seat like a cornered alley cat, she still wore her damp clothing, but had added a ratty coat which was missing several buttons. The garment was shorter than her skirt and split in places under the arm seams, and she sported a ridiculously large hat dripping with scarlet plumes that reminded him of a bedraggled rooster's tail.

He ran his gaze over the outlandish creation, astonished that something like it even existed. There had been an argument about the worthless hat before they left the detention house. Much to his embarrassment Pell had accused the matron of stealing it. At last the girl had found it in a clothing storeroom near the prison office, and, after shoving the hat on her head, walked from Holloway like a duchess.

Next she had insisted they go by a rotting tenement in Whitechapel so she could tell her best friend, Kid Glove Rosie, what had happened. Alex had remained in the carriage and watched a motley group of indigents cheer Pell as if she were royalty. They were still cheering as the vehicle rolled away into the predawn darkness.

Now he studied her face, looking for some resemblance to her father, the officer he knew so well. Other men he knew in high places had bastard children and promptly forgot them—but not the general, he thought with a mixture of pride and aggravation.

Pell scooted forward on the carriage seat, her eyes twinkling. "If I'm really a flaimin' 'eiress and wallowin' in velvet like you say, I'll tell you whot I wants," she proclaimed with childlike eagerness. "I wants to eat those fancy little birds with paper ruffles on their legs till I bust. And I wants to buy red dresses and neck ribbons till I don't 'ave a place to put 'em anymore." She paused for a breath, then went on with the enthusiasm of a starving man sitting down to a Christmas feast. "I'll need several carriages, and I wants to go to Covent Garden every day and show my friends 'ow I look dressed up in jewels and fine silk gowns with trains on 'em so long they drags out my tracks!"

He repressed a smile. "You will have your share of food and fripperies . . . but you'll be moving in different circles now. Your fortune will bring new obligations—and new friends. Besides that, your father asked me to protect you from anyone who might try to take advantage of your new position." He let his gaze roam over her face. "Don't you remember him at all?"

She felt tears prick her eyes as she looked at Victoria Embankment, where the Thames glistened like a river of silver. The first traffic had emerged and produce wagons from the country now rattled toward the center of the city.

"Blast if I knows," she said at last. "I seems to recollect a right proper old gent in slap-up fine clothes whot used to visit Mum from time to time when I was a little girl. But then we moved, and Mum cried a lot, and I never saw the old gent again." She heaved a great sigh and nervously fingered the armrest at her side. "Mum took up with Dandy Dan Dolan after we left the old gent. He was a gambler and ridin' 'igh on his luck when we met 'im." For a moment a knot of emotion welled within her throat. "Then 'is luck ran out."

As pink light flamed behind London's skyline, she swallowed hard, and looked at Alex again. "Right fond of 'is drops Dandy Dan was, an 'e beat us both. 'Is breath was always strong enough to crack a mirror and 'is swearin' 'ad a regular tune to it. Mum died when I was nine and Dan came after me, so's I smashed 'im on the 'ead and took off. Surprised 'im proper, I did. Fair made 'is timbers crack. Never seen 'im since. Bet somebody sliced 'is gullet. Either that or 'e died drinkin' cheap gin."

A flicker of surprise darkened Alex's eyes. "You've been on your own since you were nine?"

"Yeah, but it didn't matter none," she answered lightly. "I met Kid Glove Rosie and she got me into fruit-sellin'."

The chilly morning air had given her the sniffles and she wiped her nose on her sleeve.

Alex leaned forward and gave her his handkerchief.

She slowly accepted it, his action prompting a pleased glow within her. "Why, thank you, guv'ner," she ventured softly as she dabbed at her nose. "For the likes of me, 'andkerchiefs 'ave always been for showin', not for blowin'."

Alex smiled a little, but said nothing.

When he smiled, even a bit, she noticed a quickening thrill within her, and she wondered why this should be. Searching for a way to make him smile once more, she began to chatter. Having no idea what a grand figure like himself would be interested in, she went on about her life, regaling him with juicy tidbits of information.

But she fell silent as the hackney wheeled past Trafalgar Square and rumbled onto Haymarket. Here in the heart of the theatre district everything glistened with morning brightness. She had never seen this part of London from the luxury of a carriage and everything looked so magnificent that she trembled with excitement. When Her Majesty's Theatre appeared, she pressed her hands against the pane. "Gaa, 'ave a look at that, will you!"

Soon the hackney turned onto Leicester Square. For a while she listened to the clip-clop of the horses and the creak of the carriage, but then she turned to Alex, and suddenly blurted out, "Well, 'ow did it 'appen? 'Ow did the old bugger die?"

Alex's face softened again for a moment. "He was suffering from heart trouble and was very weak. One night last week he simply went to sleep and never woke up."

"You talks like you knew 'im personally."

He shifted upon the seat. "I did. I knew him in India—we were stationed together at Delhi. I was his staff judge advocate for ten years."

Confused by the lofty title, she wrinkled her nose. "Whot the 'ell does all that mean?"

"I was a military solicitor," Alex explained in measured tones. "General Fairchild, your father, was the commander of the 42nd Regiment of Foot. I gave him legal advice, read appeals, tried court marshals."

"Whot brought you back to London?"

"My older brother died a few months ago. I came back to settle his estate."

"And now *you're* a bleedin' lord, right?"

"That's correct. I'm an earl."

Alex sighed, and, crossing his legs, studied her face. He noticed she hardly opened her mouth when she spoke; it gave her speech a whining nasality that reminded him of the sound made by an ailing screech owl.

When Mayfair came into view, she became quiet, and, with an expression of awe, gazed at the tall magnolia-colored columns fronting the mansions. In this white-gloved world everything looked prosperous. A new barouche rolled past, glittering with black paint, and a few well-dressed gentlemen were now out, leaving for their offices. At long last, she turned from the window, and caught Alex's eye. "Why did the old sod do it? Why did 'e leave me somethin'?" she asked in a husky voice.

"I believe he wanted to make up for the life you lived," he said gently.

"But I was just an accident. Mum told me so. Nobody wanted me!"

"Evidently the general cared for you. He hired a detective to locate you when his health forced him to return from India."

"Why didn't 'e try to find me before?" she asked, clenching her small hands into fists.

"He couldn't," Alex answered smoothly. "You must understand, he was in India for many years."

Silent, she stared at the purple lilacs that blazed over Mayfair's black iron fences and pulled in a long breath. Alex could tell she was trying to gain control of herself before she looked at him again. "Whot is it you are now?" she asked in a bewildered voice. "I forgot."

"I'm your guardian and you are my ward. You must remember the words."

She regarded him sternly. "I ain't livin' with you without somebody else there, you knows. I wasn't raised on prunes and proverbs. I knows whot goes on in this old world, I does!"

Amusement rose within him that she could imagine he found her attractive with her smudged face, disheveled hair, and tattered clothes. But in all honesty, he had to admit that he actually *did* feel oddly drawn to her. Perhaps it was her finely molded face or the spirit he saw in her flashing eyes that touched something within him.

He let his gaze move over her. "My late mother's sister, Aunt Violet, will be sharing the mansion with us." With a pang of doubt, Alex considered his beloved, but dotty aunt, wishing there had been a better, more reliable chaperone, but being so long overseas, he could think of no one else. "She's kindly agreed to leave her little cottage in the country to chaperone you. She will take care of you every day while I'm at the House of Lords attending to my own business. And I'm hiring teachers for you who will be in and out of the house all day."

After the carriage turned onto Adam's Row, it gradually slowed and finally came to a stop before his Mayfair mansion.

Pell stared at the stately building with parted lips. Rising three gleaming stories, the Georgian mansion sat well back from the street and was surrounded by huge leafy trees. Dew still sparkled over the velvety lawn, and behind the building's Corinthian columns, tall windows glinted in the morning light.

Alex stepped from the carriage, then extended his hand and helped Pell to the paving stones. Her hand trembling a bit, she slid it away from his grasp and exclaimed, "Gawd's nightshirt! A whole crew of poor sufferin' bastards must 'ave broke their friggin' backs buildin' that great 'eap!"

Alex cocked his brow. "Young lady, while you're my ward you'll keep your vulgarisms to yourself and say nothing that would blister Aunt Violet's tender ears."

She gave him a cocky grin. "Keep your shirt on, guv'ner. I was just a bit surprised."

As she adjusted her hat, Alex clasped her arm. "Let us understand this before you enter my household. You must obey me in all things. If you misbehave you will answer to me personally. Do you understand?"

Her large eyes reflected her emotions as clearly as water reflects the changing color of the sky, and they now clouded with defiance. "Yeah, I understands." But then she pulled herself from Alex's hold. "The same to you with knobs on it, guv'ner!"

Chapter 2

$\sim\!\!\infty\!\!\sim$

At six that evening Alex sat at his library desk reflectively sipping a small glass of Old Bushmill's Irish whiskey. He had spent an unproductive day at the House of Lords, his concentration shattered by his thorny personal problems. In his hand, he now held one of his late brother's past-due bills—this one owed to a fashionable carriage-maker. Other similar statements were piled around him, all a testament to the last earl's reckless life.

Standing, he slowly crumpled the bill and tossed it on the desk, then, picking up his drink, he paced about the room. His father had been as much of a wastrel as his brother, and by now little of the family fortune remained. He could still remember the Christmas Eve when he was ten and how he had returned from boarding school, homesick and yearning to see his family. Dressed in his uniform and holding two presents in his lap, he had sat quietly in the drawing room waiting for his father and brother to come home. Only in the wee hours, after he had fallen asleep in his chair, did they stumble into the mansion, too drunk to notice his presence. After being helped to bed by the servants, they slept away Christmas day in an alcoholic daze while Alex sat at the dining table by himself.

Now, the large family estate in the Cotswolds, Stanton Hall, and the Mayfair mansion itself were heavily mortgaged, and if Alex couldn't come up with a large sum of money within a matter of months he would lose them both.

Sipping more whiskey, he ran his gaze over the familiar library. Outside, rain pattered against the windows, but the cozy room was filled with warmth and light. It was a man's room and smelled of teak, leather and old books. In the corner, a richly carved grandfather clock began to toll the hour, and the deep chimes made him think of a place halfway around the world.

This was the time when he and General Fairchild used to have their first drink of the evening, a sundowner, on the veranda of the officers' club in Delhi. The sound of the dripping rain flooded his mind with memories. He remembered leaving the Punjab on a train one rainy night; he could almost hear the sound of the clicking wheels, the rattling coaches, the throaty whistle as the train rattled through Rajasthan and Berar toward the port of Bombay.

Lord, how he had hated coming back to England to take up his responsibilities as a stiff-collared earl! As Alex paced and sipped his drink, he recalled ten wonderful years spent in India, an India of great sprawling plains and teeming jungles. At this moment he could almost feel the blistering heat, smell the fragrant bougainvillea blossoms, and see the gleam of a tiger's eyes as the animal lurked in the moist darkness waiting to attack an unsuspecting supply convoy.

In India there was constant danger and disease, but there was also challenge and excitement to move a man's heart and stir his blood. There had been skirmishes with fractious zealots, hunts for rogue elephants, dangerous expeditions to Burma, and treacherous ascents of the rocky Khyber Pass. There had also been fellowship with gentleman officers in plumed shakos, and comforting release in the arms of doe-eyed native women dressed in bright saris.

His life overseas had been good because it had purpose and meaning; in a moment of deep understanding, he realized that he would have to find a purpose for his life here too. With a set jaw, he decided that his purpose would be to pay the mountain of debts his father and brother had incurred and restore his family honor. Somehow, someway, he would make his life count for something here in England. He was now Lord Tavistock and must shoulder the responsibilities that came with the title.

There was, as well, the question of the girl. What a devil of a predicament that was! He almost wished that he'd told the general he couldn't possibly serve as her guardian. But he never could have refused his old friend. In many ways Alex felt closer to the general than to his own profligate father whom he had seen little of since childhood. A true friend, the general had taken him under his wing in India and guided him through a maze of military politics until his colonelcy was secure. After all that had passed between them he owed him not one favor, but many.

He'd made a promise to his old friend less than a month ago, during a visit to the general's sickbed.

The old officer's room was spacious but filled with fearfully elaborate furniture and trinkets from India. Red flames danced in the marble fireplace, warding off the chill of early spring. The over-warm chamber smelled of medicine and whiskey and the old man had been propped up in a huge canopied bed with pillows under his head. Silver hair crowned his head; his side whiskers and mustache were in need of trimming. Chi Chi, a boisterous pet monkey, scampered over the general's silken counterpane, chattering and playing with a ball.

In India the general had always dressed in a fine uniform, his back ramrod-straight, a swagger stick in hand. Now he had lost weight and he looked pale and defeated and terribly out of place. Alex saw at once that the man known as the Fox of the Punjab was dying, for the message was written on his face and in his eyes. Seeing him this way was so painful Alex wanted to leave, but he forced himself to take a chair beside the rumpled bed as if nothing had changed since they were in India, as if he were sitting down for a staff meeting in Delhi.

The general looked at him with sympathetic eyes. "Sorry to hear about your brother, Alex. Rotten shame. I read about it in the *Times*. Glad you could get back so swiftly to tidy up legal matters."

Alex thanked him for his concern and they spoke of India for a while. Then a great silence fell between them.

Feeling he should end the painful visit, Alex stood to leave. Just then Hadji, the general's Indian servant, entered the room carrying a tray with a teapot, china, and small sandwiches. Dressed in tightly fitted pants, a knee-length shirt, and a turban, the slender man's movements were slow and graceful and he reminded Alex of a benevolent shadow. He remembered the servant from Delhi and when their eyes met a smile flashed on the Indian's dark face.

"Colonel Alexander Chancery-Brown, my heart is being so glad to see you again!" the servant said, placing the tray on the general's bedside table. He looked up, his large brown eyes brimming with pleasure. "I am hoping you will stay a bit longer."

"Yes, stay. I told Hadji to prepare tea," the general added. "I have some fine Darjeeling you'll enjoy."

Alex knew it would be impossible to leave now so he took his seat once again. He and the old man talked of nothing in particular while the tea steeped, then, during an awkward pause, the general suddenly blurted out, "Blast it, I'm damn awkward with this small talk. I invited you here to ask a favor. This is very difficult for me."

"How can I help you, sir?" he asked quietly.

The old man struggled up on his pillows and looked toward Hadji. "I've changed my mind. Get rid of that blasted tea and bring us some whiskey. I want a drink."

Hadji looked at his master sternly. "Sahib, the doctor is saying you drink too much whiskey. I think—"

"Damn that prissy doctor," Fairchild cut him off. "The stuff works better than my blasted pills. Bring me a drink and give one to Alex, too! We've some important business to discuss."

The servant opened a nearby liquor cabinet and took out two glasses. The general struggled higher up in the bed, a resigned look on his face. "No use beating around the bush," he said. "I have a daughter and I want you to take care of her after I'm gone." The old man's eyes were bright and keen, but moist with emotion.

Shock rippled through Alex, but he remained quiet, sensing this wasn't the time to speak.

"She's my by-blow, of course. As you know, my wife Sabrina and I never had any children of our own." A bitter look crossed his face. "Right now, even as we're talking, Sabrina is on the other side of town socializing with her friends, just waiting for me to die, I'll wager."

Alex knew that although Sabrina's blood was blue, her heart was as cold as ice. Once, in India, the general had confided that the marriage was no more than an arrangement of convenience engineered by Sabrina's father.

There was a moment's pause before the old man added, "I sired the girl over eighteen years ago . . she goes by the name of Pell Davis." He breathed deeply and relaxed against the pillows once again. "The mother was a common woman, but warm and engaging. She was a singer. I met her in a tavern one night after one of my rambles. I came in out of the rain and there she stood, pretty and fetching in her cheap gown, entertaining a crowd of men with her lovely voice. One thing led to another and soon a child was on the way."

Hadji handed them both glasses of whiskey, then scooped up the chattering monkey and left them.

"How can you be sure the girl is yours, sir?" Alex asked as the old man sipped his whiskey.

"I provided shelter and food for this Davis woman for years after I met her. She saw no one but me, and she seemed quite happy. Then one day she demanded that I take the girl into my home. I knew it wouldn't work. Sabrina wouldn't have accepted Pell and she would have made the child's life miserable."

He looked up with glassy eyes. "The mother and I quarreled bitterly about it. She was swollen with hurt pride and told me to my face that Pell didn't need money from a father such as myself." He shook his head. "The woman was beautiful, but foolish. The only way she could think of to hurt me was to deprive me of the child. After we separated she met some flashy gambler and the pair vanished into the city with the girl. Shortly afterwards I received orders to sail for India in one month's time. Of course there were countless things to do, but I used every spare minute to walk the East End. Unfortunately, I never found the child.

"After the army sent me home due to my illness, I hired a detective," Fairchild continued. "He found the girl living in a tenement in Whitechapel in a wretched place called Cat and Wheel Alley."

"You trust this detective?"

The old man propped himself up on an elbow, his eyes flashing. "Yes. He's a damn good man. He asked the girl many questions about her mother—only things I would know. The girl answered everything correctly. Pell always had exceptional eyes, too. They are deep-blue, almost violet. I never forgot them."

"You want *me* to look after the girl, sir?" Alex asked, hoping he had misunderstood him.

"Yes. God knows I won't be here much longer." Despite his weak appearance, determination still lurked in his faded eyes. "I made a bundle in India, y'know. I'm leaving half of it to Pell."

Alex chuckled softly. "She won't have any idea how to spend it, sir."

"Exactly. That's your part in the game. I want you to be her guardian for six months. Teach her how to handle money; don't let her buy anything on credit and don't let anyone take advantage of her. More importantly, make a lady out of her. I've set aside an extra allotment for her coming-out ball. I want it done up in style."

The old man shifted his weight and looked up sternly. "During her transformation my lawyer, Mr. Peebles, will deliver an ample monthly allowance for her upkeep, but the funds will be put in your hands. I've decided to leave all my ready cash in Peebles's safe. I've known him for years and trust him implicitly. If I left my money in the

Bank of England, Sabrina would have it cleaned out before I was cold in the ground, and Pell, poor child, would get none. Six months after my death everyone will be called to Peebles's office."

"Everyone?"

"Yes. I'm leaving Sabrina the other half of my estate. It seems the decent thing to do. I'm putting her on an allowance for six months just like the Davis girl. Later they will each get their share of my estate when it is liquidated."

General Fairchild now began coughing violently.

Alex moved to his side, and taking his glass, eased him back against the pillows. "Don't try to talk, sir. You must rest now," he advised firmly.

Still coughing, Fairchild struggled up, holding out his frail arm. "No, we must talk, and you must help me," he pleaded. "I'm at my wit's end, and you're the only one who can help me!"

Alex studied the old man's red face and troubled eyes, then placed a hand on his shoulder, trying to calm him.

"It will be a perfect arrangement," the general continued in a rough voice, his coughing fit now passed. "While she's living with you, you can monitor her progress."

Alex's eyebrows went up as he suddenly realized that the general expected him to take her into his home.

"I want you to find her a good husband before your guardianship is over. Make sure he is someone who has his own money. I don't want any fortune hunters getting her inheritance. Of course you'll have to invent a background for her—use your own judgment. When the gentlemen find out she's an heiress, they'll all come knocking at your door. Mr. Peebles will have the distasteful duty of informing Sabrina she has to share my fortune, but I've instructed him to withhold all details about the girl."

"Let me understand this correctly," Alex said with growing misgiving. "You want me not only to play guardian to the girl, but also to live with her. Come now, sir, if you're really concerned with her reputation she shouldn't be living under my roof."

The general laughed. "Yes, I know all about your reputation with the ladies, but you'll find a chaperone. You must have some unattached female in your family. The old biddies may gossip a little, but anyone who knows you will understand you take the responsibility seriously." The old man looked him in the eye. "Besides, I need a man with courage, someone who can stare down the snobs if her story gets out and they whisper she's a bastard."

Before Alex could reply, the general had opened a nightstand drawer and pulled out a card. "Here's the detective's name and address. I'll have an agreement drawn up between us—a contract, if you will. Peebles will take care of it. Come here Friday afternoon and the papers will be ready for your signature."

Alex accepted the card, knowing he couldn't refuse the man who had done so much for him. After a few words of farewell, he said good-bye to his old friend and promised to return Friday.

Friday came and he visited the general for the last time. Mr. Peebles was there and they all drank whiskey and acted as if everything was normal, even though the general was so weak he could scarcely raise his head. Although Alex was filled with concern about the arrangement, he signed the papers, feeling he couldn't possibly refuse.

A few nights later, before the general could arrange a meeting between Pell and Alex, he died in his sleep, undoubtedly thinking that he had taken care of his long-lost daughter. The news saddened Alex, but he took some satisfaction in knowing that this old friend had died with a peaceful mind.

Alex sat down at his desk and placed his drink aside, then, opening the drawer, took out a copy of the agreement. Damnation, he thought dully, scanning the stipulations listed in fine handwriting. It wouldn't take much to convince him he should put a roll of money into the girl's hand and take her back to the East End. Then he looked at his signature on the agreement and remembered how much the general had meant to him. Besides that, he had given his word as an officer and a gentleman.

"I've been looking for you, Alex."

Gowned in a blue afternoon dress that contrasted nicely with her silvery hair, Aunt Violet stood at the library doors. She was a plump, soft-faced woman who at the moment looked tense and extremely tired. Like an old memory, the spicy-sweet scent of her patchouli perfume drifted toward him, a scent he remembered from his childhood when she reminded him of a fairy godmother. Now his fairy godmother looked completely done in—her blue eyes twitched a bit and her jeweled hand held a crumpled handkerchief instead of a magic wand. "Well, it's been quite a day, dear," she commented in a shaky voice. "But I did my best with the poor child."

"You have my sympathy."

Aunt Violet seated herself in a velvet-upholstered chair and absently twisted her handkerchief. "Yes, indeed. The creature shrieked all morning while I was disposing of her clothes."

"I can imagine," Alex drawled.

"And her colorful language made Buxley terribly upset. I cannot imagine a person acting as she does."

Alex raised his brows. "You might understand if you had seen the section of London where she was living."

Suddenly a strange look passed over Aunt Violet's face and she touched her forehead. "My, in all the excitement I think I've misplaced my spectacles." A troubled look on her face, she glanced about the room. "Have you seen them, dear? I must have them to read my novels, you know."

Alex knew she was addicted to the romantic fiction of Charles Reade and G. W. M. Reynolds and devoured their books voraciously. How unfortunate, he thought, that someone with such a romantic soul had never remarried. With a smile, he touched the crown of his head. "You haven't lost them, darling, you've just pushed them back on your head."

Looking embarrassed, the old lady gingerly touched the little half-spectacles perched atop her head. "Yes, well, there they are, aren't they? And it's a good place for them too," she said airily. "I believe I shall just leave them there in case I need them." She batted her eyelashes and gazed at Alex with a vague expression. "Now whatever were we talking about, anyway?"

"We were talking about the girl," Alex said gently.

Aunt Violet took a deep breath and patted her frilly bosom. "Oh, yes, yes, how could I forget?" She dabbed her handkerchief over her brow, then continued speaking in a quavering voice. "The maids carried the garments to the refuse barrel on the tip of a poker. Of course, she fought everyone to keep her precious hat. And it took three strong girls to hold her down and scrub her. To hear her squeals, you'd think she was melting like a sugar cube in hot water."

She pushed back a lock of hair that had escaped her bun. "When we laced her up in a corset, she ran down the upstairs hall barefooted, saying we were trying to squeeze her in two pieces. And when we tried to put shoes on her, she said they hurt her feet and curled her toes under like a child. And her hair . . . what a time we had with her hair! When we were combing out the tangles, she broke away from the maids and crawled out an open window onto the roof of the portico porch—in her underthings no less!"

Alex suppressed a smile. "How did you ever get her back in?"

Aunt Violet tapped her forehead and nodded wisely. "I offered her chocolate bonbons—a whole box of them, I'm afraid. She ate all of them while we finished her hair."

"Did you bring her to the dining room as I requested?"

"Yes, of course," she answered, gazing at him with tired eyes. "She sat there glum-faced, dressed in one of the upstairs maid's Sunday frocks. She was solemn as a judge—that is, until the food was served. Once the maid brought out the serving cart she . . ." Aunt Violet made a helpless gesture with her hands.

Alex raised his brow a fraction of an inch. "I believe I know the exact phrase you're searching for. She ate heartily?"

"Oh, merciful heavens, yes. How she devoured the food! I could scarcely eat for watching her. The child asked for second helpings of everything, and she belched, actually belched, after dessert!" Aunt Violet fanned herself with her lacy handkerchief. "I sent out for a few gowns. They were delivered late this afternoon. I'm afraid they cost one hundred and fifty guineas altogether."

Alex nodded, glad that the general had set aside quite a large sum of money for this purpose.

The old lady slowly rose from her chair. "It may take a while before I can persuade her to come down to dinner," she added in an apologetic tone. At the library entrance she paused. "Don't expect too much, now. We've just begun, you know. And we have so far to go!"

Alex stood and picked up a small picture from his desk. It was of himself, Major Hempstead, and General Fairchild. The picture had been taken after a pigsticking expedition in Bihar and the three were wearing pith helmets. Now he and Hempstead were separated by thousands of miles and the general was dead. It was hard to believe that the outlandish creature upstairs was his daughter, that the blood of one of England's finest military men ran in her veins.

Knowing he was now too involved in the situation to retrieve himself, Alex contemplated his plans for Pell. Surely the elocution, math, and history teachers he had hired for her would suffice. And of course a dance instructor would be needed to prepare her for the coming-out ball. Yes, he thought with a satisfied smile as he placed the picture aside. He would simply check on the chit's progress now and then. Firmly putting the problem of Pell Davis from his mind, he went upstairs to dress for dinner.

Thirty minutes later Pell walked about the softly lit library dressed in her new finery. As she moved, she brushed against delicate objets d'art and stumbled in her high-heeled shoes. Clutching the back of a chair to balance herself, she gasped and glanced about, glad that there was no one to see her. How out of place and awkward she felt! In her old loose comfortable clothes she had known who she was but now confused emotions stormed within her. Taking a deep breath, she told herself she couldn't let these high-falutin' nobs intimidate her. They might have restricted her breathing with a tightly laced corset, but they couldn't touch her heart or pride.

Scanning the interesting room, she spotted a group of framed military medals hanging on a narrow strip of paneling between the bookshelves. As she walked behind the desk and neared the colorful display, her gaze came to rest on a small bronze Maltese cross under glass. Thinking it was unusually pretty, she tracked her fingers over the glass, then, wondering just what the medal significd, she removed it from the wall and held it in her hands. Lost in thought, she didn't hear the steps in the hall.

Alex walked to the half-open library doors, and, adjusting his cuff links, paused before entering. Leisurely raising his gaze, he stared at a lovely lady who held one of his medals in her hands. For an instant, he thought she might be an unannounced visitor who had arrived for dinner. Then, with a sharp flash of surprise, he realized that the lady was Pell.

Clad in pink silk with tiny black polka dots, the girl who had rolled on the dirty floor of Holloway House of Detention just that morning now looked delightfully feminine. Her bustled gown had a snug bodice that clung to her slender waist and a low neckline that flattered her creamy bosom. Black lace flounces finishing the sleeves dripped over her slender hands.

With her soft blonde hair, long dark lashes, and rosy cheeks, the child reminded him of a Rubens angel—something he knew very well she was not! Yes, she was absolutely gorgeous and, unlike so many timid debutantes, she projected an aura of vitality that filled the library with life and warmth. He had hoped that she would look merely presentable. She now looked far more than presentable; she was smashing. Every rascal in London would want to bed her and he would have to contend with them all!

When Alex entered the room, Pell looked up with a start, and quickly laid the medal on his desk. She let her gaze wander over his tall frame. Dressed in dark evening clothes, he looked the perfect Mayfair gentleman, but his firm jaw and sun-bronzed face bespoke a life of adventure and command. And there was something sensual about his mouth that had a puzzling effect on her. For a moment neither spoke, then she asked, "Well, 'ow do I look? They worked on me for 'ours, you know."

He moved leisurely toward her, studying her quite openly. "You look very lovely indeed," he replied in a deep resonant voice. "In fact, the transformation is stunning." He paused near the desk, and she sensed that he was collecting his emotions. A twinkle in his gray eyes, he glanced at the framed medal that lay on the desk, only inches from her fingertips. "I see you're admiring one of my medals."

She glanced at the medal, then back at him. "Yeah. Whot is that funny little cross anyway?"

He raised a brow. "That *funny little cross,* as you put it, is the Victoria Cross, this country's highest military decoration. It was presented to me for surviving a three-day siege when Indian zealots stormed the compound there. My colleague Major Hempstead, and I—along with some other incredibly lucky bastards—were pinned down under attack with no food and water and precious little ammunition." He gave her a half-smile. "You hadn't planned on filching it, had you?" he asked in teasing tones.

Defiance flared up within her as she looked at his amused face. " 'Ow dare you accuse me of somethin' like that?" she stormed, crossing her arms and walking away from the desk. "When you accuse me of stealin', it just exasperates things between us!" She paused and glanced back over her shoulder. "I may just run off an' marry a lord, or a duke. Just so's I won't 'ave to listen to you no more."

Alex chuckled.

"Whot's so funny?" she snapped, tapping her foot on the floor.

"The word is *exacerbate,* and do you actually think a lord would marry someone who speaks as you do?"

"Why not?" she retorted. "I'm a bleedin' 'eiress, ain't I? The aristocracy is always 'ard up for money. I knows 'cause Kid Glove Rosie told me so."

"It doesn't matter how much money you have," he drawled. "If you have your sights set on a fashionable marriage you'll need to improve your grammar, diction, manners, and almost everything else. I've already engaged several teachers for you and they will start arriving for daily lessons tomorrow morning." He took a few steps toward her. "Don't you understand you must change? No one in society would marry you no matter how much they needed the money. Your presence would prove embarrassing."

Pell felt a stab of hurt at his words, but, not wanting him to know his comment had touched her, she quickly composed herself. She looked at his stern face, a knot of angry frustration lodging within her breast. "I don't know," she said roughly. "I just don't understand this laidy business." She bit her lip. "And I don't think I can do it." To her shame, her voice broke slightly.

"Of course, there are advantages to being a lady."

She raised her chin. "Like whot?"

"When you speak and act properly people will treat you with more respect."

She met his bemused gaze without flinching. "They treats me with respect *now* or I'll give 'em a pastin' they'll never forget!" Tossing back her curls, she walked to the window and let out a long, frustrated sigh. She was slowly beginning to understand how much hard work becoming a lady would take—but in her heart of hearts she was also beginning to understand that she must try.

At last she turned and locked gazes with him. "Gaa . . . whot a person 'as to do in this world to get along," she said. "It's shockin' 'ard, it is. I still don't believe you, but just in case there's a chance in 'ell you might be right, I'm goin' to give this laidyship business a try." She put her hands on her hips. "But as soon as I gets my fortune, I'll be out of 'ere quicker than 'ell can singe your 'air!"

She expected a sermon, but surprisingly he simply inclined his head in acknowledgment of her words.

She took a few steps toward him, then, noticing that her bustle had shifted, she whacked at the tilted undergarment, trying to straighten it.

"What in heaven is wrong with you now?" Alex drawled as he walked to her side.

She scanned his amused face. "Whot's wrong, the bloke asks. I'll tell you whot's wrong. I've been scrubbed and washed all day till my bleedin' 'ide is nearly wore off, then they's yankin' and tuggin' at my 'air, then they comes at me with this contraption and laces me up till I can't breathe, then they attaches this big wire basket to my behind and sticks some tight shoes on my sore feet and tells me 'ow gorgeous I looks! And now my bustle is on crooked and I can't get it straight. That's whot's wrong!"

Alex's lips quirked upward as she adjusted her lopsided bustle. "Your hair is completely different now. How do you like it?"

She moved to his desk and examined a beautiful black lacquer box, wondering what it might be. "Oh, I don't know. I sort of likes it, I guess. Least they ain't yankin' at me no more."

At this moment a maid poked her head into the library and announced dinner. Seeing Pell, her eyes widened and she quickly left.

Alex stood silently for a moment, then offered Pell his arm.

She felt angry and unsure, and she had no idea what the gesture meant. "Whot's the matter? Do you think I can't walk by myself?" she asked in an uncertain tone.

"It's the custom for a gentleman to escort a lady into dinner," he said quietly. "Your father would want your manners to be perfect. He would want you to be well acquainted with all the social niceties."

"I'll bet the general never 'ad to eat dinner with a wire basket tied on 'is bum either," she muttered tiredly.

When she reached his side, he slid his hand down her arm in an intimate caress, then placed it atop his own. To her surprise, her heart fluttered and she flushed with pleasure. Wondering why she should feel so confused yet excited, she took a few more steps, then made a face. "Gaa . . . 'ow do women walk in these tight little shoes?"

He grazed his fingers over her small white hand and smiled to himself, deciding for the first time that women did wear an abundance of useless, constricting clothing.

"I 'ad a good pair of boots last winter before some low-life stole 'em . . . and I wish I 'ad 'em right now," she piped up as they walked from the library.

"Why?" he asked with a chuckle.

"They keeps my feet warm; and I sleeps in 'em—that way I'm always ready for an emergency." She sniffed the air, which carried the mouth-watering aroma of a well-cooked beef roast. "I 'opes we's got a lot to eat, 'cause I feel emptier than a banker's 'eart. Why, I'm so 'ungry I could eat an ox and three pigs."

As they entered the dining room, a tender feeling shafted through Alex and he felt rather sorry for the little rapscallion, for he knew she would have to endure much more than an uncomfortable bustle and tight shoes to fit into the stuffy London society he knew so well. After escorting her to a place at the table, he sat down himself, and as they waited for Aunt Violet, he listened to her rattle on about a variety of things from the price of strawberries to the best place to buy used boots.

He realized that despite her speech and manners she was a very bright girl. Perhaps turning a pig's ear into a silk purse might be an interesting project after all. Yes, she was undeniably beautiful, though he preferred lush brunettes.

She wasn't his type at all. But plenty of men *did* like lively bits of blonde fluff, so finding her a husband wouldn't be a problem, he thought with some relief. It was nothing he couldn't handle. Nothing at all. He would simply assume the role of a firm but benevolent uncle. In six months his obligation would be over, she would be married to some fat merchant, and he would remember the whole episode as a ridiculous lark.

Chapter 3

⌒⊂━◯⊃⌒

The next morning after breakfast in her room, Pell came down the stairs dressed in a soft pink gown trimmed with rosebuds. Tension knotted inside of her for Alex had told her he wanted to test her knowledge before he left for the day and her tutors started appearing.

Once in the black-and-white tiled entry hall, she noticed that a door stood ajar toward the rear of the long room, beckoning her to investigate a part of the mansion she hadn't seen before. Curiosity guiding her footsteps, she pushed the door open and discovered a large chamber floored with intricately laid parquet squares. Three large crystal chandeliers hung from the ceiling, and morning light filtered about the edges of the room's pulled drapes, flickering over a cluster of dainty straight-backed chairs.

The sparsely furnished room puzzled Pell for a moment, then, as she gazed at a grand piano draped in white sheeting, she realized that the chamber was a ballroom. "Gaa," she murmured to herself, " 'ow rich the earl must be to 'ave a special room just for dancin'!"

As she gazed at the elegant ballroom, she thought of all that had happened since she arrived in the West End. Her life was just like a bleedin' fairy tale now, she thought with awe. Her head still spun when she considered the stroke of luck that had brought her to this fashionable part of London, all glitter and magic. How different from the squabbling, fighting, swearing, scolding, cursing streets of Whitechapel with the herring vendors before the tenements, and the cobblers in back of the tenements, and the Irish in the passageways.

But it seemed there was a price to be paid for these lovely things she now enjoyed. One had to observe scores of tiresome rules and give up every vestige of independent thinking, and speak only in a certain way. In that respect, the Mayfair mansion seemed no more than a gilded cage. "Well, I'll 'ave to stick it out," she mumbled under her breath, "until I can get my in'eritance from 'is nibs."

After she left the ballroom and quietly closed the door behind her, she walked into the library where Alex had told her they should meet. Sighing with pleasure, she scanned the book-lined room with wide eyes. The library held the scent of teakwood and projected a warm masculine ambience that filled her with pleasure. Seeing a large world globe, she twirled it about for a while, then sauntered to a lamp with crystal prisms and flicked the tinkling glass back and forth with her fingertips.

Next, she spied an etagere filled with a collection of exotic daggers, and with parted lips walked toward it. A shaft of morning light sparkled over the double-edged scimitars and bejeweled weapons, tempting her to run her fingers over their carved handles. Kneeling on the carpet, she carefully picked up one of the daggers from the bottom shelf and examined it, guessing it came from India. As she brushed against the etagere, several of the knives on a lower shelf toppled off onto the thick Oriental carpet. With a gasp, she gathered them up and replaced them, then, with a sinking feeling, she noticed a long horn-handled dagger was missing. Getting down on her hands and knees, she crawled under a long writing table, and, after a bit of looking, felt a wave of relief as she found the missing weapon.

"What in God's name are you doing?" came a firm voice.

No one needed to tell Pell that the voice belonged to Alex. Her heart lurching, she grabbed the dagger by the handle and lifted her head, smacking it on the bottom of the table. After rubbing the sore spot for a moment, she stared at Alex's polished boots, then ran her gaze over his tall frame. Dressed in a finely tailored Bond Street suit, he towered over her, a curious glint in his eyes. He wore the large ruby ring she had noticed the first moment she saw him, and light now glinted off the stone.

"Crawl out of there so I can have a look at you," he added in an uncompromising tone.

Lord, he was so close she could smell the spicy scent of his bay rum cologne and see a muscle working in his jaw. As he extended a strong hand to help her to her feet, a nervous pulse fluttered in her throat and she hid the dagger behind her back. Once on her feet, she pulled her hand away from his, wishing she were anyplace but the library.

Alex crossed his arms and paced before her, watching her rub the back of her head. Lord, what was the chit up to now? he wondered, studying her guilty expression. If all students were as unruly as she, no wonder schoolmasters always looked out of sorts. "What *were* you doing crouched beneath the writing table?" he drawled in an amused voice. "Inspecting the underside of the furniture for dust?"

She held out the dagger by the long handle. "Some of these funny knives started fallin' from that fancy rank in the corner and I was—"

He sighed and put out his open hand. "Here, give me that rhino dagger before you hurt yourself."

" 'Ere you goes, guv'ner," she said brightly. Before she laid the dagger across his open palm, she swept her gaze over the elaborately carved handle. "Gaa, that rhino devil must 'ave been a right 'orny little bugger in his time."

Alex wanted to smile, but he composed his face, and, after placing the dagger on the writing table, studied her, pleased with her appearance. "You look soft and demure this morning—just the way a young heiress should," he remarked in a satisfied voice.

She gazed down at the fluffy pink gown and plucked at one of the rosebuds decorating the bodice. "Ain't it a bit

plain? And look at these fussy little rosebuds . . . rosebuds
are for little girls." She jauntily cocked her head to the
side, shaking her blonde curls. "I don't see why I can't
'ave somethin' red, with a low neckline and some black jet
beads quiverin' on the shoulders with every step I take,
and some red plumes in my 'air to add a little flash. I saw
a poster of an actress whot was performin' at Drury Lane
dressed like that one time, and I think I would look quite
fetchin' that way too."

Alex smiled. "Believe me, all you would fetch dressed
like that is trouble. We're grooming you for society, not a
music hall." He glanced at a leather chair by the library
windows. "Now have a seat over there so I can ask you
some questions."

Reluctantly, she walked to the chair and gingerly sat
down, stealing a glance at him as he shuffled through the
mail on his desk. As light washed over his features, she
studied him, finding his jaw firm and strong and his mouth
surprisingly sensuous. She had a suspicion that a host of
intense emotions lurked beneath his suave, witty exterior,
but he kept all his feelings so checked it was hard to guess
what he was thinking at any given time.

Alex put the mail aside and let his gaze rove over her
graceful body and innocent face. How deceptive appearances were, he thought to himself. To see her sitting there
all pink and pretty with her creamy complexion and fashionable gown, one would think she had never set foot out
of Mayfair—that is, until she opened her mouth. "Have
you been to school?" he asked at last.

She moved uneasily in her chair, then lifted her chin.
"Of course I've been to school. I went to three years of
Ragged School before I 'ad to quit. I can read signs, and
the writin' on boxes, and even parts of real books," she answered proudly.

Alex knew Ragged School was the common name for a
Whitechapel institution that offered free lessons to indigent waifs, and he felt relieved that she would at least
know her alphabet. "Your teachers are coming this morn-

ing and when they get here I want you to work hard," he said in an encouraging voice. "It's a great opportunity to learn and I'm sure you'll have many questions for them."

Her face brightened. "I sure will. I 'ave questions I've been savin' up for years, wishin' someone could answer them." Blinking her eyes, she looked at him earnestly. " 'Ave you ever wondered why dogs wag their tails from side to side instead of up and down? And do you think elephants snore? And 'ave you ever wondered why a cat always lands on its feet? And why doesn't a spider ever get caught in its own web?"

Alex moved toward her and studied her animated face, thinking that her mind reminded him of a bed of Indian army ants—incredibly active, but going in dozens of directions at the same time. Too amused to try to stop her babbling, he simply let her run on, wondering what she would say next.

Getting to her feet, she looked up at him with sparkling eyes. "There's a bloody lot of things that 'ave bothered me for years. No one 'as been able to tell me why everybody says, 'It's rainin' cats and dogs.' Why don't they say 'rainin' cows and pigs'? And 'ow come a goose is a goose, but two gooses are geese? And two mouses are mice, but two rats is just plain rats. And why doesn't someone invent a language that we can all speak, even those Chinamen on the other side of the earth eatin' rice this very minute?"

As she continued with her cheerful chatter, Alex sat down on the corner of his desk and stared at her, his spirits lifted.

She spread her hands and gazed at him with wide eyes. "Did you ever wonder about all the lightnin' that strikes the earth?" she asked in a hushed voice. "Whot 'appens to it? You'd think it would all gather up together and cause a shockin' great earthquake. And whot about all those old nursery rhymes? Why would Jack *want* to jump over a candle stick? And why would a weasel pop?" She paused to take a long breath. "And did you ever wonder why all bald men 'ave lots of 'airs in their noses?"

Alex laughed in sheer surprise. "No. I never noticed."

"Well, it's true," she said emphatically. "The next time you're around a bald-'eaded man, just look in 'is nose."

Alex stood and rubbed his jaw. Enough was enough, he thought, remembering that he was supposed to be asking the questions. "I'm sure your teachers will have a busy day indeed, but now I have a few questions for *you*. Before we start, let me hear you recite your vowels," he said firmly, as if he were speaking to a child.

"I ain't five years old," she sighed. "Ask nicely."

He cocked a brow. "Very well. *Please* recite your bloody vowels."

There was a note in his voice that told her she should not challenge him. Still, it nettled her that she was being tested like a child. "*A, e, i, o, u,*" she rattled off in an unpleasant nasal tone.

For a moment chilly silence throbbed between them, then Alex slowly walked to her side, a determined look on his face. "From now on you will concentrate on enunciating—not worrying why dogs wag their tails from side to side instead of up and down."

She ached to come back with a saucy comment, but bit her tongue.

"Now I want you do to a simple sum," he went on. "How much is twelve and twelve?"

She smiled broadly, relieved the question was so easy. "Why, I knows that! A dozen plums and a dozen plums is two dozen plums—that is, unless some of the plums are mushy and you 'ave to throw them away, then you might come up with twenty plums or eighteen plums or whatever you 'ad left."

Alex ran a hand through his hair and sighed. "Very well, that's the general idea."

He walked to the globe and tapped his finger on Egypt. "Can you tell me the name of this country?"

Her heart beating a little faster, she moved to his side

and peered at the globe, then, with a rush of relief, she smiled and said, "Of course I can tell you. That's Egypt. I saw it on a big map they 'ad at Ragged School. But nobody really cares whot it's called 'cause all they's got there is sand and mummies." She raised her brows. "You know, those dead people they pickle and wind up in sheets?"

Alex turned his head so she couldn't see him smile, then walked back to his desk. "All right," he went on, studying her worried face. "I want to ask you a history question. How did the first King Charles meet his death?"

She moved back to the leather chair and sank down, chewing her bottom lip.

"Go on," he prompted. "Answer my question."

Suddenly a smile broke over her face and she snapped her fingers. "The Round'eads decaptivated the blighter, they did!"

"They did *what?*"

She rolled her eyes, and, drawing a finger across her throat, lolled out her tongue. "You knows, they cut off the bloke's 'ead."

It took every ounce of discipline Alex could muster not to laugh. *"Decaptivated* is a malaprop," he said, feeling bemused, but increasingly frustrated with her at the same time.

She blinked. "Whot's a malaprop?"

"It means using a word that sounds somewhat like the one you intended, but is wrong in context."

She sighed wearily. "All right. I'll try again. I suppose somethin' like that could sound a little concentric anyway."

Alex blew out his breath and rubbed the back of his neck.

She went on, "You knows from pictures whot I saw in books, it looks like someone put a great pot on those Round'eads' noodles, then just lopped off the blokes' 'air with a dull knife. Why would they wear shockin' strange 'aircuts like that? And Old King Charles seemed a regular good bloke. Seems those Round'eads was uncommon 'ard on 'im, they was."

Alex gazed at her, thinking she reminded him of a beautiful but rebellious child. He knew she was trying to get him off the track so she wouldn't have to answer any of his questions. He was pulled between compassion and anger, but knew it would be a mistake to let her think she could best him in any way. "Enough of your chatter," he said, lifting his hand. "You need to settle down and be serious for a while. A little study never hurt anyone."

She arched a brow. "Well, maybe so, but I just don't want to take a chance of bein' the first victim."

Alex frowned. "I'm beginning to think you need someone to make sure you *do* study while I'm gone."

Pell clutched the arms of her chair and scanned his stern face. "I don't know why you always get so 'uffy about everything. You're just bein' a great bully, you are!" She was about to open her mouth with another pert comment when Buxley walked into the library wrapped in an air of stiff dignity.

Tall and portly, the bald butler was dressed impeccably in dark breeches and a fine swallow-tailed jacket. He slid Pell a cold glance, then gazed at his master with troubled eyes. "There is a gentleman here to see you, milord. An Indian gentleman, I believe. I suggested he go to the servants' entrance, but he stubbornly insisted on remaining on the front doorstep. Will you see him, or shall I send him away?"

The only Indian gentleman Alex presently knew in London was Hadji and he wondered if he might be in some trouble. "No, I'll come see him," he answered, dismissing Buxley with a wave of his hand. As the servant lifted his chin and grandly exited the room, Alex realized he had been staring intently at the butler's nose. Lord, Pell Davis could drive a man distracted with her outrageous notions.

Glancing at her defiant countenance, he picked up an elocution book and tossed it into her lap. "Make use of this while I'm gone," he ordered, and then strode from the library.

Left alone, she gathered her swirling emotions about her, and stared at the book, feeling a bit guilty that she had exaggerated her reading ability to him. Actually she could only make out a few words, although she secretly yearned to be a good reader. She trailed her fingers over the gold-bound volume, apprehensive about the difficult lessons she would find inside.

Then loud voices floated from the entry hall, catching her attention. Who was the Lord High Chamberlain of Grammar reprimanding now? she wondered idly. Laying the book aside, she rose and walked to the black-and-white-tiled entry hall, feeling a gust of cool air. At first she saw only Alex and Buxley standing near the threshold of the open front door, then she noticed outside on the walk an Indian man dressed in white with a knapsack strapped on his back. Rain lashed against his slight form and spattered down about him. Interest perked through her when she heard the dark man mention her father's name.

"Yes, sahib, I am telling you General Fairchild was a good master, but his lady is now throwing your humble servant into the street. This is as I feared. When the general is becoming ill I am already seeing the handwriting on the floor concerning my future." Moisture soaked the Indian's turban and it drooped to the side as he spoke. "Before the general is passing to his illustrious reward, Mrs. Fairchild is swearing to him she will keep me, but now she is saying my services are not required. She is a reptile in the weeds!"

"I think you mean snake in the grass," Alex said dryly.

"Yes, you are not talking from both sides of your head at once!" He held his slender hands together before his face in a gesture of respect, then fell to his knees. "I am now devoting my humble life to you. I will be ironing your shirts, and polishing your shoes, and washing your feet—each toe separately!"

"You're being ridiculous, Hadji. Stand up," Alex commanded.

"No, sahib. I cannot, for I am showing my great esteem for my new master!" the servant exclaimed, hastily adjusting his soggy turban. "Serving a master is the only thing I am knowing. When Mrs. Fairchild is throwing me from her house, I am thinking I will contact my good friend Colonel Alexander Chancery-Brown. Coming today in the rain is a regrettable necessity, but I must strike while the pistol is hot!"

Pell studied the lithe Indian, realizing that in the past he had not only been connected with her father but also with Alex. She immediately liked his graceful movements and the soft musical tone of his voice, and hoped there would be some way she could help him in his plight.

"This is not India and I'm not a colonel anymore," Alex said.

"No, you are now a great lord and needing many servants to wait upon your glorious person."

"I don't need any more servants," he said, then he glanced at Pell. "Or any more problems." Alex looked at the butler, who seemed disgruntled to be involved in the conversation. "Isn't there an employment service near here that places domestics, Buxley?"

The man pressed his lips together. "Yes, I believe so, sir," he replied thoughtfully. "Now let me remember where it is."

As Alex and his butler turned to confer with each other, Hadji's backpack popped open and a monkey scrambled out. The Indian made a futile attempt to catch the animal, but it quickly scampered over a muddy rose bed beside the front door, then darted into the entry hall and hid behind a tall Chinese vase.

With some amusement, Pell realized that Alex had no idea the monkey was in the entry and a thrill of delight ran over her. Surely the animal's presence would provide a much-needed diversion from her studies. In one sense she and the monkey were in a similar situation, she mused wistfully. He was trapped in a strange place where he did not belong, just like she was.

Without permission Hadji could not enter the mansion, so he remained on the doorstep in the rain and gazed at her pleadingly. Finally he put a slender finger over his lips, begging her to keep the secret. While Alex was engrossed in a deep conversation with the butler, the servant looked at the monkey, who periodically peeked from the safety of the Chinese vase. Taking advantage of Alex's turned back, the Indian motioned frantically, but the little creature refused to move.

Alex turned and gazed at Hadji, feeling some responsibility for him, but not knowing how he could use his services. "Go to the servants' entrance and tell Cook I said to give you a hot meal and hackney fare. Then proceed to the employment service and they will place you. Buxley tells me it's located on Leicester Square."

"But, master, I am begging you—"

Suddenly Alex caught a wet unpleasant odor. Raising his hand, he scanned the entry. "Wait a minute. What's that awful scent? Something smells like a wet dog, only worse."

As he looked around for the source of the odor, he noticed Pell and Hadji exchanging worried glances, then the Indian stared at the gray heavens and mouthed a chant that Alex recognized as a Hindu prayer. "Hadji, what in the devil are you praying about?" he asked, studying the servant's face.

Rain trickling from his chin, Hadji innocently batted his eyes. "I am giving thanks to Vishnu for providing such a kind master."

Just then the monkey scampered from behind the huge vase. Pell burst out laughing as it clasped Alex's leg with its muddy hands, then glanced up and chattered affectionately.

As Alex bent to dislodge the monkey, Hadji rushed inside to assist him. "No, no! You villainous monkey!" the servant cried, trying to pick up the animal. "You must not be ruining our esteemed master's clothing. It is most impolite!"

Screeching, the monkey scurried over the tiles and clung to Pell's skirt, peeking out from behind the frothy material.

Hadji fell on one knee and gazed at Alex with sad eyes. "Ten million pardons, sahib. This is a trick he is unfortunately learning from another vile monkey. Please be assured I am teaching him otherwise, now that we are abiding with our illustrious master."

Pell scooped up the animal and held him against her bosom, caressing his little hands that were now clean since he had wiped them on Alex's once immaculate breeches. "Why don't you leave the little bugger alone? 'E ain't 'urtin' anyone." She pointed her finger at Alex. " 'E's scared of you, 'e is. You 'ave 'im all wrought up, you do. Pick on someone your own size!" The monkey nuzzled against her and chattered happily.

Hadji gazed at them with a smile, then regarded Alex with imploring eyes. "Oh, sahib, already you are seeing how much benefit we are being unto you. Chi Chi is liking the young lady very much. In India many great ladies have such a pet to entertain them. I myself once worked for a Brahamin's wife. I was her majordodo."

"Majordomo, Hadji. The word is *majordomo.*" Alex straightened his jacket while Buxley stooped and tried to brush the mud from his master's breeches.

"Whatever you are wishing me to call it, sahib," Hadji said. "And once before, I was a baby-watcher to an English family. As you can see I am being most versatile. I will serve you however you see fit."

As Alex's strong self-possession returned, an interesting idea popped into his head. "Baby-watcher, you say?" he asked with a half-smile.

"Oh, yes, sahib."

For a tense moment no one spoke, then Alex studied Pell and thoughtfully remarked, "On second thought, perhaps your services are needed here, Hadji. I'm employing you to watch Miss Davis. Your duties will be confined to her. It's not a baby you'll be watching, but an infant none-theless."

"I'm not an infant!" Pell burst out. "I'm a full-grown woman, I am!"

"That," Alex countered, "is debatable." Thinking he had partially solved a troubling problem, he turned and walked away, feeling rather satisfied. "I'm changing and going to the Carlton," he called over his shoulder. At the foot of the stairs he paused and glanced at Hadji. "As your first duty, give that mischievous primate a bath."

Pell sucked in her breath, her eyes wide. "Give me a bath? I knew this was a den of inequity when you brought me 'ere, but I didn't think you'd stoop to this. I'll bathe myself!"

Alex glanced sideways at her in surprise. Then he turned, and, shaking his head, ascended the stairs. He was still laughing when he closed his bedroom door behind him.

Chapter 4

A week later Pell sat in the drawing room reading aloud from her elocution book. She had worked with the teachers, and, faithful as the rising sun, Alex had come around every day to check her progress as he was doing right now. Usually he arrived in the morning, but today he had a late session and had stayed home for lunch, deciding to test her before he left for Parliament at two o'clock.

He paced about the large, luxuriously furnished chamber, concentration tensing his rakish face. He wore a fine jacket with a velvet collar and trousers with a broad stripe down the sides, and Pell couldn't help noticing how the clothing emphasized his well-built shoulders and the strength of his arms and muscled thighs.

The spring rains had finally vanished and sunlight streamed into the room, highlighting a shaft of dust particles and bringing out the lurking scent of lemon polishing oil. Pell sighed wearily and turned another page, distracted by a trill of bird song filtering into the room from the partially opened windows.

Soon her eyes ceased to focus on the book in her lap and she stared at the lacy shadow panels, which were moved by a gentle breeze. Lord, what she would give to be outside in the fresh air selling fruit again instead of cooped up in the stuffy drawing room studying. With deep regret, she thought of her words to Alex about being a lady, realizing he would *never* let her forget them.

45

Still pacing, he glanced at her and inquired, "Why have you stopped reading?"

She looked at him and sighed. "I need to rest. I ain't some kind of blinkin' talkin' machine, you know."

He turned full-face toward her and met and held her gaze. In his countenance she saw nothing but determination. "Keep reading," he ordered, his deep-timbered voice shot with authority.

Annoyance washed through her. Would the incessant lessons never end? Choking back her frustration, she lifted her chin and read: " 'The ladies decided to visit the 'orticulture exhibit at 'Arrods Department Store.' "

He frowned. "No, that's not right. Try it again, please."

Placing the book on a table beside her, she stood. She desperately wanted to please him, yet at the same time she was afraid of him and angry at him for forcing her into being something she was not. It seemed the only thing she had left that she could call her own was her pride, and she guarded it fiercely. The skirt of her blue silk dress rustled softly as she walked toward him. "I've been tryin' to learn this for days," she said in a tight voice. "I think I needs to rest . . . to go outside a bit."

Alex looked at her defiant face. He had never met anyone as obstinate in his entire life, and it had become an issue with him that she learn to speak properly. "You agreed to these lessons and you must keep working. Now try saying 'Handsome heroes always have friends,' " he said with quiet emphasis.

Her lips trembled and he noticed a suggestion of tears in her eyes. "Handsome heroes always 'ave friends," she uttered in a broken voice. "'Ow was that?"

He gave a weary sigh. "I'm afraid you dropped the last *h*."

Drawing in a long breath, Pell walked back to her chair and sank onto the soft velvet cushion. Couldn't Alex understand she was still confused about her unexpected change in station and felt terribly out of place every time she made another faux pas? She tried to rise above her depression, but her throat ached with despair. "Sometimes I feels like a performin' dog," she murmured throatily.

Alex swept his gaze over her bowed head and slumped shoulders, sensing she was on the verge of breaking down. With a twinge of guilt, he realized that he had been oblivious to her feelings. Perhaps without realizing it he had been pushing her too hard. "You must relax and stop fighting me," he said gently.

She raised her head and looked at him, her eyes moist with emotion. "I ain't fightin' you. Lord, I'm up early every mornin' and I works like a 'orse with these bloomin' talkin' lessons. Why, I'm so tired of talkin' my jaw 'urts every night," she said roughly. She took out her handkerchief and dabbed at her eyes. "I'm always studyin', or tryin' on clothes, or learnin' somethin' new—and I'm always makin' mistakes." She sniffled and blew her nose.

"You say *I* correctly all the time now, and you've learned to pronounce other words. You've made progress," he said in a lighter tone.

"No, I ain't," she said dejectedly. "I talk 'alf like a laidy and 'alf like whot I really am. I talk like some kind of mixed-up race'orse with a zebra 'ead and a jackass butt." She put the handkerchief away. "I talks terrible."

Alex smiled at her words. "A mixed-up racehorse with a zebra head and a jackass butt? Now there's an animal I'd like to see." He studied her sad face. "When people try to change they always make mistakes at first," he said calmly. "That's not important. What is important is that they learn from their mistakes and they *do* change."

Amazement touched Pell's heart. He wasn't demanding she recite another drill; he was talking to her as if she were his equal, and it warmed her spirit.

"When I was a boy, when I first went to boarding school, I went through a fearful time and made many mistakes. And my first years in the military as a lieutenant weren't very pleasant either."

She couldn't imagine him as a fearful boy or an uncertain young officer, but she was surprised and honored that he would confide in her, for he had never mentioned his past before.

Alex looked at her sitting there like a lost child on the verge of tears. Everything in him told him that at this moment her self-confidence was very low and she needed some kind of success to lift her spirits. Besides that, a little fresh air would not be a bad thing. "I suggest another type of lesson today," he said indulgently. "And I think this is a lesson you will enjoy because you'll get to go outdoors."

A soft smile curved her lips. "Outdoors? Except to go to the dressmaker's with Aunt Violet, I haven't been outdoors in ever so long. What kind of lesson am I goin' to 'ave outdoors?"

"Croquet. Have you ever heard of it?"

She blinked. "No . . . I 'aven't. It must be a game just for earls, and dukes, and toffs like that."

He walked to her chair. "Actually, many people enjoy croquet. It's a game in which players use mallets to drive wooden balls through a series of wickets set out on a green." He tilted a brow. "It's a skill you'll need, because as a debutante, you will be invited to many house parties where the guests often play croquet."

She looked up at him, her smile widening. "You mean we're goin' outside where the sun is shinin'? We're goin' to hit balls? And walk on the grass, and smell the flowers? We're goin' to play?"

Alex smiled and nodded. "Yes, that's exactly what we're going to do."

Pell smacked the croquet ball, then laughed as it rolled over the velvety grass stretching behind the mansion. With its stately oaks feathered in light-green and fragrant lilac hedges, the well-trimmed lawn was a sight to please the eye. A light breeze filled with the sounds of warbling birds wafted over her, and as she looked back over her shoulder at Alex she could feel her spirits rising by the second. "I wonder whot my old friends would think if they could see me this fine day, playin' croquet with the Earl of

Tavistock? I wish they *could* see me. They'd be so jealous."

Alex regarded her with a smile. "Humility isn't one of your strong suits, is it? Keep your eyes on the ball, you little pagan."

As his approving gaze met hers, she noticed a twinkle in his eyes and felt a ripple of excitement she did not understand. Ignoring the tingling in her stomach, she looked back at the lawn and tried to concentrate on the croquet game. Tightly clutching her mallet, she held her breath and took a swing at the ball.

Alex gazed at her, his own spirits lifted by her sense of play. How beautiful she was in her blue silk dress and perky straw sun hat with ribbon streamers—and how like a child she was! Only fifteen minutes ago her eyes had glistened with tears, and now a smile wreathed her face. His lips quirked upward as he observed the awkward way she held the mallet.

He walked behind her and put his arms around her, clasping her hands. "You're gripping the mallet wrong. Hold your hands this way." He pulled her a bit closer, enjoying the feel of her soft silken body in his arms and the fresh scent of her hair, feeling his body stir with passion.

When he had taken her through several swings, he turned her about in the circle of his arms and studied her expectant face. Her soft, caressing gaze stirred a host of conflicting emotions within him. After a moment he said, "You know, we must be thinking about finding you a suitable husband in a few months—some firm, solid, stable man."

She lifted her brow and made a little face. "Um, 'e sounds delightful. But whot about love?"

"Love, my dear, is for the butchers and bakers of the world—not the heiresses," he said dryly. "The idea that you can leave everything to the heart is a dangerous illusion." He glanced at the ball. "Now try again."

She slipped from his arms and swung at the ball, this time with greater success. After it had rolled through the next wicket, she walked toward it, pausing several times to make a curtsy.

"What on earth are you doing now?" he asked with a laugh.

She turned and smiled broadly. "I'm practicin' my curtsy—for when I meet Prince Alfred."

He strolled to her and smiled. "And what makes you so sure you're going to meet the prince?"

"Well, don't you suppose when I gets all my inheritance and I'm invited to some big fancy duke's 'ouse to play croquet, I'll meet 'im there?" she answered with a hint of impatience. She tipped her head to the side and grinned. "You knows, I had a pet mouse named Prince Alfred once, but I just called him Alfie most of the time."

Alex raised his brows and smiled. "You had a pet mouse named Prince Alfred?"

Tossing her curls, she slid him a sidelong glance. "Of course I did. One night after Rosie 'ad gone to bed, I was sittin' up late, and I saw the mouse dart across the floor. The next night I put out some crumbs, and kept feedin' 'im till he got real gentle-like. Once 'e let me get close enough to touch 'is tail."

He bent his head slightly forward. "But you still haven't told me why you called him Prince Alfred."

"Well, I've seen plenty of pictures of 'Is 'Ighness in the shops and all, and my little mouse 'ad the same kind of eyes . . . all soft and brown and kind of dreamy. And 'is whiskers reminded me of the prince's thin little mustache," she finished with a laugh.

Alex let his gaze roam over her lovely face. "I like it when you laugh. I haven't been around anyone who really laughed in years. There used to be lots of laughter at Stanton Hall before my mother died."

A wistful look misted her eyes for a moment, then she tapped the ball through the wicket and gazed up at him again. "Where is Stanton 'All anyway?" she asked lightly.

"It's in Gloucestershire—in the Cotswolds. It's lovely in the country with the soft green hills and stone cottages. I'll take you there someday." He strolled beside her for a moment, watching her graceful movements, then he gently caught her elbow. "Where did you get the name Pell?" he asked. "I've never heard it."

She paused and smiled. "It's an old Welch name. My mother started to name me Penelope, but she decided it was too extentious for . . . for someone like me."

Alex laughed. "She was right. I've always thought 'Penelope' was somewhat pretentious myself. I'm glad she named you Pell instead. It's a strong, good name and suits you well." Warmth coursed through his veins as he looked at her standing there in her ruffled blue gown and straw hat with its silk streamers fluttering over her shoulder. How perfect she was with the sunlight splashing over her silvery hair and creamy skin. And what a striking effect she had on him, filling him with delight and a pleasure tinged with uneasiness, as if there was something almost dangerous about her.

She smiled at him, then clutched the mallet incorrectly once again.

Forgetting himself, he moved behind her and wrapped her in his arms to adjust her awkward grip. Once again the same feelings he had experienced earlier came flooding back, only this time with such a powerful force that he couldn't fool himself into thinking he had just imagined them. For a few forbidden moments, he imagined what it would be like to crush her soft hair in his hand, flutter kisses over her silky skin, and feel the length of her body pressed against him.

Then like a thunderbolt the realization hit him that the feelings were entirely inappropriate. He had a great advantage over her in experience, knowledge, and social position, and he was her guardian, not her seducer. Something deep within him told him that he must extricate himself from this exceedingly dangerous situation—immediately. Letting his arms slide away from her, he stepped back.

"I'm afraid I lost track of the time," he said brusquely,

without even checking his timepiece. "I won't be able to help you anymore today. I must go."

She turned, a puzzled look on her face. Only a moment ago they had been talking and laughing together. Now his expression was unreadable. What had happened to alter his mood so drastically? "But earlier you said you 'ad a late session," she stammered. "You—"

At that moment all Alex could think about was removing himself from the temptation of her exquisite face and shapely body. "I said I must go," he repeated hoarsely. "I've explained the rules to you. My absence will give you a chance to practice by yourself for a while."

Without another word, he walked back to the house leaving Pell hopelessly bewildered. Had she said something wrong, or displeased him in some way? Depression once again spread through her and she noticed an aching sense of loss. Letting out a great sigh, she watched him enter the mansion.

Try as she might, she just couldn't understand his changing moods. Then, with a little surge of happiness, she thought of someone who might be able to help her. Aunt Violet was his only living relative, and by their behavior, she could tell they were very close. Feeling a bit better, she tapped the croquet ball through the wicket. The old lady would be napping now, but as soon as she awoke, Pell would ask her to come to her bedroom. For days Aunt Violet had been wanting to see her in a particular gown. She would model it for her, and while they were together she would turn the conversation to the subject of Alex. Perhaps she would be able to find answers to his puzzling behavior.

At five-thirty that evening, Pell twirled before the cheval glass in her bedroom, modeling her newest gown for Aunt Violet. A sparkling powder-blue creation, the gown was scooped low in front and featured small puffed sleeves and an exaggerated bustle. Tiny silver beads spilled down the sleek bodice and swirled onto the gown's swept-back skirt. Simple but elegant, the fanciful creation shimmered within the light cast by a crystal lamp on the dressing table.

With a flick of her wrist, Pell smoothed back her hair and looked at the old lady, suddenly noticing that she was wearing earrings that did not match. She started to mention it, then she bit her tongue, and smiled instead, realizing how much she really liked her. Aunt Violet was so sweet and kind. What did it matter if she mixed up her earrings and constantly lost things? "The gown is stunnin' fine," Pell said in an awed voice. "I loves it!"

The old lady beamed with delight. "It is lovely, isn't it?" she replied, fluffing the gown's gauzy sleeves. "Of course, it's your looks that makes the dress, dear."

Pell touched the beaded hair ornament over her right ear and watched it glisten in the wavering gaslight. "All I know is it's the prettiest thing I've ever seen."

Hearing a chattering noise, she glanced at her canopied bed and watched Chi Chi batting at a dangling tassel. Sometimes, as today when Hadji was running an errand for Aunt Violet, she kept the little animal within her sight. Blinking his curious eyes, the monkey slid from the silken counterpane and scampered over the carpet toward her. Once at her side, he tugged at her skirt, then, imitating her earlier action, he held out his hand and twirled in front of the tall gilt-framed mirror.

Laughing, she scooped him up in the crook of her arm. "You saucy little imp," she crooned, affectionately caressing his small ears. His eyes bright, he reached out with nimble fingers to pick at the shiny beads decorating her bodice.

With a swish of her pink taffeta gown, Aunt Violet hurriedly walked to Pell's side. "No . . . no, Chin Chin," she chided, moving his hands from the gown with fluttering fingers. "You mustn't destroy the dress before Alex has seen it."

Pell smiled, but said nothing, for she had given up hope that Aunt Violet could remember the monkey's name. And now that the subject of Alex had been broached, she wouldn't have to bring it up herself. Surely this was her golden opportunity to discover why he acted so strangely around her—warm and open at times, then cool and distant at others.

With a sigh, she sank onto the small padded chair before her dressing table and put Chi Chi on the floor, watching him chatter happily as he nestled against her legs. Taking a deep breath, she looked up at Aunt Violet, struggling to put her difficult questions into words.

"Oh, you look so sad, dear. What's the matter?"

Pell shrugged, then began speaking in a strained voice. "It's 'is nibs—'e's somethin' else, ain't 'e? Sometimes 'e confuses me so. Why is 'e so concerned with doin' everythin' just right?"

"He was in the military, dear, and his whole life was based on duty and rules." A thoughtful look crossed the old lady's face. "I really believe he has repressed his emotions under the weight of the duties and responsibilities of his position. And now that he is an earl he has even more obligations. Of course, he has always been a perfectionist."

Pell turned about on the chair and gazed into the dressing-table mirror, which reflected a host of glittering crystal containers. She thought about telling Aunt Violet that she found him terribly attractive, that every time he touched her shoulder or brushed her hand, her heart raced a little faster, but she pushed the impulse aside. After all, who was she? Only a problem he had taken on out of a sense of duty to her father. How could anyone as grand as Alex ever take notice of her? "I just don't understand 'im," she finally said, skimming a puff into a bowl of face powder and dabbing it on her nose. "Sometimes 'e's nice and warm like a regular 'uman bein', then sometimes he's all cool again."

Aunt Violet laid a plump hand on her shoulder. "What's wrong, dear, did you two have a tiff?"

Pell sighed again and put the powder puff in its box.

"Not really. We were playin' croquet and things were goin' fine—and 'e was treatin' me like a real person. We were laughin' and talkin' about Stanton Hall and Prince Alfred and everythin', then he put 'is arms around me to show me 'ow to 'old the croquet mallet, and 'e got all cold-like, and left me standin' there by myself." She twisted about and looked into the old lady's compassionate eyes. "Why would 'e do a thing like that?"

Aunt Violet blushed and stammered. "Well, I . . . I . . ." She fanned herself with a lacy handkerchief. "My, isn't it awfully warm in here, dear?"

All at once Pell realized that despite her innocent appearance, Aunt Violet understood something about Alex and men in general that she did not. "Sometimes we can talk just fine," she went on, "then other times talkin' to 'im is like tryin' to play a 'arp with a 'ammer." Frustration welling in her throat, she picked up a brush, and, turning back to the mirror, hastily swiped it through the loose curls about her face.

"Now, don't be getting yourself so upset, dear," the old lady advised, caressing her shoulders.

Pell put down the brush. " 'E's the most peculiarest man I ever met," she said with a miserable sigh. "I never knows which end is up, and besides that 'e's got me workin' so 'ard . . . I'm . . . I'm just at my wit's end. And I 'ave a predomination things are goin' to get worse!"

Aunt Violet smiled. "It's *premonition*, dear." She moved away, and, twisting a handkerchief in her hands, walked back and forth behind Pell. "I . . . I know you're frustrated, but Alex has so much on his mind. And then there is his background. He had such a sad family situation."

Pell turned about on the chair and stared at her. "What do you mean by that?"

"My sister—his mother—died when he was just a boy. He was very close to her and it hurt him deeply."

Pell had wanted to ask Alex more about his past this afternoon, but sensed it wasn't the time. Now she quietly listened.

Taking a long quivering breath, Aunt Violet continued, "Then he endured such a great romantic disappointment. Oh, it was heartrending. Sadder than anything I've ever read in one of my novels."

"Romantic disappointment?" Pell asked, unease stirring within her.

"Yes, he was a captain then and made all the ladies' hearts beat faster—as he still does. Of course, all the debutantes and even some of the married women were scheming to get his attention, but he fell in love with a Gloucestershire girl. She was from a good Cotswold family." Aunt Violet paused and caressed her temple. "Now let me see . . . the family estate was located in either Chedworth or Cirencester." Fluttering her eyelashes, she continued pacing. "Or maybe it was Moreton-in-Marsh."

She let out a long audible breath. "Actually I cannot remember, but the girl was from a good family and had come out that very year. She and Alex were to be married the June before he went to India, but that winter the poor girl caught a severe chill." Aunt Violet sniffled a bit and dabbed at the corner of her eye with her handkerchief. "The chill turned into pneumonia. The doctors tried to save her, but in the end they could do nothing. That March, she just faded away." She laid her ringed hand over the lacy froth at her throat. "What a great tragedy that was for Alex."

Pell sat in silence. Just to know that Alex had gone through such a tragedy filled her with compassion, yet at the same time she felt a tingle of jealousy toward the girl. "She just faded away," Pell echoed softly. "Whot was 'er name?"

Aunt Violet stared blankly across the room and fingered the little curls about her hairline. "It was Carolyn Ramsay. She was beautiful . . . so beautiful with her black hair and pale skin." She glanced at Pell and smiled. "Alex has always been partial to brunettes, you know."

Disappointment settled over Pell like an autumn mist. Alex had once been in love, and, from Aunt Violet's description, with a beautiful creature with raven hair who possessed all the qualities she herself did not.

Suddenly Chi Chi shrieked and Pell sensed rather than heard someone in the hall; when she turned about, Alex was standing at the threshold, looking very large. As always he cut a dashing figure, but now he also projected a slightly distant air, and the warm twinkle she had noted in his eyes earlier in the day had vanished.

Her heart shook like a bit of jam at the sight of him, for despite her confusion at his actions, his nearness during the croquet game had left her hungry for his touch. It troubled her deeply that she had so little control over her emotions when he was near, especially when he obviously only considered her an obligation. Vowing to give him no idea of the way she really felt, she took a deep breath to steady her nerves.

With leisurely grace, he moved toward her, his dark hair gleaming in the lamplight, his face calm and composed. When he was a few feet away, he paused to sweep her with a look of appraisal. As his gaze traveled over her, a warm blush stung her cheeks. "You're . . . you're back already," she stammered, feeling unsure how she stood with him.

"Yes, I came home a bit early," he said evenly. "There is something we need to discuss."

Aunt Violet flushed and cleared her throat. "I . . . uh, I need to speak with Cook about dinner," she said hurriedly. "I'll talk to you both later." Her face darkened and she glanced about the room. "Now where did I leave my handkerchief?"

"You tucked it under your cuff," Pell answered softly.

The old lady glanced at her sleeve and slowly removed the handkerchief as if it were a great treasure. "Well, I *did*, didn't I? Yes, here it is." After nervously patting her hair, she clutched the bit of lace to her bosom and left the room, leaving the scent of patchouli behind her.

Pell ran her gaze over Alex. " 'Ave I made another mistake? Or did you come to tell me I'm gettin' another teacher?"

He straightened his shoulders and studied her critically. "I came here to tell you I've spoken with the director of a musical ensemble and also a caterer this afternoon. I've decided on a date for your coming-out ball. We'll hold it on the fifteenth of June—that will give us six weeks to perfect you. The season will be at its zenith in June and everyone will be in London."

Too stunned to reply, she rose and watched him pace back and forth across the soft-hued Oriental carpet. Although she tried to maintain an aura of bravado so he wouldn't have the satisfaction of knowing how uncomfortable she really felt in her new surroundings, the thought of being put on display before the elite of London society frightened her thoroughly.

Pausing, Alex crossed his arms and studied her pale face, regretting that he had to put such a burden on her at this time. Then again, he knew it was all for the best. What had happened this afternoon made him very aware that he needed to find her a suitor as soon as possible. Setting a date for the coming-out ball struck him as the best way to speed along the whole process. "Your father wanted you to make a debut," he continued, trying to sound enthusiastic. "I will lead you in the first dance myself."

Pell's heart fluttered in her breast as she stared at his determined face. She would actually be rubbing elbows with those glorious creatures she had previously seen coming home from balls in the wee hours of the night as she wearily pushed her handcart toward Covent Garden. At that time the gentry had seemed so grand and glittering in their satins and jewels they might have come down to earth on a shaft of starlight. Now she was being asked to socialize with these very people.

Swallowing the lump in her throat, she met his gaze. The look in his eyes told her it would be impossible for her to change his plans. All the old fears she had ever had, and a host of new ones, came rushing into her mind. "But whot are you goin' to say when they ask about my past? Whot will you tell everyone?" She studied his cool gray eyes, wondering if they harbored a glint of mischief.

His mouth twitched upward as he paced across the carpet once more, looking as if he might actually be enjoying himself. "I will invent a plausible story for you," he said, thoughtfully rubbing his chin. "I think you will be from Newcastle. No one of importance goes there. We will say you were orphaned at an early age and reared in a convent and then a finishing school. I will paint your dead father as a wealthy philanthropist. Now that you are of age and have come into your fortune, you are in London for your social debut. Because of your father's connection with my family, I have elected to sponsor you." A hint of humor flashed on his face as he stopped to stare at her. "How does that sound to you?"

"It . . . it sounds like a lie," she stuttered.

He arched a brow in amusement. "Something the aristocracy is very familiar with, let me assure you."

"But I won't know whot to do," she said, feeling a rush of panic. "I—I won't know whot to say. I'll make mistakes."

He regarded her thoughtfully. "Yes, doubtless you will—but I'll accelerate your program and in the end you'll survive," he commented with a ring of finality. "May I remind you that this is what we have been working toward? In six weeks it will be time for Cinderella to go to the ball." His keen eyes analyzed her reaction for a moment, then, without a word of farewell, he turned and walked briskly from the room.

Numb with shock, Pell picked up Chi Chi and absently caressed his head. As the magnitude of Alex's plan sank in, she experienced a feeling of great nostalgia for the days when her biggest problem was selling a peck of overripe berries before sunset.

Hurt twinged through her as she speculated on Alex's reason for scheduling the ball as early as possible. Perhaps he thought the sooner he gave the affair, the sooner he could find her a husband and be done with her.

And while she wasn't sure about the meaning of the word *accelerate,* from the way he had said it she knew it would mean more studying and work for her. Feeling as if she had been given a death sentence, she stared at the empty doorway, wondering how on God's green earth she would be able to meet the cream of London society in six short weeks.

Chapter 5

Three weeks later, Alex leaned back in his desk chair and scanned the London social register, ticking off the names of those guests he wished to invite to Pell's coming-out ball. Since the croquet game, he had done everything he could to avoid her, but to his dismay, thoughts of her constantly lingered in his mind.

Today he had spent the early afternoon riding in Hyde Park, thinking of both her and the ball, and after returning home, he had gone straight to the library, not bothering to change his whipcord jacket, pearl-gray breeches, and varnished boots. Aunt Violet stood by his side, gowned in a lavender silk creation trimmed with white lace; a cameo brooch that she had forgotten to fasten sat crooked on her bosom, threatening to slip from her dress.

Alex tapped his pen on the list and frowned. "I suppose we must invite the Earl of Bockingford and his daughter, Lilly. Bockingford is getting a bit senile now, but he can still bore you on any subject."

His aunt ran a ringed finger down the list and sighed. "Yes, I'm afraid so, dear." A thoughtful smile graced her lips. "You know, Lilly is being courted by a young Frenchman now. The man is an artist of some renown, and from all reports, quite amusing. Shall we invite him also? Having someone from the arts might liven things up a bit."

Alex shrugged and waved his hand. "Very well. If you think the man will add a bit of color, let's invite him." His brow tightened as he continued down the list. "We can't overlook the Duke of Featherston." He put a check by his name. "The duke has a remarkable talent for brightening up a room when he leaves, but I see him at the Carlton every day and he is an important member of the House of Lords."

Aunt Violet chuckled and sat down beside him. "I know coming-out balls bore you, dear, but some social lubrication is necessary if we are to launch the girl into society."

Alex glanced at his aunt and smiled, then reached over to fasten her brooch. "Yes, but in Pell's case, perhaps *catapult* would be the correct word."

His aunt chuckled. "You know, in many ways the girl is so sweet. She sees life through such childlike eyes and it takes so little to make her happy. And don't forget how lovely she is. Why, just this morning the dressmaker said she had the handsomest figure she had ever seen."

Alex cocked a brow. "Yes, she makes a smashing impression if she doesn't speak. Perhaps we can tell everyone she was stricken with a rare disease as a child and is now mute. Actually it might enhance her value on the marriage market."

Aunt Violet toyed with her lace froth. "I've been wondering about something," she stammered. "Do you think we should invite Sabrina Fairchild?"

Alex considered the general's sharp-tongued window, deciding that her presence would be too great a threat to Pell. "No, definitely not. The girl will have a hard enough time without Sabrina here to sabotage her efforts at being a lady. I'm hoping we can avoid her completely until the six months are finished."

"Oh, it is all so much." Aunt Violet, clasped her hands over her bosom. "We only have three weeks. Do you think we can possibly get the child into presentable shape on time?"

Alex slumped back in his chair. "Who knows how she will perform. She has made *some* progress ... but not a lot. Her teachers tell me she's still dropping *h*'s like a trail of bread crumbs through the Black Forest."

"Well, we must be positive," the old lady advised, looking at him earnestly.

Alex looked at her soft face and smiled. "We will serve lots of champagne and hope for the best. At least that will make you happy."

"It will?"

He laughed and patted her arm. "Yes, darling, you love champagne."

"I do?" She fluttered her eyelashes. "Oh, yes ... *I do."*

He handed her the list, then draped his arm about the back of her chair while they both studied the column of names. For a moment there was only the sound of his pen as it squeaked over the slick paper, making checks. Lost in thought, he raised his gaze up as Buxley entered the library with an annoyed look on his face.

"Here is your mail, milord," the butler announced, handing him a thick stack of letters. "Will there be anything else?"

Alex flipped through the mail, finding several letters from his brother's creditors. When he spotted three crudely addressed letters, he sat forward and lifted his hand. "One moment, Buxley," he drawled, his interest stirring. "It appears that these letters are for Miss Davis. Did they also arrive today?"

"Yes, milord," the butler replied with a sigh. "And I'm so glad you stirred my memory." He reached into his vest, withdrew a ragged note, and handed it to his master. "A rather down-at-the-heels creature came by while you were riding and the ladies were at the dressmaker's." A disgusted look flitted across his stern features. "The woman had the effrontery to come to the front door. She left this message for Miss Davis."

Raising his brows, Alex took the note and absently laid it aside. "That will be all for now," he remarked, looking at the list once more.

The butler walked to the library doors, then glanced

back over his slightly stooped shoulder. "She really was a most dreadful creature, sir. I think you should read the note immediately." Solemnly composing himself, he lifted his chin and left the room.

Alex leaned back against his chair, realizing that the servant was as big a snob as any member of the House of Lords. Still, he had sworn to General Fairchild that he would protect his daughter from fortune hunters and swindlers. While Aunt Violet made more checks on the list, he opened the note and ran his gaze over the scrawled writing.

It seemed Pell had been called upon by a Miss Kid Glove Rosie, obviously *the* notorious Kid Glove Rosie of Cat and Wheel Alley fame. The note was harmless enough and he rather enjoyed the colorful language and humorous grammar—until two lines hit him at the bottom of the page. Rosie would be back sometime today and she "needed a fiver shocking bad."

Concern filled his mind as he surmised that the other letters for Pell were probably also requests for money. Perhaps the residents of Cat and Wheel Alley had formed a committee and elected Rosie to collect everyone's dole at one time, he thought with amusement. He put down the note and shoved the letters aside.

Aunt Violet gave him a quizzical look. "What's wrong, dear? You look as if something is amiss."

"It seems that Pell's impoverished friends have already begun a money-gathering campaign." In his mind's eye he imagined a long line of shabby costermongers queued up in front of the house, waiting for handouts on the night of the coming-out ball. He had always harbored some sympathy for the underclass himself, which his years in India had only deepened, but he also felt protective of Pell, and realized that her great fortune put her in a vulnerable position. Turning to his aunt, he clasped her plump arm. "Would you ask the girl to come to the library? I want to speak to her."

Aunt Violet smiled and stood up. "Of course, dear."

After his aunt had left, Alex stared meditatively across the library, thinking of his ward. The spitfire had courage aplenty and a type of rough wit that often amused him, and she had touched his senses as had no woman before. But what slow progress she was making scholastically! Perhaps she was unconsciously fighting her transformation, he mused, recalling how intelligent she really was.

"Aunt Violet said you wanted to speak with me."

A pleasurable warmth washed over him as he turned his head and saw Pell standing by the open library doors. A new gown of bright-pink silk outlined her dainty figure, and its décolletage scooped low, revealing a graceful neck and a distracting amount of creamy bosom.

Pride rippled through him. True, she still wasn't totally presentable, but, as the dressmaker had observed, she was strikingly lovely, and he took great satisfaction in the small progress she had made toward becoming a lady. He remembered how soft she had felt in his arms when he lost control of himself while they were playing croquet. Suddenly he felt a strong urge to hold her again.

He skimmed his gaze over her. "Yes . . . come in."

She entered the room, a cascade of glossy blonde ringlets bouncing against her shoulders. As she neared his desk, he noticed a hint of apprehension hovering in her eyes.

"These letters arrived today," he announced, running his fingers over the smooth envelopes. "They're addressed to you."

She gazed at the envelopes with wide eyes, then exclaimed, "They *are* for me! Look, there's one from Annie, and Louie the Lump, and one from Irish Mary, too." Her face aglow, she picked up the letters, ripped off their ends, and dumped out the folded contents.

Alex sat quietly while she paced in front of his desk, devouring the short letters. Her eyes sparkled with happiness and her lips moved as she read to herself. A bit surprised, he found he was touched at the transparency of her feel-

ings. Lord, what would it feel like to be that young and in-
genuous, he wondered wistfully.

When she had laid down the last piece of grimy paper,
he steepled his fingers and caught her gaze. "The letters
are requests for money, aren't they?" he asked in a serious
tone.

She arranged a lock of straying hair that had escaped
from her upswept coiffure, then twisted her slender hands
together. "Well . . . yes, there are a few requests, but—"

He rose and walked around his desk. "Your father left
strict instructions for me to protect your inheritance from
disreputable people and I'm wary of all requests for
funds," he said smoothly.

"They ain't—" She bit her lip. "—I mean they *aren't*
disreputable people. They're just down on their luck. They
need some help."

Frustration tightened within Alex's chest as he strolled
across the room, his hands locked behind him. "Perhaps
you're right, but there is a chance your old friends will
need *some help* until your inheritance is completely gone,"
he observed dryly. He looked over his shoulder at her, at
the splash of color she presented standing in front of the
dark library paneling. "I'm trying to protect your interests,
and I suspect if you start giving now there will be no end
of it when you come into your full inheritance."

She took a deep breath, her snowy breasts swelling
against the neckline of her gown. "It's my money. I can
give it away if I like."

He studied her, realizing that despite her saucy tongue
she was really very innocent about human nature. "No, actually you can't. Not until the six months have passed and
you are no longer my ward."

There was a discreet cough at the door, then, looking
flustered, Buxley entered the library once more, his patent
leather shoes squeaking on the carpet. "A Miss Kid Glove
Rosie is here to see Miss Davis, sir. Should I show her in,
or would you prefer—"

Before he could get out another word, Rosie breezed

into the library like a battered man-of-war and shoved past him. "Out of my way, Baldy. I've come to see my friend, I 'ave, and I won't be put off by the likes of you!" A much-washed black gown and a gray shawl garbed her stout body; black kid gloves with several of the fingers missing encased her blunt-fingered hands. A chip straw hat with crushed flowers sat rakishly on her head, and she carried a closed parasol under her arm.

Alex remembered seeing the woman the day he and Pell had gone by the Whitechapel tenement, and he groaned inwardly as she darted her gaze about the room and moved forward, her taffeta petticoats rustling crisply. Her eyes widened with delight when she saw Pell standing at the end of the artistically appointed chamber. *"Pell.* You looks like a bleedin' princess!" she cried in a warm, throaty voice. "Is it really you, girl?"

Pell beamed with joy and she rushed forward and threw her slender arms about the fruit-peddler in a tight embrace. "Rosie. Oh, I've missed you so. I thought you'd never come!"

The older woman held her at arm's length, confusion clouding her plain face "Whot's this, now? You not only look like a bleedin' princess, you're beginnin' to sound like one, too."

She twirled Pell about and examined her fashionable clothes, then reverently caressed her cheek. "Bloody 'ell, you washed up nice, didn't you?" She blinked her eyes and slowly scanned the opulent library as if she were trying to memorize everything in the room.

Buxley, who was now quite red-faced, spread his fingers and approached Rosie from behind, but she heard him and whirled about. "You ain't got enough brains to butter a muffin, 'ave you, Baldy?" she asked, poking him in the stomach with the tip of the tattered parasol. "I'm 'ere visitin' my friend, and I intend to stay a while."

His face set in determined lines, the butler clasped her arm, but Alex languidly moved his hand and motioned him from the room.

With a smile, Rosie drew in her breath and gazed at Alex. "So this is the captain 'imself, is it?" she said in an awed voice as she moved toward him. She chuckled deep in her throat. "Gaa, he's a real looker, ain't 'e?"

Alex inclined his head. "Good day, Miss Rosie."

Her eyes widened. "Listen at that. The sound of 'is voice is so polished you could skate on it!" A sly smile played over her lips. "I think I'm goin' to call you the *professor.*"

As she stared at him, a serious look sobered her face. "You're a smooth talker all right, but that don't mean you're a real gentleman." She glanced at Pell. " 'E ain't 'urt you, 'as he? 'Cause if 'e 'as, I'll 'ave a bloke 'ere so fast it'll make your 'ead spin." Hands on her hips, she threw Alex a threatening stare and walked closer, her skirts swishing smartly.

His emotions tottered between amusement and disgust as he looked into the woman's angry face. She needed a dentist badly and he caught a whiff of the same pungent aroma he had noticed in Holloway House of Detention.

"We takes care of our own in Cat and Wheel Alley, Professor," Rosie proudly proclaimed.

He overcame a great urge to smile. "I'll try to remember that," he said in a solemn voice.

Pell hurried to Rosie, trying to defuse the situation. "No, it's all right. 'E ain't 'urt me."

Rosie slid Alex a glance sharp enough to draw blood. "Maybe not, but 'e's sure as 'ell ruined your talkin'. You talks all flat and funny now. Listenin' to you is like watchin' milk spurt out of a water pipe. It fair messes up me mind, it does."

Pell clasped her friend's arm and edged her toward the desk, trying to distract her. "Why didn't you tell me you were comin'?" she asked, caressing the older woman's shoulder. "I would 'ave asked the cook to make tea."

Rosie stared at her with puzzled eyes. "I *did* tell you I was comin'. I was 'ere just this mornin' and I left a note sayin' I was comin' back this afternoon. Didn't you get it?"

With slow deliberation, Alex walked to his desk and, smiling faintly, presented Pell with the scrawled note. When she had finished reading it, she glanced at Alex, feeling a pang of hurt, then she looked back at her friend. "No, I didn't get your message until now," she replied sadly, placing the grimy paper on the desk. "I'm sorry."

Rosie blew out her breath, and, not waiting to be asked, flopped down upon a nearby chair. "I'm sorry too, luv. Sorry to be puttin' the bite on you, you bein' such a fresh 'eiress and all, but Minnie is dreadful sick and needs to see a doctor. I rubbed her throat with coal oil and fed her 'oney and whiskey stirred together, but she ain't pickin' up a bit." She glanced up and frowned. "'Er forehead is blazin' 'ot and I'm worried crazy about 'er."

"Yes, of course . . . I understand," Pell said, remembering how often she had been sick in Whitechapel and had no funds to see a doctor. She unclasped a large locket which she wore on her bosom. Inside she kept a little paper money, which Alex issued her in tiny amounts. She never had more than five pounds at one time—simply insurance that she would have cab fare if she were to be separated from Aunt Violet for some reason while they were away from the mansion. She pressed the money into Rosie's dirty hand, then gazed at Alex, irritated by his aloof manner. "'Ere you go, luv," she said, moving her gaze back to her friend. "And tell Minnie I 'opes she feels better."

Rosie stood, glancing at Alex with apprehension, then an awful silence crashed in about them all. At last, she swung her knitted shawl over her shoulders and hugged Pell tightly. "Well, I guess I'll be goin' now," she announced, her husky voice a little unsteady. After taking a few steps toward the door, she glanced back at Pell. "Will I ever see you gain, luv, you bein' an 'eiress and all?"

Pell swallowed hard and smiled. "Of course you'll see me again. Now that you know the way, come again."

Rosie gave a worried sigh. "Oh, luv, you *sound* so different . . . you *look* so different. Whot 'ave they done to you?" She shook her head. "They've changed everythin' about you. Didn't they leave you a little piece of yourself?"

Tears welled in Pell's eyes. "I'm the same inside and I always will be. You 'ave to believe that."

The older woman pressed her lips together and nodded her head. "I'll try, luv. I'll try." She shot another stern look at Alex. "There's people watchin' you, Professor, just don't be forgettin' that."

Alex kept his face straight and inclined his head, but Pell noted a twinkle in his eyes.

Rosie gazed at her friend one last time and her eyes were soft and gentle. "Well, I guess I better be gettin' on with it. No use for the likes of me to be dallyin' around Mayfair." Bracing her shoulders and lifting her chin, she walked toward the library doors with a determined air.

Just as she was leaving, Buxley returned with the gardener. He glanced at Alex and in imperious tones asked, "Is this woman presenting a problem, milord?"

Before Alex could reply, Rosie paused and squinted her eyes at the butler. "Put your 'ead in a bag, Baldy. I was just leavin', and a good thing, too, or you and that petunia-picker would both get a lesson you'd never forget!" With that, she pushed past the gardener who stared at her with wide eyes, then she glanced back at the butler. "If you goes out today, cover up that bald 'ead of yours. I 'ears birds are attracted to shiny objects."

Buxley and the gardener followed her from the library, and Pell listened to angry voices issuing from the entry hall, then the sound of the large front door slamming shut.

Wondering what would happen next, she joined Alex at the front window and watched Rosie march down the walkway with Buxley and the gardener at her heels. At the wrought-iron fence she turned to have an animated discussion with them both. When Buxley approached her in a threatening manner she gave him several smart whacks on his shoulder with her parasol, then whirled and strode away.

Pride warmed Pell's heart that her friend had bested the lordly butler and she wondered why Alex was so amused. "Why are you smilin' so?" she asked, irritated at him.

He turned and raised his brows. "What else can I do? Though a lord of the realm, I have just been threatened by a Whitechapel harridan. And Buxley has received a mortal wound to his pride. I'm sure he'll never recover from it."

Her frustration growing by the second, she noticed again the glint of humor in his eyes. Why, all this meant nothing to him. It was just an amusing incident among the lower classes that would soon be forgotten. "Why didn't you talk to 'er? Why didn't you make some kind of conversation?" she demanded.

He frowned down at Pell. "And what was I to say? 'Where did you get that lovely hat you're wearing today, Miss Rosie? What is the price of strawberries today, Miss Rosie? How many people have you whacked with your parasol today, Miss Rosie?' I hardly think there is great potential for a friendship between us," Alex replied with heavy irony. Aggravation twinging through him, he watched Pell march back to the desk.

"Why didn't you tell me about this?" she demanded, tapping her foot and waving the note at him.

"I saw it myself just before you came into the room," he drawled in an off-hand manner. Taking his time, he walked to her and raised her dainty chin in his hand. "I'll have none of your temper tantrums today," he announced, looking into her blazing eyes. "And you will not question my honesty or integrity."

Pell felt a stab of hurt and her throat ached with humiliation. Why was *she* always wrong? Why did *she* always have to do the explaining and make the adjustments? And what gave him the right to say who she could see and who she could not? "I likes Rosie and she likes me . . . and I don't see why I can't see *all* my old friends," she fumed, crossing her arms. "I'm not in the 'abit of castin' people off because I've 'ad a piece of good luck." His eyes glinted dangerously, but empowered by her anger, she plunged on. "The Whitechapel costermongers may be poor, but at least they 'ave some feelin's in their 'earts and blood in their veins, not like some people I know whose veins are filled with pure ice water!"

Alex blew out his breath, thinking she would never understand. Couldn't she see he was doing everything he could for her? When she was stubborn and unreasonable like this, she made him as angry as a charging rogue elephant! "We've been over this ground before," he said in a steely voice. "Why can't you grasp the idea that you are not some feckless butterfly that may dart between the classes as you please? You're an heiress now and you must be cautious, for there are many people who would take advantage of you."

Pell gazed at his stormy countenance and clenched her fists, digging her nails into her soft palms. "I grasp the idea all right, but it's just another one of your rules. And I've 'ad enough of your bloody rules and you always pushin' me to study 'arder!"

"Don't use profanity just because you're emotional," he said coolly. "It ill becomes a lady."

"Bein' a slave driver ill becomes a gentleman!" she shot back. Thinking she might burst with frustration, she clenched her teeth. "Ooh, I just can't wait to choose a 'usband and get out of this blinkin' prison. That is, if I don't run away first!"

His blistering gaze made her shrink back. "When you marry, *I* will select your husband. And this talk of running away is utter nonsense. Can't you see I'm trying to do what your father expected, and protect you!"

"I can see fine. I think *you're* the one who's blind!" Lifting her skirts a bit, she hurried toward the library doors, then paused and turned about, spreading both hands in frustration. "I'm a 'uman bein' with thoughts of my own, I am," she proclaimed, her voice breaking with emotion. "You can't force me into some kind of mold, like I was nothin' more than a bloody Christmas puddin' you could cook up any way you want!"

As she ran from the room he stepped forward and yelled, "Come back here!" He heard the large entrance door slam shut. Clenching his fists, he ran after her, and it wasn't until he was in the hall that he caught himself. Lord, what was he doing? He'd let her prod him into losing control like some young whelp. Pushing down a strong impulse to pursue her, he called for Hadji, then ran a hand through his hair and strode about the hall.

In a matter of seconds, the Indian scurried in and waited for his master's instructions with expectant eyes.

"Follow Miss Davis, Hadji," Alex ordered in a rough voice. "She has thrown a tantrum and left the premises. I expect she simply needs to calm down, but I want to see that she comes to no harm. Now go."

"Yes, sahib. And from now on I'm watching her every move with a fine-tooth comb."

As soon as the servant was gone, Alex walked back into the library and went to the window. Crossing his arms, he watched the Indian hesitate as he looked up and down the street, then race off in the direction of Hyde Park.

Her hot words had left him confounded and aggravated. What had he done to provoke her so? he asked himself with a weary sigh. Nothing, nothing at all, he reasoned, trying to ignore the voice within him that was saying that he might have been more sensitive to her feelings. Even as he wrestled with their troubling differences, he fantasized about the silkiness of her skin and the curve of her full lips. What he would give for the chance to relive those last unfortunate moments with her, he thought, clenching his fists again. How differently he would handle things. As the sound of deep chimes resonated from the old clock, he sat down at his desk and tried to focus his mind on the guest list . . . but he found the silence in the room strangely disturbing.

* * *

Pell stood under the arched opening of a Hyde Park gazebo, idly tossing pebbles into a puddle of water. Honeysuckle covered the small structure and a gentle breeze
filtered through the latticework walls, carrying its sweet
scent. It had rained the day before and the air smelled
damp and humid and the atmosphere felt close.

Her heart beat wildly, for she had raced down Park
Lane, pausing only after she had entered the park to impulsively scoop a handful of pebbles from a rose bed.
Even now, after she had been in the gazebo a good five
minutes, a great lump of emotion still wedged in her
throat.

She sailed another pebble into the murky water, trying
to vent her emotions. How dare Alex forbid her to give
money to her friends! *Splash.* Another pebble followed the
first. How dare he say he controlled her purse strings!
Splash. Of course he actually did, but he didn't have to
say so! *Splash.*

With a long sigh, she tossed away the rest of the pebbles,
and, crossing her arms, pulled in a breath of the cool air.
The sweet honeysuckle fragrance lulled her senses, but it
could not push away the despair overwhelming her. It had
been so good to talk with Rosie. So good. Seeing a familiar
face made her realize how much her life had changed since
she had met Alex. But the visit had also deepened her home-
sickness and made her feel awkward and guilty about her
good luck. Besides that, it had pricked her conscience and
made her want to help those she had left behind. But how
could she do that, when she was still adjusting to her new
surroundings and felt so insecure herself?

Thoroughly miserable, she looked across the velvety
grounds of Hyde Park and took another deep breath, trying
to hold back her tears. The green lawns were circled with
railings and tall leafy trees, and the constant movement of
hackney cabs caught her eye as they moved off with new
fares. On the street there was the sound of clopping
horses, and, closer in, the music of warbling birds and the
scent of lush greenery. The peaceful atmosphere lifted her

spirits a bit. Here she could be alone and think; here she didn't have to worry about grammar and deportment; here she could be just plain Pell Davis, rather than a lady in the making.

As she watched the strolling people, a flash of familiar white clothing caught her eye, then she flushed with embarrassment. Running toward her this very minute was Hadji. Surely Alex had sent him to track her down! She started to leave the gazebo, then looked down at her colorful pink gown. Why had she chosen to wear the dress today? she thought with irritation. Of course she stood out like a bright target; even in busy Park Lane, Hadji had easily followed her. With a spark of defiance, she decided to hold her ground. After all, the Indian was as nimble as a jungle cat—flight would be useless.

She bit back her tears, then took a seat on the circular bench inside the gazebo and waited for her pursuer.

"Are you all right, missy?" he called out as he covered the last bit of ground between them and entered the shelter. "I am watching your pink dress and running very quick to catch up with you. I am thinking you are faster than two shakes of an elephant's tail."

Pell leaned over and rested her chin upon her hand, staring at the dappled pattern of light on the gazebo floor. "'*E* sent you, didn't 'e?" she asked dully.

Hadji sat down beside her and wiped a sleeve over his damp brow. His thin chest rose and fell deeply. "Oh, yes, missy, I am afraid I am being the pig in the middle," he said between long breaths. "But I am being worried about you myself."

"You don't 'ave to worry about me. I know whot's whot and who's who. I used to live on the streets, remember?"

He looked at her sharply. "I am remembering, but you are now a fine lady and some scurrilous person might accost you."

She laughed at the ridiculous word, then leaned back and rested her shoulders against the latticework, enjoying the breeze that caressed her neck and shoulders.

The servant edged closer and gently touched her arm. "Why are you constantly fighting with our illustrious master? It is troubling him greatly. I am assured of this."

She looked at his perplexed face. "Troublin' 'im? Nothing ever troubles 'im. He's cool as the mornin' breeze, ain't 'e?"

Hadji continued to stare at her.

She gave a long sigh, realizing he didn't understand. "I've been workin' like the clatter wheels of 'ell and I still can't please 'im. 'E's always so ramrod-straight about everythin'—like 'e was still in the army." She rolled her eyes. "I know 'is motto. *Do your duty. Obey the rules. Never be late.* I'm surprised 'e don't sleep in 'is uniform with all 'is medals pinned on 'is chest. 'E probably gets up in the middle of the night just to polish 'em the same time he winds 'is watch!"

She made an exasperated sound and closed her eyes. "I just need a few minutes alone without 'im correctin' my grammar or talkin' to me like I was a child. Sometimes I 'ardly know who I am. I feel suffocated by the whole business and just want to be myself again." Feeling especially defiant, she opened her eyes, and, looking at the servant again, raised her chin. "'E can't make me do it, you know. I'm a free person, I am!"

Hadji widened his eyes. "Oh, missy, I am thinking he *can* make you do it. He is a powerful man and General Fairchild's will gives him authority over you. The general would not have selected Lord Tavistock to be your guardian if he didn't consider him a capable person. The general is being an excellent judge of character and if he were alive today he would be turning over in his grave. You must try to please his lordship."

"I want to please 'im," Pell said irritably, "but 'e makes me mad because 'e's always tryin' to force me to be somethin' I'm not. 'E's tried to change me so much I 'ardly know who I am. Sometimes I wonder if there's any of the real me left."

"Yes . . . it is a great problem."

In a softer voice she added, "Oh, 'Adji, sometimes I get so 'omesick I can't stand it. Believe it or not, I miss the East End. I miss the costermongers and the 'awkers. I miss the smells and the stinks, and the noise and the oaths. I miss the casual livin', and not 'avin' to answer to anyone. I miss speakin' to friends on the street, and 'avin' an easy feelin' about life. No bustles. No corsets. No tight shoes with wobbly 'eels on 'em." She sighed wearily and clasped his slim hands. "Everythin' is clean and safe 'ere, but it seems there ain't no excitement, nor feelin', nor real livin.' "

After her long speech, he sat quietly for a while absorbing it all. "It seems you are desiring the colorful life you once lived," he commented at length.

She looked at him and swallowed back her threatening emotions. "It's not just that. Alex makes me all confused inside. 'Alf the time I'm afraid of 'im and sometimes 'e 'as a mockin' tone in 'is voice that rushes ice down my spine and makes me feel about as big as an ant. I don't understand 'im. It seems like 'e's sealed off somethin' deep inside 'imself." She felt like telling Hadji her pulse fluttered whenever she saw Alex, but shyness overcame her, and she held her tongue.

A concerned look crossed the Indian's face and he nodded thoughtfully. "I am noticing this myself. Perhaps he has received a great wound in one of his previous lives." He patted her hand solicitously.

Pell thought of what Aunt Violet had told her—about Alex losing a beautiful girl he loved deeply before he went to India. Perhaps this was the great wound that made him guard his emotions so carefully. Too disturbed to speak, she just quietly for a while and watched a group of toddlers throw bread crumbs to the birds, then she looked back at the little man who had become her friend and confident. "I know I shouldn't fight with 'im, but sometimes it just feels good to say whot I really feel." She shook her head. "Gaa! 'Ow I work on 'is bleedin' talkin' lessons, but

I still can't get it all right. There seems to be a knot in my tongue."

"I think the knot is being in your head and heart, and not your tongue, missy."

She studied his soft dark eyes. "Whot do you mean?"

He scooted closer and placed his hand on her shoulder. "When I am first learning to speak English I am having a most difficult time. You know, as they are saying, you can lead a horse to water, but you can't make him think."

She smiled at his mistake, thinking in this case it was quite appropriate.

"Well, I am fighting my teacher, the esteemed Reverend Windwimple, because I am being afraid of losing myself," he added.

"Losin' yourself?"

"Oh, yes. He was my first master, and a minister of the Church of England, sent to Delhi to make Indian converts. I am feeling him gobble up my mind a little more each day. I am assuring you, my life was no bed of lilies, and soon I am thinking the best part of me will drift away like a leaf on a stream. But then as I am gazing at an ancient banyan tree, the noble tree is teaching me a great lesson. I am thinking that inside the banyan tree is the same sapling that is now a large tree. As the tree grew it added many rings of wood—but is not the heart of the tree the same? When I began knowing the very heart of me would always be the same, and I would not *lose* any of myself, but only *add* to myself, then I began to learn—slowly at first, but before you could say Tom Robinson, the English words began to stack up like beans in a pile."

She looked at him, considering his words, wondering if he could possibly be right. As she thought of the poor progress she had made in her lessons and her recent argument with Alex, she hung her head and a wave of depression rolled over her.

Hadji pressed his slim hand over hers. "Don't be sad, missy. You will be progressing with time. You must be remembering that London wasn't built in a day."

She tried to smile, but her lips quivered too much.

"I am making you a bargain," he added.

"A bargain?"

"Yes," he said, looking upward and scanning the gazebo. "I am not reporting the whereabouts of this curious little chamber, but you must try very hard to not run away again. I am thinking as you better understand your life as a lady you will not be finding a need to escape. When you must escape, escape into your mind as I do."

Tender emotion welled up within her as the servant's words fell upon her heart. "Thank you, 'Adji," she said softly. "Thank you for talkin' to me like this . . . and I'll be thinkin' on your words."

He smiled at her gently. "Come, we must be going back."

Her mind filled with deep questions, Pell pondered Hadji's statement as they walked across the park. Was he right? Was the knot in her mind and not her tongue? And if it was, was there time enough left to untie it before her coming out ball?

Chapter 6

Listening to the muffled sounds of chimes floating up the staircase, Pell crept from her bedroom and closed the door behind her. Dressed in a lacy silk nightgown, she walked to the second-story landing in her soft kid slippers, then, guided by a shaft of moonlight, moved down the stairs on her way to the kitchen.

Still disturbed by her argument with Alex, she had pondered Hadji's soothing words, but to no avail. She still felt angry and frustrated. Apprehension about the coming-out ball also loomed in her head like some frightening medieval gargoyle, preventing sleep and making her decide the knot inside of her was simply too tight to untie. The realization left her shaken, but at the same time with a sense of blessed freedom. Why should she ignore the truth? Only one alternative presented itself—she must pluck up her courage and leave Alex's mansion tomorrow morning.

At the bottom of the stairs she spotted a finger of light streaking from the library and her heart lurched. Evidently Alex was still up working at his desk. She started to slip past the partially open doors, but couldn't resist the temptation to peek into the room. A red ascot at his throat, Alex had slipped a paisley silk dressing robe over his shirt and breeches, and now sat back in his high desk chair, a troubled look on his face.

She shivered a little, knowing her chill wasn't prompted by the late-night coolness that hung in the mansion's great hall. She started to back away, but suddenly his gaze locked with hers, and there was an openness in his expression that touched her heart and made it difficult for her to leave the threshold.

"Up so late?" he asked thoughtfully. "Are you ill?"

"No," she replied quietly. "I couldn't sleep. I thought I'd make some warm milk."

He smiled at her, triggering a warm softness within her. "Come in and I'll give you a whiskey. It'll be just the thing to make you sleep."

Moving slowly, she entered the library, telling herself that it didn't matter because in the morning she would be gone. "Spirits make me talk too much," she said. "And I don't want to get detoxicated." She reached the leather chair before his desk and gingerly sat down on the edge of the cushion.

Alex rose and gave her another smile that ignited a small glow within her. "I won't let you get intoxicated, and sometimes talking is very good medicine indeed," he replied as he walked to the grog tray. He poured two whiskeys, and, returning to the desk, offered her one of the crystal toddy glasses. "Why don't we declare a truce for a few minutes . . . possibly be friends?" he proposed in his deep voice that affected her more than she wanted to admit.

The warmth in his gray eyes melted her resistance. "All right," she answered cautiously, wrapping her fingers about the glass. "And if we can't be friends, we can be fellow whiskey-drinkers."

He laughed and placed his strong hand on her shoulder, sending a rush of tingly warmth over her arm. "Yes, I'll settle for that," he replied, taking his seat behind the desk again.

For a moment, they sipped their drinks in silence, then, as she scanned his desk, her gaze rested on the beautiful black box she had seen there before. "That fine lacquer piece on your desk," she ventured quietly. "I've often wondered about it. Is it for stationery?"

He grazed his fingertips over the beautiful object. "No,

it's a music box. My father gave it to my mother one Christmas years ago. It came from the Orient and was one of her favorite possessions." His face took on a dreamy look. "When I was a child I remember her opening it every day. After she died my father placed it on this desk, so he could be near it, I suppose. Despite his troubles, he loved her deeply, and it was always understood that no one should move it."

A blush warmed her cheeks as his lazy gaze roamed over her. There was a new softness in his eyes that made her pulse flutter. The ticking of the clock was the only sound to break the silence.

He held her eyes for a second, then, with an amused expression, unexpectedly asked, "Are you still angry at me because I'm trying to cook you up like a Christmas pudding?"

The question startled her, and she thought it was rather unfair of him to ask her that with her sitting here defenseless in her nightgown and slippers. But she knew she had to reply. She sipped some of the fiery whiskey, then looked into his questioning eyes. "Yes, most of the time," she answered, shifting back into the soft chair.

He smiled and nodded.

She sighed, then went on, "And there are other times . . ." She paused and bit her lip.

His eye color deepening, he caught her gaze. "Yes?" he gently prompted.

She glanced down at her glass, realizing there were tears in her eyes. "Sometimes I actually likes you—just a bit." She dared not meet his gaze and was relieved to hear him chuckling softly.

"Yes. Well, I suppose even the blackest rascal has a few good points," he replied casually.

Lifting her head, she met his eyes.

He looked at her thoughtfully for a moment, then said, "During our argument you mentioned your old friends. Do you actually miss your old life that much?"

The whiskey had stirred her memories and loosened her

tongue, and she found herself relaxing. "Oh, yes," she blurted out at once. "I miss it all the time."

He placed his glass aside and cupped his chin. "Really? Tell me about it. What do you miss the most?"

"I miss lots of things. I miss gettin' up in the mornin' and seein' the sun rise and seein' the dew sparklin' over everything."

"Really? You miss getting up that early?"

"Yes, in a way I do. Everythin' is so fresh and lovely then. I used to get up at four o'clock every bloomin' mornin' and walk to Covent Garden, never 'avin' a bite to eat afore I left. Sometimes I'd eat a bit of bread and butter I wrapped up and took with me, but sometimes I didn't eat till ten at night when I came 'ome."

Pell paused to sip more whiskey, then drifted into her memories once again. "I'd push my bloomin' cart over the flagstones and drag it over the curbs for miles. My arms would ache, and my feet would rub against my boots, and my bones would creak, but I'd walk on. The sky would just be gettin' a bit pink when I got to the market. Then I'd stand there shiverin' while I 'aggled with the old women over the price of things, and afterwards I'd wash the fruit at the pump, my fingers achin' with the cold water. By the time I was finished the gas man would come around with his ladder to turn out the lamps and the square would start fillin' up with people. Vendors and cook's 'elpers, and women 'oldin' cryin' children, and footmen, and merchants, and all kinds of people. And the wagons, and carts, and vans, and barrows, and 'ampers would be so thick a person could 'ardly walk around them!"

"I suppose you were a good bargainer?" he remarked in a dry tone.

She raised her brows. "I'm a fine 'and at bargainin'. I know whot fruit is worth, and I know 'ow to sack it up where it sells best. The sacks must look biggish-like or people won't buy 'em."

"You obviously took pride in your work. It almost sounds like you yearn for your hard life."

By now she felt quite at ease with him, and she sipped more liquor, hardly noticing its fiery bite anymore. "I don't miss the work and long 'ours, but I miss the excitement of Covent Garden. I miss the crowds and the apple women sittin' on the crates smokin' their pipes, and the little flower girls with their violets smellin' all sweet and tender, and the greengrocers in their long aprons, and the country men in their rough clothes."

She heaved a wistful sigh. "It's quite a sight, you know. The flagstones are littered with nutshells, and grape skins, and squashed fruit, and the air smells like bruised peaches and spice and lemons, and someone is always cookin' somethin' good over a little fire they've made on the flagstones. Maybe it's just sausages or fried potatoes and onions—but it always smells wonderful in the chilly air." To her surprise he said not a word, but watched her intently as if he were interested in her words.

Alex gazed at her sitting there as innocently as a child in her silky nightgown, holding the crystal glass in her hand. With her soft eyes and tousled hair, she reminded him of an angel that had just slipped from her bed. But it was her words that touched his heart and touched his sympathy, and he devoured them all, realizing that she was really opening up her heart to him for the first time. How hard her existence had been and how vulnerable she really was, he thought as these bits of her life coalesced in his mind. And doubtless there were thousands like her— nameless gray souls, walking the honeycombed maze of streets that was Whitechapel. At that moment, a vague unformed idea took root deep within him that he should sponsor some kind of legislation in Parliament to promote the welfare of London's poor.

"When I 'ad sold a lot of fruit the day before," she went on, "I would buy fried potatoes and eat 'em from a piece of folded newsprint with coarse salt sprinkled on 'em from a big barrel. They were so 'ot through the paper they almost burned my 'ands, but they tasted lovely."

Now that she had started, she felt a great urge to tell

him more about her old life, and she smiled at the memories filling her mind. "And there was a sound to the place," she said in a dreamy voice. "Kind of a low growlin' roar goin' on all the time, but it was a pleasin' sound 'cause it was filled with life. And when I was there loadin' my apples and berries and melons into my cart it seemed like I was part of a big 'cart that was throbbin' right in the middle of London itself."

A thoughtful look softened Alex's features. "I have often wondered what it would be like to live such an elemental life. If you say another word I shall resign my seat in the House of Lords and buy a stall in the Billingsgate fish market tomorrow morning."

She smiled at his words, then felt somewhat embarrassed that she had revealed her secret thoughts in such a way. "I . . . I didn't mean to run on about my life," she stammered. "I didn't mean to bore you."

He regarded her with smoky eyes. "Nothing about you is boring. I pity the man who falls in love with you. He's in for quite an exciting time."

A warm blush stung her cheeks.

He sat quietly for a moment, then said, "I enjoyed your story. It was one of the best I've ever heard—and the way you told it shows me you have made progress since you came here."

Alex looked her pleased face, glad that he had said the words. And he knew he should say more. Drawing in a long breath, he struggled with his emotions, realizing he owed her an apology. Standing, he slowly walked around his desk and looked down at her upturned face, large eyes, and moist, sweetly curving lips. "It seems that I've been rather insensitive where you are concerned. You're right, you know. You aren't a Christmas pudding, or an army recruit," he said as his throat tightened, "or an obligation. You're a human being with a sense of dignity . . . and I regret that I've treated you the way I have."

His words struck a deep chord in her, and she knew she couldn't blame the glow she felt on the whiskey, for the feeling was too warm and sweet. Her heart full to over-flowing, she thought of their weeks together. Despite his firm manner, he had earned her respect for he had been honorable and stuck by his word. All of that made what she had to say only that much more difficult. Tears stung her eyes as she bit her bottom lip and looked into his strik-ingly handsome face. "I appreciate your words," she stam-mered, trying to push down her emotions, "but . . . I've decided to go. That's whot I came into the room to tell you."

His eyes suddenly darkened and a muscle clenched in his jaw.

She rose and walked behind her chair. "I've thought on it long and 'ard and I've settled it firm in my mind. This laidyship business ain't for me—surely you can see it ain't workin' out. I ain't mad no more. In fact, I feels kind of calm and peaceful-like inside." She let out a long breath. "Just tonight as I was tossin' and turnin' in my bed, I re-alized no one can make a lark out of a sparrow—not even you." She hung her head. "It's best I leave first thing in the mornin'—quick and proper-like."

Alex felt as if someone had just hit him in the stomach. His sense of loss was so acute he could feel it aching like an actual pain about his heart. For a moment despair en-gulfed him, then he told himself perhaps he could per-suade her to change her mind before she walked out of his life.

Moving to her, he gently clasped her shoulders. "I know you're discouraged and homesick, but as I said you *have* made progress since you arrived here. And anyone who can describe their life the way you just did has a great fa-cility for language, a real feel for it—a love, I'd even say." He smiled. "And unlike so many people you actually have something to say. Grammar and enunciation are details that can be learned—what you have in your heart cannot."

He looked at her standing there in her nightgown, taking in his words. If any other woman had appeared so before him she would have seemed flirtatious or indecent, but

Pell projected an air of natural innocence. Wanting to comfort her, he gathered her closer, then ran his gaze over her delicate face, knowing that what he was going to say was not suave or witty, but a bit reckless. "Can't you see you're worth more than a dozen of those empty-headed debutantes who have never tasted life, or really lived, or given a thought to another human being besides themselves in their whole empty lives?"

She sensed that he expected no response to his question, and as he feathered his hands down her back, rubbing his thumbs in wonderful little circles, she felt he was trying to keep his raw emotions in check. The gentle tone she had heard in his voice made her pulse scamper, and as he traced his fingers in widening arches, radiant pleasure spread over her back. She was amazed and pleased at his tenderness, and the look she saw in his eyes made her heart soar.

Gently he moved away from her, then walked to his desk and opened the black lacquered music box. As he did so, it issued a trill of soft tinkling notes, playing a waltz popular in the London music halls years ago. Caressing her with a tender gaze, he returned, and, standing in front of her, extended his hand. "May I have this dance, Miss Davis?" he asked in a husky voice.

It seemed that he had unlocked something deep within her, and she smiled her answer, then felt his warm hand at her waist. As he clasped her other hand and began to move her about the library, the warmth and closeness of his body touched her senses, and like a spark of fire, a deep unspoken knowledge streaked between them. She wanted him to keep holding her, keep dancing with her—and from the look on his face he wanted it too.

Alex gazed at her loose unbound hair and saw the outline of her slim body under the silky nightgown. His heart had lifted when she entered the room and it now beat steadily and deeply. Lord, she was the most desirable woman he had ever seen, he thought as he pulled her closer, feeling his body stir with desire. As they danced in the quiet, shadow-filled library the sweet tinkling music wrapped itself around them with a sensual magic, enclosing them in a romantic world of their own, a world that Alex never wanted to leave.

Here in the stillness of the night, he didn't want to be her guardian, or her teacher, or her advisor. He only wanted to hold her in his arms, and kiss her, and make love to her, and keep her from leaving him. A part of him warned against it and told him he was being reckless, that his behavior was shocking. But at this moment he couldn't restrain himself. They danced a few more measures, then, as the tinkling music began to slow and grow softer, he paused, and, gathering her closer, tightened his arms about her.

Pell looked at his glittering eyes, and for a moment the air about them throbbed with tension. She could almost feel the magnetism flowing between them like a warm light, and her heart turned over in her bosom. His virile appearance made her body warm and languorous, and the desire in his eyes startled and thrilled her at the same time. As he lowered his head and brought his lips near her face, a shudder ran through her and she relaxed in his cushioning embrace, overwhelmed with excitement.

She sighed contentedly. Then, soft as down, his lips feathered over her cheeks and eyelids and the pulse in her throat—then they were on her mouth, making her blood race and her flesh tingle. With a will of their own, her arms clutched his powerful shoulders, and as he deepened the kiss, her breasts strained against the silken nightgown and ached with an unexpected sweetness. At the same time a hot quickening sensation flared up deep within her. She had never experienced the overpowering passions of the flesh before, and this glorious new world of pleasure made her dizzy with delight.

She could smell his male scent and feel the stubble of his beard on her face as the kiss became more insistent. As he brushed her lips with his tongue, a tremulous urgency ran through her and she moaned in ecstasy. Her breath was coming quick and shallow now and they were kissing ravenously, lost in a mist of desire. Her heart fluttered crazily, and, pressed close to his hard chest, she felt shaken by the passion that flashed between them. Her head spun with delight, and, near to swooning, she realized her legs were becoming weak.

Alex had kissed many women in his life, but as he devoured the softness of Pell's lips a heady sensation rose within him. With her, all the joys and passion of his younger years came rushing back, making him feel as fresh and real as she herself was. As he swept his hand over the silken nightgown, caressing her gentle curves, he brushed his fingers over her breast and felt her hardened nipple.

Then, like a heavy hand on his shoulder, his sense of responsibility warned him that he was in dangerous waters, that he must stop the kiss. Calling upon all of his control, he slowly raised his head, then looked down into her starry eyes. "I think you should go to bed now," he said in a raspy voice. Hardening his jaw, he gently eased her soft body away from him.

Surprise flickered in her eyes, and her lips began to form the word *no*. But then she slowly bowed her head. When she raised it a moment later, a sad look flitted over her face. "Yes," she whispered, "I suppose it's shockin' late."

Alex scooped her into his arms, and as he carried her from the library and began his ascent up the darkened stairs she snuggled against him, and the warmth of her body and scent of her hair made his heart beat faster. At her room, he opened the door and entered the shadowy chamber, which was lit only by one small bedside lamp. After settling her in the bed and pulling the silken comforter up about her, he sat down on the mattress beside her and took her hand.

"Your father has given you a wonderful opportunity that makes the tale of Cinderella pale in comparison," he said in a quiet voice as he caressed her fingers. "He has given you a precious gift. Won't you stay and take advantage of it?"

Emotion choked Pell's throat as she looked into his expectant eyes. His voice sounded so warm and earnest and she wanted to respond to him, but doubts still lingered in her mind. "Whot you're talkin' about—me bein' a laidy—would take a miracle."

A smile hovered at the corners of his firm mouth. "Miracles don't happen in a flash of fire, you know. Sometimes the greatest miracles occur a little bit each day in quiet, unspectacular ways."

She sank deeper into the lace-trimmed pillows, pondering his words.

"You see, the great thing about human beings is they have the power to change, regardless of their backgrounds," he went on. "If the will and spirit and intellect are there, they can be molded into wondrous creatures."

Wondrous creatures. The words stirred her heart, for she had never heard anyone speak this way. And she had never thought of herself as having the potential of being a *wondrous creature.* Feeling thrilled and frightened at the same time, she caught a brief glimpse of what she might become and the knots in her mind and heart loosened a bit.

For a moment neither of them spoke. Then she said softly, " 'Aven't 'ad enough, 'ave you? Well . . . I guess I could give it another try."

Joy rose up in Alex's chest like a warm tide. Feeling a great rush of relief, he gazed at her lovely face that was now suffused with hope. "You must promise that you won't try to run away," he said huskily.

She nodded. "I'll 'ang around a bit longer, I suppose. After all," she said, glancing about the luxurious room and gaving him a soft smile, "I'm livin' quite snug 'ere, ain't I?"

Alex returned her smile, then placed her small hand atop the comforter, and rose to leave the room. Once outside of her door, he paused and heaved a great sigh. Lord, he was scared. Scared down to his bones about what he had let himself do and how thoroughly she had gotten to him. Not just physically, although that was there too, but she had touched his mind and heart and a secret place deep in his gut.

What would she think in the morning, he wondered somewhat ruefully. Perhaps she would decide she had imbibed too freely or just dreamed that they had danced, and kissed, and almost gone farther. But in his heart he knew he was grasping at straws. Taking another deep, steadying breath, he walked toward his own chamber. Thank God the coming-out ball was fast approaching. Doubtless she would find a suitor there and he could begin to let her go. The Lord knew it wouldn't be easy, but he would have to dredge up his courage and do it. After all, he had given his word to an old friend to protect her, and as a gentleman his honor demanded it.

The next morning Alex left the mansion early, and after eating breakfast alone, Pell walked toward Aunt Violet's bedroom, holding Chi Chi in her arms. To her surprise, she had slept well the night before. Of course the whiskey might have had something to do with that, she thought with a smile. Or perhaps it was because she and Alex were no longer quarreling and her heart was at ease.

How completely different the world seemed now than it had yesterday afternoon. In one way, the things that happened last night seemed like a fantastic dream, but in her heart she knew they were not. Every time she remembered Alex's words of encouragement and their passionate kiss, she trembled with emotion. For the first time, it seemed that he might have some real regard for her. Perhaps Aunt Violet would know for sure. It stood to reason that being an expert on romantic novels, she must know something about real love also.

Pell paused at the open door and gazed into the old lady's bedroom. It was about nine and sunlight flooded through the lacy shadow panels illuminating the cluttered chamber, which smelled of buttered toast and morning chocolate. With its lacquered curio cabinets, huge tester bed draped in silk, and soft wing-backed chairs, the room seemed a tiny island of peace and comfort. Still in her ruffled nightcap, Aunt Violet sat in a chair reading a copy of Charles Reade's *Love Me Little, Love Me Long*. She had the sniffles and had ordered breakfast to be brought to her room, but was so absorbed in her novel that she had scarcely touched the food on a silver tray beside her.

When Pell coughed discreetly, the old lady looked up from her book, then took off her spectacles and put them in her lap. She was wearing a pink morning wrapper with a marabou collar, and there were two mismatched bed slippers on her plump feet. "Oh, there you are, and you have little Ching Chong with you," she said with a smile as she laid the book aside. "Come in and sit down, dear."

Pell took a seat beside her, then absently caressed Chi Chi's head, trying to pose her difficult questions. After moistening her lips, she stammered, "Aunt Violet, do . . . do you think Alex has any regard for me?"

The old lady leaned forward, accidentally brushing her spectacles to the floor. "Oh, yes. I'm sure he does." She cupped Pell's face in her soft hands and looked at her tenderly. "He's told me he thought you made a smashing impression in your new gowns, and you often amuse him with your comments. All of this was spoken quite freely while you were not present, so I know it is true." She batted her eyes thoughtfully. "And from other little things he's said, I think he admires your courage."

With a flush of pleasure, Pell picked up the spectacles and handed them to the old lady, who put them on crookedly. It seemed almost impossible that Alex had said all of those nice things about her, but encouraged by his words from last night, hope swelled within her heart. If he actually had some regard for her maybe she could change that regard to real love, she thought, a shaft of happiness filtering through her. She enjoyed a moment of pleasure, then, as the practical part of her mind gained control, she began to worry about the ball.

With a sigh, she put Chi Chi down and moved to a large gold-framed cheval glass. The image of a striking young beauty dressed in a royal-blue day dress reflected back at her. The fanciful creation revealed the gentle curve of her breasts and emphasized her tiny waist. In all honesty, she had to admit the gown's bright color and black lace trimming brought out a sparkle in her eyes, and its perky bustle made her feel very fashionable.

Turning about, she studied the old lady's kind face. "I'm still a bit scared. Whot about those fancy people at the ball? I might do somethin' wrong ... commit some impropery."

A blank look settled over Aunt Violet's face, and then she laughed softly. "Oh, you mean *impropriety*. Well, if you do make a social blunder, just smile and keep dancing, dear." She rose and caressed Pell's arm. "Men are inclined to be very indulgent with beautiful women, you know. I'm sure you'll be a great success."

"But whot will I say to all those people?"

"Oh, that will be no problem. I'll help you memorize a list of suitable comments. I've found there is no need for you to be original in your thinking when you are dealing with the aristocracy. In fact, you scarcely need to think at all. Why, I've been talking to them for years without thinking!"

Chi Chi scampered to Pell's side and gazed at her with pleading eyes. Picking him up, she carried him back to her chair and sat down, caressing his head again. "I'm goin' to work real 'ard for the ball now. I'll practice my talkin' lessons and manner lessons, and pay more attention to my teachers. I want Alex to be proud of me."

Aunt Violet sat down and took her hand. "Don't become a lady for Alex, dear," she said earnestly. "Do it for yourself. I know most of this year's debutantes and you are prettier and brighter than any of them. It's what your father would have wanted for you."

Pell listened intently to her words, thinking they made good sense. Just as Alex had told her, she had been given a great gift, and she realized that becoming a lady was up to her and her alone now. When she thought of doing it for herself instead of to fulfill an obligation, everything seemed easier and her goal came into focus. And if Alex believed in her abilities, maybe she really could become a lady, as impossible as it sounded.

Aunt Violet picked up the romantic novel and pressed it to her bosom. "My dear, I'm sure you will be a success, and I'm so hopeful for a romance in your future. I'm such a believer in love, you know. Just the thought of you succeeding in that way thrills me so."

With surprise, Pell realized that she was talking about the possibility of a relationship with Alex, and it lifted her spirits even more.

"I cannot interfere, and you must find your own way," the old lady continued, "but I will tell you this—no matter what the cost, love is the finest thing around. I do believe the most lonely place in the world is the human heart without love."

Pell took in her words, wanting more than anything to become a lady now. "It's just the readin'. There's so much to remember. Sometimes I feel like I'm goin' as slow as a snail on crutches!"

Aunt Violet laughed and handed her the open copy of *Love Me Little, Love Me Long.* "Of course you can read. You're such a clever girl! Here, try reading just one page of this, dear. Your attitude is so wonderful today I'm sure you will do well."

Pell put Chi Chi on the floor, then, with tremulous fingers, lifted the book before her. As she stared at the page, she felt a warm force well up within her, and in that moment, in her heart of hearts, she knew she *would* be able to read.

As she began reading in a soft voice, Aunt Violet smiled, a glint of happiness shining in her eyes. Pell was reading very slowly, but well. Not tripping over her words, but pronouncing them beautifully in a pleasing voice.

When the old lady reached over and caressed her hand, she glowed with pride.

"Yes, yes, that's it, dear. Keep on. Don't stop."

When Pell had finished the page her throat was dry, but it didn't matter. Nothing mattered now. Not the tight shoes or the worrisome bustle, or the hated elocution book—for she had read a whole page of words.

Aunt Violet hugged her tightly, then gazed at her with sparkling eyes. "Why, that was wonderful, dear. See, you *can* read. You've passed that hurdle with flying colors!"

Pell picked up Chi Chi again, then sank back into the chair, marveling at the little black words on the page before her. What magic they held! And she read a whole page of words correctly without dropping an *h* or an *ing*, or whining through her nose, or making noises like a squeaky gate.

Perhaps, just perhaps, she did have it within her to become a *wondrous creature*, as Alex had suggested. She lifted her chin and straightened her shoulders, now more determined than ever to do well at the ball. With a thrill of expectation, she wondered how Alex would respond to her in the future, now that she had untied her mental knots and was really making progress toward becoming a lady.

At that moment, a little sense of power welled up within her and she felt totally alive and at least two inches taller than she had the day before. It was all so exciting, she thought. Exciting and very scary.

Chapter 7

One hour before Pell's coming-out ball was to begin, Alex stood in his drawing room thoughtfully sipping a glass of Irish whiskey. Dressed in long-tailed evening wear and a white cravat, he was ready to receive his guests, who would soon be arriving in elegant carriages pulled by finely bred horses with crested bridles. Feeling tension build in his chest, he strode back and forth before the marble fireplace, which was filled with a large basket of sweet-smelling gladiolas.

Ice tinkled in the glass as he brought it to his lips and thought about the evening that he had kissed Pell, the image of her face burning in his mind. With vivid recollection, he thought of the warmth of her body and the silkiness of her skin, and the remembered sensations filled his loins with a dull ache. Since then, he had been scrupulously correct and formal in all his dealings with her, but his body stirred with desire every time he saw her.

He had never mentioned the incident and neither had she, although she had blushed deeply the next time she had seen him, and for several days her voice trembled when she spoke to him. He had dredged up the last iota of his discipline to put the evening behind him, but despite his best efforts, he fantasized about her constantly. How could he forget the taste of her lips under his or the feel of her lush body against him? The very memory of the midnight interlude made his blood race with longing. As he sipped his drink, an odd sense of relief washed through him, for he knew if she found a husband tonight the agony of wanting her and not being able to have her would be over.

Noticing the familiar spicy-sweet scent of patchouli, he turned and saw Aunt Violet enter the elegantly decorated room. She was dressed in a modestly cut blue silk ball gown which became an older lady; white gloves covered her plump arms and blue plumes adorned her silvery hair. The gown boasted a train edged in purple ruching, which also decorated the garment's gathered sleeves and large bustle. Waving a fan of blue ostrich plumes to cool her flushed face, she lifted her skirt from the polished floor and walked toward him, her features tense with worry.

When she reached his side, he ran his eyes over her and with a spurt of amusement noticed that her gloves were inside out. "Your gloves, darling . . . you need to turn them."

She glanced at her spread hands and batted her eyelashes. "Oh . . . and so I do. Now how on earth could that have happened?"

Alex knew that in her nervousness about the ball, she had probably stripped them on and off several times and without noticing had put them on inside out.

"Is Pell ready?" he asked, watching her tug off the gloves. "The guests will be arriving soon."

"Yes, dear, she's ready, and she looks wonderful," Aunt Violet replied, slipping the turned gloves over her arms. She placed a hand over her large bosom that rose and fell with excitement. "I've never seen such a charming debutante. I'm sure the young dandies will all be agog tonight."

A dart of jealousy shot through Alex's chest and for a moment he wanted to lock his front door and not permit the guests into the mansion. Then the rational part of his brain told him he was being ridiculous. After all, his goal was to marry off his ward, and tonight would be a perfect time to look over the perspective suitors. Yet something deep in his soul rebelled at the thought of another man touching her.

"Alex, you look strange, dear. Are you all right?"

He hastily glanced away, then looked back at her and lifted his brows. "Yes, of course I'm all right. Why shouldn't I be all right?"

She stared at him, her eyes wide. "My, you are a bit touchy tonight, aren't you? Well, it's perfectly normal. The girl's whole future could hang on this evening." She frowned and searched his face. "I'm concerned about you trying to pass her off as an industrialist's daughter, dear. You know how reluctant the aristocracy is to accept those below their station."

"Pell's background may be imaginary, but her money is very real, and the aristocracy is always impressed with money," he said, trying to project a composure he did not feel. He sipped more of his drink and paced about restlessly. "American heiresses are invading the country in droves and marring impoverished aristocrats every season. If the *ton* will accept foreign heiresses, they will accept an English one from Newcastle."

"I suppose you're right. She has improved greatly in all respects, but I'm still concerned. She talks well enough now if she's concentrating, but a bit of stress will send her back to her old voice. And she's confused about the story you've concocted for her." Aunt Violet batted her eyes thoughtfully. "The whole deception seems so shaky," she added, pressing a lace handkerchief against the base of her throat where a pulse fluttered nervously. "Doesn't your conscience ache?"

He shrugged negligently, then placed his drink on a table. "No, it doesn't ache; it hasn't ached in years, for I no longer possess that overrated commodity. I find it to be perfectly dispensable—just like one's appendix. In this cold world one must be more tactful than truthful to be a social success. You know the pompous group we've invited tonight would never give her a chance if they knew she was illegitimate."

She nodded. "Yes, I'm sure you're right, but what will you do when a suitable husband has been found? Surely the man must know about her real past."

Alex smiled, trying to quell the strange sadness in his heart. "I will leave that decision in the girl's hands. The general instructed me to find her a husband, and I assure you he wasn't opposed to making adjustments in the truth." He glanced at the bronze gilt mantel clock that now chimed the half hour. "Did you ask her to come down?"

"Yes, the maid was just finishing her hair. I'll see what is keeping her." Fanning herself vigorously, Aunt Violet walked across the room, then paused and glanced over her shoulder. "The whole affair *is* rather exciting, isn't it?"

His mouth quirked upward. "Yes, the same way dashing in front of a coach is exciting."

After his aunt had left, Alex picked up his drink and walked across the carpet. At the windows he watched the streetlights glowing warmly against a night sky. He could see well, for a full moon flashed through the clouds and shone over the treetops, and light pooled onto the paving stones from the mansions across the street.

He sipped the potent whiskey, letting it loosen his mind and stir his memories. Aunt Violet had worked tirelessly and General Fairchild's money had been spent lavishly to make the ball a success. Extra footmen and maids had been hired, and the front hall was garlanded with roses. The ballroom itself was a bower of greenery and Parma violets, and since the event was to begin fashionably late at nine, a cold buffet would be served at midnight. The musicians, who were already tuning their instruments, had cost a fortune and Pell's gown was worth a shocking sum. All this expense and energy to launch one small fruit-peddler into society, he thought with amusement. Just as he placed the glass aside, the rustle of silk caught his attention and he turned about, marveling at the sight before him.

Pell stood just inside the drawing-room doors. Dressed in a fantastic cream-colored gown decorated with clusters of tiny pink rosebuds, she stood out like a white flower against the green silk wall covering. Her waist looked unbelievably small and her silky bosom swelled over the gown's low décolletage in an enticing manner. The gown's short puffed sleeves were heavily gathered and edged in expensive lace, which was also lavished on the large bustle and long trailing skirt; rosebuds twined in her upswept hair that cascaded over one shoulder in silvery ringlets.

A thrill of excitement shot through Alex as he continued drinking her in. Her face could only be described as that of an angel. Pearls hung from her ears and roped her neck and slender wrists, and long white kid gloves emphasized the shape of her lovely arms. She carried an expensive ostrich-feather fan with a mother-of-pearl handle. The lamp's glow caught on her watered silk gown with every movement she made and it shimmered and glistened in the light, dazzling and pleasing the eye. All told, she was exquisite—as breathtaking as a nimbus of sparkling stars.

Alex felt something akin to awe. At the same time he knew that every man at the ball would fall in love with her and pain twisted his heart. She looked like a bloody princess, and she was beginning to talk and act like one too. Damned if she wasn't. And he had created her. Created the vision of feminine beauty that stood before him from a dirty ragamuffin who had once wiped her nose on her sleeve.

Pell's heart turned over in her breast as she looked at Alex standing across the room, by the windows. Dressed in formal evening clothes with a white tie and military decorations blazing on his breast, he was magnificent. He had said not a word about their passionate incident, but she constantly recalled the smoldering desire in his eyes, and remembered the thrill that had coursed through her when, for one glorious moment, they had dropped their roles and been simply man and woman. How she wanted to feel his arms about her once more.

With a dart of pain, she wondered if the kiss had been no more than an accident—something that would never happen again. Even though she wore fine gowns and had a different way of speaking she had no idea how aristocrats really behaved. Perhaps they bestowed meaningless kisses on foolish girls all the time. Alex had made no promises. Perhaps the kiss meant nothing at all.

And after all, how could someone as important as him have any feelings for her? Despite her wealth, she was nothing more than a Whitechapel guttersnipe blessed with a stroke of unbelievable good luck. She might deceive everyone else in the ballroom tonight, but he would know her for what she was—a bastard giving the performance of her life.

Alex watched her as she walked toward him with practiced grace. A few feet from his side she made a sweeping curtsy, her silken skirt rustling softly. Her lashes dark against her cheeks, she bowed her head in a formal greeting.

As he studied her delicate features and creamy skin, he found her to be perfect, and a deep, almost savage physical longing for her pulled at his heart and loins. He wanted to tell her how beautiful she was; he wanted to tell her that his heart ached at the sight of her. Instead, he reined in his emotions and quipped, "No red plumes or black jet beading tonight?"

She looked up and smiled softly. "I know it's kind of plain, being all white, but Aunt Violet said it's all I could wear."

Taking her small gloved hand in his, he raised her from her curtsy. The innocent statement touched him, and at that moment he realized that no matter how dramatically she changed her appearance or speech, she would always be a Cockney at heart.

"Well . . . do I look all right?" she asked, looking at him for approval.

"Despite the disappointing lack of a red plume, you look just as a young girl should for her coming-out ball," he replied smoothly. "In fact, I expect to hear a flourish of harp music at any moment."

She met his gaze with agitated eyes.

"What's troubling you now?"

"I'm as nervous as a fly in a glue pot. I'm afraid I'll

make a mistake this evening. I might do something foolish or sound ignorant when the young men ask me questions."

"Good God," he replied softly, "no one expects you to be Toby the learned dog, who can spell, read, and tell the points of the sun's rising." He stepped back, skimming his gaze over her. "Don't you realize that the less you know, the more the men will like you? Men look for purity and submissiveness in their wives, not intellectual brilliance."

He walked to the grog tray and poured himself another whiskey, then returned and raised her small chin. "Now, pay attention. I want to ask you some questions."

"Questions?"

"Yes . . . The nicest thing about telling the truth is that one does not have to remember what one said. Unfortunately, we will not have the luxury of telling the truth this evening." He studied her face, amazed that she still looked so fresh and childlike after the life she had led. "I want you to tell me about your past—the past I've invented for you."

Uncertainty shadowed her large eyes. "Are . . . are you sure I must say these things?"

"Absolutely. Honesty might make your character, but it will ruin you completely in the social world."

She heaved a pained sigh, then moved away from him. "Very well," she began. "I was born in Newcastle to Shelton Davis and his wife Elizabeth. My father was a wealthy industrialist and phi-philanderer." She gave him a worried look. "What's a philanderer again?"

He touched a hand to his temple and smiled. "The word is *philanthropist*. That means a good man who gives to the needy. Remember that." He studied her as she walked about the room, lamplight washing over her delicate profile. "Tell me about your youth."

She turned toward him with a swish of silk and taffeta. "My parents died when I was very young. I had no brothers or sisters, or relations to take me in." Looking thoughtful, she paused a moment, then went on. "Although your father was of the nobility and mine was not, they were distantly related. They also attended Oxford together and were the best of friends. Before my father died he made the Earl of Tavistock my guardian."

Alex smiled to himself, noticing she had added the part about Oxford herself. With her colorful imagination, she would no doubt add a long-lost cousin who resided in Bath before the evening was over. She pronounced her words carefully, almost stiffly, he thought, but no more so than many debutantes. With the assistance of luck and a lot of champagne, no one should notice. Feeling that she now had a grasp on the tale, he relaxed and enjoyed the bittersweet moment, knowing once she had been introduced to society nothing would be the same between them again.

Warming to the tale, she paused and toyed with one of her ringlets. "Your father never took me into his home, but he planned my education and saw to my affairs. I was gently reared in the Convent of Saint Bartholomew by the good nuns, then attended a nearby finishing school. It had been agreed that when your father died, the responsibility of looking after me would fall to the new Lord of Tavistock. After your elder brother was killed, you became my guardian and have chosen to sponsor my coming-out ball."

How well she had done, he thought proudly, charmed with her beauty and innocence. For one lingering moment he feasted his eyes on her, almost wishing she hadn't learned her lessons so well. Then, with a sense of deep loss, he realized it was time to let her go. "I think you finally have it," he said quietly.

She lifted her dainty brows. "Yes, I have it . . . the question is, will they believe it?"

"Never mind about that," he said lightly. "We've set our course and must go on without flinching. From this night on *never* tell anyone about your real past—this is extremely important, and a vow we must both hold to."

She nodded thoughtfully.

"Tonight I want you to engage our guests in conversations about the weather and other trivialities—only those topics. Don't talk about politics, religion or illness. And don't laugh too loudly. Do you understand?"

She nodded again. "Yes, of course I understand," she replied with twinkling eyes. "I understand that you're the greatest lawgiver since Moses."

He smiled crookedly. "I see your natural spirit of rebellion has conquered your stage fright." He paused and said, "Don't forget to smile. Smile until your face aches and you can't smile a minute longer."

"Yes, I'll try," she answered softly.

A moment of charged silence filled the air, then he said, "I think you should go upstairs and rest until you are called. When you come down I'll escort you into the ballroom myself and present you to the guests."

She nodded and gracefully moved to the drawing-room doors, holding her back straight and her chin raised a bit, just as he had taught her. She glanced back as she put her slender hand on the knob. "Thank you," she said quietly. She lowered her dark lashes for a moment, then met his eyes once more.

There was a tender look on her face that tore at his heart. For an instant, his chest tightened with deep feeling—then he pushed it aside, and scanned every inch of her appearance. "If you drop an *h* tonight I shall personally throttle you," he drawled at last. "Do you understand?"

A smile tugged at her lips. "Whot's the matter, Professor? You afraid I'll embarrass you? I can talk like a friggin' angel now, I can." She glanced at the trimming on her dress. "But I still 'ates the bleedin' rosebuds!"

When she slipped from the room and closed the doors behind her, Alex found himself smiling. There wasn't another woman in London who would have spoken those words. There had been a number of women in his life, but he had never been acquainted with anyone who had piqued his interest like this saucy guttersnipe. In that quiet, secret moment, he admitted to himself that she was the cleverest and most amusing girl he had ever known.

True, the chit could be frightfully infuriating, but she was certainly never boring. With her flashing eyes and impudent tongue, he could only wonder what the evening would hold for her.

Regret flooding through him, he thought of her in her tattered rags—when she had been his and his alone. Now she was no longer the Cockney girl he had plucked from the detention house, but the most ravishing creature he had ever seen—and some man would claim her as his own.

He walked to the window and looked outside again. He saw the long front walk, which had been covered with a crimson runner and sheltered with a green-striped awning. A moment later, there was the clip-clop of horses and a carriage drew up in front. Gentlemen in top hats and tails got out and assisted laughing women in sparkling dresses from the vehicle while his hired footmen stood at attention.

With a weary sigh, he girded up his strength, then turned and walked from the drawing room into the large, flower-decked entry hall, preparing himself for what he was sure would be the worst evening of his life.

Pell stood with Alex in the large black-and-white tiled entry hall scarcely able to breathe. She could hear strains of music wafting under the ballroom doors and the murmur of expectant voices. All those people were waiting. Waiting just for her—Pell Davis of Cat and Wheel Alley.

For one insane moment she wondered if she would meet someone to whom she had once sold fruit. What if they recognized her? Then she told herself she was being silly. Who would have given her a second look when she had been a shabby fruit-peddler? She was now an heiress and she must remember it; she must remember that the blood of a brilliant man ran in her veins and it was time to begin her new life.

After she had taken several deep breaths, Alex nodded

at a footman and the door opened to reveal a melange of color and music and loud applause. Pell's heart lurched, but she lifted her chin a bit higher, and, remembering her instructions to smile, stepped forward to greet the cream of the aristocracy.

Alex guided her through the crowd to a receiving line where Aunt Violet waited. A dowager in a rose silk dress approached Pell and smiled sweetly. The woman's skin was as old and wrinkled as used tissue paper, but diamonds encircled her thin neck and bony wrists. "So you are Alex's little heiress from the north," she commented in a friendly voice. "I'm so glad to meet you, my dear!"

Pell's heart hammered furiously as she stood in the line greeting her guests. Trying to smile, she clasped the older woman's outstretched hand. "I'm so glad you could come," she answered, carefully pronouncing each word. She forced herself to speak softly and gently as she had been taught, even though her cool hands trembled ever so slightly.

As the dowager moved on, Pell glanced at Alex, who towered by her side. With his broad shoulders, jet-black hair, and aristocratic features he was undeniably attractive, and she noticed a host of feminine gazes flickering over him as the guests milled about the ballroom, visiting with each other. She had to admit there was something seductive about him, and ironically his brooding expression only deepened his dangerous appeal.

Another hand was thrust toward her. With a feeling of pity, she looked into the sallow face of a thin girl garbed in a yellow dress. The gown did little for the painfully shy girl whose mousy hair had been crimped into tight little ringlets.

"May I present Lady Lilly," Alex said. "I have known her father, the Earl of Bockingford, for years."

A deep blush stained the girl's cheeks. "I came with Papa. Claude Dubois, my escort, sent word that he had been unavoidably detained. Perhaps he will arrive later. He is just over from Paris and a fine artist."

Lilly's eyes glistened as she spoke of her absent escort and Pell guessed that the artist was her first beau. The girl now walked past Alex, and he inclined his head and chatted a bit before passing her on to his aunt, who stood to his left.

Alex now introduced the portly Duke of Featherston, who had snowy-white hair and walked with a cane. Sweeping into a low curtsy as he took her hand, Pell smiled at him, and said stiffly, "How do you do, your dukeship?"

For a moment the old gentleman blinked his eyes, then he laughed and raised her from her curtsy. His eyes dancing with mirth, he looked at Alex. "Did you hear that, Tavistock? She called me *your dukeship*. Can you imagine? *Your dukeship.*" He kissed Pell's hand. "Oh, she's a saucy one. Charming, very charming indeed!"

As the old man waddled away, Alex threw Pell a sidelong glance. "You address a duke as *your grace*—not *your dukeship*. Remember that."

Trying to forget her mistake, she glanced about the ballroom at the gentlemen who were assembled here tonight. What an impressive assembly they made in their tailcoats—but in her heart, she realized that many of them were here vying for her hand simply because she was an heiress.

Surrounded by palms, a group of musicians played in one corner, while servants walked about carrying refreshments. Hothouse blooms covered every surface, their sweet scent mingling with the aroma of melting candle wax. Decked out in a spotless white tunic with a mandarin collar and an impressive turban, Hadji made his rounds about the warm chamber, serving chilled champagne to the dowagers. From their smiles, she could see the ladies liked the Indian servant, who was having something of a coming-out party himself. Once Hadji caught her eye and a grin flashed on his dark face, prompting her to smile in spite of herself.

Finally the last of the receiving line passed and Pell

gave a long sigh of relief. But before she could catch her
breath, the orchestra began to play the *"Valse Bleu"* and
she realized it was time for Alex to lead her in the first
dance.

She trembled as he took her hand and led her to the center of the polished floor. It seemed that every eye in the
room was upon her, and her heart thudded heavily for she
still expected someone to rush forth and reveal her identity. Her mind flashed back and she saw herself at Covent
Garden. She felt her fingers aching with the cold, smelled
the bruised fruit, and heard the noise of the crowd, and a
wave of insecurity crashed over her. But, dredging up every last bit of her strength, she told herself, *No! I will not
crumble. I have gone this far and been accepted. I shall go
on and never look back.*

As she looked into Alex's eyes and he rested a warm
hand on her back, a sudden thrill rushed through her. The
intense look on his face made her draw in her breath, for
in his eyes she read open admiration. She felt almost
afraid. Then as he swept her into his arms, her pulse scampered with excitement and she exhaled a sigh of contentment, glorying in their shared triumph.

As they glided about the dance floor, her head spun with
giddiness as if she had already consumed a whole bottle of
champagne. Tonight there was only warmth and light, and
she could almost feel life itself singing through her veins.
In the circle of his strong arms, she glowed with security,
and a flush of joy warmed the core of her being. During
this magical moment the gates of paradise had swung open
to reveal a shining new world that took her breath away.
She was a debutante . . . a grand lady . . . the society princess of her dreams.

Chapter 8

There was a burst of applause as Alex took the first step and began to sweep Pell about the dance floor, then other couples moved about them, light glistening over the ladies' jeweled throats and brightly colored dresses. Their laughter mingling with the swelling music, the women glided by in clouds of tulle and flashing silks. Her spirits buoyant, Pell gazed up at Alex's bronzed face as they waltzed across the ballroom. "You dance very well, milord," she said cheerfully.

His gray eyes lit with amusement at her carefully articulated words. "You needn't try your charm on me," he said with a wry smile. "Have you forgotten that I helped teach it to you? Behave yourself, or I'll find you a grouchy, one-eyed husband with arthritis—who snores."

Pell laughed softly, then, brimming with fresh confidence, took advantage of the light moment. "What about you? Has the thought of marriage ever crossed your mind?" she asked, hoping he might open his heart to her.

He quirked a brow. "I've noticed that men with wives have half as much pleasure as they did before they entered the bonds of holy matrimony."

Pell gave him a playful frown. "But everyone praises marriage as a good thing."

"Perhaps," he replied in a warm, teasing tone. "But I've also noticed many men praise it as they do horseradish—with tears in their eyes." His amused expression gradually sobered. "Besides love never lasts ... or at any rate, the circumstances have never been right for me."

Pell imagined that after he'd lost his fiancée there had been many women in his life and he had become more cynical with each love affair. "But what about an heir?" she continued. "Who'll become the next Lord Tavistock when you're gone?"

A faint smile played over his lips. "How soon you rush me to my coffin. I have a younger cousin in Hertfordshire who is counting heavily on becoming Lord Tavistock. He would be devastated if I produced an heir."

His dry jests and light, bantering manner lowered Pell's spirits a bit. Was he really this cynical, or just saying these things to cover the pain of losing Carolyn Ramsay? If the lovely brunette had meant so much to him that it still hurt him to talk about his engagement, how could she possibly win his heart?

All too soon, the music faded away, and gallantly Alex inclined his head, then raised her hand to his lips. Warmth rushed up her arm. The pressure of his lips on her hand re-kindled the memory of the night they had danced at midnight to the sound of the tinkling music box, and a warm radiance blossomed within her.

Before she had time to completely compose herself, a sandy-headed young man dressed in impeccable evening clothes came forward to claim her for the next dance. From the reception line she recalled that his name was Lord Mitford, and that he had just taken a seat in the House of Lords. His evening clothes fit him to perfection, but they could do little to hide the thinness of his body or his awkward manner. With an uncertain smile, he took her gloved hand and led her away from Alex, who watched her with warm eyes for a moment, then began moving among his guests, dutifully speaking to each one.

As the waltz began, Lord Mitford held her gingerly, as if she were made of fine china. "Are ... are you enjoying the summer?" he stammered.

"Yes, but I've noted the heat is a little regressive." She

blushed and hastily put a hand over her mouth, but he only coughed and flushed deeply once more.

Halfway through the dance she missed a step, but he laughed it away as if she had done something clever. While they talked, she noticed he flushed and stuttered continuously. Still, from the light in his eyes, she knew he found her attractive.

When the dance ended, he slipped out a handkerchief and dabbed perspiration from his brow, then swallowed hard, making his large Adam's apple bob up and down. "I'll ask Mother to invite you to tea," he announced, his high voice cracking. "She's a lovely woman. I'm sure you would adore her."

Pell smiled and watched him bow formally and then walk away, almost bumping into another couple.

Next she danced with a student from Oxford, and as they whirled about, she spied Alex moving around the dance floor, holding a pretty young woman in his arms. Jealousy rose up within her, but she told herself he was only doing his duty as a host. Aunt Violet now sat with the other chaperones in one of the dainty gold chairs ringing the ballroom, and she smiled proudly every time a young man swept past her chair with Pell in his arms. As man after man partnered Pell, she glowed with the success of the evening that had exceeded her wildest dreams.

After Pell had rested and drank a glass of champagne, a boyishly handsome young captain wearing a military uniform with several decorations strode to her side, then escorted her to the center of the ballroom. She had forgotten his name, but breathed a sigh of relief when he announced, "My name is Blasingstoke, Miss Davis—Captain Blasingstoke of Her Majesty's 32nd Regiment of Dragoons. I've just been reassigned here after a tour in India."

While they danced her gaze strayed to the medals on his chest, and he proudly described how he had won the colorful ribbons. As his liquor-scented breath flowed over her, she noticed his red face and glassy eyes. After he had finished describing his heroic deeds, he raised his brows.

"Yes, life on a far-flung military outpost can be very difficult. Supplies were scarce and sometimes we didn't see the paymaster for three months at a time."

"How awful," Pell said carefully. And then Blasingstoke went on about his experiences in India, though Pell couldn't help thinking that the place sounded much more interesting when Alex was doing the describing.

When the dance ended, the captain bowed and pressed her hand warmly. "Your servant, Miss Davis," he proclaimed with passion-heavy eyes before giving her a last lingering look and walking away.

Almost immediately, another gallant bowed and claimed her for a waltz. Standing on her tiptoes so she could peek over the tall man's shoulder, she noticed Alex's new partner was especially attractive. Seized by a rush of jealousy, she fought down her feelings as she danced her way through quadrilles and polkas, and was swept from the arms of one man to the next. But the vision of the beautiful woman smiling up at Alex lingered in her thoughts.

Just before the buffet was served, a raw-boned landowner named Squire Stubbs claimed Pell for a waltz. He wore his evening clothes uneasily, and looked as if he would have been more at home in tweeds. "I shall ask Tavistock to bring you to my place in Kent for a fox hunt," he proposed in a loud country voice.

Despite his bluff good humor, she felt uncomfortable in his arms, and in his eyes she noted a primitive yearning that disturbed her.

"I can just imagine how beautiful you'll look seated on a fine horse," Squire Stubbs continued.

Pell's eyes widened. "But my sympathies will be with the fox, sir," she blurted out without thinking.

She blushed, for she thought she had been too honest, but the beefy man laughed heartily and replied, "Have no fear, my dear, I'm amused by your frankness. Perhaps you have no taste for the hunt, but you obviously have other virtues."

It had been so all evening, she suddenly realized, her

confidence growing by the minute. Even if she disagreed with the gentlemen, they seemed to think her very clever. She had noted that their eyes would at first widen a bit, then gleam with longing, and like a child who had just learned to add sums, she reveled in the wonderful new power within her grasp.

At midnight a buffet of cold salmon, quivering jellies, and light soufflés was served and Squire Stubbs escorted Pell to the heavily laden table. Aunt Violet had engaged a popular singer and the woman now performed at the other end of the room, drawing the attention of most of the guests. The squire lingered by Pell's side for a moment, then, seeing an old acquaintance whose horse had just won an important race, he walked away to congratulate the man.

"I see you have stolen Squire Stubbs's stout country heart," came an amused voice.

Pell turned to see Alex towering beside her.

"Alex ... it's you," she said, putting a hand to her throat.

An easy smile played over his mouth. "How do you feel?"

Glancing about, she saw they were alone. "Excited but still a bit scared," she said quietly. "Nothing gets the blood pounding like waiting to be exposed as a fraud before all of society. I can promise you it's very thrilling."

He laughed lightly. "But you must finish the course."

"Actually, it's like an enchanted dream. I can't believe I'm a part of it."

He cocked a brow and ran an approving gaze over her. "You're doing wonderfully well, you know."

She felt a blush sting her cheeks. "I've made a few mistakes."

"I'm sure no one noticed," he replied in an encouraging tone. "You don't have to worry now. The worst is over."

Pell glanced downward, then looked up into his warm eyes. "Yes, at first I thought I would be unmasked, but it seems they've accepted me."

"You've charmed them all. Not only the gallants, but the ladies as well." He glanced at the matrons who nodded and smiled broadly at the two of them. "They've not only accepted you, they've taken you to their hearts." His eyes shone with pride as he caressed her arm. "I'll expect a rush of invitations for you tomorrow. Doubtless I'll have to hire a secretary to handle them all."

After the buffet, the music began once more, and as if by magic a new partner appeared to lead Pell away. As he took her into his arms, she cast a lingering look at Alex, and with a twinge of regret noticed that he partnered a slender young lady with raven-black hair. She struggled to put the sight from her mind, and as the dance wore on, she started relaxing and enjoying herself again. She had been afraid a tragedy would happen, but discovered that Aunt Violet's advice about men was right. She had made mistakes with a number of her partners, but had managed to recover with a smile on her face. It seemed that if one was lucky enough to have a pretty face, men were very forgiving, and indulgent too.

Around two o'clock, Pell spotted an elegant young man dressed quite differently than the rest of the gentlemen in the ballroom. Garbed in a black velvet dinner jacket with heavy lace at his throat, with smoldering blue eyes and a mass of golden-blond hair that hung almost to his shoulders, he seemed to have stepped from a romantic oil painting. His striking image interested Pell deeply. He danced with Lilly, but seemed quite bored and cast a longing gaze at Pell, which she couldn't help returning with a smile.

When her partner escorted her to Aunt Violet for a rest, the man in the velvet jacket abandoned Lilly and hurried to her side, boldly stepping in front of the gentleman who had signed Pell's card for the next dance. She thought his actions a bit aggressive, but flushed with pleasure at his determination to dance with her.

"Mademoiselle, forgive me for being rude, but I must have one dance with you before the evening has passed."

He glanced at the buffet table which was now being cleared. "It will soon be time to go and I will have missed my opportunity."

He spoke in heavily accented English and Pell knew he had to be Lilly's French artist. "You're Claude Dubois, aren't you?"

The beautiful young man with the golden hair nodded and smiled. *"Oui.* Unfortunately I arrived late, after you had already received your guests." He placed a ringed hand over the lace at his throat. "A mistake I will always regret."

The gentleman who had been cut out glared at Claude, but the Frenchman blithely continued, completely ignoring him.

"Mademoiselle, one dance, I beg of you, or I shall be quite desolate."

Pell looked at Aunt Violet for guidance.

The old lady smiled and patted her hand. "It's all right, dear. I shall tell the orchestra leader to announce there will be an extra piece this evening. Everyone will like that anyway." She glanced at Claude, then the guest, who glowered his disapproval. "I'm sorry, sir, but it is your obligation, I think, to preserve Anglo-Franco relations."

Claude needed no more encouragement and swept Pell onto the dance floor just as the music began. Over his shoulder, she could see Lilly throwing her a jealous glare, and Alex observing them with interested eyes.

As she and Claude melted into the sea of dancers, she found herself wanting to ask him many questions. "I know you're a painter, sir. Do you have work on exhibit here in London?"

"Mais oui. I have recently arrived from Paris and some of my work is now hanging in the Royal Institute of Art. I was trained at the French Academy of Fine Arts and have received many awards. Fortunately I have been received well in London also and intend to stay in the city indefinitely."

"It seems that you're doing well," she said in precise

tones, trying to speak very properly in front of such a gifted artist.

"*Oui.* Very well indeed. Some of my paintings have sold for as much as five thousand pounds."

The astounding price shattered Pell's fragile discipline again. "Five thousand pounds!" she blurted out. "Ding dong bell and bloody 'ell! Ain't you doin' yourself proud?"

A shocked look flew over Claude's face, then he laughed richly. "How well you mimic the Cockney dialect. You are amusing as well as beautiful. Where did you hear words such as that?"

Pell moistened her lips. "Uh . . . from my maid," she lied. "She's always saying such things. I constantly have to correct her." Trying to steer the conversation away from her blunder, she fluttered her eyelashes and said, "Tell me about your work."

He caressed her with his warm gaze. "Ah, now I understand. You're an artist yourself, *n'est-ce pas?*"

A warm blush crept to her cheeks. "Well . . . I do paint a little, but I'm just a student," she stammered.

Claude smiled wisely. "We all begin as students; then, with competent teachers, we progress."

He held her a little tighter than necessary as they whirled about the dance floor. She found his comments about the English aristocracy amusing. He had a way of saying the simplest things and making them funny.

At first she smiled at his words, then giggled, and at last laughed merrily. When she laughed a little too loudly, she impulsively hid her head against Claude's shoulder, trying to cover her mistake.

"What is it, *chérie?*"

"I'm making a spectacle of myself. I'm laughing too much and too loudly."

"Nonsense! This is your coming-out ball. You may laugh as much as you want." He sighed wearily. "I only wish we were in Paris. How dull these English can be! In Paris we take life less seriously." A warm smile flickered over his lips once more. "You must visit me at the Royal Institute of Art. I lecture there most afternoons."

Standing on the other side of the ballroom, Alex crossed his arms and studied Pell as Claude swept her about the dance floor. Now here was something a little different than he had seen tonight, he thought with growing interest. He didn't remember the young man from the reception line, but a guest had told him the fancified gallant was a French artist. The fellow was dressed like a prince and he had a smooth attitude about him that said he considered himself royalty indeed. And Pell was laughing in his arms, laughing as if she was having the time of her life!

When the dance ended, Pell noticed Alex studying her with crossed arms, and a flicker of excitement shot through her, for without a doubt a jealous look glinted in his eyes.

"Don't forget, *chérie*," Claude reminded her as he kissed her hand. "You will find me at the Royal Institute of Art if you ever wish to speak with me."

The man that Claude had cut out now returned and waited impatiently for his dance, and after casting a lingering glance at Pell, the artist bowed and reluctantly left.

As Pell went through four more dances and a spirited galop which would end the evening, all she could think of was the fiery look in her guardian's eyes. Glancing over her final partner's shoulder, she watched Alex's movements closely, and when the last strains of the music drifted away, she saw him standing by the open ballroom doors ready to bid his guests good-bye.

Now Lord Mitford, Captain Blasingstoke, Squire Stubbs, and all the young gallants circled about her, praising her charms while they said good night. She stood there, the center of attention, as they clustered about her with wide smiles on their faces. What a glorious evening this had been! All about her men were vying for her favors and she was lost in the sheer pleasure of it all. Why, every gentleman she had danced with had complimented her in his own way, she thought, realizing even more deeply the effect she had on men. It was a power she had never even known she possessed.

A smile on her lips, she let her gaze wander past her clamoring suitors and rest on Alex's handsome face.

At last, the guests, musicians, and additional servants had departed and the mansion was silent. Standing by the library windows, Alex pushed back the lace shadow panels and watched the first rays of dawn pinken the sky. He could scarcely believe that he had created the toast of the social season from a dirty-faced ragamuffin, just as Pygmalion had created a vision of feminine beauty from ivory. With a smile, he thought about how, in the beginning of their relationship, Pell had been just about as yielding as a block of ivory herself. The Greek myth had ended happily with Aphrodite solving Pygmalion's problems. Alex wondered how the story of Pell Davis and Alexander Chancery-Brown would end. It seemed that Aphrodite had made precious few appearances this balmy summer of 1880.

Somewhat puzzled at the workings of his own mind, he watched rosy light touch the rooftops of the neighboring mansions. Since he had engineered this clever feat, why didn't he feel more elated? he wondered with irritation. He should be bursting with triumph; instead, he felt a vague sense of loss. He had brought an open bottle of champagne into the library, but as his lips touched the half-filled glass in his hand, he decided he had no taste for it.

Letting the panels fall back in place, he lowered the champagne, then walked to his desk and placed the glass aside.

Standing at the open library doors, Pell let her gaze travel over Alex. He had loosened his tie and a lock of dark hair fell over his aristocratic brow. His rugged features now held a sensuality that sent a ripple of passion skittering through her body. A tingling sense of expectancy rising within her, she quietly entered the room. Hearing her footsteps, he looked up, and his lips parted in a smile, showing a flash of strong white teeth.

Filled with a sense of awe at her overwhelming beauty, Alex gazed at Pell. In the white gown with dawn light washing over her, she projected a delicate, ethereal air that touched his heart. Composing his emotions, he widened his smile and tried to hide his contemplative mood. They had both worked very hard for this victory, and tonight should be a time for celebration. "Will you have a last glass of champagne to celebrate before you retire?" he asked warmly.

Moving with studied grace, she came to the desk. "Yes, but just a sip. I'm afraid I've had far too much already."

Pell's heart brimmed with anticipation as she watched him walk to the grog tray and pour a glass of champagne. When he returned to her side, she accepted the cool glass and tasted a sip of the tangy wine.

They were both silent for a moment, then Alex gave a deep chuckle. "What a night we've had."

"Was I acceptable?"

"Acceptable and more. It was all an immense success. You looked regal . . . as if you were in a world of your own."

"I *was*. I was scared to death. My heart raced like crazy at the beginning of the ball."

He laughed a little. "Did you see Lord Mitford when I first escorted you into the room? He was so overcome he spilled his drink on his waistcoat."

She sipped more champagne, then giggled. "He seemed to be in a state of nerves all night . . . blushing, and coughing, and stammering."

Alex picked up his glass and smiled. "Yes, I understand he's quite under his mother's thumb." He looked at her with appreciative eyes. "You had them all agog, you know. Captain Blasingstoke was completely overwhelmed. I saw him after his dance with you and he looked quite shaken."

"I'm not sure he could feel anything . . . I think he was almost drunk."

Alex frowned and sipped some champagne. "Hmmm . . . I vaguely remember him from India. He comes from a good family, but turned into a bit of a hard-drinking braggart overseas."

Pell began slowly pacing about the library, idly tracing her fingertips about the rim of her glass. "Squire Stubbs said he was going to invite us to Kent for a fox hunt," she said lightly.

A scowl darkened Alex's face. "That bounder? He's a great landowner, but also the biggest scoundrel since Casanova. I'm surprised he has time for the hunt with all his womanizing." For a moment a tense silence throbbed between them, then, looking more serious, he walked to her side. "You were fabulous this evening," he said in his deep, velvety voice, sending tingles over her arms.

"I always thought I didn't know how to be a lady," she murmured softly.

"Tonight you were a lady and more." His voice was warm and full of pride.

She placed her glass on a bookshelf and gave him a cocky smile. "Well, I 'ad a slap-up fine guardian. That explains it all, don't it, guv'ner?"

He chuckled, then, moving so close she could see the dark flecks in his irises, he added, "I'm sure many men fell in love with you tonight, but you must promise me that you will not accept any of their proposals of marriage until you speak with me."

Aching to try out her new seductive powers, she touched his sleeve. "Yes, there is so much I don't know about men. I don't know what to do when they pay me all those flowery compliments . . ." She ran her hand over his arm lightly. ". . . or what to do when a man does that." She could feel the warmth of his body and smell the scent of his bay rum cologne, and she sensed a raw, primitive feeling rapidly welling up between them.

As she gazed into his eyes, they glittered with a hungry intensity, and a powerful sensation surged through her, filling her with a burning longing. The thought of what might happen if he completely let himself go made her heart hammer with excitement.

Alex looked down at her lovely face. Lord, he'd been forced to watch men touching her like this all evening and his discipline hovered near the breaking point. All those men dancing with her, and caressing her, when he wanted to hold her in his arms himself. They were all insufferable—Mitford, and Blasingstoke, and Stubbs, and that fancy French artist. He traced his fingertips over her smooth cheek. She was so desirable with the pink light washing over her delicate features and silvery hair, and there was something young and defenseless about her that touched his deepest feelings. He tried to throttle the ever-building desire racing through him, but he felt his discipline giving away like a ship tearing from its moorings.

She looked up at him through lowered lashes, and the raw desire she saw on his face made her pulse race out of control. "Do you think all those men were paying me those flowery compliments because they want to get my fortune?" she asked in a raspy whisper.

He was very still. As a muscle flicked in his jaw, he set down his glass. His eyes deepened with passion as they had the night they danced and the sight of them made her heartbeat thud in her ears. His hand was clenched and he was searching her face intently as if he was trying to draw the thoughts from her head. He studied her for a moment longer, then his hand rose to cup her chin, and he put his arm about her, pressing her against him.

"No, you are absolutely wrong," he added huskily. "It is because they all wanted to do this."

A thrill ran through her as he lowered his head and brought his lips near hers. With a sob of pleasure, she raised her arms and slipped them about his broad shoulders, wanting him as she had never wanted anything in her life. When his firm lips brushed over hers, warmth coursed through her in a golden flow and the room seemed to whirl about her.

Raising his head, he looked into her eyes and murmured

roughly, "You're so lovely. You were the loveliest woman here tonight. How I would like to forget who we are." The urgency of his husky voice resounded through her, sending sparkles of fire through her blood.

"Yes," she whispered thickly. At this moment she knew without a doubt that she was in love with him. In love with his strength, his mind, his wit, the gleam in his eyes.

As he lowered his head again and settled her against his hard chest, she felt his heart thud against hers and realized he was struggling with an intense desire he could not control. Then seconds later she could think of nothing else, for she burned with a hot yearning beyond description. His lips were devouring hers and his hand was at her back, creating a glowing warmth that radiated upward to her shoulders and downward to the small of her back.

As his tongue flicked possessively over her lips, her breasts tingled with a rapturous pleasure that left her weak and tremulous. Lord, what was happening to her? Her breath came fast and hard, and she was quivering, her nipples straining against her silken chemise.

Alex used his tongue expertly and now slipped it between her lips and plunged into her mouth, and before she could believe it was happening, his hand was at her breast. She could feel the warmth of his fingers through the thin fabric of her gown, and a flame of rapture shot through her. Her neck and face flushed with warmth.

He pushed the low-cut gown from her shoulders, and, raising his head, fluttered hot kisses over her face and quivering eyelids. Then his hand deftly scooped into her bodice and cupped her breast, his warm fingers sweeping over her silky fullness. Now his mouth kissed the pulse in her neck, and, speaking tender endearments against her ear, he grazed his thumb over her aching nipple, making her moan with pleasure. As she listened to his deep voice, a chill raced over her arms, and a sweet warmth surged between her thighs.

As he lovingly rolled her nipple between his fingers, she felt her coiled desire unwinding and spreading outward, and she gasped and buried her head against his neck. Then when she thought she would faint with longing, their mouths met in another passionate kiss. As his invading tongue searched her mouth, aching need spilled through her, matching his own hunger. Light-headed with ecstasy, she reveled in the deep kiss that left her weak-kneed and on the verge of swooning.

She thought she might explode with pleasure, then, gradually, the kiss cooled a bit, leaving an emptiness inside her. With puzzlement and a sense of loss, she felt his body tensing before he slowly lifted his head. With tender movements, he adjusted her bodice and eased her away from him. In the dawn light his face was all harsh angles and planes and he looked as if he were carrying a great burden.

A pulse throbbing in his temple, he gazed down at her with eyes full of pain and longing. "This can never be," he said in a raspy voice. "I've sworn to your father that I would take care of you. And I can hardly call deflowering you proper guardianship." He turned from her, and, letting out a weary breath, walked across the room to the windows.

Her body still glowing from his touch, she looked at him, wondering what she could say. Her lips trembling, she took a few steps toward him and murmured, "Alex?"

"Don't you understand?" he said quietly, still staring out the window. "You should go to your room. Go while my courage holds."

In her heart she yearned to stay with him, but his firm tone prevented further conversation. As she moved to the library doors, joy rose within her like a swelling tide. For a few golden moments they had been one in spirit, and there had been no barriers between them. For a brief span, she had once again glimpsed the fire within him, and now that the barrier had been lowered, the exciting possibilities that fact suggested thrilled her deeply. Wrapped in a sense of warm euphoria, she left the library and softly closed the door behind her.

Alex heard her go but did not move. Emotions storming within him like crashing waves, he clenched the edge of a bookshelf and watched the sky brighten with pale light. Even now after she was gone, his loins stirred with desire and his hands hungered for the warmth of her skin. Straightening his shoulders, he took a deep breath and tamped down his runaway emotions, telling himself she would soon be married to another man and out of his life.

After he had regained a measure of composure, he pondered the future with misgiving, wondering what it would hold for a man as passionate as himself. Even under the best of conditions, he had to admit the days ahead looked treacherous. How could he squire Pell about town and hand her off to the other men standing in line for her attention, when all he wanted to do was take her into his bed and keep her there? If truth be told, he thought, running a hand through his hair, he felt like a man standing on the edge of a rocky cliff waiting to fall into an abyss.

Chapter 9

"**L**ift your chin, Hadji," Pell admonished. "If I'm going to make you look like a Hindu prince, I need to see your face."

Since her coming-out ball Pell's life had been a social whirlwind, but when a free afternoon appeared, she indulged in her favorite pastime—oil painting. Today, dressed in a splattered smock, she sat before an easel in the library, trying to capture Hadji's likeness. Gone since breakfast, Alex was not scheduled to return until early evening, so the huge chamber, which now held the scent of oil paint and linseed oil, was hers alone.

The heavy velvet drapes had been pulled back and late-afternoon light flooded into the chamber, illuminating Hadji's tense face as he shifted uncomfortably upon a stool placed near the easel. "I'm begging your forgiveness, missy," he said, lifting his chin a bit higher. "I am momentarily forgetting that I am being a regal prince this afternoon, and my mind is dwelling upon my villainous pet. He is getting up on the wrong side of the mattress this morning and I am thinking he is not to be trusted."

Pell laughed softly. She touched her brush to the flesh-colored pigment, then lightly brushed it over the canvas. As her hand worked on the portrait, her mind considered her new life. She was performing the lady role very successfully, but she felt bored and hemmed in. She longed to spend more time with Alex, who always seemed involved in his own affairs. With a sad heart, she thought it almost seemed like he was burying himself in his work, trying to avoid her.

Though he had kissed her passionately the night of the ball, it seemed he had decided he must resist her because of his loyalty to her father. To her, it seemed that if two people cared for each other they should act on their feelings! With mounting frustration, she picked up another brush and dipped it into some scarlet pigment, deciding it would be fun to paint a ruby in Hadji's turban so he would look like a great maharaja. As she began outlining the jewel, she thought of Alex again. How exasperating he could be! After all, hadn't he felt something for her too the night of the ball?

As she worked on the ruby, she remembered reading a difficult passage for him a few days ago. His eyes had shone with pride when she finished the passage and he had praised her abilities with great warmth. By the expression on his face when he had said these things she sensed that he felt more than a guardian's joy for his ward's victory. Then again, maybe he didn't feel anything for her, she thought with a prick of despair. Maybe he didn't care for her beyond the boundaries of his responsibilities because he knew the truth about her origins. Sighing, she realized she didn't know for certain how he felt about her. She had so little experience in affairs of the heart.

As she enjoyed the way the creamy pigment glided over the canvas, a commotion arose in the hall, then Chi Chi came scampering into the room dragging a top hat behind him.

His face flooding with alarm, Hadji jumped up from the stool. "Oh, missy, I am telling you the devious creature is not to be trusted!" he exclaimed. Bending on one knee, he retrieved the hat and shook his finger at the monkey. "You should be ashamed, Chi Chi! You are embarrassing me in front of missy." He gestured excitedly at his head. "And I am getting many gray hairs worrying over you—soon my head is being as white as that of my venerable grandfather."

Hurried footsteps resounded in the hall and a moment later, Aunt Violet rushed into the room gowned in a frothy pink silk creation trimmed in heavy lace. A puzzled look on his face, Mr. Peebles followed a few steps behind. With his aristocratic nose, white hair sweeping back from his forehead, and bushy eyebrows, the portly solicitor was a fine representative of London's legal profession. Garbed in a quietly fashionable suit with a satin vest and gold watch fob, the elderly man sported all the gentlemanly accessories except a top hat.

Pell felt a rush of joy, for she always enjoyed seeing her father's old friend, and she noticed that Aunt Violet's face glowed like that of a love-smitten schoolgirl. Obviously Mr. Peebles had made a conquest.

Aunt Violet clutched the lacy froth at her throat and gazed at the chattering monkey, who covered his eyes. "Upon my word, Ching Chong. Have you misbehaved again? It's very impolite to steal hats, you know."

Hadji bowed reverently, then brushed off the top hat with his sleeve and handed it to Mr. Peebles. "Ten million pardons, your solicitorship. I am most humbly apologizing for the actions of this unworthy creature."

With a shriek, the monkey leaped to the stool, and from there jumped onto the Indian's shoulder. Chattering loudly, the animal stretched upward and snatched at his turban.

Crying, "No, you must no longer be stealing turbans!" Hadji disentangled Chi Chi's hands and righted his tilted head covering. "You are now living with our illustrious master," he added, looking sternly at the monkey as he clutched him tightly in his arms, "and you must be putting your wicked life behind you."

Pell laughed. "I've never heard of a monkey living a wicked life."

Hadji's eyes widened. "Oh, but this one did, missy. He was belonging to an Indian monkey man. Chi Chi would dance about while the man is playing the flute, and the animal is doing many good tricks, but at other times he would be riding atop the man's head in an open basket.

His evil master is teaching him to snatch turbans and hats from pedestrians' heads and toss them into the basket." He sighed wearily. "After General Fairchild is purchasing Chi Chi for his own entertainment, I am working diligently to reform the little creature, and was hoping he would turn over a new wheel, but alas, sometimes he is regressing to his old ways."

Everyone laughed, but Hadji flushed with embarrassment and looked sternly at the monkey he held in his arms. "If you are persisting in this scurrilous behavior, I am sending you back to India, then you must be propelling your own canoe." With concerned eyes, the servant looked at Mr. Peebles again. "Please be accepting a multiplicity of apologies for this unfortunate incident, sahib," he said as he backed toward the library doors, pausing to bow several times before he slipped from the room.

After Hadji had left, Mr. Peebles neared Pell's easel, his blue eyes twinkling merrily. "I just stopped by to speak with Alex, my dear, but I find he isn't home yet." He swept a warm gaze over Aunt Violet who now stood at the easel herself, looking at the painting of Hadji. "Actually this gives me a wonderful opportunity to visit with you lovely ladies for a while," he went on.

Pell put her brush in a jar of linseed oil and smiled. "Yes, we don't see enough of you."

Bowing his head, the solicitor gallantly kissed her hand, then, turning a bit, pressed Aunt Violet's plump hand to his lips, making her brush prettily. "And now, good lady," he prompted, looking at her warmly, "do you suppose I could beg you out of a cup of tea?"

The old lady's eyes brightened and she beamed at Mr. Peebles. "Yes, of course. Why don't we *all* have tea?" she said, glancing at Pell. "I've already asked the maid to set a table in the drawing room." She smiled again, looking ten years younger. "It will be fun . . . just the three of us."

Pell laughed and started cleaning her brushes. "Yes, with my Hindu prince gone I can't work any more today."

Aunt Violet took the solicitor's proffered arm, and as

they walked toward the library doors, she glanced up and fluttered her eyelashes. "Have you read the novels of G. W. M. Reynolds, sir?" she asked in a tremulous voice. *"Loves of the Harem* was excellent and *The Empress Eugenie's Boudoir* was quite stirring indeed."

Pell noticed a glint of surprise in the solicitor's eyes, but smiled to herself as he escorted Aunt Violet away as if she were a girl of eighteen. After Pell had removed her smock, she walked through the hall and joined the pair in the drawing room. When they were all seated around the tea table Aunt Violet poured for Mr. Peebles. "Sugar?" she asked, gazing at him as if in a trance.

"Yes, please," he replied, returning her affectionate look with one of his own.

Pell noticed that, never glancing down, Aunt Violet added not one, but five lumps of sugar to his tea. Studying the couple's faces, she saw their two gazes still locked in mutual admiration. With some amusement, she cleared her throat, and, blinking, Mr. Peebles looked at her and smiled. Picking up his cup, he sipped the tea and cringed in surprise, then, after glancing at Aunt Violet to see if she had noticed, gingerly forced down another sip.

After Aunt Violet had filled the other cups, the solicitor searched Pell's face. "You look a bit sad, my dear. Is something wrong?"

She sighed and shrugged. "Oh, it's nothing, really. I just thought that after my coming-out ball I would be given more freedom, and have time to do things that I'm interested in."

He looked at her sympathetically, and, grimacing a bit, drank more of the over-sweetened tea. "Don't worry, everything will soon seem worthwhile," he said encouragingly.

Pell sighed. "There are so many rules, and it seems that since I've been launched into society I have less time than before," she said wistfully. "In the mornings there are sessions with dressmakers and riding lessons in Hyde Park, then in the afternoon obligatory visits and leaving cards.

With all the formal dinners, garden parties, and receptions I never get to go anyplace of interest to me." She sat back and crossed her arms, watching as the solicitor finished his tea with a little shudder. "I thought that being a lady would be fun," she added in a disappointed tone, "but it's a lot of hard work!"

Mr. Peebles put down his empty cup and chuckled. "Yes, a fruit-vendor may take her fun were she may, but a lady must always be a lady." He reached across the tea table and touched her hand. "A few months can make a great difference in our attitudes, you know. I'm sure things will look different to you later."

When Aunt Violet started to pour him a second cup of tea, he captured her eyes with his, then leaned forward and quickly put his hand over the sugar bowl. "I think, dear lady," he said gently but firmly, "that I'll have cream this time."

Giving him a tender look, she picked up a silver creamer and started pouring liquid into his cup. Just then, footsteps heralded another arrival, and, turning about on the settee, Pell saw Alex standing just inside the drawing-room doors. Her heart lurched with joy, for, dressed in an elegantly cut frock coat and sleek breeches, he looked incredibly handsome.

Aunt Violet held out her soft, ringed hand. "Come, join us for tea, dear," she said sweetly. "I have raisin scones, and you always like them so much."

Pell flushed with pleasure as he walked toward them with purposeful steps, then paused and gave her an unconscious smile.

"You're back already?" she murmured, basking in his presence.

"Yes, I managed to get away a little early today."

Mr. Peebles stood and shook hands with Alex, and when they were all settled about the tea table again, the old man caught his eye. "Did you know they're having a new exhibit at the Royal Institute of Art?" he asked. "They've brought some of those Impressionist paintings over from

France . . . some of the work exhibited at the Boulevard de Capucines."

Alex accepted his tea, then set down the cup and relaxed into his chair. "Yes, I hear it's all the rage—setting the art world on its ear."

The solicitor cleared his throat and transferred his gaze to Pell. "Why don't you take Pell?" he suggested, laugh lines crinkling around his eyes. "I'm sure an art-lover such as herself would enjoy it."

Pell glanced at Alex as he considered the proposal and then returned her gaze, his eyes glinting indulgently. "Yes, painting is a desirable accomplishment for a young lady, and I see merit in her work." His face softened noticeably. "And I think the general would want her to be exposed to some real art."

She held her breath, hoping she understood his words, then he gave her a smile that sent her pulse racing.

"Be ready tomorrow at one and I'll take you," he said, settling the matter with good humor.

A happy glow spread through her. She would be permitted to go to the Royal Institute of Art. She was going somewhere *she* wanted to go for a change instead of to another dull party. Yes, she thought, picking up her teacup with a broad smile, with the help of Mr. Peebles she had won an outing at last—and better still, a chance to spend an afternoon with Alex. Then, with a little ripple of excitement, she realized she would also be seeing Claude Dubois.

Alex and Pell stood in the east gallery of the Royal Institute of Art studying a misty Impressionist painting by Renoir titled *Gust of Wind*. All about them there was the sound of murmuring voices and feet moving over the parquet floor, and above their heads warm afternoon light streamed into the high-ceilinged chamber, bringing out the scents of oil paint and picture varnish. At last, Alex rubbed his jaw and sighed. "I think it looks like blowing leaves."

Pell clasped his arm and laughed. "Blowing leaves?

Don't you have any imagination? It looks like birds with spread wings!"

Alex cocked a brow and gave her a slow smile. "You're quite set in your opinions, you know. Am I always going to have this much trouble with you?"

She slid him a teasing smile as they moved past the long line of gold-framed paintings. "Yes, of course. You didn't expect anything else, did you?"

Alex smiled and scanned her as she paused to look at a painting by Degas. A lavishly embroidered gown of purple silk molded her curves and a matching bonnet with pink ostrich feathers set off her sparkling eyes and creamy complexion, making her look very saucy this afternoon.

With a swish of her skirts, she turned about and gazed at him, eyes dancing. "Look at the wonderful colors Degas has used in this painting. The orange is so luscious I can almost taste it."

Alex laughed and fondly caressed her arm. Warmth welled up inside him as he studied her excited expression. How far they'd come since their first days together, he thought with deep satisfaction. It now seemed that they almost instinctively agreed on many things like old friends, and just being in her presence gave him great pleasure. In public like this it wasn't so hard for him to keep his hunger for her at bay.

Clustered around them were elegant ladies and men dressed like himself in dark suits, carrying top hats in their white-gloved hands. As Pell turned back to the painting, Alex observed a trio of gentlemen casting a speculative gaze in her direction.

With a radiant expression, Pell looked up and smiled. "I think I've seen enough here," she said, tracing her fingertips over the edge of the huge frame. "Let's move on to the west gallery. I don't want to miss a thing."

Alex took her arm with a proprietary air and proceeded through the noisy chamber, and as they strolled along he spotted many notable socialites newly arrived in London for the season. Suddenly a tall thin man emerged from the crowd, and as their eyes met Alex recognized him as Lord Mitford. The young lord nodded and blushed deeply, and for a moment it seemed he might greet them but, looking flustered, he coughed and hurried on his way.

"Wasn't that Lord Mitford?" Pell asked in a puzzled tone. "What on earth was wrong with him? Why did he seem so nervous?"

Alex escorted her from the press of people and paused by a roped-off statue of a winged Mercury. "Mitford is always nervous, always blushing or stammering or apologizing about something," he explained in an amused voice. "But I imagine he was especially nervous today because he asked me for your hand in marriage yesterday."

Her lips parted in surprise. *"He did?"*

He smiled at her stunned expression. "Yes. And this last week I also received fevered proposals from Squire Stubbs and Captain Basingstoke."

"But I've just met all three of them," she blurted out. "How can they propose marriage?"

"It seems you've caused a sensation. Since your coming-out ball, some calf-eyed gallant is always leaving a card at the house or approaching me at the House of Lords, asking if he can court you. I can hardly walk for them anymore." Apprehension welled up within him as he continued. "Personally, I feel you can do better than a stuttering lad, a hard-drinking army captain, or a lecherous old squire. What do you think?"

He studied her thoughtful face as she digested the news, marveling at the way she had literally waltzed into the lives of the aristocracy and charmed everyone she met.

She sighed. "I agree. I really don't like any of them either. I don't fancy being a handmaiden to my mother-in-law, a nursemaid to a drunk, or a wronged wife."

Alex laughed and felt a rush of relief. "Very well then. I'm beginning to see one must be quite ruthless to be a guardian. I shall strike them off the list with all haste, and dispatch letters of condolence to the unfortunate suitors tomorrow." He looked down at her and smiled. "Perhaps I should start carrying a pistol. Doubtless, until you're married, I'll be the most detested man in London, and one of your lovesick swains will take a shot at me."

She raised her brows. "A pistol? If all the men in London are like Lord Mitford, Captain Blasingstoke, or Squire Stubbs, you'll need a suit of armor."

Laughing together, they joined the milling crowd, and a few minutes later discovered a side gallery exhibiting a small collection of Turner's paintings. "Shall we look at the Turners?" Alex asked good-naturedly. "There's no one like him, you know."

Pell smiled. "Why don't you go ahead without me? I want to study the Impressionists a bit longer."

Casting her a lingering glance, Alex moved into the press of people thronging into the Turner gallery. Spotting the artist's huge *Fire at Sea,* he made his way to the front of the crowd, then stood before the dramatic painting enjoying its wonderful colors. For a few moments he relaxed, lost in the painting's atmospheric effect, then he felt a light tap on his shoulder.

Surprised, he turned about, and his heart beat a little faster as he gazed at Sabrina Fairchild's attractive face. He hadn't seen her since the general became ill and the couple left India, but he was struck anew at how handsome she was for a woman in her early fifties. Her figure was still trim, her black hair glossy and threaded with only a few strands of gray, and her complexion was flawless. Dressed in a mauve silk day dress that reflected a sense of taste and style, she had held the line against her advancing years with strength and grace.

"How nice to see you again, Alex," she began in her low, smooth voice. "Or should I call you Lord Tavistock now?"

Alex inclined his head. "I've always believed old friends should never stand on protocol. How have you been?"

She sighed heavily and idly ran a slim hand over her closed parasol. "I'm sure you know Phillip passed away recently," she said dully. "He'd been ill for over a year and it was no surprise . . . but he left such a strange will." She widened her eyes. "It seems I'm on an allowance for six months, like a child. Can you believe it? It's really too much."

Alex stood there silently, almost feeling sorry for her. He knew she had been forced to live the best years of her life in isolated military posts far from the glittering London social scene she loved so much. Nor had she been blessed with children of her own. He could just imagine her humiliation when Mr. Peebles had presented her with the general's will.

She touched his arm and gazed steadily into his eyes, apparently relieved to find someone to talk to who had known both her and her husband for years. "I know you liked Phillip, however I'm going to tell you something that may shock you," she said in a hushed voice. "When I heard of it, I could scarcely believe it myself, but Mr. Peebles assured me it is true." She took a deep breath and clutched his arm. "Phillip had a love child by some common woman here in the city before we went to India . . . and he left half his money to the girl," she muttered in a dazed tone. "I cannot believe he would do such a thing after all those years I spent with him in the military living God knows where."

Alex raised his eyebrows, realizing that all she presently wanted from him was a sympathetic ear.

Her eyes glistening with tears, she gazed at the Turner for a moment, then looked back at him. "Isn't it utterly astounding? Peebles would tell me nothing, but I wonder if there is anyone in society who knows anything about this wretched girl. She's almost of age, you know. I wonder where she is and if anyone is sponsoring her?" She clutched her parasol and swallowed back her tears. "I assure you," she ground out in a raspy voice, "if I can ever locate the girl I will not let this matter pass unchallenged. I gave too many years of my life to Phillip Fairchild to receive a shock like this as my reward."

The crowd parted a bit, and from the corner of his eye Alex saw that Pell was gazing into the Turner gallery looking for him. Apprehension flooding through him, he knew he must stop her from coming to him and meeting Sabrina. Straightening his back, he looked down at the widow and pressed her arm solicitously. "I can just imagine how you feel. It seems one never knows what life will bring. I wish we could talk more, but unfortunately I must be on my way now. Perhaps we will see each other again soon."

A look of disappointment suffused Sabrina's face, but she managed to calm herself and give him a little smile. "Yes, it was nice to see you. I'm sure our paths will cross again. It seems one always sees the same people during the season."

Alex smiled and bowed his head again, then turned and made his way between the people pressing forward to see the Turners. As he left the small gallery a great sense of relief washed over him, but at the same time the depth of Sabrina's bitterness shook him profoundly. She was a clever, aggressive woman and she had been hurt deeply. As he walked toward Pell he realized that Sabrina wouldn't think twice about humiliating her in front of the whole of London society, and somehow he had to prevent it. Composing himself, he pasted a smile on his face, for the last thing in the world he wanted to do was share his concern with Pell and shake her blooming confidence.

Once at her side, he took her arm. She looked up at him with an innocent smile. "Who was that nice-looking woman you were talking to? I don't remember her from my ball."

"No," Alex replied lightly, casually moving her down the gallery. "She's just an old acquaintance I haven't seen in years." With every step they took he felt more relieved, and when they passed through a throng of people and turned into the huge west gallery he felt far enough from Sabrina to pause for a moment.

"Oh, look!" Pell cried, staring at a cluster of ladies and

gentlemen crowded about a huge canvas. "There's Claude Dubois. Let's walk over and say hello." Not giving Alex time to reply, she smiled and quickly moved toward the group.

Mild irritation stirred within Alex as he recalled how the artist had laughed so freely while he danced with Pell. As they approached the painting and the crowd parted a bit, he studied the flamboyantly dressed young man, unable to control a flicker of resentment. True, the dandy was handsome; his features were finely chiseled and his blond hair hung to the collar of his expensively tailored suit jacket in flowing waves.

That was the problem—he was *too* handsome. Something told Alex the young man would not make a good soldier, for he seemed to lack internal strength. And now that he thought about it, he recalled that after the ball he had heard gossip that the Frenchman was a bounder without funds.

The artist drew a long slender hand across the canvas as he addressed the crowd. "You see, ladies and gentlemen, I have used a circular construction, which draws the viewer's eye into the painting."

With some annoyance, Alex noted that Pell's eyes glistened as she gazed at the boldly painted canvas and then looked at Claude with a worshipful expression. "Your brushwork is so strong," she breathed, her face soft with emotion.

The Frenchman beamed, then, after inclining his head at Alex and murmuring, "Milord," he walked forward and took her hand. "Mademoiselle Davis. Fate has been kind and brought us together once again."

Pell blushed deeply.

With growing interest, Alex watched the pair talk. Their gazes had locked intimately and people were drifting away as if they were disturbing a lovers' conversation. Seeing his admirers go, the Frenchman excused himself, then hurried away to kiss a few of the ladies' hands and bid them adieu.

Thinking that Sabrina might still be in the gallery, Alex started to guide Pell away, but she glanced back at Claude as he approached them again. "Let's wait a moment," she said, laying a hand on his sleeve. "I'd like to talk to him some more."

Once at their side, the artist bowed formally, then extended his hand to Alex. "*Monsieur,* perhaps you remember me from the ball?" Claude said with a wide smile. "If you have a moment, I wish to speak with you."

Alex shook his hand. "Yes, what do you wish to talk about, sir?" he drawled lazily.

"I was hoping to offer you my services as an art instructor for the young lady."

Alex sighed inwardly, knowing this was not the moment for a refusal. "She already has an instructor, but I will certainly keep your offer in mind," he replied smoothly. "Now I'm afraid we must leave." Ever aware of the threat of Sabrina, he inclined his head at Claude, then took Pell's arm.

A disappointed look flooded the artist's face, but he bowed again before they walked away.

As Alex maneuvered Pell through the perfumed crowd packing the west gallery, a strange unsettled feeling rose up within his chest. Only a blind man could have missed the look of joy in Pell's eyes when she saw Claude, or the tender look the artist had bestowed on her. With a pang of regret, he told himself that he wasn't the center of her universe anymore and she would doubtless be attracted to many men—but the admission did nothing to relieve the heaviness about his heart.

As they left the Royal Institute of Art, a fresh summer breeze washed over them, and the air was filled with the sound of horses and carriages moving about Piccadilly Circus. "Is something wrong, Alex?" Pell asked as they descended a flight of stone steps.

He looked at her and smiled. "No. There's nothing wrong. I never felt better in my life."

"What do you think about Claude's offer? I'd love to

take some lessons from him," she said, her face aglow with anticipation.

Alex sighed and looked straight ahead. "I haven't made a final decision at this point . . . but I don't think it would be a good idea."

She frowned and searched his face. "Why do you dislike him? He's gracious and always seems to have a smile on his face."

He gave her a sideways glance. "So does a crocodile—just before he swallows you up."

"It's not like you to be unfair," she said in a disappointed tone.

He looked at her again as they left the steps. "I have an uneasy feeling about the man. Something just doesn't set right about him." Spotting his carriage driver, he signaled him to bring the brougham to the curb, then glanced back at Pell, who had a little smile on her face.

"You know, Alex," she said with a touch of mischief in her eyes, "if I didn't know better I'd think you were jealous."

He raised his brows. "Me, jealous of that paint-dauber? Don't be silly." Despite his quick retort, her words had hit him like a blow in the stomach.

She gave him a playful glance. "Don't forget," she said teasingly, "you must find me a husband before your guardianship runs out. Wasn't that part of your agreement with my father?"

Trying to ignore the question, he guided her toward the brougham. Good God, what was he going to do? She had just officially entered society and he would be subjected to scores of silly young pups like Claude before the torture was all over.

As the carriage slowly jingled to a stop before them, and the driver opened the carriage door, Alex straightened his tie. After a good dinner at the Carlton, he would visit Desiree and prove to himself that Pell really meant nothing to him. He had been introduced to the lush brunette at a party after his return from India, and she had been free with her favors with him. He was astonished that he hadn't thought of the demimondaine before now, for normally he would have visited her several times a week. Lord, had his life become so centered about Pell that he never gave a thought to another woman?

Pell frowned at him as he hastily urged her into the brougham. "Why are you rushing me so? Where are we going?"

Alex smiled and smoothed back his hair, feeling better than he had in days. *"You're* going back to Mayfair. Then *I'm* going out . . . out to find the answer to a problem."

Late that night Alex walked up the steps to his mansion, cursing himself for being seven kinds of a fool. He wondered if he had lost his mind since he had become Pell's guardian, for something very remarkable had just happened. At Desiree's flat there had been the perfunctory drinks and small talk, then she had slipped her slender white arms about his neck and kissed him deeply. And unbelievably he had felt nothing. It was too much to be believed. Desiree and his body had been willing to make love—but his mind had not. More than that, the woman had been downright eager to continue their relationship, but he had left, telling her he didn't know when he would see her again.

Still somewhat dazed, he fitted his key into the lock of his front door and entered the shadowy mansion. As soon as he had closed the door behind him, he was greeted by Hadji and Chi Chi, who sat on the servant's shoulder. "Hadji? What are you doing up?" he asked in a surprised tone. The words had no sooner than left his mouth than the monkey leaped across to his own shoulder, and, stretching upward, snatched off his top hat.

Hadji immediately removed the hat from Chi Chi's grasp, then swatted at the monkey lightly. "Oh, you villainous creature," he chided, sweeping the animal into his arms. He glared down at the little creature, who squinched his eyes together as he endured his reprimand. "To think that you would dislodge the hat of our own beloved master in such a rude way. I am thinking you will surely be reincarnated as a gnat for such a wicked offense!"

After carefully placing Alex's top hat on the entry table, the Indian rushed back to the door, his eyes large and liquid. "Ten million pardons, sahib," he said, clasping his hands together. "Once again this unspeakably treacherous monkey is embarrassing me. I am thinking I myself must have been very wicked in a former life to be punished with the burden of such a creature."

Too tired to reprimand Hadji, Alex quietly walked into the softly lit library, trying to decide what *he* had done in a former life to be in his present predicament. Surely he was the only man in London who had in his care a lovely, but totally unpredictable Cockney girl, a beloved, but dotty aunt, a loyal, but extremely persistent Indian servant—*and* a mischievous monkey given to snatching hats.

As he seated himself at his desk, the familiar scents of leather, teak, and old books wrapped themselves around him with welcoming warmth, and all he wanted was to be alone and think. At that particular moment Hadji entered the library with Chi Chi still in his arms. At first the Indian looked at Alex timidly, then, putting down the monkey, who scampered away, the servant approached the desk.

"Master, I am staying up late to inform you that I have laid out your clothes and I'm also shining your shoes. I am understanding that tomorrow you are having an important day in the House of Lords."

Alex sighed. "You needn't have done that. I can wait on myself. I always have."

A frustrated look crossed Hadji's face. "I am not wanting to raise an odifferous aroma about the subject, but you are now being Lord Tavistock," he said. "It is fitting that you have a valet."

Thinking he might make a drink, Alex stood and looked at the grog tray, but before he could take a step, Hadji rushed to the assortment of glittering crystal decanters.

With a flashing smile, the servant glanced back over his shoulder. "I am remembering from India that you are liking Old Bushmill's Irish whiskey. I will prepare a drink for you, sahib."

"I hired you to help me with Miss Davis, not lay out my clothes or prepare my drinks," Alex said tiredly.

Hadji moved to his side and put the drink in his hand. "But Miss Davis is being already launched into society and I am presently doing nothing most of the day." He smiled brightly. "But have no fear, sahib. I am serving General Fairchild as a valet for many years and will also serve you most excellently in that capacity."

As Alex sat down, the servant walked in front of the desk and continued in a soft voice: "When I am being your valet I am polishing your boots until you can see your face in them. I am arranging your ties, ironing your shirts, brushing your hats, carrying water for your bath, and putting your slippers in front of the fire—being careful to not place them too close. I am also ironing your bootlaces, and even your newspapers before they appear on your breakfast tray."

Hadji took a long breath before he went on. "As to my temper, I am being faithful, unobtrusive, good-tempered, and lighthearted, as the esteemed Reverend Windwimple is instructing me. Surely such an illustrious master as yourself will not begrudge a paltry fifty pounds per annum in return for such devotion."

As weary as Alex now was, he felt his lips twitch upward. The man's verbal ability was amazing. If he had been born in England instead of India, he would have probably secured an important seat in Parliament by now. Although he felt no need for a valet, he knew the position would secure Hadji a place of honor among the other servants, and admired him for wanting to earn his keep. "Very well," he finally replied. "Your work will now include the aforementioned duties—and I expect them to be carried out very well indeed."

His face aglow with joy, Hadji put his slender hands together and bowed his head. "Oh, yes, sahib, and I am hoping you will forgive me for making hay while the moon shines, but I must grasp every opportunity for advancement." He then cast a questioning gaze at Alex. "Are you having some late-night entertainment this evening, sahib? You are looking very fatigued."

Alex wanted to say, *I just spent the evening with London's most beautiful demimondaine—just talking.* Instead he said, "I was visiting an old friend."

"And you are enjoying yourself?"

"Yes, yes, I am enjoying myself," Alex answered wearily.

"It sounds quite festive," Hadji said. "There must have been other guests there. Perhaps you were having a party?"

Alex put down the drink and scanned Hadji's expectant face, thinking that the affair had been more like a funeral. "No, there was no party. Now leave me." He reached across the desk to turn out the light, then paused and looked at the servant, unable to shake Pell from his mind. "How *is* Miss Davis tonight?"

"Oh, she is most excellent, sahib. I am just talking to her before she is retiring." A worried look on his face, the servant shifted his gaze away from Alex, then glanced downward.

"Is there something you want to say to me?" Alex asked quietly.

A frown wrinkled the Indian's brow. "It is unworthy of your attention, illustrious one. I have been keeping a thought in my heart, but it is merely the ponderings of your worthless servant."

Alex sighed and loosened his tie. "Hadji, it's late . . . please come to the point."

The servant gazed at the toes of his shoes, then pulled in a deep breath. "It is appearing to me that you are most happy in the presence of Miss Davis. I am thinking that perhaps she is filling a secret place in your being."

Alex slumped back into his chair and stared at the amber liquid in his glass. Had things come to the point that his own servant had to lecture him about his love life? "What are you suggesting?" he asked quietly.

Hadji looked up, a flush rising under his smooth brown skin. "Ten million pardons for intruding into the workings of your generous heart, but I am often seeing a smile cross your face in her presence, and your gaze is falling on her with great softness."

Alex remembered the wonderful afternoon he and Pell had enjoyed at the Royal Institute of Art until Sabrina had accosted him and they had run into Claude Dubois. He also recalled how he had bristled inwardly at the tender look the smooth Frenchman had given Pell. Could he, Alexander Chancery-Brown, actually be in love with her? Had he guarded his emotions so carefully that he had become a stranger to his own heart?

With a sigh, he put his glass aside and quietly asked, "May I go to bed now, or have you other things you wish to discuss?" He glanced at the clock. "Perhaps we could squeeze in another subject before the sun rises."

"Oh, sahib, you should be telling me earlier you are wishing to retire. It is not wise to be burning the stick on both ends, you know."

Seeing Chi Chi topple over a wastepaper basket, Alex said, "Go to bed, Hadji, and take that mischievous animal with you."

Scurrying across the room, the servant swooped up the monkey and backed toward the door. At the threshold he paused, and a serious look sobered his usually happy countenance.

"Is there something else?"

Hadji blinked several times. "Yes, sahib. I am realizing it is very late—and perhaps I am putting my foot in the soup—but for several days I have been remembering one of the wise fables from the *Panchatantra*. It is about a jackal."

"A jackal?" Alex said in a surprised tone.

Hadji moved forward a bit, caressing Chi Chi's head as he spoke. "Yes, sahib. One day the jackal is falling into a pot of whitewash and becoming as white as snow. When he returned to the forest he is telling the other animals he is a splendid creature, and for a time they are believing him."

"I don't see what this has to do—"

Hadji raised his slim hand and his eyes became very large. "Sahib, there is being a parallel in this tale to Miss Davis's situation."

"Go on."

"For a while everything is being wonderful, and the other animals are bringing the jackal many presents. Then a huge rain is coming, and it is removing the whitewash from the jackal, and everyone is seeing that he is not what he is pretending to be. When the other animals are realizing that they have been tricked, they are chasing the jackal from the forest and devouring him."

Alex lifted the corner of his mouth. "And you're afraid that the whitewash will come off Miss Davis, are you?"

The servant nodded vigorously. "Yes, sahib. People are forgiving stinginess and bad manners and other shortcomings in society, but it is making them most angry if they are discovering they have been tricked. They are disliking it more than anything else!"

Alex studied his worried face for a moment, then rose and walked around the desk. In a much softer voice he said, "Go to bed, now. We will talk of this another time."

The servant bowed and backed toward the door, then, bowing respectfully yet again, he exited the room. As soon as the Indian left the library Alex clicked off the lamp. As he himself walked from the room and ascended the darkened stairs he thought about the simple folktale, realizing it held great truth.

Whether she knew it or not, Pell still had a rather precarious toehold in society. His encounter with Sabrina today had made him realize that if she ever found out who Pell was, she would lead the social wolf pack that would rip them both to shreds, just as the animals had devoured the jackal.

The potential for disaster was great indeed, but there could be no turning back now. They would have to continue with the charade, being as careful as possible and hoping for the best. To add to his troubles, Alex knew that possible social ostracism was only one of the things he had to worry about now. Pell had totally rearranged his life in the space of a few short months and made him feel like the father of the bride and a jealous lover all rolled into one.

The sting of it all was that he was neither one, only a very tired and disgruntled guardian who now had to fully admit to himself that he not only wanted her as any sane man would, but was so emotionally involved with her that he had no desire for one of the loveliest women in London. Compared to Pell, Desiree now seemed overripe, over-painted, overdressed, and oversexed.

Damn the little minx, anyway! How in the devil had Pell managed to wind her way into his emotions so deeply? Yes, he was in serious trouble . . . with no prospects of escape.

How long could he subject himself to this torture? he wondered as he took the last riser of the stairs. He knew that somehow he had to struggle through the rest of his guardianship without touching her, for he had given his word on that promise as an English gentleman.

And he had never broken a promise—at least, not yet.

Chapter 10

Claude leaned back in the petit-point chair, and, lifting his chin, laughed deeply. "Oh, *chérie.* You are so enchanting." He picked up a lace-trimmed napkin and dabbed away his mirthful tears. "I could listen to you retell your maid's droll stories all day. You are a wonderful mimic. I've never heard anyone do a Cockney accent so well."

"Oh, I have plenty of stories," Pell said enthusiastically. "Stories about Slobbery Jim, and Gentle Maggie, and lots of other people."

"*Oui,* I'm sure you do, and I want to hear them all, but finish this tale first."

After smoothing out her blue silk gown, Pell gazed at him across the lavishly set tea table in Alex's drawing room and returned to her story, using the broad Cockney accent that came to her so naturally. "Well, after the peelers took Louise the Lump into the police station, they searched 'im and pulled this ragged paper out of 'is pocket."

"And what did it say?" Claude asked, his eyes twinkling merrily.

"It was a price list, it was. 'E 'ad everythin' written down neat and proper-like, 'e did. A punchin' was two pounds, a nose and jaw broke was ten pounds, an ear chawed off was fifteen pounds, stabbin' was twenty-five pounds, and doin' the *big* job was one 'undred pounds and up." She smiled and raised her brows. "When the peelers told 'im the list was outrageous, Louise shrugged 'is shoulders and sighed. 'Yes, maybe 'tis a bit 'igh,' 'e came back. 'But for you gentlemen I'll consider a ten-percent professional discount.' "

Claude burst out laughing again. "The way you tell these stories, *chérie,*" he said, still chuckling, "it's almost as if you knew the people yourself." After he had controlled his mirth, he poured Pell more tea. As he did so, afternoon light poured through the drawing-room windows and danced over his diamond rings, catching his shoulder-length hair. A blue velvet frock coat emphasized his wide shoulders and an intricately tied cravat set off his satin vest, making him look like a Victorian fashion plate. Smiling, he leaned toward her and she accepted the cup and saucer, noticing the spicy scent of his expensive French cologne.

As she sipped her tea, happiness hummed through her heart. Not only was Claude incredibly charming, he made no secret of his infatuation with her, showering her with extravagant compliments and courtly gestures. How wonderful it was to have a man fervently declare his admiration for her and openly lay his heart at her feet. She had yearned to see Claude for days. Then about a week after their encounter in the Royal Institute of Art, he had appeared on her doorstep with a bouquet of roses and a poem he had written about her beauty. And he had appeared the next day. And the next.

He was amusing and loved to be amused, especially with these little stories he thought came from her maid. What would he think, she wondered, if he knew she did indeed know the people in the humorous tales? What would he think if he knew the stories were bits and pieces of her old life? Returning her smile, Claude reached across the table and caressed her hand, making her feel warm and appreciated. Yes, Claude was gaining more and more of her confidence and she found herself wanting to tell him all about herself.

Hearing a heavy footstep, she glanced at the open door

and saw Buxley walking through the hall. Relief washed over her, for Alex had already told her that he had decided against engaging Claude as an art teacher, and she felt that he disapproved of him. As luck would have it, he had always been at the House of Lords or the Carlton when Claude came to visit.

Feeling happy and relaxed, Pell set down her cup. For an instant a great urge came over her to tell him the truth about herself, but she stifled the impulse; then, with a rush of pleasure, she realized she did have a little secret she could tell him. "Do you want to hear a secret?" she asked softly. "But if I tell you, you must keep it very quiet."

His eyes gleamed with interest. "I'm honored that you would put your trust in me. Be assured your secret will be safe, *chérie*."

A tense silence hovered between them for a moment, then Pell leaned forward and whispered, "Since my coming-out ball, sometimes I take walks in Hyde Park. I'm meeting a friend there—her name is Kid Glove Rosie."

Claude looked surprised, but rather disappointed at the same time. "Kid Glove Rosie? What a strange name. Who is this person?"

"A friend . . . an old friend." Suddenly Pell felt afraid that she had said too much. What if he started asking questions about her past? "She . . . she's the maid who told me the funny stories," she fibbed, feeling rather guilty. "I give her little things. Old clothes, shoes, items like that. She takes them back to the East End . . . to people who need them."

Claude chuckled, then patted her hand. "I always knew you to be amusing, and now I find you are also generous," he said warmly. "You are so giving it is only right that you should receive something yourself." Reaching into his pocket, he withdrew a velvet jewelry packet and pressed it into her palm. "Open it," he urged in a gentle voice.

When she lifted the flap, a small heart-shaped locket slipped into her hand, making her draw in her breath with delight. Popping it open, she saw with some surprise that Claude had placed his photograph inside the locket. "Why, it's beautiful," she murmured, closing the locket. "I don't know what to say . . . how to thank you."

He sat quietly for a moment, then gave her a serious look. "*Chérie,* I wasn't going to ask you this yet, but this seems to be the day for revealing secrets. I want you to come with me to Paris someday, for a visit. We'll stay in my chateau and drink champagne and have a fine time."

She gasped softly and touched her lips. "You . . . you have a chateau? I thought you were an artist."

"Can't I be an artist and have a chateau?"

She put the locket into the velvet packet and slipped it in her bodice. "I thought all French artists lived near Notre Dame in cold flats with gargoyles on the roofs," she said with a smile.

Claude laughed. "*Oui,* that is everyone's conception of a French artist, but I'm actually a man of some means. What a joke that I must conceal my fortune because I want to be taken seriously as a painter. When critics discover I am wealthy they consider me a mere amateur. Wealthy men are supposed to be patrons of the arts, not artists themselves." He sighed dramatically. "Unfortunately my wealth has become a cross to bear."

She sat stunned, thinking his secret certainly made hers pale in comparison. He was fabulously wealthy and he wanted her to visit Paris. "You would really take me to Paris?"

He smiled, showing even white teeth, and his eyes twinkled again. "*Mais oui.* I'll show you Paris as only a Frenchman can!" he proclaimed, taking her hand and caressing her fingers.

"Perhaps someday I could go for a short visit," she said doubtfully, "but Aunt Violet would have to go, too. I'm sure Alex would never approve of me going by myself."

Claude's face darkened and for an instant he looked much older and harder. She could tell he was struggling to choose his words. But before he could open his mouth Pell heard someone enter the room. She turned about in her chair and with a start of surprise, saw Alex studying her with interest. As his gaze left her and slid over Claude, his eyes clouded. She noticed he held a large white card in his hand that appeared to be an invitation.

Claude hastily released Pell's hand, then rose and bowed his head. "Monsieur, I did not know you had returned home," he mumbled under his breath.

Alex inclined his head. "Yes, that is apparent, Dubois," he drawled evenly. Turning from Claude, he swept a firm look over Pell. "Come into the library, please. I want to speak with you."

Stung that he had made no attempt at conversation with Claude and had addressed her so bluntly in front of a visitor, she blushed. "I'm ... I'm with a guest," she stammered. "Can't our conversation wait? What do you want to talk about anyway?"

Alex turned and walked away, then, as he was about to leave the drawing room, he paused and studied her unhurriedly. "I think it would be best if we spoke now, for I want to talk to you about leaving London."

Two days later, Pell sat beside Alex as their brougham clattered through the open countryside toward the Duchess of Roxbury's estate, leaving a cloud of white dust behind it. Another carriage followed, containing Hadji and a lady's maid; the second vehicle also transported luggage full of gowns, hat boxes, jewel cases, fans, and parasols—everything a fashionable lady might need for a long weekend in the country.

As the brougham jostled around a wide curve, Pell looked at Alex, who stared out the window, dark hair falling over his brow. Dressed in one of his elegant hand-tailored suits, he seemed distracted. "You're very quiet this afternoon," she said tentatively, suspecting he was thinking about his encounter with Claude a few days ago.

He gave her a dispassionate look. "My dear, it's fine to

hold a conversation, but it's also good to let go of it now and then."

With a resigned sigh, she sank back against the seat, and, taking the invitation from her reticule, held it in her white-gloved hand. "The Duchess of Roxbury, at home for the weekend of June twenty-seventh," she muttered under her breath, "Devonshire Manor, Surrey." Putting away the cream-colored card, she looked at Alex once again. "I still don't understand," she said softly. "Why did the duchess invite us, anyway?"

Alex gazed at her, and in the late-afternoon light his eyes glittered. His bay rum cologne had teased her nostrils all afternoon, and, trapped in his close presence, her body had tingled with warm pleasure. Even now as the heat of him radiated toward her and his hard thigh touched hers, a shaft of pleasure swept through her. "You're a beautiful heiress, which is something of a novelty among the aristocracy," he explained with amusement. "Society is always interested in lovely new faces."

His compliment brought a warm blush to her cheeks, but as she glanced down at her red candy-striped silk gown, she wondered if she was dressed fine enough for the duchess. Aunt Violet had helped her choose enough dresses for three changes a day, but despite her finery she felt a wave of inadequacy surge through her. True, she had successfully negotiated the coming-out ball, but a three-day house party involved countless points of etiquette, with no margin for mistakes. Licking her lips nervously, she looked at Alex again. "You told me that everyone comes to London for the season," she said, absently twisting the tassel of her reticule. "Why is the duchess hosting a house party in the country now?"

He crossed his long legs and settled back into the seat. "The duchess is in frail health and doesn't come into London for the season anymore. Receiving an invitation to her house party is a social plum. You should feel honored."

She tossed back her ringlets and sighed. "But I don't want to go to her house party. I'll have to remember which fork to use . . . and they might serve me something to eat that I can't even say, like that vishy-swishy soup."

He smiled dryly. "It's *vichyssoise*. And you don't have to pronounce it, just eat it." He swept his gaze over her. "Besides, it's all part of your schooling. That's why I accepted the invitation."

She lifted her brows. "It seems to me this endless *schooling* you're putting me through would be more interesting if it had a recess once in a while." Crossing her arms, she sank back into the soft seat and pouted. "I think you just wanted to get me away from Claude. I'd rather be in London talking to him this very minute than going to a dull house party."

He slid her a dark gaze. "I don't think he's suitable for you," he said matter-of-factly. "There's something about the man that just isn't believable."

With some irritation, Alex recalled the scene in his own drawing room a few days ago. How it had chafed him to walk into the room and see Claude fawning over Pell. Despite her saucy manner, he realized she was really quite vulnerable, and as he thought of the smooth artist, a protective feeling for her welled up within him.

As Pell studied Alex's thoughtful face, defiance flickered up within her. She wanted to tell him she was capable of handling her own affairs, but she held her tongue, knowing this was no time to start a row. But deep in her heart, she vowed to see Claude once more, if for no other reason than to bid him a decent good-bye. All she needed was a chance.

The carriage made a turn and suddenly the Duchess of Roxbury's estate came into view, set among terraces and sweeping parkland. There were stately oaks and a wonderfully kept formal garden; dozens of windows glinted like gold in the last rays of sunlight. Lined with towering oaks, a long drive approached the estate, and as their carriage turned down the shady avenue, Pell saw a cavalcade of landaus and victorias drawing up to the mansion before them.

Baggage crowded the area at the base of the imposing marble steps, and every lady had a maid and every man a valet. Liveried servants were opening the carriages and elegant men were escorting gorgeously dressed ladies up the great steps. An air of frivolity reigned, and it seemed that everyone was enjoying themselves immensely.

As their carriage slowed to a crawl, Pell's heart beat a little faster. She knew there would be high teas, late brunches, long dinners with brilliant conversation, bridge games, and croquet on the smooth lawns—and that strict formality would rule every occasion. *Ding dong bell and bloody hell,* she thought. *How, oh, how, can I survive the treacherous weekend without revealing myself as an imposter and a fraud?*

Pell bit into a cucumber sandwich and looked at the Duchess of Roxbury as she and Alex enjoyed tea with her and some of the other guests. She knew they had been especially favored for they sat with the duchess, while other guests clustered about tables, being served by footmen. She tried not to stare, but the lady's appearance riveted her. As Alex had said, she was frail, but her dark eyes snapped with vitality, and perhaps a touch of mischief.

"Would you care for more tea, my dear?" the duchess asked, then at Pell's "Yes, thank you, your grace," she filled a cup. Black embroidery decorated her gown of lavender satin; ropes of pearls and golden chains encircled her slender neck and wrists. A gauzy concoction of ribbons and lace perched atop her snowy hair, and when she moved the heady fragrance of gardenia perfume drifted across the tea table.

Pell finished her bite of crunchy cucumber sandwich, sure all the distinguished guests grouped about the tea table could hear her. She glanced at Alex, who sat by the duchess on the other side of the tea table, which was crowded with glittering silver and delicate china. His look of approval gave her just enough courage to remain seated.

After arriving and being greeted by the duchess, who

had stood in the center of the entry hall, they had been ushered into the sumptuous drawing room. With its velvet-covered settees, exquisite sideboards, and Grecian statues that might have come from a museum, the room looked like something from a fairy tale. Pell knew that while the fifty chattering guests socialized and drank tea, their bags were being unpacked and their baths prepared. She felt ill at ease among the fashionable people, but managed to get through the introductions by repeating some of the carefully prepared phrases she had learned for her coming-out ball. Still, it seemed as if she had the lightest of holds on the situation and her mask of respectability might be ripped away at any moment.

The duchess looked at Pell and smiled, then offered her a serving of lobster aspic on a crystal plate. The old lady's eyes held a friendly gleam, and for one so exalted she seemed quite warm and open.

Pell didn't care for the dish, but could think of no way to refuse it. As she watched it quiver and tremble upon the sparkling plate, she impulsively blurted out, "Thank you very much, your grace, but I make it a rule to never eat anything that's more nervous than I am."

Several of the men about the tea table laughed, but the ladies looked at each other and raised their brows. Glancing about the room, Pell saw Lord Bockingford standing nearby, his eyes dancing with interest. Dressed in another unbecoming gown, his daughter Lilly was at his side and Pell knew her remark would be reported in London.

The duchess placed the aspic on the table and smiled at Pell. "That is perfectly all right, dear. Think nothing of it." She now turned to Alex, whose mouth quirked with amusement. "What a lovely girl. She's so refreshingly candid. Sometime you must tell me how you came to be her guardian." With a gracious smile, the old lady poured more tea for everyone, then looked at Pell once again. "Can I serve you anything else? Another petit four perhaps?"

Pell moved restlessly in her chair, trying to manage an

answer. "No, thank you, your grace. As Hadji often says, 'I am being full to the brim.' "

The duchess laughed lightly. "And who is Hadji, my dear?"

"Why, he's Alex's valet," Pell answered innocently.

The duchess looked at Alex and raised her brows, prompting him to settle back in his chair with a smile. "Yes, Hadji is a rather amusing Indian fellow I met while stationed in Delhi," he explained.

Pell hesitated for a moment, then, drawn to the duchess's warmth, she scooted forward on the settee and added, "We have Chi Chi with us too. Sometimes he can be a bit lively, and Aunt Violet felt she would be more comfortable if he was with Hadji."

The guests about the tea table laughed at the implication of the innocent statement, and the duchess's eyes widened. "Chi Chi? What a strange name. Is this lively Mr. Chi Chi from India too?"

Pell put a hand over her mouth and chuckled. "Chi Chi isn't a gentleman, your grace! He's a monkey. He used to belong to an Indian monkey man who taught him to do clever tricks. Hadji has worked with him and kept him in practice."

The duchess gave Pell an indulgent smile. "They both sound very amusing."

"Oh, they are," Pell replied quickly. "Sometimes I think they're both good enough to be in a circus."

An interested murmur rose from the guests and Alex sat forward and gazed at the duchess. "Would you care to see them perform, your grace?"

The duchess laughed. "Actually I would. I've always enjoyed animals, and it isn't every day that such a novelty comes to my very home." She smiled at Alex. "I'll send someone to fetch them." After motioning to a footman, she spoke with him quietly, then turned back to her guests and poured more tea.

While the group about the tea table laughed and talked as they waited for the unexpected entertainment, Pell gazed about the softly lit drawing room. The men looked elegant in their fine clothes and the women's bright silk gowns reminded Pell of colorful flowers. She recognized a few of the gentlemen from her coming-out ball. Indeed, the moment she entered the drawing room they had regaled her with extravagant compliments.

In a matter of minutes, the footman returned to the drawing room and walked to the duchess's side. Extending a white-gloved hand, he looked at the open door. "Hadji and Chi Chi, your grace," he announced in stately tones.

A smile flashing on his dark face, Hadji proudly entered the room with Chi Chi riding on his shoulder. White silk breeches and a knee-length shirt clad his slim body and an impressive turban with a decorative gold pin sat upon his head. A proud glow rose up within Pell as the servant approached the duchess, his large brown eyes shining with happiness.

At her side, he placed his raised hands together and, bowing his head, said, "I am being most thankful, illustrious duchess, that I and my unworthy pet may be of some entertainment to you." With a graceful movement, he took Chi Chi from his shoulder and placed the monkey on the carpet. "I am now seeing if this unworthy animal will perform. I am presently on the ears of a dilemma, for I am wanting to please you, but Chi Chi is becoming most lazy in the mansion of our beneficent master Lord Tavistock."

Everyone about the tea table laughed and Pell noticed that the duchess basked in Hadji's courtly manner.

First the servant hummed a little tune and Chi Chi stood on his hind legs and chattered as he danced about in a circle. Then Hadji knelt on the floor, and, getting the animal's attention, rolled his hands in a circular motion. At first the monkey balked, but with additional encouragement he finally placed his head on the carpet and turned several somersaults, eliciting chuckles from the gentlemen and *ohhs* and *ahhs* from the ladies. As a final trick, Hadji held his spread hands above his head, and Chi Chi climbed up one of his arms, then leaped back and forth between his hands, garnering a little round of applause.

His eyes shining, Hadji tucked the monkey in the crook of his arm and bowed his head before the duchess once more. "Ten million pardons, illustrious duchess, but the worthless animal is presently forgetting the rest of his tricks. I am thinking if I continue the performance I will be ending up with porridge on my face. I am begging your gracious indulgence concerning the brevity of our humble performance."

The great lady nodded her head in acquiescence, and everyone laughed and applauded. His eyes glinting with happiness, Hadji bowed himself out of the room.

The duchess looked at Alex and smiled. "How right you were. They were both most entertaining. You're fortunate indeed to have such a unique valet."

Alex cocked a brow. "Yes, with Hadji and Chi Chi about one can always be assured of surprises."

They all talked a while longer, then, after pressing a napkin to her lips, the duchess rose to her feet and brought the tea to an end. "I have some guests who will be arriving later. I'm sure you will all be anxious to meet them, but for now, I suggest we go to our rooms to rest and dress for dinner." She looked at Pell with kindly eyes. "As to accommodations, you shall be in the blue room at the end of the upstairs corridor. I think you will find it quite comfortable."

There was a clatter of teacups and rustling of silk as the ladies and gentlemen followed their hostess's example. Engaging the group in conversation, the duchess led them away until only Pell and Alex were left standing together.

"Go and rest now," Alex said. "I'll meet you at eight-fifteen at the foot of the stairs and escort you to dinner." He swept a concerned gaze over her. "Try not to worry. Everything has gone all right so far, and the duchess seems to have a great fondness for you."

Despite his words of encouragement, Pell felt more nervous than ever. But before she could express her concerns, Lord Bockingford approached them and invited Alex to join him and some other guests for a game of bridge.

At last Pell stood by herself in the huge drawing room, wishing she could take back her comment about the lobster aspic. With Alex's encouragement and the diversion provided by Hadji and Chi Chi she had gotten through the tea, but the house party had just begun. What perils lay ahead of her? How could she possibly survive the whole weekend? she wondered as she lifted the hem of her skirt and hurried away to the safety of her bedroom.

Following Alex's suggestion, Pell left her room at eight-fifteen. Her heart raced as she descended the grand staircase wearing a gown of shell-pink satin with a swath of matching fringe across the bosom. Dark-green velvet bows and pink flowers decorated both shoulders and loops of green velvet were swagged over one hip.

When she saw Alex at the foot of the stairs, relief surged up within her. As on the night of her ball, he was magnificent in an evening suit that emphasized the trimness of his athletic body and made his shoulders seem even wider. When his hot gaze washed over her, she realized that he was analyzing her, and as she reached the last step, shyness eddied through her.

"You look lovely," he murmured, his warm eyes holding hers.

Her cheeks burned with excitement at the compliment, and, taking his proffered hand, she noticed its warmth through her long white glove. As he escorted her toward the noisy dining room, she could feel his hard-muscled arm beneath the fine material of his jacket and it gave her a measure of much-needed confidence.

"How are you feeling?" he asked.

"Kind of trembly. Like I'm in a hurry all over, but my legs don't want to move."

He laughed softly. "I'm sure the evening will go smoothly. Just relax and take deep breaths. And remember," he added as they approached the dining room, "don't move too fast or speak too quickly."

"Don't worry about that. The way I feel now I may not be able to speak at all."

Two footmen wearing red livery and white wigs stood like soldiers at the open doors. Garbed in another fantastic gown—this one of purple and silver—the Duchess of Roxbury smiled pleasantly at each couple as they entered the long chamber.

The scent of roses and burning candles enveloped Pell as she and Alex walked into the dramatically decorated room. Topped by heavy cornices, red silk drapes fell to the polished floor, their color echoed in the upholstered chairs. Three massive chandeliers sparkled above a table set with gold-rimmed china and glittering silver, and decorated with hothouse blooms. A string ensemble played softly, surrounded by palms and baskets of flowers.

Several men flicked warm gazes over Pell as she and Alex moved about the long table looking for their names, which were written on white cards and displayed in silver holders. People were still pouring into the dining room to take their seats, and as Pell sat down and arranged her trailing gown, she happened to glance at the door.

Her gaze immediately locked on a handsome middle-aged lady wearing a wine-red gown, who turned for a moment to speak to her companion. The slender lady in red carried herself with grace and dignity and seemed to be someone of importance. The woman's thick black hair was swept back into an elegant chignon and decorated with red plumes, which complemented her creamy complexion and dark eyes.

Evidently this guest was one of the late arrivals for she had not seen her at tea. After finishing her discussion, the woman sat down directly across the wide table from Alex, and, looking pleased, nodded at him. He inclined his head and smiled pleasantly, but Pell sensed his disquiet. A moment later the woman's interested gaze drifted toward Pell. As Pell studied the woman, she realized she looked familiar. Although she couldn't place her, she knew she had seen her before.

Before she could question Alex about the elegant lady, the meal began and a footman placed a bowl of consommé in front of her. Trout almondine followed the soup. With a sigh, she looked to her right, hoping to speak to the fat lord seated beside her, but he seemed more interested in eating than talking. She remembered he had gorged himself at tea and now met her attempts at conversation with grunts and nods. Cutting into the trout with relish, he ignored her smile.

Her gaze went back to the woman in the red gown, who gazed at Alex with friendly eyes; then, in a flash of remembrance, she recalled that this was the woman she had seen him speaking with at the Royal Institute of Art. Leaning toward Alex, she whispered, "Who is the lady in red and why does she keep glancing this way?"

Alex took a sip of wine and avoided her eyes. "She's no one of importance," he said, setting down his glass. "Forget about her."

"*No.* Tell me who she is," she whispered insistently. "She's the same lady I saw you talking to in the art gallery."

Unease marking his expression, he glanced at Pell, caution flickering in the depths of his eyes. "My dear, the lady in red," he drawled casually, "is Sabrina Fairchild."

Chapter 11

❧

Pell had taken a bite of fish and now began to choke on it. Coughing, she put her napkin to her mouth and tried to control herself. Alex offered her water in a crystal goblet, and several people glanced her way, but when she sipped the water, they returned to their dinner. Wiping the tears from her eyes, she leaned toward Alex once more and touched his arm. "Bloody 'ell," she whispered roughly. "I've got to get out of 'ere!"

"No, you need to stay seated and control your speech, which has just fallen to pieces."

"But I want to—"

"No," he cut in again. "Smile sweetly, and put a brave face on things. Sabrina has no idea who you are . . . but avoid her if you can."

His words made her terribly self-conscious and everything she managed to choke down sat in her stomach like a rock. Her mind whirled with unpleasant childhood memories as she recalled heated discussions between her mother and the general. As a child, she didn't understand what the altercations were about, but she did remember them bringing up the name *Sabrina* again and again. Now she sat across the table from the woman who had played such an important part in their disagreements.

As the meal progressed, tension gathered between her shoulders, and an almost overpowering urge to leave the table rose up within her. A huge roast and many elaborate side dishes followed the fish, but finally the waiters began

162

serving a dessert of sweetened strawberries in whipped cream.

Pell's gaze kept straying to Sabrina, and, trying to look away, she spotted a familiar figure standing at the half-open dining-room doors. *Hadji.* If that wasn't enough, Chi Chi was sitting on his shoulder. Pride warming her heart, she remembered how well their performance had been received at tea. But what was he doing at the duchess's dining-room doors? His lips parted with wonder, Hadji watched his old mistress with surprised interest. Putting things together, Pell guessed that Hadji had glimpsed Sabrina enter the mansion, and out of curiosity had crept to the half-open dining-room doors to watch her.

The woman had treated him none too kindly, she knew. Hadji had even told her that his former mistress had mistreated Chi Chi. And now, the monkey was staring at Sabrina with keen eyes.

The table was so wide the guests were forced to converse only with those seated beside them, but, leaning forward a bit to be heard, Sabrina looked at Alex. "It's so nice to see you again, Alex. I was sure I would bump into you again before the season was over."

Pell's pulse raced at the sound of the woman's cultivated voice and she wondered how Alex would respond.

Inclining his head formally, he gazed across the table and smiled. "Yes, it's nice to see you too, Sabrina," he replied simply.

An interested look passed over the lady's refined features. "Who is the charming young lady at your side? Surely you haven't taken a wife since you returned to England?"

Alex laughed softly. "No. This is my ward, Miss Pell Davis."

Sabrina's eyes widened. "Why, you never told me you had a ward. You never mentioned the girl in India."

Alex sipped his wine, then smiled leisurely. "Actually Pell was my brother's ward. I inherited the guardianship along with my title. Miss Davis is from Newcastle and she is making her debut this season. Her father was a great philanthropist."

"Davis?" Sabrina echoed thoughtfully. "The name is not familiar to me." She looked at Pell with contemplative eyes. "Where did you attend school, my dear?"

Afraid to respond, she glanced at Alex whose gaze clung to hers, prompting her to speak. Girding herself, she looked back at Sabrina, and said as casually as she could, "I attended the convent of Saint Bartholomew."

Sabrina's eyes flickered as she studied Pell, who stirred uneasily in her chair. "I see," she replied with a faint note of doubt.

By now most of the guests within hearing range had put down their forks and were listening attentively. The duchess, who sat at the end of the table, seemed especially interested in the conversation. Pell's cheeks burned as she realized everyone was eager to hear about her past.

She wondered if the guests sensed she was a fraud, if they guessed she was nothing more than a Cockney imposter. At that moment she felt as much like a freak as a two-headed calf.

"Did I know your mother?" Sabrina went on in a smooth, but slightly insistent voice.

Pell nervously twisted her hands in her lap, not knowing how to respond.

As she fumbled for words, Alex put his warm hand over hers. "Miss Davis's mother was in the arts—a singer dedicated to her craft. Her name will always be engraved in the hearts of those who heard her perform."

Pell felt tears of gratitude gather in her eyes as she listened to Alex's deep voice.

"What about your father, my dear?" Sabrina continued, her tone becoming more pressing. "Do you remember him at all?"

Pell had scarcely time to compose herself from the last question, and total silence now filled the huge chamber as every pair of eyes at the table watched her, waiting for her answer. Swallowing back her emotion, she raised her chin, and in a firm voice responded, "Yes, I remember my father. I believe he did much for his country. He . . . he was a great man."

Taking a steadying breath, she glanced back at the door and what she saw made her heart lurch. Chi Chi had leaped from Hadji's arms and now raced toward Sabrina, his eyes fixed on the plumes in her hair. Knowing he had been trained to snatch people's headgear, Pell realized what was going to happen and gasped in shock.

The monkey nimbly jumped into Sabrina's lap and, stretching upward, started snatching at the quivering plumes. Stiffening in shock, Sabrina helplessly flailed her hands at the animal, while men rose to their feet and the ladies' eyes widened in surprise. His mouth gaping, Hadji stood frozen at the threshold of the dining room.

Chattering happily, Chi Chi plucked away the plumes, then leaped from her lap and scampered across the table toward Pell, who grabbed them from his hands. Alex quickly moved around the table to assist Sabrina to her feet. Finally coming out of his trance, Hadji rushed forward, scooped up the chattering monkey, and dashed from the room.

The Duchess of Roxbury's face was pale with surprise, and everyone else seemed to be in shock.

Alex put his arm about Sabrina and escorted her to the dining-room doors. "My apologies for this unfortunate accident," Alex offered graciously.

Her heart racing, Pell rushed to his side and presented the plumes to Sabrina. "I don't know why Chi Chi did such a naughty thing. I'm so sorry!"

Clearly shaken, Sabrina glanced at the open door, then shifted her gaze to Alex. "Now I understand what has happened. You've taken in Phillip's servant and that mischievous monkey too." Taking a deep breath, she scanned Pell, then swept her gaze over Alex. "What else have you done for him?" she asked with quivering lips. "What else?" Her eyes sparkled with anger as she left the room.

When she was gone, Pell's heart dipped and she glanced

back at the murmuring guests who were now all talking at once. After a moment of confusion, the duchess stood and raised her jeweled hand, silencing the noise. "My dear friends," she announced in a soothing voice, "let us adjourn to the drawing room where the gentlemen will be served port, and we ladies may visit. Later there will be dancing in the ballroom."

With a great scraping noise, the footmen pulled out the ladies' chairs and the men began good-natured conversations about the latest sporting events. Clutching Alex's arm, Pell caught his concerned eyes. "I need to talk to you," she said in an urgent whisper.

He glanced at the elegantly dressed guests, some of whom were staring at them. "We must wait," he said in a firm voice.

As Alex escorted Pell from the crowded room, humiliation shuddered through her, leaving her weak. *Sabrina knows who I really am,* she thought. *She knows, and she will tell everyone!*

Alex stood by the great marble fireplace in the duchess's ballroom, watching the guests glide over the dance floor to the strains of a sweeping waltz. Gilt-framed portraits decorated the paneled walls, and five large chandeliers hung from the high ceiling, casting light over a group of liveried musicians at the end of the huge chamber.

The dancers talked as they glided over the glistening parquet. Far from ruining the festive mood, the incident with Sabrina and Chi Chi had seemed to enliven the evening. Sabrina herself had come back down to join the dancing and seemed to have regained her composure. But even as he watched her, worry plagued Alex's mind, for he recalled their conversation at the Royal Institute of Art. He knew that she was deeply hurt about the general's will and was searching for his daughter, and someone as clever and aggressive as she was would never let the matter rest. His gaze lingered on her graceful form for a while, then he observed Pell as she danced with a young lord who looked at her with starry eyes. In the drawing room a host of eager gentlemen had crowded around her, making it impossible for Alex to have a private word with her.

He'd had to endure silly young pups fawning over her at the coming-out ball, and now men of all ages stared at her hungrily. Every time she returned to his side some new gallant approached asking, "You don't mind if I dance with your ward, do you, Tavistock? That's a good man, Tavistock, don't hog the girl to yourself. Let someone else enjoy her company, won't you?"

Alex crossed his arms and sighed. Despite her remark at tea this afternoon, she was a great success—at least with the gentlemen. She was also the loveliest lady at the house party. Hadn't every man there told him so—the married ones as well as the bachelors? Feeling irritable, he suddenly realized why men with daughters of marriageable age always seemed so testy.

Catching a flash of white at the open ballroom doors, he noticed Hadji, whose worried black eyes beckoned him from across the crowded chamber and aroused his curiosity. Knowing the servant could not enter the ballroom, he casually drifted toward the doors, making his way between the dancing couples. At last he slipped into the great hall and saw the servant fall on one knee.

Looking mortified, Hadji gazed upward with pleading eyes. "Oh, illustrious master, I am realizing both Chi Chi and I have made a grievous error and we are both humbly repenting from the wickedness of our ways. The vile creature is now on a leash and tied to my bed in the attic. I am assuring you that nothing will be happening again as happened this evening."

Alex made his voice sound stern. "I certainly hope not. What in the devil were you doing peeking into the dining room anyway?"

Hadji swallowed and blinked his eyes. "I was going to my room when I am thinking I am seeing my old mistress walk past at a distance, but I am not really knowing if it was the general's widow or not. So I am following her to make sure."

"And why would you need to know if Sabrina was here or not?"

Hadji put a spread hand on his chest. "Oh, wondrous one, I am wanting to know in order to warn my illustrious master, for I am noticing that wherever she goes there is a great stirring of trouble."

Alex sighed heavily. "The animal has disrupted a dinner and embarrassed the general's widow."

The servant hung his head in shame. "Yes, glorious master. The guilt of my mistake will be an abalone around my neck for the rest of my life."

Alex stifled a smile, and, putting a note of command in his voice, asked, "Hadji, are you going to lay out my clothes for tomorrow, or should I look for another valet?"

The servant instantly scrambled to his feet. "Oh, yes, beneficent master, I am ironing your shirt, and shining your boots, and polishing your buttons, and in general preparing you for another festive day."

Throwing Hadji a last stern glare as if to warn him what would happen if the monkey escaped again, Alex walked toward the ballroom's open doors. Looking back once more, he saw the servant push his hands together and bow three times, then hurry away.

Once he was inside the great chamber again, Lord Bockingford approached him, a smile creasing his fleshy face. When the elderly lord reached his side, he slapped Alex on the back. "I must say, the bit with your valet's monkey brought a little life to the evening." He chuckled deeply. "The incident will be the talk of the season, y'know."

Alex started to explain that he had no reason to accept congratulations for the spectacle, but he knew the slightly senile man wouldn't understand, so he simply replied, "Why, thank you, Bockingford, decent of you to say so."

Bockingford raised his heavy brows. "Can't say I fathom why Phillip Fairchild ever married that woman anyway. He was always more interested in soldiering than anything else. But I suppose Sabrina's father pushed the match." A thoughtful look passed over his face. "Sabrina was very beautiful when she first came out."

Bockingford paused to sip his drink, and in a moment they were joined by Pell and Lilly, both of whom had just finished a dance.

"Lord Tavistock," Lilly chirped, "I've missed you all evening. In fact I haven't talked to you since the coming-out ball." She glanced at Pell, then back at him. "Did you meet my new beau, Claude Dubois? What do you think of him?"

A muscle flickered in his jaw. "He's really in a class by himself, isn't he?" he offered, studying Lilly's face.

He shot a glance at the open doors at the end of the huge chamber, wanting to whisk Pell away from Lilly and her father, and all the guests. But the two of them had delayed their escape long enough that a young fop now approached, his eyes locked on Pell. Obviously she had promised him a dance and he had come to claim her. Was there no place they could be alone for a few moments! Suddenly he remembered a sheltered rendezvous located in the formal gardens behind the sprawling manor house.

Knowing they would soon be separated again, he moved Pell aside for a moment, and in a soft voice said, "There's a gazebo in the gardens. Meet me there at midnight tonight. We'll be able to talk privately."

As the dandy took Pell's hand and led her away, she glanced back over her shoulder, her face flooding with relief.

Pell shivered and wrapped her shawl about her as she ran toward the gazebo, her feet making crunching sounds on the graveled pathway. As she entered the large gardens, the scents of azaleas and honeysuckle rose up to meet her and the air was alive with the sound of chirping crickets.

There had been a light shower in the afternoon and the air was moist and soft and full of the scent of rich earth.

In the night sky, clouds slipped over the full silvery moon, and a little chill rode the air. Pell's heart hammered in her bosom, but she had no idea if it was from exertion, or because she was about to see Alex alone.

As she neared the latticework gazebo, shadowy foliage blew about the little structure, making it difficult to see inside. Was there a tall man standing inside or simply more deceiving shadows? With cautious steps, she entered the wooden structure, her feet creaking over a loose board. She gasped as a strong hand clasped her wrist and gently pulled her forward.

"Alex," she breathed, looking up into his moon-silvered face. "You came."

A faint smile played over his lips. "Yes, I have a penchant for keeping my promises." Putting an arm about her, he led her to a bench that circled the inside of the gazebo and sat down, drawing her to him.

Her pulse scampered as she thought about Sabrina's parting words at the dining-room door, and she clasped his warm hand. "Why didn't you tell me it was Sabrina you were talking to at the Royal Institute of Art?" she asked with a hint of reproach.

He gave her a half-smile. "I didn't want to worry you. I was hoping there would be no need for you to meet her."

"Well, now that I have, what are we going to do?" she asked in a strained voice. "Sabrina has guessed who I am and she will tell everyone. I know she will."

Actually, concern about Sabrina's possible actions weighed heavily on Alex's mind, but he didn't want to share his worries with Pell, who had more than enough to deal with already. His common sense told him this was a crisis for her, and knowing that, he channeled his efforts into lightening her burden. "She may very well *suspect* who you are, but she can prove nothing," he said casually as he stroked his thumb over her hand. "You must remember that. She will learn nothing from Mr. Peebles or my servants, whom I have sworn to secrecy. You hold the key to this affair."

"Me?"

"Yes. I will not lose my nerve, and if you don't lose yours, your secret will be safe."

"But what if she goes to Newcastle? What if she tries to find out about my past?"

Alex chuckled. "The picture of Sabrina making the dreary trek to Newcastle is quite amusing. I doubt she would discomfort herself by leaving the London social scene she loves so much. If you put on a brave face and hold to your story, everything will be fine."

With a sigh, Pell relaxed and looked at his face. "Do you really think so?"

Alex studied her tense expression for a moment, then cupped her chin and pulled her a bit closer. In the silvery light filtering into the gazebo, he saw that worry seemed to weigh her down. "Yes, I do," he replied in a reassuring voice as he lightly caressed her back. "Everything will be fine," he added, brushing back a loose curl on her cheek.

As Pell buried her head against his shoulder he offered more words of comfort. "Don't let Sabrina trouble you so," he advised, tenderly massaging the nape of her neck. "She is so focused on herself she will soon forget you." Although he knew this might not be entirely true, he felt the fluttering of her heart against her ribs and he struggled to put her mind at rest. "Promise me that you will likewise forget her."

Gently he raised her head, watching moonlight touch her delicate features. "Yes, I'll try," she whispered in a trembling voice.

Suddenly he realized how much he wanted to kiss her soft lips, but he knew he shouldn't begin something he might not be able to stop. Tamping down his growing desire, he slowly moved her away from him. A pulse throbbing in his temple, he stood and gazed down at her puzzled face.

She held her hand out toward him. "Must you go?" she asked with an almost imperceptible note of pleading.

"Yes, I really think I should." He trailed his fingers over

her smooth cheek. "Remember, no more worrying tonight. I'll return first and wait inside the door to see that you've followed." Trying to ignore the shadow of hurt in her shimmering eyes, he moved away from the bench and left the gazebo. How close he had come to giving in to the temptation of kissing her, he thought as he made his abrupt departure.

As he quickly strode toward the manor house, his hands were still warm from holding her, and the scent of her sweet perfume lingered on his clothes, making it that much harder to keep walking. If he had stayed a few moments longer he might have done something unwise.

As his footsteps echoed over the stone terrace, he considered the situation and knew that as long as she was close to him, he would be exposed to her charms and his heart would be in constant turmoil. Hardening his jaw, he steeled his resolve, and decided he must rededicate himself to the task of getting her happily married—and very soon.

Chapter 12

A week later Alex and Pell strolled by the sun-speckled Thames near the small town of Henley. Sheltering oak limbs met far above their heads, and as they walked beneath the dark foliage, flickering shadows danced over the wide path before them. The sight of the shells, cheering people, and flower-decked houseboats made Henley-upon-the-Thames a great summer event. The day was perfect and the fragrance of hollyhocks perfumed the air. With its flags, bunting, and glittering water, the scene along the river sparkled with color.

Garbed in a suite of fine English tweed, Alex looked the perfect country gentleman, and as Pell studied his thoughtful face, she guessed he was searching the crowd for possible suitors. When they had left the Duchess of Roxbury's house party, she had sensed that his mind was working furiously. Upon their arrival in London, he had told her that he wanted to see her married by the end of the month. So saying, he had launched them both into a fevered social whirl to find her a husband. He had taken her to Rotten Row and the Goodwood Races, and today he had brought her to Henley. She had hoped—in fact, prayed—that he might marry her himself, but it seemed that it was not to be.

He now looked down at her, his handsome face dappled with shade from the trees. "The cream of Oxford University is here at the races, and you'll have a good chance of meeting an eligible man."

She sighed and gave him a sidelong glance. "That doesn't sound very romantic. It fact, it reminds me of a livestock auction. Why don't you just take out an advertisement in the *Times* saying I'm available for marriage?"

A smile flickered over his lips. "Actually, that might be quite effective. But we have to be a little more polished than that."

She stared at him, feeling more hurt by the minute by his insensitivity. Was the man blind? Couldn't he see she didn't give a damn for the cream of Oxford University? Couldn't he see she was attracted to *him?* "What makes it so important that I find a husband now?" she asked in a troubled voice. "To hear you talk, a person would think it was some kind of race."

He smiled again. "In a way it is. The season will soon be over and anyone with a title will flee back into the country and not appear until next April. The general made it clear that I should find you a husband before my guardianship was over."

As Pell studied his determined face, a small smile curved her lips. So she was to be put on the marriage block like a piece of chattel, she thought. Very well then. She would turn his own tactics against him. He might be blind, but she wasn't. She had seen how he frowned at the other men at the Duchess of Roxbury's when they paid her court. Surely he had *some* feeling for her, however hidden he tried to keep it. All she had to do was uncover it, and jealousy would be her tool. She would flirt with every man she saw today until Alex became so jealous that his wall of reserve would crash about him and he would claim her for his own.

Alex scanned Pell with pride as she walked along beside him, twirling her parasol over her shoulder. In her pink striped gown with the veil of her jaunty straw hat floating out behind her, she made quite a fetching sight, and stood out beautifully against the deep-green trees bordering the Thames. How wise he had been to bring her here to the Henley Regatta, he thought with satisfaction.

Smart carriages, many adorned with noble crests, packed the shady area bordering the river, and all about them were brightly striped tents belonging to various rowing clubs. Amid the noontime clatter of knives and forks and the popping of corks, ladies and gentlemen paraded between the tents, laughing and greeting old friends as they waited for the next race.

Here in the midst of all these people, to Alex's great surprise, Pell suddenly affected a loud chatty manner and boldly flashed her eyes at the titled men and young lordlings they met on the path. Wondering why she was acting so pert and generally high-blooded with every gentleman she met, he suddenly realized that she was flirting! Knowing smiles passed over the men's faces, and, thinking her performance rivaled some of the more polished courtesans, Alex wanted to whisk her back to their carriage, but she walked ahead, smiling brightly.

As a well-dressed gentleman paused and doffed his top hat, Pell cocked her head and gave him a smile, then she started talking—so fast that Alex was amazed.

"What a magnificent suit that is, sir," she remarked cheerfully. "How fine you look in it."

As her comments poured out like gurgling water, the surprised but delighted man hardly had a chance to answer. Looking thoroughly pleased, he smiled and answered her questions, completely ignoring Alex.

Soon Pell's gay laughter attracted several other men who drifted toward her. Now a dozen men—all wearing broad smiles—had crowded about her as she entertained them with questions and amusing comments.

A mustachioed gentleman thoughtfully looked at Alex, then shifted his gaze back to Pell. "Who's your companion?" he asked cautiously.

Pell glanced at Alex, then swiftly returned her attention to the mustachioed man. "Him? He's just my guardian," she replied lightly.

Irritation rippled through Alex. He watched her bat her

large eyes, and giggle, and toss her curls, and dimple prettily while she chattered with the gallants.

Feeling he could stand no more, he clasped her elbow and led her aside. "What in God's name do you think you're doing?"

"Flirting," she answered saucily. "Didn't you say you had to marry me off by the end of the month?"

"Yes. But I didn't tell you to act like this," he replied as he glared at the disappointed men, who started to disperse. With a disgruntled frown, he glanced at a nearby caterer's tent. "Let's buy something to eat and take it to that bench by the river so we can watch the races," he suggested tersely. He gave her a disapproving look. "I think you need to calm down a bit."

After Alex had purchased box lunches and champagne, they walked to the bench and sat down. While they ate, Alex studied Pell, wondering if she had finished flirting for the day. But when the races began and the polished shells moved out, surging ahead of each other, he knew that she hadn't, for to his embarrassment, she actually stood and cheered for the crewmen. As beautiful as she was, she attracted the eye of every man there, and before each race, the brawny crewmen, all fine male specimens and heirs to fortunes, flocked around her.

"A favor," one of them begged, falling on one knee and holding out his hand. "A token from you to bring me luck."

Smiling brightly, Pell plucked a deep-pink ribbon from her hair and presented it to the young man. "Of course, sir. And I wish you success."

A great roar went up from the rest of the crew, and minutes later they had attached the ribbon to the prow of their slender craft.

To say that Pell was the belle of the Henley Regatta would be an understatement. The captain of another crew wove a crown of wildflowers and presented it to her after he had finished his race. Sturdy oarsmen regularly made the trip up the grassy slope to present her with little bouquets of wildflowers, and, accepting them, she placed her hands over the crewmen's bulging biceps and marveled at their strength.

After winning the final race, the victorious crew which had sported Pell's ribbon on their shell, cheered hoarsely, then rushed up the bank and crowded around her in a frenzy of adulation, leaving Alex with a pile of chicken bones and a glass of warm champagne.

Seething with irritation, he stood and watched her as she walked down to their shell and they all followed, their faces glowing with admiration. Scowling, he stared at her, wondering what had prompted her to try to behave so outrageously. The little minx was up to something—but he had no idea what.

Alex's horses covered the miles from Henley quickly, and late that afternoon his brougham entered the noisy London streets, which were packed with private carriages, hackney cabs, and omnibuses. Sitting forward a bit, Pell gazed from the window.

The life and color outside the carriage only served to drive her deeper into her melancholy thoughts. Relaxing back against the seat, she tried to organize her troubled mind. Alex's efforts to marry her off had hurt her deeply and she had a hard time controlling her emotions. The last days of summer were passing with terrifying swiftness now and soon the season would be over. Worse than that, once she was married, she would be out of Alex's life altogether, and would only see him in passing once or twice a year at some dull social function.

A tense atmosphere filled the carriage. They hadn't spoken since entering London, but now Alex crossed his legs and caught her gaze. "I think I'll take you to the opera tomorrow evening," he said thoughtfully. "There is always a good crowd there during the season."

As the last rays of light slanted into the carriage, highlighting his face, she studied his expression. His jealousy at Henley had been obvious, she thought with some satisfaction. As she had planned, her flirting campaign had touched his male pride. "And what if I won't agree to go to the opera tomorrow evening? What if I won't agree to put myself on the market like a Guernsey cow?"

His gray eyes glittered in the dying light. "You must trust my judgment in this matter. I know what is best for you. You need a husband to care for you . . . and protect you."

She let out an exasperated sigh. "You make it sound like I'm a spaniel, not a woman. What about love?" she asked in a hurt tone. "Where does love come into this bargain?"

His mouth twisted dryly. "Often it does not. Sometimes love plays little in the affairs of ladies and gentlemen, especially when they will soon be receiving a great fortune."

Alex looked at Pell, thinking her actions today had been just short of brazen. "You shouldn't argue with me. It's not ladylike. And your performance today wasn't very appropriate for a lady either," he said.

She lifted her chin a bit. "I disagree. I see ladies arguing all the time . . . and I see them flirting too. They flirt at the theatre, and at the receptions and teas. Why, during the season, ladies are *expected* to flirt." She gave him a sweet smile, and in an even sweeter tone added, "We must work very hard if we are to find husbands, you know. Since we are only females we must have a husband . . . to care for us and protect us."

Alex swept his gaze over Pell. The look of triumph on her face irritated him all the more. Now it seemed she was determined to taunt him with her words. As the carriage made a turn, he saw the Carlton's white columns flash out in the dusk, and thought his club had never looked more inviting. Tapping his cane against the carriage roof, he signaled the driver, and the brougham slowed, and finally stopped.

"I'm going to eat dinner at the Carlton tonight," he said, gazing at Pell's surprised face. He smiled tightly. "Sorry, but no females are allowed to dine there during the week." He slapped his top hat on his head, and, opening the carriage door, left the brougham. Turning, he studied her frowning face. "Don't wait up." By the look on her face, he knew she was displeased, but a man had to have *some* refuge against the stings of the world, he thought, slamming the door behind him.

As the brougham rolled away, he saw her slouch down in the seat and cross her arms, then he turned, and, with a chuckle, walked up the Carlton's wide marble steps.

Chapter 13

Several days later Alex and Pell rode toward the section of London near St. Paul's Cathedral to attend a reception. Dressed in an evening gown of moss-green silk with matching plumes in her hair, Pell rested against the carriage seat and listened to the creaking wheels and the rhythmic clip-clop of the horses' hooves. The streetlights' warm glow and the twinkling windows of the Park Lane mansions should have cheered her, but their brightness only mocked her sad mood. Despite her rebellious display of high spirits at Henley, she was really thoroughly depressed. She had flirted so much she was sick of it. Keeping her vow, she had made eyes at every man she met. But to what end?

With a sinking feeling of despair, she moved her gaze over Alex, who sat beside her. His powerful, well-muscled body filled out his resplendent evening clothes, while his white shirt and gold studs flashed in the light that flickered through the carriage windows. At times she could feel him begin to respond to her, but then he would check his emotions, just as he had after the ball, and it seemed she had hardly touched him emotionally at all.

It saddened her to imagine what lay ahead of her. She knew the season was ending. The first aristocrats had already begun to return to the country. By the set of Alex's jaw, she also knew he still intended to marry her off—no matter what he had to do. What disturbing surprises lay ahead of her? Would he shackle her to some arthritic lord or irresponsible fop in his determination to fulfill his promise to her father? His kisses told her that if she could only break down the wall he had built around his emotions, she would find a deeply passionate man. But this late in the season, how could she find a way to accomplish that difficult task?

Their brougham now rattled along by the Thames, where the buildings became shabbier, the lights fewer, and the streets more narrow. At first they wheeled right along over the rough cobbles, but the horses' rhythm soon became uneven, making the carriage shudder a bit. After a short while, the conveyance gradually slowed, and finally creaked to a stop.

Alex reached for the door, but before he could step out, a liveried driver in tall jockey boots appeared, and, doffing his cockaded hat, bowed his head. "I'm afraid one o' the horses lost a shoe, milord," the man said apologetically. Holding his hat in his gnarled hand, he added, "There's a long stretch o' rough cobbles ahead. Perhaps we'd better turn back ... I don't want to lame one o' your lordship's fine mares."

Alex stepped from the carriage and was gone with the driver but a few moments before he returned and opened the door. "The driver is right," he agreed, giving Pell a thoughtful look. "I think we should take a hackney cab from here." He turned, and, eyeing the driver, who patiently waited for his instructions, he added, "Take the carriage back to the mansion, and make arrangements to have the horse reshod."

"Yes, your lordship," the man murmured, returning his hat to his head.

Trying to make the best of the predicament, Pell scooted forward on the seat and caught Alex's gaze. "The weather is fine tonight and a stroll would do us good. Why don't we walk a bit?"

He favored her with an indulgent smile and helped her from the carriage. "I'm sure we'll find a hackney soon."

After Pell had alighted from the brougham, the driver

climbed back upon the box, and, giving the reins a little slap, wheeled the carriage about. Standing together, she and Alex watched the vehicle clatter away, then vanish into the darkness.

They began to stroll along the Embankment, with the Thames somber and majestic beside them. Lights twinkled on the shore, reflecting in the inky water. Soft night air washing over her, Pell glanced about and spotted Blackfriar's Bridge looming in the darkness, its arches spanning the river like mighty arms.

Soon she could see the docks filled with the masts of boats looking ghostly in the moonlight, and when harmonica music floated upward from the river, old memories stirred her heart. When she had lived in Whitechapel, she and her old friends always had an outdoor get-together on the first Saturday night of the month in this area, and, with a flash of pleasure, she realized that they were only yards away from the old gathering place. Her heart beating a little faster, she lifted her skirts and hurried toward the river steps, irresistibly drawn to the sound of the music.

As she moved ahead, she heard Alex call after her, *"Pell,* where are you going?"

Not giving him time to ask more questions, she turned and motioned for him to follow, then raced down a flight of stone stairs, which ran down to the water's edge. As her shoes tapped over the steps, the dank reedy scent of the river touched her nostrils and she could hear lapping water and the laughter of merry people.

At the bottom of the stairs there were heaps of rubbish and planking brought up by the tide. Lifting her skirts even higher, she picked her way through it. Behind her she heard Alex's footsteps scraping against the steps, but, eager to join her friends, she rushed ahead. Then as she walked underneath an arch, she saw a small fire blazing in the darkness. On the bank of the Thames, a dozen ragged people stood about the flames, and a familiar figure stirred a boiling cauldron. Hearing Pell's footsteps on the rotten planks, the motley people standing about the fire froze for a moment, and the harmonica player stopped his music. Everyone stared her with sharp surprise, their eyes wide with wonder.

Breaking the tense silence, Kid Glove Rosie laid down her huge stirring spoon, and, blinking her eyes, slowly stepped forward. "Pell, is that you, girl?" She peered into the shadows behind Pell. "Who's the swell with you?"

Glancing back over her shoulder, she saw Alex's look of amusement as he surveyed the sight before him. Moving her hand a little, she motioned for him to come forward.

When he walked into the light and it made his elegant evening attire gleam, Rosie's mouth fell open. "Bless my liver," she gasped, clutching her throat. "It's the professor!"

Pell winked at her and laughed. "Yes, it's the professor, but don't stop the fun. I heard the music and wanted to join in . . . just for old times' sake."

An old man hobbled into the fire's glow and shook a crooked stick at Alex. "'E's a precious fine one, 'e is," he piped up. "We don't need the likes of 'im 'ere!"

The others burst out laughing.

Rosie shot the old man a hard look. "Stop that bell-clapper of yours, will ye? The gent's with Pell and she's family." Moving closer, she slid her gaze over Alex. "Besides, 'e don't look a bad sort—just a little starchy, that's all."

Pell glanced at Alex nervously.

"Why's they so dressed up?" one woman called out.

By now more ragged people crept from the shadows of the arches and drifted from a row of shabby houseboats where they slept. Chatter rippled through the group as they crowded about Pell and Alex, staring at their evening clothes.

Rosie pushed her way through the crowd and stood between the pair. "Don't you costers know anythin'?" she asked roughly. "Are you all dumb as clams? The professor's a swell, and Pell's a swell now, too. Swells always dress up fancy-like, even when they's sleepin', and usin' the necessary room, or doin' whatever else swells do."

A woman garbed in a black dress and ragged shawl came forward and touched Pell with her thin hand. "We's all 'eard 'ow you's a lady now, but we never thought to see you again. You look like a bleedin' angel whot's come down from 'eaven, you do. And to think you used to be one of us!"

The words seemed to stamp the pair with a seal of approval and the crowd relaxed and laughed a bit. Then, accepting the unusual situation, they went on with their party.

Pell was delighted to be with her old friends again, but when they were out of earshot, Alex clasped her arm and took her aside. "What's going on here?" he asked in a puzzled voice.

She shrugged. "Why, can't you see? They're having a party."

A flash of humor crossing his face, he scanned the area about him. "A party?"

Seeing his puzzled expression, she laughed. "Of course. The bridge provides shelter for the costers, and they get a good fill-up, and sometimes there's a man that comes and brings his fiddle." She raised her brows. "Every party doesn't have to be held in a ballroom and catered by Fortnum and Mason's, you know."

"Yes, this is all very interesting," he said smoothly, "but we need to be on our way if we're going to the reception."

Quickly surveying the crowd, she straightened her back and said, "Let's join *this* party instead." With a puzzled look, he opened his mouth to speak, but not giving him a chance to answer, she took his hand and added, "I feel at home here, and on occasions such as this, being poor isn't so bad." She looked into his eyes and grinned cockily. "Just consider it all part of your schooling."

Alex pursed his lips thoughtfully and nodded, and the amused look on his face told her he was beginning to enjoy himself already.

After introducing him to some of her friends, she moved away and found Rosie busily stirring her stew. As she approached, the older woman put her spoon aside. "Lor', I nearly passed out when I saw the professor. The sight of 'im is enough to make a saint swear on 'is blessed liver."

Pell laughed and caressed her arm. "Well, now that we're here and you're over the shock, we're going to join the party." She glanced at Alex, who was already talking to some of the costers crowded about him. "I want to show his lordship what *real* fun is."

Rosie's lips parted in surprise. "You wants to *eat* with us too?"

"Of course we do," Pell returned lightly. "I haven't had any sheep-trotter stew since I left the East End." She laughed. "And I know Alex has never had any in his life!"

A slow smile spread over Rosie's face as she watched the animated crowd about Alex. "Yes, this should be quite an interestin' evenin' indeed."

Soon after that, the harmonica player began a lively tune and everyone danced and laughed merrily. Feeling better than she had in days, Pell walked to Alex's side and took his arm. Several of the men opened bottles of cheap gin, and one of them made a great show of polishing a glass and bringing Alex a drink. As he accepted it, he narrowed his eyes and studied the man's face. "Aren't you Corporal Cummings? Corporal James Cummings of Her Majesty's 42nd Regiment of Foot?" he asked in an astonished tone.

The wiry little man chuckled. "Yes, sir. It be me, sir. I couldn't believe me eyes when you walked into the fire's glow. But when I came to meself, I knew it was you." The man swept an unbelieving gaze over him and shook his head. "Gawd's nightshirt, who would 'ave ever thought I'd be drinkin' gin with Colonel Alexander Chancery-Brown under the Blackfriar's Bridge!"

Alex smiled at the man's stunned reaction. "I've often thought of you, Corporal Cummings," he said warmly.

"You were with us when the Pathan tribesmen attacked the compound in Delhi, weren't you?"

The bandy-legged corporal tossed off his gin and stood a little taller. "Aye, that I was, sir. And a bloody devil of a fight it was, too."

Alex's face brightened as he reminisced with the man about army life in India, and as Pell moved away to visit with some old friends, she heard them both laughing heartily.

Later she came back to his side just as Rosie approached with two steaming bowls of delicious-smelling stew. Alex accepted his bowl with a quizzical expression, then took up a spoonful and put it into his mouth. Pell smiled when he swallowed the first bite, and continued to eat. When he had almost finished he said, "This is a tasty concoction. What's in it, anyway?"

Pell just kept smiling and let him eat on. He finished the last bite as Rosie came walking toward them. "The professor wants to know what's in your stew, Rosie—probably for scientific research, you know," Pell quipped.

The fruit-peddler looked him up and down as if she were revealing a great secret. "Well, we puts in whatever we 'appens to 'ave on 'and, we does. I found some taters with black spots a grocer 'ad throwed out, but I cut out the bad places, and added some mushy tomatoes. I always goes by the slaughter'ouse on Saturday nights. You can get lots of good things there—just like this." She pulled a round piece of flesh from her apron pocket and brandished it in front of Alex.

He raised his brows and peered at the object. "What's that?"

She stared at him as if he had lost his mind. "Why, it's a bleedin' sheep trotter, of course. That's whot we calls the stew—sheep-trotter stew. I likes to slice up about two dozen trotters and cook 'em till they're good and tender."

Alex blinked and put his bowl on a keg, then looked at Pell, who burst into laughter.

Rosie smiled and patted his hand. "That's all right, Professor. If you've kept it down this long, you'll be all right for the rest of the evenin'."

Before Alex could ask Pell any further questions about the sheep scrotum stew, a young man came by and swept her away to dance. From then on the evening flew past and it heartened Pell to see Alex dancing with the coster women, and apparently enjoying himself. She also noticed him asking several of the people about their lives. He seemed genuinely interested in them. Filled with the joy of the moment, Pell danced with all the laughing coster men, then, as the harmonica player gave them a final ballad, she finished the evening in Alex's arms.

"Having fun?" she said, looking up into his warm face.

Amusement flickered in his eyes. "Yes, actually I am," he said, holding her closer. "In fact, I'm thinking about canceling my membership to the Carlton and coming here from now on."

Laughing together, they danced a while longer, but as the bells of Saint Saviour's tolled midnight, the party began to disperse. Alex moved among the costers telling them good-bye, and, seeing Rosie, he took her aside. "I'd like to contribute to the next pot of stew, if I may," he said quietly.

She clasped his hand. "Oh, no, Professor. That wouldn't be proper, now would it? We was the 'osts 'ere tonight, and right glad to 'ave your company, we was."

After a last good-bye, Alex escorted Pell up the river steps, and when they reached the road, he looked down the Embankment Road at the twinkling lights. "Let's walk to Covent Garden," he suggested. "It's late, but I'm sure we can find a hackney at the opera house."

As they strolled arm-in-arm back toward the market-place, a late-night mist rose up from the river, blurring the golden halos about the gaslights and softening the shapes of the hulking buildings along the Embankment. Noticing the pungent scent of coffee, Pell spotted a crude stall across the street huddled under a gaslight, which illuminated a cluster of cabmen's faces. "Let's have something to drink before we go home," she said with a smile. "It's chilly and the coffee smells so good." At the stand, the cabmen stood back and respectfully touched their caps to Pell, while Alex bought coffee for a halfpenny a cup. After they had finished the steaming brew, Alex put his arm about her and they continued toward Covent Garden.

Their footsteps resounding in the darkness, Pell looked up at him. "Well, from the look on your face, it seems you enjoyed the evening," she said brightly.

He walked on silently for a moment, then, with some enthusiasm answered, "Yes . . . in fact, I've never had an evening quite like it before."

His response sent happiness spiraling through her. "I'm glad," she said quietly, snuggling against him as a chill closed in about them. "I had many happy times like this when I was young."

"I wish I could say the same for myself," he said with a slight touch of irony. "After my mother died, my father spent the rest of his life seeking mindless pleasure to blot out his pain. He was a good man, but weak without my mother's love and support. My brother became his companion, but I was too young to join in their fun. Being in the way, I was sent to a series of boarding schools and military academies. I came home for a few days around Christmas, then I was sent away again."

With some surprise, Pell realized that she had actually received more love and warmth in her rough-and-tumble childhood than he. Feeling sad for him, she tried to move the conversation along. "And then?"

"And then like every good second son, I went into the army. Once I left England my life improved and things began happening. Africa. Hong Kong. India. These are places where a man can stretch his wings and test himself," he said with a faraway look in his eyes.

He looked down at her and smiled broadly. "It was wonderful to see Cummings tonight," he said. "He made me think of India again."

She smiled. "I know you love that country. What do you remember about it?"

As they walked on, his face became more animated. "There were cricket matches in Calcutta and tiger hunts, and pigsticking expeditions, and lines and lines of scarlet tunics, and brass glittering in the sun," he said in his deep, resonant voice. "I remember the cry of jungle birds in the darkness, and throaty train whistles, and the sound of pounding rain, and the scent of sandalwood, and heat— horrific heat."

His words touched Pell. "I love the way you talk about India," she said softly. "I can almost see it myself."

He smiled. "I often see it in my mind's eye. Once a man sees India, he can never forget it." He let out his breath and it seemed that a mask had fallen away—that she was seeing him as she imagined he looked ten years ago. "I'll never forget the day I arrived in Bombay's Victoria Station. It was as if the bowels of hell had been opened into that smoky gigantic hulk of a building. What a maelstrom of frantic humanity there was, all shouting and shoving, and pushing one another to get to the trains that were hissing and screaming up to the platforms.

"There were men in long flapping shirts, and dark naked children with jangling bangles on their legs, and beggars with bowls, and Indian soldiers in scarlet turbans and tunics, and piles of cargo giving off the scents of cinnamon, cumin, and mint."

"I suppose the Indian women are very beautiful," she commented, her voice tinged with curiosity and a bit of envy.

Alex looked ahead, his eyes kindling with strong feelings. "Yes . . . they are. They have a sweetness, a grace, and they take pride in their thick long hair. They love jewelry, and colors hold great meaning for them. White is the color of sadness and mourning, while red represents joy." He chuckled. "Brides even wear a little red dot on their forehead—it's called a *bindi.*"

Pell was so engrossed in his words that she scarcely noticed that they had arrived at Covent Garden. With a shaft of disappointment, she looked across the open square and saw a cluster of hackney cabs at the entrance of the opera house. In the distance Big Ben boomed one o'clock.

At a corner, a little clot of people waited for the last omnibus, and a few street workers were spraying the square with water and sweeping it down. As they walked to the carriages, shadows shrouded the silent area, but gaslight flashed against the wet paving stones, and the *swish-swish* of the sweepers' brooms became more distinct.

The evening had been wonderful for Pell, and at this moment she felt very close to Alex. After they entered the cab and it clattered off toward the West End, she scooted a little closer to his side, wanting to continue their conversation. Feeling she had heard quite enough about beautiful Indian women, she searched for a way to change the subject and her eyes came to rest on his familiar ruby ring.

The deep-red stone, exquisitely cut, rested in a gold setting etched with exotic designs. "I've never seen a ring like that," she ventured. "In the East End we would call it a real flasher. Someone would steal it in a heartbeat if you weren't careful. I'll bet it came from India."

"Yes," he answered, glancing at his hand. "A friend of mine, Major Hempstead, asked me to invest in a ruby mine there. This stone came from that mine."

"I think I've heard you mention him before."

"I'm sure you have. He is the third man in the picture that sits on my desk—the one you always look at when you are studying your father's face." His countenance relaxed even more at the memory. "Tom had a degree in engineering and was to be in charge of all operations. I was to be the major financial backer. Although labor is cheap in India, equipment must be brought in from a distance, and I invested heavily."

He chuckled softly. "We were positive the mine would make us rich, but this stone is one of the few gems that's ever come out of that 'sure' venture." He raised his hand and studied the blood-red stone. "You can't imagine how much this one ring cost me." His eyes full of memories, he added, "Hempstead is still in India laboring away with a few natives using the equipment I bought. When I left he was still confident that the mine would produce a fortune—but I've written it off as a lost cause."

"You must have been good friends to take such a risk together."

He sighed and leaned back against the seat. "Yes, the best. I don't know if I'll ever see Tom again, but he will always remain my friend."

They were in Mayfair now, and the hackney slowed as it turned onto Adam's Row. Feeling secure and satisfied, Pell exhaled a long sigh of contentment and listened to the sounds of the clopping horses and the creaking wheels. How wonderful it was when Alex talked to her in this way, she thought warmly, looking at his shadowed face. "Thank you," she whispered softly.

He raised a quizzical brow. "For what?"

"Tonight. Everything. I haven't had so much fun in a very long time."

His gray eyes met hers and she felt happiness well up within her. Then, with a small smile touching his lips, he thoughtfully brushed his fingers over her cheek in a gesture that sent waves of delight surging through her. He was so close she could feel the heat of his body, and his manly fragrance sent her senses reeling. As if in a dream, she heard the driver call to the horses and felt the carriage slowly rock to a halt. At the same time, Alex turned, his leg pressing against hers, making her heart race out of control.

His eyes glittered. The moment seemed to Pell to last forever. Then gently he drew her face to him and lowered his head. Anticipating the kiss, she shuddered with pleasure, but suddenly the carriage door creaked open, and her heart pitched violently.

She felt Alex stiffen, and, with a gasp, she turned her head to see the driver's embarrassed face as he moved from the door. The man's intrusion had broken the magic spell, and Alex's countenance took on that formal look she knew so well. Moving away from her, he got out of the carriage and extended his hand in a courtly manner, the very gesture destroying the intimacy they had just shared.

Her heart aching, she could only alight to the pavement and let him escort her toward the house. She searched for something to say to restore the closeness they had shared, but from the look on his face she knew he had taken up his guardianship duties again.

Once inside, he paused at the library door. Looking preoccupied, he said, "I must attend to some work now. It's very late and I suggest you retire for the evening."

His words pricked her heart with pain. He was speaking to her as if she were a child, ordering her to go to bed. From his manner one would never know they had just shared a romantic evening and had been a heartbeat away from a kiss.

His gaze flickering over her in dismissal, he stepped back into the library, then closed the doors, leaving her standing alone. For a moment she could scarcely breathe and felt a hollow emptiness aching inside of her.

She had tried to make Alex show his love for her every way she could. She had been gay and lively, and she had flirted with other men to force his hand. But deep within her heart she knew that after everything was said and done . . . she had lost.

Slowly moving away from the closed doors, she began to ascend the stairs. Tiredness now swept over her, making her legs feel leaden as she took one step after the other. Yes, she was a lady now. She would soon be coming into a great fortune, but what did it matter if she lacked what she needed most, that one possession that no amount of money could buy . . . Alex's love.

Desperation clutched at her heart and almost cut off her breath. Alex would soon be rid of her, marrying her off to some suitable man, and she would never feel the warmth of his arms again. Then, in defiance of the terrible thought, her rebellious spirit surged up to save her pride. *Well, he may have rejected me himself, but he will not choose a husband for me,* she silently vowed. She, Pell Davis, would choose that man—a man who would show her the warmth and love that Alex did not.

Chapter 14

Claude's laughter echoed through the quaint Italian café, forcing Pell to pause in her story-telling. "Oh, *chérie,* what a joy you are! *Mon Dieu,* you mimic the cockney accent so well, I feel as if I am actually in the East End," he said affectionately. He glanced at an approaching waiter, who wore a long white apron and carried a tray. "After we are served, you must continue." With a warm smile, he reached across the small table and took her hand.

She clutched his fingers and smiled in return. How good it was to be with Claude again, she thought, and how like him to select such a romantic setting for their rendezvous. As the waiter arrived at their table, she slipped her hand away and straightened in her chair.

Sighing with satisfaction, she glanced around the little establishment which smelled of spices and freshly baked bread. It was tucked away in the heart of Soho, London's Bohemian district. Rickety tables and heavy sideboards laden with aromatic cheeses and bowls of ripened peaches crowded the low-ceilinged room.

As the waiter placed a bottle of wine and two glasses on the table, Pell thought of the intricate planning this meeting had required. What a piece of luck it had been to see Claude at a ball last week and have him partner her in a dance. Apprehension had shadowed her thoughts at his request to meet him in the café today, but her desire to speak with him one last time finally overrode her fear.

Thankfully Alex was at Parliament today, and a visit to Charing Cross Road to buy more romantic novels claimed Aunt Violet's attention. With a minimum of guilt, Pell had managed to tie the rendezvous in with an afternoon trip to the dressmaker's shop.

Her heart still ached for Alex, but he had returned her warmth with indifference, leaving her searching for companionship. At least Claude was attentive and diverting. To show her appreciation for his attention, she put on a brave face and entertained him with the stories he enjoyed so much.

When the waiter left, Claude poured them each a glass of rich red Chianti. They sat by a window facing Shaftesbury Avenue. Sunlight flooded through the lace curtain, dappling bright spots over his blue velvet jacket and catching in his golden hair. Placing the wicker-covered bottle aside, he smiled and lightly remarked, "Now, go on with your storie, *chérie* . . ."

Pell thoughtfully smoothed her lavender silk gown and brushed back a dangling ringlet. "Well," she said slowly, "after Louie the Lump got out of the detention 'ouse—"

Claude lifted his hand. "Louie the Lump?" he exclaimed, arching his brows. "Is that actually the man's name?"

"Yes," she replied, taking a sip of her wine. "'E 'as a large lump on the right side of 'is 'ead—but it don't interfere with 'is thinkin' any."

He laughed appreciatively as she picked up the working-class accent.

"You sees," she continued, "once when Louie was in a local pub 'e spied a bowl of fresh eggs. Bein' the natural-born thief 'e is, 'e couldn't pass up the opportunity."

Warming to Claude's twinkling eyes and ready smile, she shifted to the edge of her chair. "Now Louie didn't 'ave anythin' to carry 'em in—so 'e just took the 'at off 'is 'ead and filled it up." She put her elbow on the table and leaned forward. "And who do you think should come along just then but the pub owner 'imself. Louie was caught with the goods in 'is 'at!"

A smile played over her lips. "The owner flew into a tantrum, promisin' to summon the constable. Louie, who was already well acquainted with the official, said 'e would return the eggs, but the owner would 'ave none of it. So Louie decided to speed things along. 'E placed the 'at on the owner's 'ead, and with a stout yank, tugged it down to the man's ears." Pell paused while Claude leaned back and wiped a mirthful tear from his eye.

"The man was cleanin' egg from 'is face and cursin' to beat the devil when Louie left the pub," she said in an amused tone. "It was quite a fit 'e pitched, considerin' 'e 'ad just gotten a new 'at out of the deal."

As Claude recovered from the story, she took another deep drink of wine.

A special closeness welled up between them as they sat there, and encouraged by the Chianti's glow and the warmth of the moment, an impulse seized Pell to reveal her past to him. "And now," she said quietly, putting her glass aside, "I have another story to tell you."

Noting her seriousness, he held her gaze and waited for her to continue. "What is troubling you, *chérie?* Why has the sun suddenly left your face?"

She swallowed uncomfortably. "I'm an heiress," she admitted in a tight voice, "yet not the type you imagine." She thought she saw his eyes glaze with disappointment, but attributed it to her nervousness. "I'm the natural daughter of General Fairchild ... not a wealthy orphan from the north as Alex wants everyone to believe." He took a quick breath and she studied his shocked face. "And my mother was a singer, a common tavern wench." Fear twinging through her, she glanced at the checkered tablecloth, then risked another look at Claude, who sat pale and speechless.

"I was raised in the East End," she went on in a strained tone. "When my father's detective found me, I was a fruit-peddler." She dared not tell him she had also stooped to picking pockets on occasion, a fact that she scarcely believed herself. "Alex served with my father in India, and the general chose him to be my guardian," she finished in a soft voice.

Claude gave her a look of utter disbelief. "But what of the years before? How could your father be so cruel as to deny you his companionship when you were a child?"

She clasped her hands tightly in her lap before continuing. "He could do no better. He wanted to bring me into his home, but he knew his wife Sabrina would have nothing to do with his bastard child." She picked up her glass with a trembling hand and moistened her dry lips with wine. "Although she never saw me as a child, Sabrina now suspects who I am," she added, looking into his stunned eyes again. She let out a worried breath. "Thank God, she can't prove it, for she's blazing mad that she must split the general's fortune."

She leaned back and nervously fingered the lace on her bodice, waiting for Claude's reaction. She trembled a bit, but she also felt great release—it was good to get the weight of deceit off her shoulders. At last she was being true to herself, rather than acting a part. "You . . . you don't think badly of me, do you?" she stammered.

Her heart pounded as she searched his handsome face. Would he still accept her, or had she alienated the one person who could always bring a smile to her lips?

Emotion choked her when he reached across the table and covered her hand with his. *"Ma chérie,* how could I ever think less of you?" he said with deep conviction. "You are the same angel I have always admired, but now my admiration is even greater, for I understand what hardships you have endured."

Her lips quivered as she tried to smile. "The stories and accent that amuse you so much are both mine, of course."

His eyes softened with emotion. "Of course. And now that I know, they are even more precious to me." He brought her cool hand to his lips and kissed it. *"Mon*

Dieu," he breathed as he covered it with his own hand once more. "What a burden you have borne!"

Anxiety began to well in her throat, eclipsing the joy of her release. "You mustn't tell anyone, *ever,"* she pleaded, eyeing his sympathetic face. "It's a great secret and Alex would be very angry if—"

"The despot is always mad at you," Claude cut in. He removed his hand from hers and leaned back in his chair. "He thinks only of rules and regulations, never of life ... of pleasure. And he never allows you to enjoy yourself either!" He steepled his ringed hands and leaned forward. "I suppose he won't even allow you to spend your own inheritance?"

"Oh, he watches me very closely, I can assure you!" she exclaimed.

"Does he give you anything, or must you beg for a penny like a child if you wish to purchase a cream puff?" Claude snapped contemptuously.

Pell reined in her nervousness, trying to compose an answer. "I now receive a monthly allowance, but at the end of the season I will come into my full inheritance. It's expected to take that long to liquidate my father's investments."

"May I ask what he invested in?"

She studied his tense face. "He invested heavily in the East India Company, and made a fabulous fortune, if I understand correctly." She noticed his eyes glisten with interest, then he shrugged and made a dramatic gesture with his hands.

"But why do you stay with this dictator? You are not a child—and he is so intolerable. Just to think of a flower like you crushed under his foot makes my blood boil!"

She gazed into his blazing eyes. He was so handsome, so gallant, so protective. How could she tell him that she stayed with Alex because she loved him? "I'm in Alex's charge until I receive my inheritance and am suitably married. At least, that was my father's plan."

Claude gave her a tender look and caressed her hand.

"Come, *chérie*, let us leave this place. I have much to discuss with you and need some privacy."

An inner voice warned Pell that she should leave by herself—and now—but there was something hypnotic about Claude. Surely it wouldn't matter if she spent a few more minutes with him. Why, they hadn't even exchanged proper good-byes yet.

Taking her moment of hesitation for acquiescence, Claude stood, and quickly ushered her from the table. When they left the warm restaurant and emerged into the fresh air and noise of Shaftesbury Avenue, he hailed a cab.

After they were seated in the carriage and it was clattering through Soho's dark narrow streets, he clasped her hands, and, raising them to his lips, gently kissed them both. "My heart is heavy with a question I must ask, *chérie*," he said huskily. "It has been on my lips since I met you."

She could not raise her eyes to his, and, guessing what he might say, her breath caught in her throat.

"Marry me, my angel. I will devote my life to you. We will flee to Paris, and be married in my chateau outside the city."

His words left her reeling. She had expected that he might ask her to marry him, but was stunned that he suggested they elope to France. She glanced up at him, her heart racing. *"Paris?"* she breathed in an incredulous tone.

"Oui. The French will take you to their hearts as I have."

"But my inheritance?" she murmured.

He regarded her with warm amusement. "You can receive your inheritance there and do with it as you please." He traced a knuckle over her cheek in an affectionate gesture. "No more of this British stuffiness. No more rules or lectures. No more of Lord Tavistock's orders and frowns."

She tried to sort out her tangled thoughts. "But Alex and my father had an agreement and—"

"A mere formality," he interrupted, his smile widening. "I'm sure the general did not know Lord Tavistock was such a tyrant or he would not have entrusted you to his care. Do not worry yourself so, my angel. No court would withhold funds from a rightful heiress."

Indecision tore through her as she listened to the clopping horses and the cries of the Soho street vendors. She wanted to remain with Alex, but outside of two impetuous moments when his discipline had slipped, he had not returned her love. She remembered how hurt she had been when he shut the library door in her face after their evening at the costers' social. If only he had shown her a little attention, a little affection . . .

Her mind spun as she struggled with the thorny decision. Claude appreciated her and her company, and offered compliments, rather than criticism, but she wondered if she could ever feel for him as she did for Alex.

Claude caressed her hand, disturbing her thoughts. *"Chérie,* you must give me an answer," he pressed, leaning so close she could smell his heavy French cologne.

Now one undeniable and depressing fact hammered through her mind. Alex had offered nothing in return for her love, had made no commitment to her whatsoever— and from his behavior it seemed that he never would. Besides that, if she didn't act soon, he would pressure her to marry a man of his choice rather than her own. On the other hand, Claude was so loving and attentive, and his artistic nature stirred her imagination.

Her vision blurred as she looked into the Frenchman's expectant eyes. "Yes," she said in a broken whisper. "Let's go to Paris and be married. With your fortune and my inheritance we'll live like royalty."

Claude's eyes swam with emotion as he kissed her cheek. "Oh, *chérie,* you will not be sorry! There is so much for me to show you in Paris. So much for us to do. We will live life to the fullest . . . we will breakfast on champagne and every day will be the beginning of a new party." His voice was as smooth as his expensive silk cravat.

Pell's heart fluttered and she nervously clasped her fingers together. She was still stunned by her decision, and for a moment she had an impulse to flee from the carriage.

But now that she had given Claude her word she could not turn back. "When . . . shall we leave?" she asked in a trembling voice.

"As soon as possible," he answered, his voice raspy with excitement. "Now that you have made your decision we must go before the despot marries you to some arthritic fossil." He caressed her hair. "I will look for a convenient time and make all the arrangements. Do you know your social schedule for next week?"

"Yes, I have three luncheons, and there is a large party at Lady Shelton's," she replied thoughtfully. "Alex has already said he will not be able to go to the party, but he asked a married couple of his acquaintance to escort me there."

Claude's eyes sparkled. "Good! I've received an invitation to the same party. I'm sure we can make plans around that event. I'll send you a note. Do you know my handwriting?"

She nodded her head, remembering his distinctive scrawl from the poem he had given her.

"Then search the mail every day before Tavistock sees it."

She gave a wistful sigh. "I must say good-bye to an old friend before we leave."

"*Oui,* my love. Say good-bye to your friend. But let it be soon." He covered her hands in kisses yet again, then, gathering her close, lowered his lips to hers.

As he deepened the kiss, the thud of his heart and pressure of his hand moving over her back sent a surprising flood of warmth through her limbs. The man who held her was not Alex, but the stirring kiss demanded a response, and as the artist pressed her even tighter against him, she found herself slipping her arms about his shoulders. Despite the tiniest flicker of doubt, her heart now brimmed with anticipation about her new life, and the future glowed before her like a lovely Parisian sunset.

* * *

Kid Glove Rosie swept her gaze over Pell and let out a low whistle. "Gaa! Turn around and let me see you, girl," she commanded in an awed voice.

Clutching a paper-wrapped parcel in her hand, Pell twirled about on the floor of the Hyde Park gazebo, modeling her fashionable apple-green gown. As she did so, a morning breeze blew against her cheek and she heard the sound of laughing children playing in the park.

Rosie ran her work-worn fingers over the lace at Pell's throat, then caressed the gown's bodice, which was trimmed in darker green velvet. "You looks just like a bleedin' queen," she said in reverent tones. Her face aglow, she peered up at Pell's jaunty hat. "And whot a fine 'at. Plumes and all. You've really come up in the world, you 'ave!"

Circling her, Rosie thumped Pell's bustle, then bent and examined the gown's small ruffled train. "I'll bet Victoria 'erself ain't got a gown as fine as this!" A grin brightened her plain face as she straightened and snatched the parasol from Pell's hand. With a snap and a pop, she opened it and pranced around the gazebo, holding her nose in the air. When she had made a full circle, she called out, "Look at me ... I'm the duchess of Cat and Wheel Alley, I am. I thinks I'll carry this along with me when I'm cleanin' fish at Billingsgate today!"

Pell burst out laughing and hugged her friend, wishing the fruit-peddler was really dressed in finery to match the parasol. Instead, a drab gown garbed her bulky figure, and the straw hat with the crumpled flower that Pell remembered so well sat atop her head. It was the poor girl's uniform that she had once worn herself. With a wistful smile, she noticed that Rosie still wore her black kid gloves—just to make her feel like a lady.

These secret meetings always lifted Pell's spirits, but today a shadow lay over her heart, for she had come to say good-bye. Wondering how she would tell her friend about Claude's proposal, she took the parasol and closed it, then scanned Rosie's happy face, dreading the task before her.

"Sit down," she said quietly, placing the parasol on the bench. "I have something to tell you."

Rosie's lined face tensed with concern as she took a seat. "Whot's troublin' you, girl? Tell old Rosie."

Pell eased down by her side and clasped her rough, reddened hand. "I could always count on you for a friendly ear. Now I need you more than ever," she began, feeling emotion begin to well up within her bosom.

The fruit-peddler blinked her eyes. "Ding dong bell and bloody 'ell, whot's 'appened now?" she cried. Then a horrified expression flew over her face. "You're not—"

Pell shook her head and laughed. "No, I'm not expecting," she answered with a smile. "There's no fear of that."

"Well, whot is it then?"

Drawing in a breath of the cool morning air to steady her nerves, she carefully chose her words. Finally deciding that a sharp knife hurt the least, she simply said, "Claude has asked me to marry him. And . . . and I've accepted."

Rosie's eyes narrowed and she sat forward. "You did whot!" she exclaimed.

"I'm marrying Claude and going to Paris," Pell replied a little defensively.

The fruit-peddler's mouth flew open. "I just can't believe it. It's enough to make a saint swear on 'is blessed liver!" She sank back against the high-backed bench and stared at Pell with disbelieving eyes. "Let me see that locket you're always showin' me again!"

Realizing her task would be an uphill fight, Pell removed the locket from her reticule and put it in her friend's calloused hand.

Rosie popped it open, stared at the picture, and shook her head. "I've never clapped eyes on the gent in the flesh, but from this picture 'e's got the look of a two-pence bouquet—bright and showy, but cheap-lookin' at the same time." She snapped the locket together and tossed it in Pell's lap. "'E's pretty to look at, all right, but I 'ave a feelin' 'is looks will soon fade. 'E's too pretty for a man.

And whot do you know about this bloke, anyway? A bugger like 'im might be after your fortune."

"Claude isn't like that," Pell declared in a hurt tone as she put away the locket. "He cares for me, and he likes to have fun ... and he makes me laugh, and he's always smiling."

Rosie drew herself up in grim disapproval. "I still says 'e's after your money."

"No. Claude is rich himself," Pell laughed. "He told me so, and you can tell by the way he dresses. He's a real gentleman."

The older woman nodded her head knowingly. "Don't think 'e's rich just 'cause he dresses fancy. A whiff of rich perfume or fancy threads don't make a lord or lady," she lectured sternly. She cocked her head. "Remember that girl Katherine whot moved into our tenement about two years ago? She wore fine clothes and smelt like Marie Antoinette herself, but as I recalls, she didn't gain her wealth by in'eritance. And she didn't spend her evenin's at the Queen's cotillions, if you knows whot I mean. In fact, I 'eard she 'ad a baby by a feller whot gave 'er a long line." She winked to emphasize her point.

A pang of doubt assailed Pell as she thought of the kept woman who had flaunted her finery before the others in the tenement while they secretly whispered about her behavior. Despite the fine day, a shiver ran over her arms as she considered something like that happening to her. Then she took a long breath and told herself she was being silly. Claude was too fine to use her and abandon her.

Rosie's mouth dipped down on one side. "Runnin' away with Claude just don't make sense girl. Whot about the professor? From whot you've told me 'e was favorin' you 'imself. Whot 'appened there?"

Pell sighed heavily. "That's the problem. *Nothing* has happened since we kissed after the coming-out ball. He was in a great mood on the night of the costers' party, then that sense of responsibility of his came back. I suppose he thinks he's got to do his duty by my father and marry me to some fine lord." She blew out her breath, making the silky curls tremble on her forehead. "Besides that, he doesn't understand how I feel ... he'll never love me, much less marry me." Her heart ached as she lowered her eyes and in her mind added the thought, *I suppose it doesn't matter, because I'm not good enough for him anyway.*

They both glanced up as a passerby walked by the gazebo, his shoes crunching over the graveled path. As the sound of the man's footsteps faded, Rosie shook her head, loosening strands of hair from the dark bun pinned at the nape of her neck. "And I thought 'e 'ad 'is mind on dallyin' when 'e took you in," she commented in an amused voice.

"Oh, *dallying* is the furthest thing from his mind," Pell returned. "After my ball, I thought he felt something for me, but since then he's been his proper military self. I've tried flirting with other men. Flirting with him. Everything." Her shoulders slumped in despair. "I suppose I was foolish to think he could ever love me."

Rosie straightened her back and patted Pell's hand. "Well, I says, who needs the professor, anyway? You'll be better off without 'im." She rolled her eyes. "And I'm sure you won't be missin' that stuck-up bald-'eaded butler of 'is either. I don't think I've ever seen 'im crack a smile. 'E looks like 'e's just walkin' around to save funeral expenses." She raised her brows and widened her eyes. "But you can't be runnin' off to Paris with this Frenchie. You don't know enough about 'im. It's too big a risk!"

Stung by those words, Pell pulled away her hand. "Well, I say Claude is worth the risk." She turned from her friend's reproachful gaze and looked over the park's scarlet rose beds and sparkling fountains. "I don't have anyone else to help me," she added softly. "At least this way I have some choice in my future. If I stay with Alex much longer, he'll soon have me married to one of those old men he brings home with him from the Carlton."

Rosie grimaced. "Gaa, one of them great blinkin' toads?

Why, I'd as soon kiss a codfish as one of those old goats."
She searched Pell's face. "You're in a tough spot all right,
but are you sure, luv? Maybe you're just down now.
Maybe—"

"No. I'm sure," Pell said shortly, trying to convince herself as well as Rosie. "I'm comfortable with Claude and I
trust him." She caressed her friend's arm. "Don't worry
about me. I'll be all right."

Looking worried, Rosie pushed her loose hair under her
hat. "But whot about your money?" she rushed out. "How
will you get your fortune in France? Whot if the professor
tries to keep it? That's your money, bird. Don't let some
bloke cheat you out of it."

Pell took Rosie by the shoulders and looked into her
troubled eyes. "Claude and I have already talked about financial matters, and he has promised me that we'll get my
fortune. He's so rich he can hire all kinds of solicitors.
Don't worry . . . they'll see that it comes to me."

A look of resigned defeat settled over Rosie's face.
"When do you leave?" she asked sadly.

"Tonight—from Victoria Station on the Continental
train." Pell smiled, feeling excited just to be talking about
it.

"So soon?"

"Yes. Now that I've made up my mind, it's best that I
go."

"Supposin' you *do* run off with Claude tonight," Rosie
said crossly. " 'Ow are you goin' to do it, with the professor watchin' your every move?"

"I'm attending a party tonight. Alex can't go because he
has to prepare a speech he is giving to the House of Lords
next week. He has arranged for a young married couple he
knows, the Petersons, to escort me there. Claude will be at
the party also. We'll simply slip away together a little before midnight. By the time we're missed we'll already be
on our way to Dover," Pell explained, feeling a little guilty
about the deception.

Rosie darted a sharp look at her. "You're leavin' the country with only the gown on your back?"

"Yes, but Clause already has a portmanteau in a rented locker at the station. He has purchased and packed another gown and some personal items for me. As soon as we arrive in Paris, he has promised me a grand shopping expedition."

Her friend blew out her breath and slapped a hand on her knee. "Well, I guess you've got everythin' all planned out then," she said in a tired voice. "But I'm still worried about you." She ran her gaze over her friend once more. "I just don't trust those damn Frenchies!"

Trying to evade Rosie's probing eyes, Pell remembered her package and handed it to her. "Here," she said firmly. "Stop worrying, and take this! It's a pink gown and it will look wonderful with your dark hair." Pell had also added some money to the package for the woman who had watched over her for so long.

Rosie's eyes glistened with emotion. "Cor, another dress? You'd better stop or people will be thinkin' I took up Katherine's old job!" She blinked back her tears. "If you're goin' to Paris, I don't guess I'll be seein' you anymore, will I?"

Pell dropped her gaze. "No . . . but we can write—"

"You knows I ain't much for writin'," Rosie interrupted. She sniffled and rubbed her gloved hand under her nose, then, trying to control her emotions, reached into her apron pocket. "Oh, I saved this for you," she said with forced gaiety. She placed a large, perfectly shaped peach in Pell's open hand. "Wasn't sure if the professor was feedin' you proper," she added in a hoarse voice.

Pell felt hot tears prick her eyes. "Rosie . . . I don't know how I can thank you for taking care of me for all those years. I . . ." Her voice faded and broke off.

Rosie shook her head. "Eh? Whot's all this?" Gently she wiped away Pell's tears with her apron. "Lookin' after a little bird like you was nothin'." Then she hugged her tightly, making her bones crack.

Rising, she prepared to go and lightly touched Pell's cheek. "Bein' separated don't matter to us, does it?" she asked in a trembling voice. "You and me . . . we'll always be mates. Right?" With a big smile that didn't match the tears in her eyes, she turned and sauntered off with the package under her arm. About twenty yards from the gazebo, she paused and raised her hand in a last farewell, then wiped her nose with a tattered handkerchief, and, holding her back very straight, turned and briskly walked away.

Choking back the lump in her throat, Pell watched her go. When Rosie was out of sight, she caressed the warm fuzzy peach with her thumb, at that moment wishing she had never left Whitechapel.

Chapter 15

As the library clock chimed eleven, Alex pushed the scribbled papers to the side of his desk, his own handwriting blurring before his tired eyes. At dusk he had returned home from the House of Lords, and, without bothering to change clothes, begun work on a speech. But unresolved problems filled his mind, and he had found he could not concentrate. Leaning back in his chair, he looked at his cold, untouched dinner that lay on a small table near his desk. He knew a presentable speech would require many more hours of work.

Lost in troubled thought, he automatically glanced at the library doors as Aunt Violet swept into the room dressed in a frothy peach gown trimmed in heavy lace.

"I just came in to say good night, dear," she announced softly, clutching her patchouli-scented handkerchief as she moved across the room. Once at his side, she glanced at the untouched dinner tray and frowned. *"Why, you haven't eaten."*

Placing his fingers on the desk, Alex pushed back and stood, then, hands locked behind his back, started pacing around the library. "No, and it seems that I haven't composed a speech, either. I've been trying to write a proposal concerning affordable trade schools for poor boys. So many of them become embittered in the workhouses and come out with no marketable skills. I also have an idea about free health care for infants . . . but it seems I haven't been able to concentrate."

She walked to his side, and, as he paused, lightly clasped his arm. "Worried about all those bills, dear?"

He glanced down at her troubled face. "Yes, it's becoming increasingly difficult to look my peers in the eye when I know that most of them hold my brother's unpaid promissory notes."

She pressed her lips together, looking as if she were searching for comforting words. "You might secure that high appointment in the conservative government yet," she offered brightly, a hopeful look on her face.

He raised his brows and sighed heavily. "Yes, I suppose that possibility does exist."

There was an awkward silence for a moment, then, looking as if she wanted to change the subject, the old lady blurted out, "Didn't Pell look lovely this evening!"

Alex recalled a moment just before Pell left with the Petersons for a large party at Lady Shelton's. A gown of purple trimmed in blue clung to her graceful figure, and jaunty purple plumes adorned her soft blonde hair. The married couple had already left the library and waited for her in the hall, but she lingered behind, looking up at him with eyes that glistened with unspoken emotion.

He'd smiled as his gaze slid over her. How utterly perfect she was, he thought as he took her slim hand and turned her about. "You look lovely tonight," he said warmly, his voice husky with pride.

She blushed and pulled her cool hand away from his grasp. "Thank—thank you," she stammered.

A heavy silence stretched between them and she shifted under his gaze. He felt that she wanted to speak, but instead she bit her lip and seemed anxious to escape.

What was bothering her? he wondered thoughtfully. "Is there something you wish to say to me?" he asked quietly.

She sighed, and there was a troubled shimmer in her eyes. "No, not really. I . . ." She bowed her head, then looked up again, her face clouding with uneasiness. "I . . . I just wanted to say thank you for everything." Her voice broke slightly.

He swept his gaze over her, noticing her milk-white face and shaky hands. Was this just a case of party nerves? Had her old insecurities flooded back to seize her tonight? "Don't worry," he advised with a soft laugh as he caressed her arms. "I'm sure you'll be the belle of the ball. You always are, you know."

She nodded and swallowed hard, then quickly moved to the library doors, where she gazed at him one last time. "Good-bye," she whispered softly.

"Alex, I don't believe you've heard a thing I said," Aunt Violet chided, breaking into his thoughts.

Focusing his mind, he glanced at his aunt.

"The Petersons are a solid and reliable pair," she continued. "They'll look after the child." Giving him a last comforting look, she walked to the library doors, then glanced back over her shoulder. "I'm going upstairs now, dear. I've just started Edward Bulwer-Lyttons's *Leila and the Siege of Granada* and I want to finish the first chapter before I go to sleep." She smiled once more. "Don't work too late, now."

After she left the library Alex began to pace again as he thought of Claude Dubois. Bitterness seeping through him, he remembered a recent event where Claude had been present. Dressed to the nines and wearing an air of casual elegance, he had swept into the room, charming every lady he met. The rascal had the boldness to ask Pell for a dance, and Alex had watched closely as the pair waltzed. There had been no impropriety on Claude's part, but he could imagine a scheming mind working behind those twinkling eyes.

As Alex reseated himself at the desk, thoughts of Claude lingered in his mind. Reaching into his desk drawer, he removed a thick envelope and tapped it against his hand. He knew he must tell Pell what it contained, and soon, for he was sure it would change her mind about the artist. But with some regret, he also realized it would hurt her. Avoiding the issue had been easy; he had received the letter only yesterday, and had scarcely had a moment alone with her.

As he considered when he could talk to her, banging and scraping sounds issued from the hall, drawing his attention. Slipping the letter back into the drawer, he listened to raised voices. Seconds later Buxley hurried into the library with such a look of horror on his face that Alex rose from his chair. "What is happening?" he said in an exasperated tone.

Buxley's lips trembled as he stood at a respectful distance from the desk. "I'm very sorry, milord," he answered nervously, "but that creature is here again and she demands to see you."

Before he could say another word, Kid Glove Rosie strode into the room and shot the butler a look of disdain. His hands clenched, the man paced toward her, blocking the way to Alex.

"Outta my way, Baldy!" she snapped, weaving back and forth to move around him. "I needs to speak with the professor, and right now!"

"Madam, this is not a public place," Buxley informed her sharply. "You cannot enter this room without permission." He flared his nostrils, then threw her a disgusted look. "Merciful heavens, woman, you stink of fish!"

She narrowed her eyes. "Fish-stink will wash off, but bein' dumb won't, Baldy. Cor, it's a good thing rusty brains don't clatter or there would be an awful racket in 'ere!"

The butler drew himself up to his full height. "*You,* madam are a foul-mouthed harridan and a crude excuse for a human being. I'm sure his lordship does not wish to speak with you. Leave immediately!"

Hands on hips, she drew a slow gaze over him. "Say, does the undertaker know you're up? You better see, 'e may be gettin' a bit worried."

Buxley's mouth flew open like a trapdoor. "Well, I never!"

"No, and it's damn lucky for somebody, ain't it?" She

flashed him a crooked smile and finally maneuvered around him.

He got in front of her again and raised his hands in a last-ditch effort to block her path. Swatting one of his arms out of the way, she strode ahead, and stopped in front of Alex's desk. His eyes blazing, the butler stuck out his chin and paced toward her, but Alex waved him off. Rosie glanced over her shoulder as the butler snapped about and walked toward the library door in his squeaky paten-leather shoes. "'Ey, Baldy," she called after him, "you better put a pot on your 'ead. I 'ears there's some low-flyin' woodpeckers about tonight."

Alex tried not to smile as Buxley tightened his fists and took a deep breath that strained the buttons on his jacket. Clenching his jaw so hard his temples pulsed, the butler bowed formally to Alex. Then, throwing Rosie a murderous glare, he exited the room.

Alex scanned Rosie's grime-smeared face. "My, how delightful to see you again, Miss Rosie," he said dryly. "I see you and Buxley are getting on smashingly as usual."

She glanced at the door. "That numbskull? If God had put 'is brain in an ant, the thing would crawl backwards. I don't know why you keep 'im around."

"Dear lady, you do him an injustice. He's more intelligent than he looks."

"Righto. 'E'd 'ave to be, wouldn't 'e?"

A smile twisting his lips, Alex walked to the grog tray and poured himself a drink.

"Would you care for a whiskey?" he offered, turning and studying her worried face.

"Yeah . . . I could use a whiskey all right!" Her eyes followed his every move as he poured another drink and handed it to her.

Surprised, he watched her tilt back her head, toss off the drink in two gulps, then place the glass aside with a loud clink.

"Well, what urgent business brings you here this evening?" he asked, swirling the whiskey in his glass. "I'm sure Buxley informed you that Miss Davis is attending a party—"

Frustration flashed on her face. "I knows where she is," Rosie blurted out. "That's why I came. All day, as I was cleanin' cod at Billingsgate, I been sayin' to meself, Rosie, you can't let 'er do it. You can't let a good kid like that throw away whot she's got. It just ain't right!" As she gestured with her hands the aroma of fish wafted toward Alex, making him draw back a bit.

Trying to make sense of her ramblings, he inquired, "What do you mean, *throw away what she has?* What does this have to do with Miss Davis?"

A splutter of exasperation burst from Rosie's lips. "That' whot I'm tryin' to tell you," she wailed. "She's run off with that Frenchie! I told 'er 'e weren't no good for 'er, but she wouldn't believe me!"

There was a moment of silence in which Alex could hardly credit what she had said. The statement seemed so fantastic that he could only stare at her for a moment; then the full meaning of her words swept over him, shaking him deeply. Of course, he thought. That was the reason why Pell had acted so strange when she said good-bye. Placing his drink aside, he grasped Rosie's shoulders. "Are you certain about this?"

"Of course I'm certain. She told me 'erself. They're leavin' from that fancy party together." She glanced about the library, then looked back at him as if to keep the matter confidential. "I figures a soft Frenchie like that is just after 'er money," she whispered with a knowing look.

At the moment he wanted to throttle her, but with a great effort he forced himself to be calm. "Why didn't you come sooner?" he demanded tightly, his voice rough with frustration.

She looked at him apprehensively. "I . . . I couldn't make up my mind if I was doin' the right thing. I thought about it all day while I was workin' and after I got 'ome, tryin' to decide whot I should do." She rubbed her temples. "My 'ead near burst today from thinkin' about it. I started to tell one of the blokes at the tenement, but I finally decided you was the only one who could stop 'er from ruinin' 'er life." Tears glazed her eyes and she hung her head. "I'm sorry, Professor, I . . ."

"Never mind," he said hoarsely. He raised her head and studied her frightened face. "When are they leaving?"

She blinked her eyes. "Late tonight. They're catchin' a train—"

Forgetting himself, he shook her a little. "A *train?* Good God, just where does that scoundrel think he's taking her?" Although his voice was even, he felt his anger soaring out of control. He was furious with Claude and furious with himself for letting this happen. Why hadn't he anticipated that the artist would try something like this, and why hadn't he taken steps to stop him?

"You won't be mad at me when I tells you?" Rosie asked, looking as if he might strike her. Trying to reassure her, he shook his head, then backed off a step and smoothed down her rumpled shawl. "All right then," she said in a halting voice, her eyes still wide with fear. "I'll tell you. They're goin' to Dover by the Continental train, then catchin' a ship to France and goin' on to Paris."

A leaden heaviness filled his chest like a great stone and despair engulfed him. He yearned to distance himself from the pain of her departure as a man yearns to move away from the heat of a searing fire. At the same time, one lucid thought hammered through his head, overpowering his other emotions. He must find Pell and save her before Claude took her out of the country. He knew the Continental train left at midnight. A quick look at the clock told him he had only forty-five minutes to stop them.

As he walked from the library, Rosie trailed after him, trying to keep up with his long strides. "You'll find 'er, won't you, Professor? You won't let that Frenchie take 'er off, will you?" she implored in an agitated wail, twisting her stained apron in her hands.

Alex touched his fingers to his forehead and closed his eyes. "Calm yourself, woman. I'm trying to think." In the hall he saw Buxley, who still had a disgruntled look on his face. "Go to the mews and rouse the carriage driver, and be quick about it," he ordered. "Tell him I must leave with all haste!"

"That's right, Professor," Rosie blurted out as she clumped into the hall behind him in her scuffed boots. "I wouldn't spare a minute if I was you!"

"Is there an emergency?" the butler asked loftily. "Should I have the maid notify your aunt?"

"No. Do not disturb Aunt Violet," Alex commanded. "Simply carry out my orders, then send the servants to bed and close the house after I depart." As he watched the butler leave the hall, he realized that Victoria Station was so large that he could easily miss Pell; it would be a great advantage to have another person with him. For a moment he considered taking Buxley or Rosie, but he quickly rejected both of them, for he had never seen Buxley move faster than a stately walk and Rosie was in a state of nervous turmoil.

When he spotted Hadji quietly moving through the hall, carrying some books back to the library, he remembered how swiftly he could run. Making a quick decision, he called the servant's name.

His eyes large, Hadji placed the books on an entry table and hurried to him.

"Come with me," Alex commanded as he moved toward the front doors, leaving Rosie standing by herself in the hall.

"Yes, illustrious master, but where are we going?" Hadji asked respectfully.

Alex glanced back over his shoulder at the Indian's puzzled face. "We're going to stop Miss Davis from making the biggest mistake of her life. Now look sharp, and put some ginger in your feet!"

From inside the carriage, Alex heard the coachman shout at the horses and crack the whip over their backs. He had ordered the man to speed to Victoria Station as if his very life depended on it, and apparently he had taken him at his word, for the team clattered around another corner, making the carriage creak and tilt.

"Why would she do such a foolish thing?" Alex muttered in a rough voice, talking to himself as much as to Hadji, who sat by his side.

The servant clung to the swaying hand strap and glanced at his master. "Perhaps she is not being happy, sahib," he answered simply.

"Not happy?" Alex thundered. "Nonsense. Why, she had everything a woman could want."

"Perhaps not everything," the frightened servant corrected. "Perhaps—" He swallowed hard. "Perhaps Miss Davis is lacking love."

Alex's mouth twisted with exasperation. "But that's exactly what I'm trying to help her with! How can she be married to a suitable husband if she won't remain here and let me introduce her to eligible men?"

The carriage lurched and Alex heard the coachman exchange oaths with another driver as they narrowly missed colliding with a hansome cab. The Indian straightened himself upon the seat and peered at Alex through the gloom, his eyes large and apprehensive. "Perhaps Miss Davis is already finding an eligible male she is liking . . . even loving."

Alex clenched his jaw. Never in his entire life could he remember being as angry as he was at this moment. "Claude?" he asked curtly. "Are you saying she's in love with that fancified, limp-wristed fop? *He's* her suitable male?"

The Indian spread his trembling hands. "Oh, no. Please excuse your humble servant for being so unclear." He hesitated and glanced down in embarrassment. "Perhaps it is my illustrious master that she is favoring," he offered in a broken voice.

Feeling the vibration of the spinning carriage wheels beneath the floor, Alex braced his arm against the door and stared straight ahead at the glowing gaslights. "Me? Impossible! All we ever do is fight. There's hardly a peaceable word between us." He hit his fist against his thigh. "And if she does *favor me,* as you put it, why would she deceive me and run away?"

"Sometimes we are not seeing what is the plainest, beneficent master."

Alex let out his breath and stared from the window at the passing cityscape, where endless streets vanished in the darkness. What use was it to try to converse with a servant who talked in Indian riddles? he thought with irritation. He had felt Pell tremble in his arms the night they kissed after her ball, and knew she had been touched with passion—but passion and love were two different things. It had never occurred to him that she might actually love him, and as he pondered the idea, it shook him deeply. As he stared at the dark brooding buildings and the reflection of the moon on the Thames, he wondered what he would find at the station. Would he be in time to stop Claude from taking Pell out of the country, or would she be gone from his life forever?

Just then the carriage pulled up near the imposing entrance of Victoria Station. It loomed above a cluster of horse-drawn vans that were delivering morning newspapers to be taken all over England. Several fine equipages with liveried footmen were also drawn up to allow their owners to catch the Continental train.

Alex immediately got out of the carriage and motioned for Hadji to follow him. "Miss Davis is wearing a purple gown this evening," he said as they ran under the high-arched entrance. "Keep a keen eye out for it." Once they were into the station, which smelled of oil and soot and sulphurous smoke, Alex spied a red-jacketed porter and put out his hand. "Where does the Continental train leave from?" he asked sharply.

The man gestured toward the far end of the building, which was filled with hissing steam and the sound of shrieking whistles and slamming doors. "From the farthest platform, guv'ner," he shouted over the din. He pulled a pocket watch from inside his coat. "You'd better hurry, too, sir, if you don't mind my sayin'."

Alex strode briskly away from the man, Hadji at his heels. The station bustled with activity even at this late hour. Porters in uniforms and braided hats pushed handcarts full of leather bags after elegantly dressed couples who casually made their way to their cars. Steam billowed from engines as they prepared to get under way, and conductors slammed portable steps beneath the car doors of arriving trains.

Alex and the servant hastily made their way through the maze of platforms and luggage, searching for signs of the eloping couple. Suddenly drawing in his breath, the Indian touched his master's arm and pointed past a group of soldiers standing on a nearby platform. Beyond them, Alex saw a purple plume waving from behind a high stack of luggage.

Alex moved toward the plume and Hadji followed; in his excitement, the servant brushed against a stack of luggage and sent it tumbling to the grimy platform, attracting the notice of a shouting porter. When the pair neared the owner of the purple plume, Alex's heart sank. Jerking up her head, a large bleary-eyed matron gave him a startled look, then hurried on her way.

His heart hammering, Alex pushed through the press of people, continuing his search. Suddenly, a white-jacketed servant, carrying a food hamper to a waiting car, loomed in front of him. The man glanced up, but too late, and as the hamper sprang open, china cups and bottles of marmalade met the station floor with a resounding crash. Alex quickly withdrew several pounds and stuffed it into the dazed servant's pocket, then hurried on, allowing his eyes to focus on the huge clock at the front of the station. The straight-up position of the hands confirmed his worst fears—it was exactly midnight, time for the Continental train to depart.

He raked his gaze over the few remaining platforms and his heart lurched when he saw a blotch of purple. At last he had found them! Dressed in an impeccably tailored suit and a jaunty bowler hat, Claude escorted Pell onto the step of the waiting train, his face aglow. Evidently the couple was the last to board, for a conductor waited by the open door.

The engine's whistle screamed with a deafening blast and steam billowed from beneath the train's wheels as Alex ran with a thudding heart. Anger hardening his jaw, he swiftly closed the short space between himself and Claude and clasped the Frenchman's arm in a steely grip. Claude wore an expression of utter surprise as Alex jerked him to the platform and separated him from Pell, who gasped and whirled about on the step.

"Monsieur! What do you want?" Claude demanded, his eyes darkening in surprise.

"I'm going to see if my fist and your face can occupy the same place at the same time!" Alex growled. Before Claude could utter another word, Alex leveled his fist near his own shoulder, and with all the force of his rage smashed it into the center of the artist's face.

Claude's heels left the ground and he landed with a meaty thump on the platform. Blood bubbled from his nose as he sat bewildered, his legs awkwardly turned out in front of him. Leaning hastily to one side, he attempted to draw a leg beneath him to balance himself. Instead, his head lolled to the side, then he collapsed backward on the oil-smeared floor.

Alex now turned to Pell, who looked pale and terrified, her hands over her mouth. She trembled and her eyes widened in fear as he clasped her arm and pulled her from the step.

Puffing for breath, Hadji arrived and came to a halt by Alex's side, his mouth falling open as he looked down at Claude's crumpled form. A crowd of murmuring spectators surged forward and also stared at the Frenchman, who still lay sprawled on the platform, hair falling over his eyes, a bright spot of blood spreading over his white shirt.

"Mon Dieu," he said in a strangled voice. "You've broken my nose." He glowered at Alex. "I will see that you are rewarded for this," he muttered hoarsely. "You cannot treat me in such a manner!"

Ignoring the threat, Alex turned away from him and tightened his grip about Pell's arm. "Come with me," he ordered coolly.

Indignation flared up within Pell as she gazed at his flashing eyes and thunderous expression. How dare he do this! She would show him she was an independent person, that he couldn't manhandle her and embarrass her in front of all these people. Trembling with anger, she tried to tug away from him, but his hand was like a steel band about her wrist as he pulled her closer.

Twisting, she balled her fist and pounded on his chest with her free hand. "Let me go this instant!"

His eyes sparkling with fury, his mouth clamped in a hard line, he effortlessly lifted her off her feet, and subdued her squirming body. "Save your breath," he commanded as he turned and strode away with her in his arms. "We're going home!"

Chapter 16

Pell clenched her hands and glowered at Alex as their carriage creaked to a halt in front of the house. "How dare you treat me as if I were a naughty child to be brought home in disgrace!" she snapped, her throat tight with anger.

In the dim light coming through the pane, Alex's face was rock-hard and his eyes glittered with cold reproach. "If you act like an irresponsible child, people will treat you that way," he countered icily.

His tone inflamed her mounting rage, and in her mind's eye she relived the mortifying incident at the railroad station. Resentment surged up within her as she pictured Claude sprawled on the railroad platform, his face smeared with blood, and the expressions of the stunned people who had witnessed the embarrassing spectacle. To worsen her humiliation, she thought of Kid Glove Rosie and trembled inwardly, wondering how her friend could have betrayed her.

"I am not a stick of furniture that you may transport about as you please," she stormed, fury strangling her voice. "I am a grown woman with a life of her own!"

He flashed her a cool, sardonic look. "You are nothing but a spoiled, insolent child who knows little of real life."

The words stung her like a cut and she ached to lash back at him, but his stony countenance temporarily forbade further comment. Her breath coming fast and ragged, she scooted to the edge of the seat, promising herself that she would finish the argument inside.

Wordlessly, Alex put his hand on the door lever and stepped from the brougham. After handing Pell down to the sidewalk, he slammed the carriage door behind him with a resounding thunk, and the driver wheeled the carriage around the side of the mansion toward the mews, taking Hadji, riding on the box, with him.

Taking Pell's arm in a firm grasp, Alex hastily ushered her toward the house where a soft light still glowed from the library windows. Hurrying to keep up with his swift strides, she pulled against his steely grip and cried, "Let me go! I'm not a prisoner to be escorted back into my cell. You act as if I can't make a decision for myself!"

His lips thinned with anger. "I am beginning to wonder if you can think at all."

At the entrance he fitted a key into the lock, then, once inside the house, walked her through the shadowy hall and into the library. On the desk a reading lamp cast soft light over the room. His gaze resting on a nearby chair, he unceremoniously plopped her down upon it as if she were a sack of dirty laundry.

She instantly shot to her feet, burning to slap his face. "I won't sit here and be lectured to like a bloody criminal," she lashed out, turning to walk away.

He yanked open his desk drawer, and, taking out the fat envelope, quickly opened it. "Pity. I thought you might like to learn something of the notorious history of Monsieur Claude Dubois. It's hardly a bedtime story, but highly colorful nevertheless." Before she could answer, he started reading aloud.

" 'Dear Lord Tavistock: In response to your query about Monsieur Dubois I have been able to unearth these facts. He was born in Paris to an upper-middle-class family that occasionally associated with those on the edge of the aristocracy. Monsieur Dubois, whose real name is Gaspard Gourgaud, has many aliases. His father, who was a well-to-do merchant, sent Gourgaud, or Dubois as I shall call him, to one of the better Parisian universities. There, in his second year he fell in with bad company and was expelled from the school for gambling.' "

Pell had every intention of walking from the room, but as the unbelievable words rolled from Alex's mouth she found her legs would not move. Feeling as if the ground had vanished from beneath her, she gave him her full attention, her cold hands quivering at her side.

Alex gave her a quick glance, then brought the letter to her. "Here," he said, putting it into her trembling hand, then walked back to the desk. "I urge you to read the words for yourself."

At first, she only stared at him blankly, and he wondered if she was going to read the letter at all. Then, as if in a trance, she looked down at the pages. Finally, she lifted her hand, and with shimmering eyes, began reading haltingly, her voice rough with emotion. " 'After Dubois' expulsion from the university, things proceeded from bad to worse. His mounting gambling debts financially drained his father, forcing the poor man to disown him. The French authorities report that Dubois has been arrested and incarcerated no less than four times, usually in connection with fraud.' "

For a moment tears welled in Pell's eyes and she lowered the letter and stopped reading. As she did so, Alex studied her sad face and felt his anger subsiding. Concern rose up within him, for her shock and misery were apparent and it pained him to see her this way. He decided to take the letter away from her, but before he could move, she lifted the pages once more and continued in a rough whisper.

" 'He loves high living, and although he does nothing in particular, he does it very well, depending on others to support him. It is difficult to ascertain how many times he has duped unsuspecting women out of their income, for once they find him out, many are too embarrassed to press charges.' " Pell's voice broke. With a look of despair spreading over her face, she swallowed back her tears.

Alex walked to her and gently took the letter. " 'Although the French have no grounds to arrest him at this present time,' " he read, " 'they are highly interested in his activities. By barely staying inside the laws of the land, he often escapes incarceration; nevertheless the gentleman in question is morally bankrupt and has ruined the lives of numerous women. I find that he has no attachment whatsoever with the French Academy of Fine Art, although he must have some artistic talent for he was incarcerated for a period of one year on a count of bank-note forgery.' "

After walking back to his desk, Alex laid the pages aside. "As you might imagine, the letter is from a London detective I hired to investigate Monsieur Dubois. There is more—all of it bad, I'm afraid," he said quietly.

She dropped her eyes before his compassionate gaze and grasped the back of a chair, her legs trembling with weakness.

Claude's deceit pressed about her heart like a vice and she was too shocked for words. He had been her friend—or she had thought him to be. They had laughed and talked together, and he had sworn his love to her and won her friendship with his tenderness. Now, hearing this report, which had been written so matter-of-factly, made her doubt her own sanity. "This can't be true," she finally whispered, blinking her eyes in disbelief as she stared at Alex. "There must be some mistake. He's a rich man. He has a chateau, a fortune in France. He—"

"No, he has nothing," Alex interrupted, picking up the letter again. "A few paragraphs further into the report, the investigator states that Dubois has no assets whatsoever."

He put the letter down. "True, he has deceived a French count into thinking he is also an aristocrat. When the nobleman is in the south of France, Claude takes women to the man's chateau—but he himself has nothing. He is a fraud and a fortune hunter . . . a man who lives by deceiving women."

Holding back her tears, Pell lowered her eyes in embarrassment again. How mortified she felt! She had almost thrown away her fortune and her life on a scoundrel. In her heart of hearts she had harbored her own doubts about Claude, but she had never dreamed his past might reveal something so ugly and sordid as this. Fear knotted within her as she recalled that she had revealed the secret of *her* past to this man. How could she ever admit to Alex that she had been so foolish? Defiance flooding through her, she decided that she wouldn't tell him. At this point, why should he know? And deep in her heart she still hoped Claude wasn't as worthless as the detective's report said.

"What about his paintings?" she asked in a shaky voice. "How could the man produce such works and be as bad as the detective says?" She looked into Alex's appraising eyes, challenging him.

He paused, then replied dryly, "In his report the detective writes that Dubois purchases paintings from some of the art students who live in the Montmartre section of Paris. I have seen the students myself. Many are extremely talented, but desperate for funds. After lightly touching a brush to the canvases to soothe his conscience—if he has any—Dubois signs his name to the paintings and claims they are his own."

"But that can't be. He knows so much about art. He—"

"Talking about art and painting are two completely different things. No one has denied that Dubois is gifted verbally. Most scoundrels are, you know."

"But—"

"Think about it," he said in a gentler tone. "Have you actually seen him paint?" He cocked a brow. "No, he merely talks about it and the awards he has won; no doubt all fake like the rest of his credentials."

She now felt crushed and numb inside. The supposed artist had deceived her, and manipulated her into almost running away with him. "What will Claude do now?" she asked in a weak voice.

He measured her with a thoughtful gaze. "If he has any sense at all he will vanish from the London social scene.

I imagine he might visit the country ... at least for a while."

Her face burned with mortification. Not only had she been deceived by Claude, it seemed that Alex had known of this dark secret for some days and held the facts back from her. As she looked at him standing there so handsome and sure of himself with the lamplight washing over him, her shame blossomed into irritation. "How long have you known this?" she demanded. "Why didn't you tell me?"

He looked down at her with hooded eyes. "I only received the report yesterday. I knew you were attached to the man and I was waiting for the right time to tell you about it," he said evenly. He clasped her forearms in his large hands, bringing her closer. "I would have told you instantly if I had suspected you intended to elope with him. How could you have been so foolish?"

His accusation fueled her growing anger. "The answer to that question is very simple, milord. When a human being is freezing, that person will seek a fire—any fire, poor though it might be. I had long ago given up hope of stirring your heart, for it is made of stone." She gazed into his smoldering eyes, wanting to touch him, even hurt him. She knew she had gone too far, but the hot words spilled from her quivering lips before she could catch them. "All you have in you is an army book of regulations!"

His face hardened at her accusation and his hands tightened about her arms, biting into them. "How wrong you are," he whispered in a rough voice. The sentence was spoken with such feeling it almost took her breath away.

Alex looked down at Pell's angry face, and for a moment he felt the sting of her words. Then, with the force of a wall crashing over him, he realized that in her own way she was telling him she loved him. And at the same moment, he knew that he loved her—loved her with all his heart. And he knew that this love was a strong, vibrant, invincible love. The realization was so powerful that it swept away all concerns of duty, honor, and suitability, and as he felt his heart thudding crazily in his chest, he knew he was going to carry her upstairs and make love to her.

For a moment it seemed to Pell as if Alex were trying to see inside her very soul, then he lowered his lips to hers and she could feel his warm breath upon her face. With unyielding force, his arms went around her and pulled her against him; she could feel the buttons on his jacket pressing into her bosom. Soft tender feelings rushed over her, leaving her limp and helpless in his steely embrace. A look passed between them that shook her deeply, and in the space of a heartbeat his mouth took hers in a wild kiss, so forceful that she trembled. Realizing that to give in now meant total surrender, she twisted in his arms and pounded his shoulders with her balled hands.

Ignoring the futile attack, he slid his powerful hand over her arm, subduing her, and as he deepened the fiery kiss, pressing her closer, she knew there would be no denying him. She felt the raging fire within him, and it thrilled her. In a state of awe, she relaxed into his warm embrace, and, with a will of their own, her arms crept around his broad shoulders.

Moving his lips from her mouth, he pressed hot kisses over her closed lids, her cheeks, the throbbing pulse in her throat, and she noticed a strange sensation in her breasts that she had never known before. Her limbs took on a sensual glow, and with a shiver of excitement, she felt her nipples harden and swell against her gown. "My little love," he whispered in a caressing drawl as he moved his strong hand over the hollows of her back. His body was warm and strong and the rhythm of his thudding heart sent a dart of passion sweeping through her veins.

She could feel his starched shirt against her cheek and his lips kissing her hair, and when he easily lifted her up and swung her feet from the floor, she drew in a sharp breath. Her heart leaped as he positioned her in his arms as if she were almost weightless and moved toward the open library doors. Everything was happening so swiftly she didn't have time to speak or think, and a deep languorous need passed through her, turning her will to water.

Before she knew it, he was out of the large chamber and carrying her up the dark stairs, and for an instant her consciousness seemed to dim. Alarm rippled through her, making her weak and confused. Who was this passionate stranger, this man she had never seen before? With a start of fear, she realized he had shown her only one side of his personality up until now, concealing the wild passionate side that he reined in with a curb bit.

Then as his bedroom door drew near, her heart pounded furiously and she opened her mouth to cry out, but he shifted her in his arms and kissed her again, muffling her voice. Clutching his shoulders, she quivered at the power and tenderness of the kiss and her head spun wildly, forestalling her protests. In the bedroom she heard the door close behind them and excitement spiraled in the pit of her stomach. She had never been in his private chambers and the semidarkness and musky man-scent of the room wrapped around her like a velvet cloak. When he laid her on the bed, she sank into the soft mattress; nearby, a small bedside lamp cast a soft glow over his determined face. Her senses whirling with fear and pleasure, she glanced into his fiery eyes. "Why are you doing this?" she asked in a broken whisper.

A hungry look raced over his features. "Because I can ... and I've wanted you since the moment I saw you." There was passion in his voice, and the words sent her blood racing with anticipation. She realized that what was happening was mad, *insane*, but she knew she couldn't stop it if she tried. It was as if destiny had bound them together and the passion they had both tried to repress rushed to the surface, demanding satisfaction. As if in a dream, she felt him pluck the plume from her upswept hair and remove several hairpins, so that her loosened locks fell in a cool cascade about her shoulders.

He sat down beside her and feathered hot kisses on the inside of her arm. There was a tender expression in his eyes that made her pulse throb with excitement. When he buried his face against her neck and nuzzled her throat, she could feel his warm breath and hear his ragged breathing. Then, raising his head, he swept her hair back from her forehead and gazed into her eyes. "My darling, how I fought this happening, but I can't anymore ..."

His eyes were shining with love, and a rapture glowed through her unlike anything she had ever known. She felt tears prick her eyes and there was a constriction in her throat. "Please ... let me stay with you."

Alex looked down at her exquisite face and savored her feminine beauty. Her eyes were shiny and sparkling with passion, and her lips were slightly parted. In the diffused light, her long lashes cast shadows on her cheeks, and her silvery hair fanned out on the pillow in a tangle of silken curls. For the first time in his life, he felt that he understood the great love that inspired poets and painters ... the love he had been waiting for all of his life. As impossible as it seemed, he had found that love in this childlike girl of the streets who was waiting, just waiting for him to awaken her sensuality. "Yes, my angel. It seems I've wanted you forever," he murmured, tenderly sliding his hands over her arms.

Pell's heart fluttered madly as he stood and slipped off his jacket and shoes and carelessly cast them aside. As he leaned over her, the manly scent of his cologne radiated toward her with the heat of his body and sparked her mounting passion. Soft light burnishing his bold face, he removed her shoes, then sank to the bed again. In one fluid movement he pulled her close, and with an agonized groan caressed her hair. Ecstasy sparkled through her like fireworks as he gathered her in his arms and then took her mouth in a deep kiss. At that moment Pell felt she was encompassed by a warm glory and everything around them dimmed in comparison.

As the kiss became more possessive, he eased his tongue into her mouth, and when he tightened his arms about her, hunger sang through her veins, making her slowly slip her fingers into his crisp black hair. The kiss melted into a soft intimacy that made her quiver in delight, but even then, it was fired with a new urgency that bespoke heart-shaking passion. With a low moan, he buried his hand in her hair and ran his fingers through her locks, then swept them over her breast and waist, hungrily tracing her curves. It seemed that they were starved for each other, and that the barrier between them was down. They were one, and a wonder unlike anything she had ever known flowed through her.

Confronted with a last-minute surge of doubt, she moved against his broad chest, but he pressed her into the bed, and, gently easing down her low-cut gown, he fluttered hot kisses over her shoulder. Then, taking her mouth once more, he scooped his hand into her bodice. For long moments he cupped her breast and ran his open palm over its softness as if he were enjoying its weight and silky texture. She didn't understand the rapturous new feelings welling up within her, but when he tantalized her aching nipple with feather-light strokes of his fingers, breathtaking passion rocked her body, leaving her defenseless against him.

Raising his head once more, he trailed little kisses over her pulsing throat, and she drew in a sharp breath as he took her hand and placed it over the long hot swelling in his breeches. "See how much I want you?" he said huskily, the sensuality in his voice stirring wild primitive feelings within her. The hardness of his manhood both intimidated her and filled her with a delicious shock as he held her trembling hand in place. "Yes, that's the way, my darling," he said, moving his fingers over hers, encouraging her to caress him.

Doubt and fear assailed her, but she felt a flame leaping within her, stoking her courage. As she slowly complied, he groaned in pleasure and eased down her deeply cut décolletage, freeing both her breasts from her tight corselet. She flushed with embarrassment, but as he moved his hand over her bare breast and slowly rolled the nipple in his fingertips, she almost swooned with delight. She had guessed that he was capable of deep passion, but her own wanton response startled and frightened her. Sensing her fear, he moved his mouth over hers again in a slow shivery kiss while his fingers drew at her aching nipples. Warm blood stung her cheeks; currents of desire raced over her, making her writhe against the cool silken counterpane.

In one languid movement, Alex sat up and unbuttoned his shirt, then lightly cast the garment aside. Sinking into the mattress again, he took her mouth once more and eased up her skirt and petticoat to explore her thighs. When she moaned in delight, his mouth moved to a rosy nipple and lovingly suckled it while he pushed down her bloomers. She sucked in her breath and felt a hot flush rising from her bosom as his tongue deftly flicked at her sensitive peak. Fiery waves of pleasure rolled from her breast, and, gaining in strength, shuddered through her body. Lord, what was happening to her? she wondered, scarcely able to believe such intense sensations existed.

His hand caressed her smooth buttocks and quickly brushed over the cleft between her cheeks. When he removed her bloomers, her heart thudded crazily. She drew in a sharp breath as his fingers seared a path to the seat of her desire and caressed it with electrifying touches. As the juncture between her thighs throbbed with a tight aching sweetness that drove her to a fever pitch, she held her breath, suspended between modesty and desire. Almost delirious with passion, she wanted to weep with the pleasure and intensity of it all.

"Let me make love to you," he whispered as he raised his head, urgent need flaring in his smoky eyes. "I'll show you passion as you've never known." As he spoke he leisurely grazed a thumb over her swollen nipple, making her skin flush with warmth.

"Yes," she sobbed, her lips trembling. The feelings he had elicited in her body were so intense she felt as if a light were shafting through her body, filling her with a pleasure beyond words. Taking her hand, he put it over the swelling in his breeches again, and slowly moved his hand over hers. He groaned in delight, and a few moments later unbuttoned his breeches. She gasped in surprise as the fiery shaft spilled forth and rested in her palm. Her heart fluttering madly, she gingerly explored him, shocked and thrilled by the hardness of his aroused flesh.

Her heart racing out of control, she gazed at him through a mist of emotion as he caressed her hair, then raised her hand and gently kissed her fingertips. The power and intimacy of the moment sent her senses reeling. This was the imperious Lord Tavistock whom she had feared and secretly desired for months. As his fingers deftly loosened the long row of buttons down her back, her heart nearly burst with love and desire for him. She trembled as she thought about losing her virginity, then told herself it was now too late to worry about the future, for he had brought her body to a state of trembling need.

Gently urging her to a sitting position, he eased the gown over her head and tossed it aside. Her rustling petticoats followed. As she sat on the edge of the bed, he knelt before her, and his lips found her mouth while his fingers untied the cord at the top of her corselet. Giving it a firm tug, he pulled it from the eyelets. The constricting garment slid to the floor, and her bare breasts spilled forth, to be caught in his warm hands. Still kissing her deeply, he grazed his thumbs over her sensitive nipples, then, after pressing kisses over her throat and breasts, he suckled each of the coral peaks, drawing on them long and steadily, making her close her eyes and clutch his shoulders as she moaned in delight. At last he tenderly kissed her lips, then stood, and, lifting her a bit, settled her upon the mattress.

Alex gazed at her as she lay there defenseless before him in the soft rosy light, totally nude except for her black stockings and garters. A reverent feeling stirred his spirit as he considered the perfection of her gently curving body and delicate face. This was his woman, the woman he loved above everything else; she was so exquisitely lovely that his heart ached at the sight of her. The thought of awakening her to womanhood, of seeing her blossom into a lush rose, sent his blood racing. Lord, how he wanted her, wanted to bury himself in her velvety depths this very moment.

Pell felt the cool night air wash over her bare breasts and thighs as she watched him divest himself of the rest of his clothes. Soft light washing over his fine muscular form, he towered before her, his huge shoulders, hard chest, and flat stomach riveting her gaze. Hair tapered from his broad chest down to his aroused flesh, which stood proudly from his shadowed groin. As her eyes ran over his magnificent body, she thought of how long she had feared him, wanted him, desired him. But never in her wildest dreams did she think he would be so breathtakingly perfect. Her heart raced as he clicked off the light and laid down beside her.

Her breath catching in her throat, she watched his dark head bend over her breasts, then she felt him take a nipple into his mouth again and leisurely swirl his tongue about it. A glowing sweetness now pulsed between her legs and she slipped her arms about him, pulling him closer. When his fingers caressed her soft mound, deep, drugging passion spread through her veins and she felt ecstasy streak through her like sheet lightning. Taking her mouth in a hot kiss, he stroked her secret places until she was nearly mad with desire. One of his hands caressed the nape of her neck while the other strayed between her thighs and brushed the hair of her mound, gently teasing it before he separated the moist folds. Finding her swollen bud, he stroked his thumb back and forth, urging her to open her legs. She shuddered with pleasure and he deepened the kiss, thrusting his tongue into her mouth as boldly as his searching hand was gentle, and she was lost in a world of rapturous desire.

The heat of her passion flushed her face and neck, and, lifting his head, he spoke to her with soft words of love, tenderly stroking her body and flowing hair, reassuring her and giving her courage. When he roughly nuzzled her neck and pressed his hard manhood against the inside of her bare thigh, she let out a heart-pounding moan and trembled with desire. As he supported himself on one elbow and leaned over her, she opened her quivering legs, and, with an almost unbearable longing, ached for him to enter her. Taking his time, he kissed her breasts and stomach while his hand moved between her legs, working her desire to a white-hot heat. At last, he moved over her. She felt the tip of his long hardness slide into her, and she buried her face against his shoulder and moaned softly.

"Quiet, my darling," he whispered gently. "The pain will last for only a moment, then a golden tide of pleasure will wash it away."

She gasped at the sting of entry, but he kissed her deeply and, as he had said, the pain quickly melted into lulling pleasure. As he began to move, the hair on his chest teased her bare breasts, stirring new excitement within her, and with a gasp, she clutched her arms about his muscled shoulders. At first she traced her fingertips down his back, then she slipped her hands to his tight buttocks.

Now he lowered his hips until he was farther inside her, and for a few moments he was motionless. Then he began to move once more, stroking her firmly and deeply this time, slowly, deliberately. Pell shivered with delight and felt a languid satisfaction steal through her as he increased his speed, confidently controlling each stroke. A mounting pleasure built inside of her and as she relaxed, he increased his speed.

Lifting his lips from hers, he whispered, "Put your legs about me, my darling."

Moaning with pleasure, she complied and was able to accept the full length of his huge shaft as he stroked her more deeply now. On fire for him and trembling with eagerness, she clutched his buttocks, pulling him toward her.

"It's too soon, love," he murmured, raining kisses over her face.

Shuddering, she clutched his shoulders, marveling at the length and power of his fiery maleness. Stroking, caressing, whispering endearments, he moved rhythmically until she thought she would faint from the fire building in her loins. Sighing with emotion, she totally abandoned herself to passion, and he thrust into her faster and harder as he urged her toward sweet fulfillment. She was unaware of everything but him, and it was as if they were no longer two people, but one, their hearts singing together.

With a cry of joy, she clutched his lean hips, wanting the pleasure to go on forever. At last his hot seed burst inside her and she shuddered with a heart-shaking climax.

For long moments, they glided to the heavens, then they slowly floated earthward together, their spirits bound in ecstasy. With tender kisses and soft caresses, they clung to each other. As she struggled for breath, he turned on his side and held her in his arms, caressing her full creamy breasts. Even now, the secret place between her legs throbbed sweetly, pleasure radiating from her loins and rolling over her stomach and legs.

As he moved his hands over her body in the wake of their overpowering passion, tears slid from her eyes and her skin glowed from his touch. She could feel his heart beating against hers as he cradled her in his arms. At last her breathing slowed and she felt herself sinking deeper into the mattress.

As she floated on a hazy sea of satisfaction and fulfillment, exhaustion overtook her and she slept in total pleasure for a short while, dreaming wonderful things. Then she felt Alex stir at her side, and she clasped his hand and slept again, drifting into velvety darkness.

Chapter 17

⟨~~ ୨୧ ~~⟩

Sleepily, Pell opened her eyes and watched rosy light filter into her bedroom from between the draperies. The second-story window stood open a bit and cool air wafted into the room, bringing with it the deep-throated trill of a lark and the sound of the milkman's rattling delivery wagon. For a moment, confusion muddled her thoughts, then, as she stared at the diffused light, joy flooded through her in a warm tide, for she remembered that she and Alex had made love. It touched her deeply that although she had fallen asleep in his bed, he had carried her back to her own bed so her honor wouldn't be compromised.

Contentment filled her as she felt the soft sheet against her naked breasts, and her body tingled with wonderful new sensations. Delightful memories crowded her mind as she thought of their lovemaking and she tried to remember everything about it: the feel of Alex's muscled back under her fingertips, the look in his passionate eyes as he caressed her breasts, the musky man-scent of him, the feel of his warm breath upon her cheek, the sound of his low husky voice as he urged her toward her climax. For a while she let herself float upon these memories like a lily upon a sun-warmed pond, but then her mind began to spin.

Pushing herself up on the lace-trimmed pillows, she tried to remember everything that had happened and been said last night. Despite her initial protests in the library, she had enjoyed every minute of their lovemaking. She remembered he had spoken tender endearments and praised her beauty—but he had never told her outright that he loved her. Nor had he made any commitment of marriage to her. As these thoughts hit her full force, her stomach felt heavy and nauseous. Surely he would have no use for her now, except as a lover. Someone in his exalted position would never marry a guttersnipe who had given herself to him like a common woman of the streets. Knowing he was an early riser, she wondered where he was at this very moment. Perhaps he had gone to the Carlton for breakfast, hoping she would leave before he got back, she thought, depression seeping through her like molten lead.

Flushing with embarrassment, she wondered if anyone had heard them make love, then she told herself that Aunt Violet had already retired when they came home from Victoria Station. As for the servants, they were in the attic fast asleep after a hard day's work. No, she was sure no one knew of their lovemaking but her . . . and she would never forget it.

She ran a hand through her tousled hair, despair overtaking her. In her heart she knew she could have resisted him, but she had abandoned herself to a maelstrom of passion and thrown away any chance of respectability. How could he ever bear to look at her after what had happened?

True, he had carried her to his bedroom and masterfully awakened all her senses, introducing her to a secret world of unknown pleasures. But in all honesty, she had welcomed his advances, and her own body had burned for fulfillment. Her throat ached with tears and she closed her eyes once more, praying for strength. She felt as empty as a drained eggshell. Despite all her teachers' efforts she was still the same foolish Cockney wench she had always been.

She pressed a hand to her throat, trying to think what she must do to salvage the scraps of her dignity. With an exhausted sigh, she propped herself up on one elbow and glanced around the room, seeing her purple gown and discarded undergarments draped over the back of a chair. Obviously Alex had brought them with her when he carried her back to her room. Blood stung her cheeks and her heart pounded faster as she remembered how he had skillfully removed her clothes and lightly cast them aside. She had been ecstatic with joy then, just as she now had to deal with the consequences of her rash actions. Controlling her racing thoughts, she suddenly realized that she must put on her clothes and leave Alex's mansion—and his life.

Quickly getting out of bed, she opened her wardrobe and selected a gown, comforting herself with the thought that she had always been able to take care of herself. With or without her father's fortune, she didn't need Alex or any other man to see to her affairs. After she had dressed as best as she could without the assistance of a maid, she began pulling other gowns from her wardrobe. She would need just a few things to tide her over until she could make a fresh start, she thought, trying to stir up her courage. As she frantically tossed garments on the unmade bed, she felt a great urgency to leave before she had an embarrassing encounter with Alex.

Returning to the wardrobe, she pulled out a pair of shoes and added them to the pile on the bed. How would she carry everything? she wondered with a rush of panic. If she could locate Hadji at this early hour, she could probably talk him into finding a portmanteau for her. Doubtless he would try to dissuade her from leaving, but she would stand firm in her resolve to go.

As she searched through her clothes, she thought of her reticule and remembered she had left it in the library when Alex carried her upstairs. The reticule made her think of Claude, for she always carried his locket there. Fresh hurt stabbed through her as she remembered his deceit and the sight of him sprawled on the railroad platform.

Hearing footfalls in the hall, she froze, hoping desperately that it was a maid, but knowing by the heaviness of the step that it was not. Her heart lurched and she stiffened when she heard a soft rap on the door, then the sound of it opening. Humiliation rose up within her at the thought of seeing Alex, but then, with a flash of insight, she realized that the only things she had brought into this house were the clothes on her back and her pride. The maids had burned her ragged clothes, but they couldn't touch her pride—no one could take it away from her.

Swallowing back her embarrassment, she turned about and looked up into Alex's face, her heart fluttering. A fine paisley silk dressing gown garbed his large frame, and he looked as if he had not slept. His features were drawn, but his warmly erotic eyes, glistening with sensuality, and tousled hair heightened his masculine appeal and made her want him all the more.

She stood motionless, loving him and hating him at the same time, as she had loved and hated the passion that had brought them to this pass. Her heart raced wildly and she could not speak.

"What are you doing?" he asked quietly. His voice was calm, but concern lingered in his tone.

"Leaving, as you can see," she answered, trying to hold back her emotions.

He leaned back against the door, his eyes wide and intense. "How can you even talk about leaving?"

She struggled to control her faltering voice. "What role can I play? I'm no longer the amusing Cockney wench who used to entertain you. As your mistress I would be a reminder that you—that both of us—betrayed my father's trust." Her lips quivered. "And even if you *did* offer marriage, we both know that I'm not suited to be your wife."

A strange look passed over his face, and then he straightened, the hint of a smile playing about his lips. "On the contrary," he drawled, "I feel that you would make an excellent wife."

His resonant voice sounded deeply within her and it seemed that all the breath had left her body. Her heart pumped even faster now, and for an instant her eyes dimmed with tears. Could she actually be hearing these words? Surely she had misunderstood him.

When he walked to her and clasped her shoulders, her

heart fluttered and she felt as if the morning sun was traveling within her, filling her with its warmth. "I want you to become my wife," he said in his deep voice that sent excitement darting through her. "We'll get married quietly in a few days. Afterwards we'll go to my estate in the Cotswolds."

She pulled in a trembling breath. His proposal had totally disarmed her and she gazed at him in awe. He had said the words she'd secretly hoped he might say one day, but in the deepest part of her heart never believed she would hear. For a fleeting second, tingling joy expanded within her, then sudden heartache made her throat tighten with sadness. He didn't love her, really love her. He was only fulfilling his duty.

"Leave me with a bit of my pride," she finally managed in a rough voice. "You don't mean what you're saying. We were born in different worlds, and we belong in different worlds. You can't be certain what will happen if—"

"Hush," he interrupted, caressing her shoulders with firm sweeping strokes. "I've been up all night and have given the matter a great deal of thought. I'm sure this will be best." His eyes kindled with a tender look. "You're just tired . . . overwrought."

"But I—"

He moved his warm hands over her arms, gentling and soothing her as if she were an upset child. "Everything will be fine. And just think . . . when we're married you'll be the Countess of Tavistock."

His closeness made it difficult for her to move or even think. She had vowed to leave, but faced with such emotion she found herself weakening. She had started melting when he first entered the room, and now the sight of his tall, heavily muscled body and rakish face stirred memories of their night of love and made her blood race with longing. Searching for words, she stared at him, unable to speak.

"Well, what do you say?" He gave her a soft smile and raised his brow.

She studied his intense eyes, knowing her will was sliding away by the second. "We haven't settled things," she muttered helplessly, her heart beating hard against her rib cage.

He laughed softly. "We'll settle them as we go along— just like most people." His eyes glistened with emotion, and as he molded her softness against him, her flesh tingled with anticipation. Lowering his head, he brushed her lips with his and sent a racing flame of passion through her body. She trembled against him; then his arms were about her, pulling her closer. When he hungrily took her mouth, she yielded gladly, relishing the warmth, and taste, and scent of him.

Alex pulled her closer to him, feeling her pounding heartbeat against his chest and her quickened breathing. How refreshing and exciting she was, he thought, savoring the warmth of her body and sweet scent of her hair. He slowly traced his hand over her tense back, making her relax into his embrace. He had kissed dozens of women before, but none could compare to Pell. She was so fresh and genuine, so unlike any other woman he had ever known.

Gently breaking the kiss, Alex smiled down at her. "In the military we're taught to take silence as compliance ... so I'm assuming you've accepted my proposal."

Her heart too full to speak, she gave him a tremulous smile and nodded.

He studied her face for a moment, then kissed her cheeks and eyelids. She had become so precious to him, he couldn't bear to think of anyone hurting her. After taking her hand and kissing her cool fingertips, he eased her away from him. "When Aunt Violet awakes, I'll speak with her about the marriage," he said in a warm, satisfied tone. "I'm sure she'll be delighted." For a moment, he watched light catch in her long locks, then, with great tenderness, he brushed back a wisp of hair from her rosy cheek. After filling his eyes with her to set her image into his mind, he finally turned and walked from the room.

Pell felt heavy layers of uncertainty and fatigue wash

over her. She moved to a chair by the window and sat down. Her mind whirled as she watched early-morning traffic move along Adam's Row below her. There was so much she had wanted to say to Alex, so many arguments she had wanted to make, but his promise of intimacy and sweet passion had overwhelmed all her good intentions.

As the events of the last five minutes sank in, her heart leaped with excitement. Alex had actually asked her to marry him, and she, Pell Davis, a former fruit-vendor and occasional pickpocket from Cat and Wheel Alley, was going to be the next Countess of Tavistock. Sinking back into the chair, she blinked in disbelief, marveling at her transformation. Finding out she was an heiress had left her shaken, but learning that she would soon be a countess was too much to be believed!

She suddenly wondered if she could act the part of a countess. After they were married she would technically belong to the aristocracy, but would she really fit in? Would she be able to fulfill her position and not compromise Alex or make him ashamed of her?

She and Alex has already conspired to deceive the whole of London society, an unforgivable sin in the eyes of the aristocrats should it be discovered. The loyalty of Alex's household was unquestionable—but there was one man whose loyalty was in doubt. Claude Dubois. What would happen if he returned to London? The very idea of it filled her with terror—she must *never* tell Alex that she had been foolish enough to reveal the secret of her real identity. What would Claude do with the information? she wondered, her heart beating a little faster. It seemed her whole future rested on that question.

Three days later, Pell whirled about as Aunt Violet knocked, then entered the bedroom, followed by a maid who carried tea and toast on a silver tray. "You didn't come down for breakfast, dear, and it's ten o'clock already," she announced with a smile. "I thought you might want a little something to calm your nerves, this being your wedding day." Dressed in a rose-colored gown and wearing a little ribboned ornament in her hair, the old lady looked soft and sweet, and the tender emotion in her eyes touched Pell deeply.

"Yes ... thank you," Pell answered, hastily brushing back her loose hair.

Aunt Violet took her hand and pressed it affectionately. "My dear, I can't tell you how excited I am that you're going to be Alex's bride ... that you'll be in the family." Her eyes glistened with tears of happiness. "It's all so romantic, more romantic that anything I've ever read in my novels." She fluttered her eyelashes. "I had hoped this marriage might occur, but to see my hopes materialize is thrilling beyond belief. It's as if fate itself had destined you to be together."

Pell felt a rush of tenderness for Aunt Violet, and with amusement, noticed that her hair ornament was drooping to the side. After securing it so it wouldn't slip from the old lady's hair, she kissed her wrinkled cheek. "Thank you, Aunt Violet. I always felt you were on my side." She gave a soft chuckle. "Even from that first day when you offered me a whole box of chocolates to get me down from the roof of the porch."

They laughed together, then Pell watched the maid place the tray on a table near the bright bedroom windows and pour tea. The girl joined Aunt Violet, and the chattering pair removed the wedding dress from a heavily carved wardrobe and fluffed out its trailing skirt.

As the pair talked, Pell retied the sash of her silken wrapper and sat down by the window to drink her tea and think. After many hours of troubled soul-searching last night, she had finally drifted into a fitful sleep, then an hour ago she'd awakened with a start and realized it was her wedding day. Somewhat guilty that she had slept so long, she'd gone to the windows, pushed back the lacy panels, and watched the summer sun glint over London's rooftops. Too nervous to eat, she had paced about the bedroom, trying to sort out her thoughts.

Since Alex had asked her to marry him, he had spent his nights at the Carlton out of a sense of correctness, and life had taken on an unreal quality. All the servants had cheerfully accepted the news, and Aunt Violet had fussed about, notifying the society papers, planning a small wedding, and accompanying Pell to the dressmaker's shop.

Pell now surveyed the gorgeous gown as Aunt Violet gently laid it over the foot of the bed—it was made of creamy white satin and embroidered with pearls. Alex had insisted that she have an equally lovely powder-blue traveling gown for their trip to the Cotswolds later today.

At times it seemed that he was really interested in pleasing her, and during these periods, her spirits soared. But when a preoccupied look clouded his eyes, sadness pressed about her heart, and she scoffed at the idea that he might really love her. How could he love her when they came from such drastically different backgrounds? As she sipped her tea, she thought of the aristocracy. Would those who really belonged to that world accept her, or would they laugh behind her back?

Aunt Violet glanced at her worriedly. "You're dreaming again, dear," she chided in a tender tone. A ringed hand at her throat, she moved toward the improvised breakfast table. "I must go downstairs and see how things are coming along, but the maid will dress you." Pulling in a long tremulous breath, she patted Pell's arm. "Now don't look so worried, love. Everything will be just fine. Hurry and get dressed and I will bring up your bridal bouquet when we're ready for you." Fanning her face with her patchouli-scented handkerchief, she hurried from the room.

When the maid lifted her brows and smiled, Pell put down her teacup and rose, knowing what was expected of her. Forcing down her troubled emotions, she sat on a padded bench at the end of the bed so the girl could smooth silk stockings and embroidered wedding garters on her legs.

Then she stood, and, slipping off her wrapper, allowed the girl to fit a corselet about her camisole and bloomers and lace it up as tightly as possible. Next she stepped into high-heeled satin shoes and a petticoat, and the maid tied the dangling petticoat tapes. At last, with the girl's help, Pell eased in the heavy wedding gown, feeling the cool stain skim over her body. When the maid had fastened a long row of tiny buttons down the back of the gown, she turned Pell about and said, "I'm all finished, miss. If you'll move to the vanity table, I'll arrange your hair."

At the mirrored vanity, the maid brushed Pell's hair until it was glossy and shiny, then, pulling it from the nape of her neck, twisted it into a high chignon and secured it with shiny pearl-studded pins. Bending, the girl arranged the rest of Pell's naturally curly locks into long shining ringlets and let them fall to her shoulders on either side of her head. After dusting her mistress's cheeks with powder and rouge and applying a faintly tinted lip salve, the servant stood back and proudly clasped her hands.

Taking a deep breath, Pell lifted her chin. In her own eyes she saw doubt, but she couldn't be second-guessing herself and backing out of her commitment. She had made a decision and she must follow through with it. She must behave as a sophisticated lady, not an emotional guttersnipe.

The maid began attaching a long wedding veil to Pell's hair, letting it flow down the back of the silky gown. "After I'm done 'ere, I'll be goin', miss, and give you a little time to yourself." When the girl had finished, someone rapped on the door, and Pell glanced up, expecting to see Aunt Violet again.

Instead, Hadji peeked into the room, Chi Chi sitting on his shoulder. His eyes large and curious, the servant quietly entered the chamber; as the maid left and closed the door behind her. The Indian smiled and bowed his head. "Oh, a thousand pardons, missy, I am not wanting to be a peeking Harry, but I am needing to speak with you."

With a smile, Pell held out her hand, and the servant knelt by the vanity to put the chattering monkey on the carpet. Bringing a red rose from behind his back, the Indian presented it to her with proud eyes. "I am noticing that in England brides wear white, but it is not being so in my country," he explained gently. "In my country brides are wearing red, for it is the color of joy. I am thinking that you must have something red today to bring you luck."

Pell took the rose and brushed it against her lips. "Thank you, Hadji," she whispered as she inhaled the bloom's heady scent. "I'll always remember that you gave me a red rose on my wedding day." Trying to conceal her inner turmoil, she smiled and added the rose to a small bouquet already on her vanity.

His eyes perplexed, the servant placed his slim hand over hers. "Missy, I am being greatly confused, for I am noticing a shadow of unhappiness in your eyes. Surely I cannot be seeing this. I am thinking how far you have matriculated since you arrived here, and in less than an hour you are being a countess."

Battling her stormy emotions, she rose and moved away from the vanity. "I know. I still can't believe it myself," she replied softly. "It doesn't seem possible."

A wide smile brightened the servant's face and he walked toward her. "It is seeming very possible to me, for I am realizing that it is your kismet."

"My kismet?"

"Yes," he said matter-of-factly. "Kismet is what the gods in their wisdom have decreed for your life. *Your* kismet is being a countess."

She gave him a soft smile. "Do the gods make countesses out of fruit-peddlers?"

"Yes," he stated emphatically. "If the wondrous ones are desiring this, it is being within their magnanimous power."

She gazed at him. "I don't know," she murmured thoughtfully. "In the East End we believe that if fate throws a knife at you, you can catch it by the blade or the handle. Maybe being a countess isn't my kismet . . . maybe I'm doing the wrong thing. Maybe Alex is just marrying me out of duty."

Hadji's eyes grew alarmed. "Oh, no, this cannot be! I am knowing my illustrious master for years in India. He is being a fine soldier of the queen, and a flawless aide to the great General Fairchild." He looked at her sternly. "But even the great Fox of the Punjab cannot make Lord Tavistock do something he is not wishing to do. Believe me, I am knowing my turnips on this subject!"

Suddenly a great screeching noise arose from the vanity, prompting Pell to look in that direction. There in a cloud of face powder Chi Chi moved among a collection of cosmetics as he surveyed himself in the mirror. Before Hadji could reach him, he showered more face powder over himself, and in his excitement sent several crystal perfume bottles crashing to the floor.

At this unfortunate moment, Aunt Violet entered the bedroom with a wedding bouquet of white roses trimmed with pink ribbons. Seeing the havoc at the vanity, she dropped the bouquet on the floor and clasped a hand to her throat, exclaiming, "'Pon my word, Cho Cho, you'll destroy the bedroom!"

Hadji snatched at the monkey's tail just as the animal slid to the floor, dragging a lace cloth and several jars of face cream to the carpet. "Cease your wicked play, you naughty creature!" he cried. "You are greatly overthrowing the lemon cart!"

Wondering when the chase would end, Pell watched the servant and Aunt Violet follow the monkey about the room until they had him hemmed in a corner. At last, the Indian pounced on the shrieking animal, and, after scooping him in his arms, stood and righted his tilted turban. With a heaving chest, Hadji gazed at Pell and gasped, "Oh, missy, it is coming to me like a belt from the blue! If Satan is ever having a contest for mischievousness, Chi Chi will be winning in a gallop!" Still breathing heavily, he clutched the monkey tightly in his arms and left the room.

Leaning against the wall, Aunt Violet fanned her flushed face with her handkerchief. "I don't know what we shall do if Hadji doesn't control that creature," she said in a tremulous voice. She fluttered her eyelashes and took a long breath. "Just to think, that today of all days the little creature should pull another of his pranks." She smoothed back her hair, then, as piano music wafted up the stairs, she calmed down a bit and picked up the bridal bouquet. "I just came up to tell you the vicar is here, love," she breathed, her eyelids quivering with excitement. "You mustn't keep him waiting."

The incident with Chi Chi had temporarily distracted Pell, but all of her doubts about the wedding now rushed back to unnerve her. Trying to control herself, she pulled on long white gloves, and, taking the bouquet in her arms, looked at herself in a tall cheval glass in the corner. She knew the gown's low décolletage, short puffed sleeves, and elongated waist were becoming, but she also knew she looked pale and tense beneath the delicately applied makeup.

For a moment her head swam with excitement, and she seemed to hear a strangely familiar voice—her own before she met Alex—saying, *Gaa . . . you looks like a bleedin' princess, girl.*

A strange twinge of sadness passed through her, for she knew she was saying good-bye to Pell Davis of Cat and Wheel Alley forever. When she ascended the stairs again to change into her blue traveling dress she would be the Countess of Tavistock.

"Do hurry, dear!" Aunt Violet urged as she lowered the misty bridal veil over Pell's face. "Just remember, Alex is waiting at the foot of the steps."

Her mind a tumult, Pell left the safety of her bedroom. As she trailed one hand over the smooth banister and descended the first steps, she heard the hired pianist playing the wedding march. Then, rounding the sweeping staircase, she saw Alex standing in the entry hall.

His smartly tailored suit showed off his broad shoulders and emphasized his trim, hard-muscled body, and he looked so resplendent, a great tenderness for him welled up within her. Excitement sped through her veins as she studied his face. His features were strong and held a worldy expression, but also nobility.

His countenance was impassive, but she knew he was skilled at hiding his emotions. What was going on behind those smoldering eyes? What was he feeling? When they had made love she felt an honesty in his wild passion, but now it seemed he had veiled his emotions once again.

As Alex gazed at Pell, his breath caught in his throat. Awed by her beauty, he thought she looked lovelier than he had ever seen her, including the night of the coming-out ball. In the shimmering white wedding gown that revealed her figure to perfection, she appeared young and ethereal, but also elegant and very desirable. There was a touch of color in her cheeks, but her eyes were large and frightened, making him want to protect her all the more.

Concern twinged through him as he thought about the circumstances of their marriage. He had certainly not found her a rich husband. He had in effect compromised her and failed in his duty toward her father, and the feeling was constantly with him. But, he thought with a sigh, the temptation had been too great. Now that she was his, he resolved to always do the best by her . . . to indulge her like a dear child. He knew she was still somewhat unaware of the threat that Sabrina presented, and he vowed to himself to shield her from that potential disaster. But above all, he'd conceal his serious financial problems from her. He wasn't marrying her to give her a whole new set of problems. From here on, he wanted her life to be one long summer day. It was only what she deserved . . .

When she reached the last step, he clasped his warm hand over hers, and for a moment their eyes met. As he took her arm, he tried to make some of his vitality flow into her body and give her strength. But as he guided her toward the drawing room and the music grew louder, he could tell that she was feeling overwhelmed.

So as not to seem surreptitious, they had invited a few guests to witness the ceremony, including the Duke of Featherston and Lord Bockingford and his daughter Lilly.

They now stood, gazing at Alex and Pell as they walked toward an elderly vicar in dark clerical robes who was positioned at the end of the chamber with a Bible in his hands.

Aunt Violet and Mr. Peebles smiled at them from the front row, and Hadji stood quietly at the side of the room.

Alex held her eyes with his own, and, raising her gloved hand, pressed it to his lips. The gesture was formal and precise, but he meant it to give her the strength to go on with the ceremony.

The next several moments passed like a dream to Pell. First the pianist finished the wedding march and the guests took their seats. Pell swallowed nervously as the ceremony began in earnest. With a trembling voice, she pledged her troth to Alex. He repeated his vows quietly.

When the service was at last over Alex lifted her veil and gently gathered her to his chest. She could feel his steely muscles through the fabric of his elegant jacket. Briefly, she allowed herself to relax in the circle of his warm arms. When his mouth came down on hers, she shuddered and was swept away on a tide of joy. As the kiss deepened, liquid fire spread through her body, making her quiver with delight. With a fiery blush, she remembered the feel of his hands on her body the night they had made love. The thought seemed too private for the moment and she felt a sense of relief when he raised his head. Then as she looked up into his eyes, she saw a fleeting glimpse of something she didn't understand.

What were the shadowed emotions lurking in the depths of his eyes? Was it love and compassion—or doubt and regret?

Chapter 18

After their wedding luncheon, Pell and Alex had left London from Victoria Station, and late that afternoon arrived at Cheltenham where a carriage from Stanton Hall waited for them at the railroad platform. Now there was the nicker of horses as the driver halted Alex's well-sprung brougham on the hill overlooking the huge Gloucestershire estate. Dressed in her new powder-blue traveling gown and a fashionable feathered hat, Pell looked through the carriage window at the huge manor house and grounds sprawling before them in the summer twilight.

Built in the Elizabethan style and constructed of the honey-colored stone for which the Cotswolds were famous, the house glowed against the protective greenery and wooded hills. Smooth green parkland, dotted with grazing deer and a silvery lake, shone in the sunset and made Stanton Hall look like something from a child's picture book. "It's lovely. Really lovely," she commented in a soft voice.

Alex put his warm hand over hers. Wearing a superbly tailored coat of olive-green, tan breeches, polished boots, and leather gloves, he cut an elegant figure and had caused a stir at the Cheltenham railroad station. "Yes. I wanted you to see it from this vantage point," he said, his voice tinged with pride. "It's been in my family for centuries, though I haven't been here since I got back from India. It would be a pity to lose it."

252

She twisted about on the carriage seat and scanned his face. "Lose it? Why do you say that?"

He shrugged and gave her a smile. "It was nothing. Just a figure of speech."

Pell studied him for a moment, pondering his words, but then the driver called to his team and the carriage rolled on toward Stanton Hall, whose windows glinted golden in the sun's last rays. Pell thought the flowering hawthorns bordering the dusty lane gave a fairy-tale quality to the scene. After a short while, the brougham slowed and turned onto a great U-shaped estate drive approaching the great manor, and her heart beat a little faster.

Just as twilight deepened into the first shadows of the evening, the carriage came to a halt before the great marble steps of Stanton Hall. Brisk footsteps rang over the marble, and a footman garbed in green and gold livery opened the carriage door and helped her alight to the graveled drive. Alex followed, and escorted her up the imposing entry steps, where the manor's great door was swept open and another footman stood respectfully aside.

With a rush of pleasure, Pell scanned the softly lit entry hall with its Grecian statues, alcoves and suits of armor, and impressive carved staircase. Then there were more footsteps, and a tall, gaunt man garbed in country tweeds that hung loosely on his frame entered the hall and bowed his head at Alex. Projecting a studious air, the man had high cheekbones and a thin face, and wore spectacles perched on the end of his long nose. "Milord," the steward said humbly as he raised his head and looked at Alex. "It's a great honor to have you here after all these years. You've been sorely missed."

Alex nodded a greeting, and put his arm about Pell. "Let me present Mr. Potterfield, my steward," he announced with congeniality.

Again the glum-faced man bowed his head, this time at Pell, then he muttered, "Milady . . . I hope you had a pleasant journey from London. Welcome to your new home." They had discussed the steward on the train from

London, and she knew that the man had served the Chancery-Brown family for most of his life.

His hand at her back, Alex directed her toward the drawing room while Mr. Potterfield walked at his side, looking greatly relieved to see him.

"I trust that you received my letter?" Alex asked.

"Yes indeed, milord," came the quick reply. "I had the housekeeper prepare your room and everything is in readiness for your visit." He awkwardly cleared his throat. "If possible, though, I need to speak with you at your earliest convenience, sir."

Alex escorted Pell into the classically decorated drawing room, and indicated an elegant white brocade sofa with petit-point cushions. As she sat down she could hear the servants bringing luggage into the great hall, and carrying it up the staircase. While Alex walked back to the drawing-room doors to speak quietly with Mr. Potterfield, she gazed about. It was a breathtaking room, appointed with antique French furniture, its walls hung with dark, gilt-framed landscapes, and lit by twinkling chandeliers with creamy candles. Soft-hued carpets covered the parquet floor, and huge bouquets of sweet-smelling summer flowers rested on every buffet, perfuming the room. As the Countess of Tavistock all this belonged to her, she thought with awe.

The steward lingered at the doors for a good five minutes, but when he finally said good night and departed, Alex went to the grog tray. "Would you care for a sherry before dinner?" he asked warmly. His deep voice stirred her and brought a pleasant tingle of anticipation to her body. He poured himself a glass of port, and as he brought the sherry and sat down beside her, their hands brushed and she felt a glowing tide rise up within her, making her heart race.

After tasting the sweet sherry, she looked at Alex and cocked her head. "Why did Mr. Potterfield look so glum?" she asked. "He seemed to have the weight of the world on his shoulders."

Alex relaxed against the sofa and laughed. "He looked glum when I was a boy, and I see he has not changed. I'm beginning to believe the man was born glum."

"He seemed eager to talk with you," she went on. "Do you think there's some trouble?"

"No, not at all. I imagine he just wants to go over estate business," Alex answered with a light laugh. "The estate dairy probably needs a new roof, or the sow has produced an exceptional litter this year." He took her hand and kissed her fingers. "I'm sure there's nothing to worry about."

Just then, there was a rustle of silk, and a heavy older lady, who was wearing a lacy head covering and a black taffeta dress with chatelaine keys dangling at her waist, stepped inside the drawing room. A pleasant smile brought color to her cheeks, and her eyes sparkled with happiness at the sight of Alex.

Standing, he cast a warm gaze at her, then with some deliberation, set his glass aside. A smile playing at the corners of his mouth, he walked to the doors and took the lady's plump hand, then escorted her back to the sofa. "This is Mrs. Harris, the housekeeper at Stanton Hall," he explained with affection in his voice. Amusement glinted in his eyes as he added, "Actually she is a wizard, and if you need anything while we're here, just ask her. She will provide it, even if she has to make it materialize from thin air. When I was a boy I used to beg her for chocolates, which she never failed to produce."

Laugh lines crinkled around the woman's eyes. "Now that's quite an old story for you to remember, Master Alex!" she said, her shoulders shaking with mirth. She looked at him with tender eyes. "It's so nice to see you again. How you've been missed!" she added pleasantly. She had a wonderful country voice, warm and mellow. She smiled at Pell, and, clasping her hands before her, nodded her gray head in respect. " 'Tis a great honor to meet you, milady," she murmured quietly. "Stanton Hall has been needing a mistress for years."

"Thank you," Pell replied. Putting down her sherry, she took in the woman's honest face. She was short and heavy, and at first sight plain, but she radiated such an expression of kindliness, Pell was immediately attracted to her.

Mrs. Harris turned back to Alex. "Your clothes have already been unpacked, and dinner will soon be ready. Shall I have it served in the dining room?"

Alex gave Pell a sidelong glance. "No," he answered emphatically. "I imagine the countess is exhausted after our long trip from London. We'll have dinner in our room this evening."

Pell felt herself blush at his words, but with the familiarity of a trusted servant, the woman only smiled knowingly, then bowed her head once more. "Yes, very good, Master Alex," she replied with a hint of amusement before turning and walking away with swishing skirts.

His eyes twinkling, Alex took Pell's hand and raised her from the sofa, then, hugging her close, he escorted her toward the drawing-room doors. "You *are* tired, aren't you? You certainly look very tired to me," he said playfully.

Pell chuckled and snuggled against him. "Yes, I'm very tired indeed. Why, I can hardly wait to get into bed."

Their laughter echoed through the marbled entry hall and up the sweeping staircase leading to the second story. The bedroom door was slightly ajar, and when Pell entered the chamber a thrill ran through her. A row of windows stood open to permit a flow of balmy summer air, and in the old-fashioned style, the chamber boasted two adjoining dressing rooms. A huge half-tester bed with side and back curtains sat against one wall, and gas lamps on bedside tables pooled light over a fringed silk counterpane.

The window curtains were of pale-rose silk with thin shadow panels inside them; a sofa upholstered in matching silk stood by the fireplace. A great gold-framed mirror hung on one wall, reflecting a writing desk and a rose-colored Oriental carpet of the finest pile. The spacious bedroom also contained ornate chairs, heavy wardrobes, and china bric-a-brac. "Oh, it's the prettiest room I've ever seen!" Pell cried, taking off her feathered hat and placing it on a table.

Alex smiled as he watched her face light up like a child's on Christmas morning. Her fair hair was brushed back from her forehead and her ringlets bounced against her shoulder as she moved about the room, lightly tracing her fingertips over the beautiful furniture. Her eyes danced with pleasure and she was so innocent and unspoiled it lifted his heart to see her enjoying herself.

She had been thrilled with the train trip from London and sat forward on her seat when they arrived in the Cotswolds to marvel at the sleepy hamlets and lush green hills. After living in India for so long, Alex's return to the Cotswolds was a homecoming, and she had made it very special. "Look at that old house," she would say excitedly. "Isn't it beautiful? I wish I could paint it!" Her laughter came from her heart and shone in her eyes, and he couldn't remember when he had looked forward to life with such relish. He felt that he too was now seeing life with new eyes.

After a meal had been brought to their room and they had eaten at a table by the windows, Pell pulled the bell cord for a maid. In the dressing room, while the maid loosened the long row of buttons down Pell's back, she studied the charming nook. Done in country chintz, the little room had a soft chair and a vanity, and there was a basin with a cake of scented soap, a can of warm water, and towels of the softest damask. Pell noticed that the maid who had unpacked her luggage had already laid a nightgown over the chair.

After she slipped from her traveling gown, the maid helped her out of the rest of her clothing, and, giving her a quick curtsy, left the dressing room. Pell now pulled the pins from her hair, letting it fall in cool waves about her shoulders, then slipped on the fine lawn lace nightgown that Aunt Violet had given her as part of her trousseau. Blushing, she looked at her rosy nipples through the sheer material, but she told herself that Alex would have extinguished the lights by the time she returned to the bedroom.

As she walked into the softly lit chamber, she saw him standing by the bed wearing a long robe of navy-blue silk. He had already darkened all the lamps but one, and that light now gleamed over him, making him look even more impressive than usual.

Alex studied Pell as she stood there in the thin nightgown with her soft blonde hair falling about her shoulders in lush waves, thinking she looked like an angel. With his eyes, he traced each feature—her violet eyes, her straight little nose, her delicate chin—and committed them to memory. When he turned off the bedside lamp, shadows engulfed the room, and he shed his silk robe and let it fall to the carpet; then, feeling the coolness of the air against his bare skin, he walked across the moonlit room, wanting to hold her in his arms.

Already aching with pleasure, she watched him come toward her, the moonlight gleaming over his thick hair, well-defined chest, and muscled thighs. In the shadows, his nude body had a soft hazy quality about it, and just the sight of him made her weak with passion. When he wrapped his strong arms about her and lowered his head, it filled her with a joy that could only be expressed in total surrender. As he pressed her against his hard chest, she put her arms about his neck, and when his lips found hers, it seemed that her spirit was flowing toward him. Now his lips became more insistent, and she felt a rising flame within her. Her heart raced out of control.

Raising his lips from hers, he looked down at her moon-silvered face. "This is our wedding night, my darling, and I want it to be very special. Let's forget all that led to this day and start afresh tonight."

She gave him a shy glance from beneath her lashes. "Yes . . . that would be wonderful. Although you've taught me many things since we first met, I'm looking forward to learning some very special new lessons."

Alex chuckled softly and lifted her gown over her head

to remove it, then pulled her against him once more, feeling her soft bare breasts against his chest. When his hands moved over her possessively, she sighed with pleasure, and he pushed her bloomers from her hips, taking time to knead her silky flesh as he did so. As the undergarment slid to the carpet, he felt her lift her foot and lightly kick it out of the way.

Scooping her into his arms, he carried her to the bed while she laid her head against his shoulder, cuddling close. The bed was turned down, and the linen sheets and pillowcases, embroidered and edged with lace, flashed in the moonlight spilling into the room. Gently he laid her down, and noticed that in the silvery rays her eyes were bright with passion, her lips slightly parted, and her curls were fanned out in a shimmering halo about her head.

Pleasure radiated through Pell as she gazed at Alex's shadowed face, and before he slipped into the bed beside her, she caught a glimpse of the proof of his aroused passion. He now trailed little nibbling kisses over her ear, her shoulder, and the hollow of her neck. "Mmmm . . . . you taste delicious," he said playfully.

"I'm glad you approve of me," she said with a giggle.

He raised his head and cocked a brow, and in the moonlight she saw a mischievous smile on his lips. "Approve of you? *That,* my girl, is the understatement of the century. Don't you know how breathtaking you are?"

As he took her into his arms and kissed her once again, a surge of longing rose up within her, and that sharp sweet sensation throbbed between her thighs once more. They kissed so deeply that Pell's mind whirled with desire, and the passion he aroused in her both frightened and delighted her. She'd never dreamed that love could be this way—so wild and sweet at the same time—and as his hands moved over her, every nerve tingled with awareness.

She felt his hand brush her breast, then his fingers stroked over her sensitive crest until she glowed with a tender feeling beyond words. When he raised his head and transferred his mouth to her nipple, she moaned with ecstasy. "What have you done to me?" she murmured softly. "I'm already on fire for you." With a contented sigh, she reached up and caressed his muscled back and worked her hands down to his tight buttocks, feeling the power and strength of his body.

As he took her mouth once more, his hand searched between her thighs, making her pulse race out of control, and the excitement he aroused in her sent a tidal wave of pleasure crashing over her. She could feel the heat of his maleness pressed against the inside of her thigh now, and as he relentlessly stroked her secret places, an ever-building passion swelled within her, demanding release.

Lost in pleasure, she clutched his back, and it seemed they were one person united by a physical need beyond their control. Soon he was above her, and, raising his head a bit, he gently pressed her into the mattress with his weight. She could feel his beating heart as he positioned himself and lowered his torso to her bosom, and she moaned softly.

"Yes, let yourself go," he whispered. "Let your soul flow into mine."

Her arms and legs moved instinctively, and, filled with love and tenderness, she pulled him toward her. Grazing her face with kisses, he continued to stroke her until she trembled with desire, and clasped his buttocks.

"Are you ready for me, love?" he murmured hoarsely.

"Yes . . . please, now, for I can wait no longer."

Taking her mouth once more, he raised himself to protect her from his weight, then he eased deeper into her. With a low groan, he began to thrust and she felt a pulsing ecstasy between her thighs. Powerfully, he moved against her, leisurely stroking over her and engulfing her with unspeakable joy. Then, on the verge of her fulfillment, he eased off, only to begin once more, so that he could prolong her pleasure as long as possible. Finally, as a crest of overwhelming desire rose from the core of her being, she felt herself pulse about him in trembling release. He surrendered himself to shuddering pleasure, and joined her as their spirits soared heavenward together.

She whispered his name and he held her gently until their passion had ebbed away. Afterwards they floated in the tranquil state between wakefulness and sleep, and Pell reveled in a contentment that left her feeling cherished and warmly satisfied. As she slipped into a peaceful sleep wrapped in Alex's arms, her last thoughts were that she was now his bride and the Countess of Tavistock. It was all so wonderful. Wonderful beyond relief. She felt like a princess, and tomorrow she would explore her new realm.

Pell awoke to find sunlight streaming through the cracks in the drapes and making bright patterns on the carpet. With a yawn, she rolled over, eased up on one elbow, and, with a surge of disappointment, found that Alex had left the bed. She had already grown used to the warmth of his body beside her, the touch of his hand upon her, and sorely missed his presence; then she told herself he probably had to attend to some early-morning estate business.

Lazily, she sat up and stretched her arms, thinking she had never enjoyed a better night's sleep. With a little smile, she remembered their passionate lovemaking, knowing that it had left her so contented and relaxed, she was bound to wake with a glowing sense of happiness.

Quickly getting out of bed, she slipped on Alex's discarded robe and went to the silken curtains. Pushing them back a bit, she opened one of the diamond-paned windows and looked out, getting her first glimpse of the grounds surrounding Stanton Hall in the morning light. As a breeze touched her face, she saw balustraded terraces, velvety lawns, and white swans gliding upon the lake. Leaning out a little farther, she breathed in the fragrance of the wild roses climbing up the manor walls. How wonderful life was! The sun was shining, she and Alex were married, and she already loved this part of Gloucestershire.

After one last look, she returned to the bed, and slipped under the covers once more. Then she sat up and pulled the bell cord hanging beside the headboard. A few minutes later there was a soft rap on the door and Mrs. Harris entered carrying a beautifully appointed silver breakfast tray. Once again dressed in a black taffeta gown, she was smiling broadly. "Good morning, milady. I hope you slept well. I'm sure you needed a good rest after the excitement of the wedding and your journey from London," she remarked, placing the tray on a bedside table. Her eyes warm, she poured tea and removed the silver covers from the breakfast dishes, releasing the aromas of country bacon and eggs, porridge, toast, and jam. Despite her large meal the night before, Pell realized that she was hungry again.

"Where is Alex?" she asked softly as the housekeeper bustled to the drapes and pulled them all the way back, flooding the bedroom with golden light.

"Master Alex is out and about with Mr. Potterfield. He didn't want to wake you, but asked me to see to your needs." The older woman pushed up her sleeves and smiled brightly. "Is there anything you would like to do today, milady?"

Pell thoughtfully sipped her tea, then set down the delicate china cup. "Actually there is. I'd love for you to show me Stanton Hall."

Mrs. Harris beamed with delight. "Of course, milady. I'll send a maid up to dress you, then meet you downstairs a little later." She turned and walked to the bedroom door.

An hour later Pell walked about the vast mansion while Mrs. Harris told her the history of Stanton Hall. Last night when Pell had first arrived she was wrapped in a state of euphoria; everything had appeared beautiful in the lamplight's soft glow. But now in the slanting rays of day, she noticed that the furnishings seemed oddly frayed and worn. In the library, although the room was filled with valuable books from ceiling to floor, their bindings were torn and in need of repair. As Mrs. Harris pointed out famous paintings in the drawing room, and told her how they had been acquired, Pell noticed that some of the frames needed another coat of gilt.

It was the same in the conservatory, the ballroom, and the many bedrooms. In fact, before the tour was over, Pell realized that most of the manor's furnishings needed to be refurbished. In places gold fringe hung from frayed window hangings, and legs wobbled on antique tables. Besides that, the servants' liveries shone with bright threadbare spots on the elbows and knees. Of course Alex had spent a long time in India, but his father and brother had lived in Stanton Hall at least six months every year. Why hadn't they maintained it properly?

As she and the housekeeper walked through the drawing room, Pell paused and took the good lady's arm. "Can you tell me why things look so worn?" she asked.

Mrs. Harris laughed, and brushed back her gray hair. "Milady, this is an ancient house—one of the oldest in the land. Things are bound to seem a bit run-down here, aren't they?"

"But even the servants' liveries are threadbare," Pell persisted.

The housekeeper laughed nervously and glanced aside, failing to meet her gaze. "Well, milady . . . you see," she stammered, twisting her plump hands, "it's just that an Earl of Tavistock hasn't lived here in a while and there's a lot of catching up to do. Now that Master Alex has returned from India, things will be looking up, I'm sure."

Pell gazed at the housekeeper's kindly face, not wanting to press her further, but feeling there was more to be learned. What had happened to send the manor into such a state of disrepair? It just didn't make sense, she thought, her heart swelling with frustration.

Several days passed and Alex indulged Pell in every way possible. During the cool twilight, they strolled in the gardens and he pointed out the names of each of the flowers and told her in which century the ancient trees had been planted. At this hour, they often rode over the Gloucestershire hills and laughed as they raced to some ancient oak. He asked her which dishes she preferred and told

Mrs. Harris to see that they were prepared; although he was always gone when she awoke, there were fabulous breakfasts in bed, served on a silver tray.

At night before they went to sleep, he would cuddle her against him in the great canopied bed and read her poetry by Byron and Keats. When the books were put away, he often gave her a long massage, and then made love with such passion and tenderness it left her breathless.

But despite his attentiveness in the evenings, she scarcely saw him during the day, and when she did, his eyes harbored a faraway look, as if his mind was dwelling on a problem. She knew there was something going on at Stanton Hall that she didn't understand, and it was putting a burden on Alex that she wanted to share.

About noon one day, she came down the sweeping staircase and heard Alex's deep voice floating from under the library door. "Well, that should be all for now, Mr. Potterfield, but we must work more on this particular problem before I return to London."

"Yes, indeed we must, milord," came the man's concerned voice. "I'm making a trip to Cheltenham tomorrow and should have that information you want very soon."

Pell heard steps inside the library, then the door opened and Alex and Mr. Potterfield stepped into the hall. After bowing his head at her, the steward turned and quickly hurried down the hall. Dressed in casual country attire, Alex was as handsome as ever, but she noticed that there were tense lines about his eyes and mouth.

"Is anything wrong?" she inquired.

He gave her a soft smile and caressed the side of her face. "No, nothing that should worry you. I was just discussing some more business affairs with Potterfield," he explained.

"Well, you look like you just bet your last quid on a losing horse," she said good-naturedly.

He arched a brow and kissed her forehead. "You're quite a worrier, aren't you?"

She sighed, determined not to let him gently turn her

aside. "But I know *something* is wrong," she continued, lightly clasping his arm.

He studied her face for a moment as if he was making a decision, then he patted her hand and smiled broadly. "Really, love, as I said earlier, Potterfield and I are just discussing some dreary estate business that would bore you silly." He took her elbow and escorted her toward the dining room. "In fact, after luncheon today I'm afraid I'll be tied up in another session with the man." He looked down at her and smiled. "No one has attended to matters in so long that a mountain of details have piled up, all requiring attention."

Frustration rose within Pell's heart. Since they had been married, Alex had indulged her like a child, but she wanted to be treated like an adult and be a helpmeet to him. How could she do this when it was becoming increasingly difficult just to get his attention? Then as they entered the dining room, an interesting idea popped into her head. It was obvious that Alex would not take a well-needed rest if she didn't do something drastic to divert him. With a smile, she knew exactly what that drastic action would be. It was all very simple—tomorrow, she would kidnap him!

The next afternoon, Alex tooled his open gig along one of the rutted country roads bisecting his estate. Frowning, he remembered his puzzlement when, half an hour ago, he had found a note in the library stating there was a dire emergency at the Milbanks' farmhouse requiring his attention. As best he could remember, the crofter was a fine tenant who had never given his family a bit of trouble. What could have arisen to prompt the old man to summon him from the manor house on his honeymoon?

It would have been wiser, he thought, to send Mr. Potterfield, but the man was presently in Cheltenham, taking care of estate business. Guilt pricked Alex's heart as he considered how little time he had been able to give Pell since they had arrived here. And dodging her questions about estate business was becoming increasingly uncomfortable. But after all she had gone through, he was determined he wouldn't burden her with the fact that he was in immediate danger of losing Stanton Hall.

Passing through a slumbering hamlet half-cloaked with leafy oaks, he drove on for a while, then, rounding a bend, eased the gig from the road into a grassy field shaded with ancient trees. In the distance, he could see the Milbanks' farmhouse, a small thatched cottage with a garden bright with blossom, and around it, old stables and outbuildings.

After tying his reins to the low-hanging limb of a tree, he headed through the grassy field toward the farmhouse. About him the fragrance of earth and summer vegetation rose up to meet him. He was fifty yards into the field when he heard a voice from behind an ancient oak saying, "Pssst. Over 'ere, guv'ner!"

Surprise and a bit of irritation washed through him as he walked toward the thick-trunked tree, wondering if some child was playing a trick on him. When he was almost there, Pell stepped from behind the oak holding a picnic basket in her slender hand, a soft blanket draped over her arm. She was dressed in a simple floral-printed cotton gown and her hair was loose and flowing in the gentle breeze. A mischievous little smile played over her lips as she cocked her head and gazed up at him. "Well, it took you long enough. I thought you'd never get here. I'm starving!"

Alex laughed and clasped her shoulders. "How did you get here? I found a note saying there was a dire emergency at the Milbanks' farm that only I could handle."

She chuckled throatily. "To answer your first question, one of the grooms brought me here in a carriage. As to the second question, there *is* an emergency—and it's me, and you are definitely the only one who can handle the situation."

Alex studied her with interest. Her long silvery hair was parted in the middle and gave her a look of simple innocence, in striking contrast to the seductive glint in her eyes and the bold invitation of her full lips. Laughing again, he hugged her against his chest, charmed with her cleverness. "Why, you little minx! You're a devious one, aren't you? What would you have done if I'd sent Potterfield out here?"

She blushed and gave him a provocative glance from beneath her long lashes. "I suppose I would have been very embarrassed indeed!"

Pell gazed at Alex and they held hands and laughed together. Garbed in an open shirt with tight buff-colored breeches and polished Hessians, he looked the part of a country squire to perfection. And it pleased her greatly to see that he had taken her little joke with good humor and seemed to be enjoying himself.

Taking the blanket and picnic basket from Pell, he put his arm about her, then as birds twittered in the trees, they strolled into the field, the warm sunshine on their backs. "Now that I think about it," he commented thoughtfully, "I remember coming here several times for picnics when I was a child."

Pell snuggled against him as they walked. "Yes, Mrs. Harris said it was one of your favorite spots, and that the Milbanks would be honored to have you picnicking here again." She looked up at him and smiled. "I think you'll enjoy the food. I asked the cook to pack something special."

Once they were well into the field, Alex selected an appropriate spot, and after he had spread the blanket over the velvety grass, they sat down upon it. They were in the partially forested hills of his large estate, sheltered under a secret bower of overhanging limbs; in the distance woolly lambs gamboled in the lush grass, and a silver creek twinkled in the sunlight. Fifty yards away, a stable made of Cotswolds stone stood out white and creamy against a thicket of dark-green trees. Overhead, small clouds blended together, making great white mounds against the blue sky.

When they had placed the contents of the picnic basket

upon the blanket, Alex uncorked a bottle of chilled champagne that the cook had packed in cracked ice. Taking two long-stemmed crystal glasses from the basket, he splashed bubbling wine into one of them and handed it to Pell.

Feeling free and easy like a child on a school holiday, Pell sat cross-legged with the skirt of her simple scoop-necked dress spread over her legs. After opening the carefully wrapped packages of thinly sliced ham, cold chicken, dark bread, and delicate pastries, Alex snapped out a linen napkin and laid it in her lap, then he gave her the best of everything. As they ate, the trill of a bluebird and the pleasant tinkle of a lamb's bell were the only sounds to disturb the drowsy woodland silence.

After a while, smiling, he said, "You look as if your mind is a hundred miles away. What are you thinking?"

She sipped the champagne and twirled the long-stemmed glass between her fingertips. "Nothing really." As she scanned his tanned face and twinkling eyes, warmth coursed through her. "I was just thinking how pretty it is here. How different it is from the grime of the East End." She sighed. "I was also thinking how different *I* am. How my life has changed. Things have happened so fast it makes me dizzy." She laughed a little. "It always surprises me when the servants call me *Countess.*"

He brushed back a lock of her hair, displaced by the gentle breeze. "You will become accustomed to it in time."

They ate quietly, pausing as Alex related something about the Cotswolds or pointed out a nearby landmark. Full and satisfied, Pell sipped more champagne, then eased back on her elbows to scan the scenery. On the horizon the clouds had built into puffy mountains, and as the quickening breeze refreshed her face, she noticed that the air had cooled a bit.

With the huge trees, grazing sheep, and thatched cottages in the distance, the scene could have come from a Gainsborough painting. Yes, everything was perfect here. Perfect except for one puzzling problem—the problem of

Alex's preoccupation with estate business. Since they had been married, he was relaxed and attentive, as he was now—as long as she didn't ask him any personal questions. Alex now took the glass from her hand and placed it aside, interrupting her pensive musings.

"I'll vow your mind is not here today!" he chided, his eyes sparkling with humor.

Trying to organize her thoughts, she lay on her back, spreading her hair out behind her.

He propped himself on one elbow and studied her face. "Perhaps I should do something to bring it back."

She watched sunlight glint on his ruby ring as he traced a finger over her cheek. His face hovered so close over hers, she could see the desire in his eyes, and it tugged at her heart. She loved it when he was like this—so warm and full of affectionate teasing. The casual smile on his face gave her the courage to broach the problem that had filled her mind since the day she had arrived at Stanton Hall. "Alex . . . sometimes I feel that you don't trust me," she murmured.

He lifted his brow. "Why do you say that?" he asked, his voice edged with surprise.

"Because you're so vague when I ask you about your business affairs or what you and Mr. Potterfield are discussing. Because you won't tell me what's bothering you. I want to help you and share your problems, whatever they might be."

His face tensed for a moment. "We've been through this before, darling," he said lightly. "It's of no significance."

"But . . ." she began.

He put a finger over her lips. "Let's not discuss it any further," he said huskily. "Why should we talk about dull business matters or skinny Mr. Potterfield when there are other, more pleasant things to do?" His eyes twinkled. "After all, I was told there was an emergency out here."

Pell's heart pitched as she studied his erotic gray eyes and firm mouth. She had to admit that his masculine demeanor drew her to him like a fly to a honey pot. Still, why must he treat her like an child, too immature to understand anything more than trivial social matters?

As she struggled to understand the conflicting feelings within her, he lowered his head and brushed his lips against hers, spreading passion through her body like liquid fire. Trembling, she felt his breath on her face, and, melting with desire, she put aside her worries. After all, didn't she have weeks in the Cotswolds to discover what was troubling him?

Raising her arms, she twined her fingers in his hair, and when he pressed his hard chest to her bosom, she felt the arousing thud of his heart beating against hers. She loved the warmth and the scent of his body as it mingled with the fragrance of the grass and wildflowers and the heady scent of rain hanging in the moist air. As his tongue caressed the fullness of her lips, her desire blossomed into a deep urgency for his touch.

Then, to her great displeasure, a raindrop plopped on her leg, and another fell on her arm and shoulder. Soon, soft thunder growled in the sky and heavy drops splashed down faster and faster, bringing them to a sitting position.

Disappointment shadowing his eyes, Alex raked back his damp hair and pointed at the stable. "Let's take cover there, till the shower passes," he suggested. Moving about the blanket, he tossed wrapped food parcels into the basket, and, getting to her knees, Pell helped with the hasty packing. In a matter of seconds, they both ran for cover, Alex carrying the basket, and Pell clutching the blanket which flew out behind her.

Laughing, they entered the ancient stable, which held the scent of must and leather, and, pausing to catch their breath, peered through the murky light. Tossing back her damp hair, Pell looked about and saw three empty stalls, a tangle of harness hanging from the walls, and on the other side of the building, a large mound of fresh hay.

Alex set the picnic basket on the stable floor, then, taking her shoulder, held her still as he brushed a leaf from her hair and gently wiped raindrops from her bare arms. A mischievous look on his face, he took the blanket, and, throwing a pointed look at the haystack, said, "My military training has taught me to use any equipment available . . . which in this case happens to be a haystack." Cocking an eyebrow, he teasingly asked, "Does this bring any possibilities to your mind?"

Pell put a hand to her chin and pretended to consider the situation. "Mmmm . . . let me see. What *could* one do with a haystack? I know . . . we could feed a team of hungry horses—if we had one," she replied laughingly.

"You'll have to do much better than that," he chided. "Why, your lack of imagination is appalling." With a devilish glint in his eye, he moved to the haystack and spread the blanket over the mound of hay, then, before she could protest, came back and scooped her into his arms. Her laughter bounced against the beams of the low-ceilinged stable as he tossed her on the blanket and lay down beside her. As she shook with mirth, he slipped off her shoes, and, pressing her into the springy hay, fitted his hard body against hers.

Rain drummed on the roof of the stable and the sweet scent of hay rose about them as he trailed kisses over her face and neck, then swept an amused gaze over her face. "Since you've displayed such a shocking lack of imagination, I'll have to instruct you in the proper use of a haystack." He gave her a look of mock severity. "And I suggest you pay close attention since you may be tested again at a later date."

She laughed and ran her hand through his wet hair. Then as she looked into his eyes, she became quiet and still, and caressed his jaw with her fingertips. She loved him until her heart ached, and his warm jesting mood made her want him to share his problems with her all the more. If only their life could always be as simple as this afternoon, she thought wistfully, still wanting to understand this strikingly handsome man who lay beside her.

His eyes growing more serious, he loosened the drawstring at her neckline and pushed the loose cotton gown from her shoulders. Lovingly he cupped one of her full breasts, then the other.

Alex had only to look at her questioning eyes to know that she wanted to share his problems . . . but he had no desire to tell her that he might soon be a ruined man. He only needed a little more time to get his financial affairs in order, he reasoned. Why should he shatter her dreams when he valued her so much—when all he wanted was to keep her life as cloudless as a summer day. "Are you happy?" he asked softly.

Drawing in a long, shuddering breath, Pell slipped her arms about his neck and sighed. "Yes . . . I'm very happy."

His eyes darkening with passion, he took her mouth in a deep kiss.

She shivered with excitement when he freed both of her bare breasts from her thin shift and tenderly grazed his thumb over each aching nipple. This afternoon, he had diverted her from her serious questions with his charm and silvery tongue, and she decided to enjoy the moment and pursue her concerns later. How could she do otherwise?

As his tongue thrust into her mouth, his hand pulled up her long skirt and petticoat, and, with practiced skill, eased down her bloomers until they dangled about her stockinged feet. Raising his lips from hers, he reached down and flicked away the undergarment, then rained kisses over both of her exposed breasts, making her quiver with pleasure. She gasped as he twirled his tongue about her hard nipples, each in turn, finally nursing one while he rolled the other in his fingertips.

His attentions suffused her body with a hungry glow and she moaned and writhed under him, sinking a bit deeper into the hay. She truly felt like a wanton country wench, for her skirt and petticoat were up about her waist, while her bodice was off her shoulders, exposing her bare breasts to his warm lips. Blood stung her cheeks as her naked hips rubbed against the soft blanket, for she realized she couldn't really account for her bloomers, and guessed he had tossed them somewhere in the hay.

Quickly, he lifted himself a bit and made some adjustments in his clothing, then, as he leaned over her and took her mouth in another kiss, she felt his pulsing hardness brush the inside of her bare thigh. Shivering with desire, she thrust her tongue up to meet his and instinctively clutched his hot brand, thrilled with its silky texture and marble-like hardness. As she caressed its velvety tip, he slipped his hand into the moist triangle between her thighs, and, finding her aching bud, relentlessly flicked over it until she thought she would swoon with pleasure.

Her heart thudding, she felt him move over her, and, in a matter of seconds, the tip of his shaft slipped into her warm, welcoming sheath. Her senses whirled with the lush sensations enveloping her: the sound of the rain splattering against the stable's slate roof, the taste of his silky tongue against hers, the feel of his warm hand on her breast, the pressure of his hardness sliding into her and filling her to bursting. Isolated in the rude stable, they seemed to be the only people in the world, and for this blissful moment they had successfully banished their problems. For this breathtaking instant, they belonged to one another, and one another alone.

When he was fully inside her warmth, she groaned and ran her fingers over his hard shoulders and muscled back, feeling a burst of deep erotic pleasure. For a moment he was still, then he began to stroke her deeply and firmly and she wrapped her legs about him, her heart swelling with tender feeling. She trembled as he increased his tempo and lunged into her again and again until she flushed and quivered with pleasure. With a moan, she dug her fingers into his broad shoulders and tightened her legs about him, burning with passion. When she began to shudder with an explosive climax, he thrust into her deeply one last time, then held her against him as they pulsed together in a heart-shaking climax. With a burst of fiery passion, their love swept them to the stars and they throbbed in moments of tender fulfillment until their passion had subsided and they rested together, bathed in love.

He held her gently and showered kisses over her face as their hearts slowed and their shallow breathing became more regular. Caressing her hair, he gently rolled to his side, bringing her with him. As he trailed his fingers over her back, she was lost in clouds of peace and satisfaction, and lulled by the sounds of the gentle rain, she slid into a peaceful sleep.

Chapter 19

Three wonderful days slipped by after the picnic in the rain. On the afternoon of the fourth day, Pell and Alex arrived back at the estate, having just made an obligatory social visit to neighbors.

Alex stepped down from the carriage and helped her to the ground, then, the white gravel crunching beneath their feet, they strolled to the entrance of the sprawling manor house. Pell was thinking about their relationship as she walked by his side. She still harbored doubts about the reason he had married her, and his lack of openness troubled her not a little. But since the picnic, she was sure she could nurture his trust and affection for her until it grew as large as her love for him.

The heady fragrance of the climbing roses that twined about the ancient door touched her senses as a footman bowed them into the house. Alex put a hand to her waist and she could feel its heat burning through her gown. The sensation ignited her desire, and she found it very satisfying to think that they would be alone this evening to dine, talk about their day, and later make love.

In the drawing room, she took a seat on the sofa and Alex poured her a glass of wine. His eyes warm, he presented her with the small glass of amber liquid. "Have a sherry, darling?"

Alex looked down at her sitting on the sofa and felt a rush of tenderness. She wore a yellow silk gown with a touch of lace at the neckline and looked as fresh as a summer's morn. Her eyes were as warm as the smile on her soft lips. She was so innocent. He wondered if she had given any thought to Sabrina since they had left London. He told himself that it didn't matter, because he had done enough thinking for both of them, pondering the problem of the general's widow almost every waking hour. He was sure that she'd heard of their marriage by now, and she was certainly clever enough to put all the facts together. No doubt, she was even now hatching some scheme to discredit Pell.

Hearing a discreet cough, Pell saw Mr. Potterfield standing near the threshold of the drawing room, the corners of his mouth turned down. Her spirits dipped at the sight of his thin, bespectacled face, and in her heart, she already knew what he was going to say.

Fulfilling her fears, the steward approached them with a grave face. "I've been working on the books all afternoon, milord, and I must speak with you in the library," he announced. "I'm sure we're in for a long session this evening."

Alex became very still and looked at the man's humorless face. He'd had his heart set on dining with Pell tonight, and the steward's intrusions were becoming more frustrating each day. What a temptation she was, he thought, begrudging every hour he had given to Potterfield. Then, with a long sigh, he told himself that getting his financial house in order was the best way of protecting her. After all, he wanted her life to be perfect from now on, and the scandal of losing everything he owned would only add to her troubles. It was a shame that now that he had found the woman of his dreams he couldn't live happily with her.

Regretting the words he knew he must say, Alex eyed Pell's discontented face. "I'm sorry, love ... but I can foresee that we'll not be able to dine together tonight. I'll have Mrs. Harris send a tray to your room, then I'll join you later."

Pell sighed. Still, she inclined her head in acquiescence,

then watched him and Mr. Potterfield leave the drawing room. Frustration tightened within her bosom as she admitted to herself that Alex would probably work far into the night, and she would be asleep when he finally came to bed. For a moment she thought of finding Mrs. Harris, just to have someone to talk with, then realized that this evening she was hungry for companionship that only Alex could satisfy.

Sudden tiredness slipping over her, she placed her sherry on a little table, then walked from the room herself. A moment later, she passed the library and heard the murmur of the men's concerned voices already engaged in deep conversation. *He's locked himself in there again and shut me out,* she thought. Then, feeling small and petty, she pushed down her resentment and told herself that the men were simply handling dull business matters that had built up after Alex's brother had died. Still, just what were they discussing that required such attention?

As she paused to stare at the closed library door, she experienced a great urge to press her ear against the thick panel, or to simply walk in and ask what he and the steward were talking about, but her pride held her back. She wanted Alex to share this part of his life with her of his own accord, not because she had pressed him.

Depression weighing upon her spirit, she started walking up the sweeping staircase that led to their huge bedroom. About halfway up the stairs, she noticed several bright patches high above the steps and realized that some of the pictures had been removed from the wall—pictures that had been there before she and Alex went on their social call. As she stared at the plastered expanse, trying to decide what had happened, she remembered that Mrs. Harris had told her the paintings were valuable. Perhaps the paintings had been taken out to be cleaned, she reasoned.

But as she continued up the stairs, she recalled how surprised she had been that the manor's furnishings were in need of repair, and doubts crept into her thoughts. How could Mrs. Harris afford for the paintings to be cleaned when she was obviously on such a tight household budget? Pell entered the bedroom, and leaned against the closed door. Blinking, she noticed that a painting was missing here too! At that moment, a strange sense of insecurity slid over her. What was happening at Stanton Hall?

The next morning she woke with a start, for she had been dreaming about Claude. In her dream, she saw him sprawled on the platform at Victoria Station, an expression of vengeance twisting his face. She realized that her dream had materialized from her worries about the possibility that the artist might reveal her past, and in so doing compromise Alex. For the hundredth time she chastised herself for being so open with Claude; she wanted to confess to Alex how foolish she had been, but she felt too embarrassed. No, she thought, she could never tell him.

The sound of twittering birds as they stirred to dawn's first light outside the partially opened windows told her it was about five in the morning. For some reason it flashed through her mind that less than six months ago at this hour she haggled for fruit at Covent Garden. Now, as the Countess of Tavistock and mistress of Stanton Hall, she lay between silken sheets, Alex at her side.

As she had expected, he had come to bed during the wee hours of the morning and there had been no time to talk about estate business. But when would they talk? she wondered, now becoming more fully awake. How cleverly he changed the subject if she mentioned any of his private affairs!

Her brain in tumult, she rose and quietly slipped from the bed, feeling the cool carpet against her bare feet. At the window, she pushed back the lacy shadow panels and drew in a long breath of chilly air heavy with the scent of country greenery. In the east an apricot blush warmed the sky and gilded the tops of the rolling Gloucestershire hills, promising another beautiful day.

But what promise did her life hold? Would Alex ever trust her enough to completely confide in her? she wondered sadly. Could she take the warm intimacy they had shared on the picnic and transform it into a deep abiding love?

With a shiver of awareness, she heard the rustle of sheets and the creak of springs, and, glancing back at the bed, saw that Alex was now awake. Her heart swelled with warmth at the sight of his huge body tangled in the bed coverings. He was completely nude except for a bit of the sheet that rode low over his slim hips, and he looked so appealing that her breath caught in her throat. As she drank him in, dawn's golden rays touched his tousled hair and heavily muscled arms, highlighting his air of rugged masculinity.

His gaze never wavering, he beckoned her with his eyes, and she was irresistibly drawn to him. Feeling her heart beat faster, she came back to the bed and sat on the edge, a smile on her lips. Alex's hand reached upward and worked into the bodice of her gown, then his finger nimbly circled her nipple, making it harden and tingle pleasantly. "Take off the gown," he commanded sleepily.

"Now?" she murmured with a soft chuckle.

"Now."

She loosened the tiny buttons, then stood and let the gown slide over her body and pool around her feet. She shivered a bit as the cool air from the open window caressed her bare back, and, leaning forward, she gazed into his glittering eyes as he pulled back the sheet, fully exposing his large frame. When she saw his erection, blood stung her cheeks, excitement stirring within her.

With strong arms, he pulled her down beside him and she slipped under the sheet, relishing his warmth and nearness. She could feel his hard chest pressing against her, and savored the rhythm of his evenly beating heart. Tenderly, he cupped her breast, then lowered his head and suckled her flesh, sending little shivers of pleasure over her body. As he twirled his tongue about the hardening nipple, exquisite feelings shot through her, making her gasp with desire. Impulsively, she clutched his smooth hardness, already feeling herself becoming moist and ready.

Alex gently turned her on her back, and, sliding down in the bed, began kissing her parted legs, eliciting delicious sensations within her. All the time, his fingers tantalized her aching nipples, while his mouth worked ever closer to the moist triangle between her trembling legs. Near her seat of desire, he slowly licked the inside of her silky thighs, increasing the tingling anticipation of what was to come until she throbbed with wanting. Blood roared in her ears and pleasure spread between her legs.

Soon his mouth had progressed to her mound and his probing tongue searched for her swollen bud. She moaned as she felt his warm breath upon her inner flesh, and when he taunted her with loving persistence, she gasped, and, clutching the sheet, called his name. Somewhere within her, her spirit stirred like a flower opening its petals to the warm sun. After moments of intense pleasure, she cried out in joy and shivered convulsively, wild sensations sweeping through her quivering body.

Filled with deep, glowing satisfaction, she lay quietly for a while, soaking up every last drop of the powerful climax. Moving to her side, Alex pulled the sheet over her cool arms and held her against him as they both relaxed and drew strength from one another. As he caressed her shoulders, his hard chest rubbed against her bosom, stirring the embers of their passion. With a soft murmur, she trailed teasing fingers over his back, then worked them up his neck and twined them in his silky hair. When he took her mouth again, his long hardness brushed against her thighs; sighing, she reached downward, her fingers finding the object of her desire.

Passion now swelled from the core of her being, and with a spurt of hungry desire, she gently moved from his arms. With a few graceful movements she was on top of him and leaned forward, her breasts near his face. His eyes glinted, and in the dim light she saw a sly smile curve his lips. "What is this then, you bundle of Cockney mischief?" he asked in a rough murmur. "I suppose you will soon be challenging my seat in Parliament as well?"

She gave a soft laugh. "I know you put great store in good value. I thought perhaps you would like to receive a full measure of reward for all my expensive riding lessons."

He laughed, then, slowly teasing her nipples, brought her face downward and took her lips. In a matter of seconds they both trembled with desire, and he put his strong hands at her waist and carefully positioned her where she could find his hardened shaft. As she eased herself over his steely brand and felt it fill her to bursting, she murmured with satisfaction, and, closing her eyes, began to move instinctively. Alex moaned with desire, and, clutching her smooth buttocks, repeatedly thrust inside her warmth while she tightened herself about him and rocked up and down, teasing him with her slow movements.

Alex's heart leaped as she raised her mouth and her eyes fluttered open. A look of tender sensuality graced her face and her eyes glistened with desire. She smiled, and he returned her smile, their gazes meeting and holding in a warm caress. He had guessed that she was deeply passionate when he first met her, but it thrilled him that she was being so adventurous in their lovemaking. Astonished, but pleased with her wild hunger, her trailed his hands over her cool back and curving hips, pulling her closer. How he loved this tempting little seductress, and how he wanted to pleasure her. "My darling. My wanton angel," he whispered huskily.

Aching with pleasure, she applied herself to her task; he thrust upwards, slowly at first, then faster and faster. As he continued his movements, a powerful erotic hunger flashed over her, carrying her to the heights of desire. She ached for fulfillment and his savage rhythm was almost too much to bear. Then as he gave one mighty lunge she felt his warm seed jet inside of her. Still he continued thrusting until they both shook in a throbbing climax that left them gasping for breath.

Trembling with emotion, she let herself fall over his body and they melted into each other for a moment; then, tenderly caressing her hair, he moved her to his side and kissed her face. Warm and drowsy, she lay in his arms, wrapped in an exultant feeling that nourished her mind, body, and spirit. Nestled in the hand of love, they dozed for a while, then she felt his warm hand caressing her back and sweeping over her smooth buttocks. With a twinge of surprise, she flicked open her eyes to see him propped up on one elbow, a crooked grin lifting the corner of his mouth. "Again?" she whispered. "I cannot believe it. How do you do it?"

Shrugging a broad shoulder, he lifted his brow and sighed. "It's a gift," he said with mock seriousness.

She chucked softly, but when he reclaimed her mouth and rolled her nipples between his fingers, new fire flamed deep within her. Drifting into pleasure once more, she closed her eyes and soon felt his hand steal between her legs and slid into her damp tangle of curls. As he skillfully moved his fingers between the tender folds, fiery waves of sensation rolled through her, until moisture once again dampened her thighs.

Kissing her eyelids, he carefully positioned himself over her and slipped the tip of his hard shaft into her warmth; as he slowly pressed in and out, in and out, teasing her with entrance, an aching arousal swelled within her womanhood, demanding release. Moaning with pleasure, she clasped his tight buttocks and urged him toward her, wanting him to take her fully. His moist breath tickled her ear as he growled, "Yes, my darling, I understand," and then he complied with her wishes and thrust into her with his hard throbbing manhood.

Now he began an erotic movement as old as time. Completely surrendering to his masculinity, she opened wider to him, and, wrapping her legs about him, adjusted to his rhythm. Faster and faster he pounded into her, taking her possessively. Just as she was about to shudder with pleasure, he instinctively eased off, then increased his rhythm again, drawing out her enjoyment as long as possible. Passion darting through her veins, she clutched his shoulders, and in her excitement, dug her fingers into his back as they reached a state of fiery ecstasy. At last they exploded together in a storm of desire and she felt herself pulse about his hardness in long moments of exquisite release. Blood pounding through her glowing body, she sank into the mattress, totally satiated and spent in the aftermath of their glorious passion.

When their racing hearts had slowed, Alex rolled to his side and cradled her in his arms and they collapsed in a floodtide of satisfaction and fulfillment. His warm hands skimming over her arms and breasts, he murmured soft love words, stirring a melting sweetness within her. "I want to see more of the countryside today," she said drowsily, still floating on love's rosy afterglow. "After breakfast, let's take a carriage and go out again."

He pulled her closer and kissed her forehead lightly. "I can't, my darling. There's more business that Potterfield and I have to discuss this morning."

Disappointment rose within her and she started to protest, but when she glanced at Alex, his eyes were closed and his chest rose and fell deeply. Raising up on one elbow, she gazed at him, relishing the luxury of just being able to lie there beside the man she loved as he slept peacefully. Brushing back a lock of dark hair from his forehead, she considered how he had tried to please her, and she thought of their passionate lovemaking. Their afternoon in the stable and this dawn tryst made her believe that if she were patient for just a little longer, he would open his heart to her.

As she snuggled against him, a deep sense of peace overcame her, and all she wanted to do was sleep contentedly at his side. Just before she drifted off, she told herself that she would humor him and let him have the morning with Mr. Potterfield—but in the afternoon he would be hers and hers alone!

* * *

About nine o'clock, sharp light streamed into the bedroom, washing over Pell's face. Blinking her eyes against the brightness, she eased up on one elbow and glanced about. With a tug of sinking disappointment, she discovered that Alex had dressed and quietly left the room, leaving her to sleep. Sitting up and stretching leisurely, she basked in the lingering glow of their love that still clung to her body like an exquisite perfume. As she moved from the bed and slipped on a wrapper, contentment radiated to the womanly core of her body, and she brushed back her loose hair, feeling wonderfully rested and satisfied. After a long leisurely bath and a good English breakfast taken on a tray in her bedroom, she felt fully alive and ready for a bit of play.

Wondering what she would do to entertain herself until Alex finished his morning conference, she cast about for an idea to distract herself, and thought of all the beautiful flower gardens about the manor house. Yes, surely she could find enough there to keep her busy until noon.

Two hours later Pell shielded her eyes and scanned the lush lawns rolling in front of Stanton Hall as she strolled back to the manor house with a full basket of fragrant blossoms. As the sun warmed her back and the blooms flooded her senses with their heady aroma, she realized that, like the manor house itself and the furnishings inside, all this now belonged to her, when a few months ago she had scarcely owned a change of clothes.

She'd been wandering through the lush gardens for quite a while, snipping the blooms she thought most lovely. Now as she entered the great hall, she met the housekeeper carrying the morning post in her hand. "I'll take the letters, Mrs. Harris," she said cheerfully, shifting the heavy flower basket over one arm. "I'm on my way to the library myself."

The older lady smiled and nodded as she handed Pell the stack of letters. "Very good, milady."

Quickly glancing through the envelopes, Pell noticed one with unusually ornate handwriting that had no return address. In the library, her gaze went to Alex, who was dressed in the casual tweeds and polished boots of a country squire. He stood with his back to her reading a local newspaper, but turned as she said, "Did you finish your business with Mr. Potterfield this morning?"

He laid the paper aside and his mouth curved into an easy smile. "Yes, as a matter of fact I did," he answered, his voice reflecting his relaxed mood.

"Good, now we can spend the whole afternoon together!" Smiling, she crossed the room and gave him the letters, saying, "Oh, I met Mrs. Harris in the hall . . . here's the mail." She watched with interest as he shuffled through the envelopes, setting aside the one with the florid handwriting. She turned to place her basket on a nearby table as she heard him ripping it open.

Alex flicked his gaze over the letter in his hand. As he expected, it was from Sabrina. The beginning of the letter was formally worded, like many of the congratulatory letters they had received since their hasty marriage, but as he read further, he could almost hear Sabrina's silky voice purring.

> Alex, although I'm sure you're enjoying your honeymoon away from the bustle of the city, we're beginning to miss you here in London. Really, do you plan on staying in the Cotswolds forever? We in society are beginning to wonder what you're doing. What could possibly be delaying you for so long? Ah, well, I suppose you have become so involved with your little wife that you've forgotten the rest of us—although we certainly have not forgotten you. Again, my congratulations on your unexpected marriage.

Alex clenched his jaw in frustration as he folded the letter. One of the reasons he had brought Pell to the country was to quiet rumors, but obviously Sabrina was bent on stirring them up again. Reading between the lines, he could see that she was suspicious of them, and he realized that they would have to return to London to monitor all the rumors she was creating. If nothing else, he and Pell needed to attend a few social functions and appear forthright. On top of that, he had business in the city, and Pell's important meeting with Mr. Peebles was fast approaching. As he glanced at Pell, who was just finishing arranging her blossoms in a blue-and-white Chinese vase, he decided that there was no reason to tell her that Sabrina was trying to tighten the noose around their necks.

As she settled the last bloom in place, Pell turned and looked up at him with an appealing smile. "Why don't we take a long ride this afternoon?" Her eyes twinkled. "Or go back to the Milbanks' farm?"

She looked so much like an excited child that he dreaded breaking the news to her. "I'm afraid that won't be possible now," he answered.

Pell felt a surge of disappointment, and by the look on his face she knew something was troubling him. Her mind alive with questions, she walked to him and placed her hands on his chest. "What's wrong? Was there bad news in the letter?" she asked softly.

A shadow clouded his eyes. "No, not really," he replied dryly, slipping the letter into its envelope. "It was just another letter of congratulation like so many we've received. But after luncheon, ask Mrs. Harris to see that our things are packed . . . so we can leave for London."

At first her mind refused to register the statement, then her spirits sank like a rock plunging into a pond. "Lon-London?" she stuttered. "But why? I thought we would be staying in the Cotswolds for several weeks. The country is lovely here. Why must we go back to London now?"

His gaze flickered over her. "No more questions for now," he said lightly as he put the letter into his jacket pocket and strode toward the door.

Resentment swelled within her. "There's never time for questions, is there?" she lashed out. "Why did you ever marry me if you're going to keep secrets from me?"

He paused and turned around, annoyance darkening his

eyes. "Isn't it enough that I want you more than I've ever wanted any woman?"

"I understand that you couldn't share your life with me when we first met—when you were my guardian alone—but I expected things to change when we married!" she exclaimed.

He gazed at her with unreadable eyes. "There are some business affairs that you should not concern yourself with. Trust me to take care of them."

The authority in his voice kindled her anger. "Are you afraid that sharing your secrets means we're really, truly married? Is that why you never answer my questions?"

Drawing himself up to his full height, he stared at her, frustration tightening his features. "I'm not prepared to talk about this now. Perhaps you'll get all your answers back in Mayfair," he said quietly. Turning and walking from the room, he left her standing hurt and alone, struggling to grapple with the problem that had put a sad end to the honeymoon that had begun so gloriously.

Chapter 20

Two days later, Pell sat at a table in the butler's pantry of the Mayfair mansion, interviewing a prospective maid. A soft smile on her face, Aunt Violet hovered by her side, silently overseeing the procedure. The small room smelled of cleaning oil and silver polish, and a feeling of nervous expectation charged the air. After riffling through a handful of tattered references, Pell glanced up at the slender blonde girl, who stood before a case of porcelain dinnerware. "It says here that you're a laundress as well as a maid. Is that correct?"

The girl shuffled her feet on the stone floor and licked her dry lips. "Yes, milady," she replied in a quavering voice. "I was a laundress fer a while, and I've done other kinds of 'ousework. I'll be 'appy to work fer you any way you sees fit." Her fingers trembling, she brushed back her tousled hair, then wiped her hands on her long apron.

Compassion filled Pell as she studied the girl who resembled herself less than six months ago. The maid spoke in the same nasal voice, and in the girl's eyes she saw the same hunger and desperation she had known.

It seemed as the Countess of Tavistock she now stood on a great hill, and, looking back over the past months, she could see everything very clearly. At this moment as she gazed into the girl's frightened eyes, she realized how much she had accomplished since Alex had rescued her from Holloway House of Detention. He had bullied her and pushed her, and she had hated him at times, but he had done it anyway. And with his assistance, she had soared over the great chasm that existed between the lowest and highest social classes in England.

Aunt Violet placed a hand on her shoulder and coughed discreetly, shaking her from her thoughts. Straightening in her chair, Pell smiled at the girl, who now blotted perspiration from her brow with a tattered handkerchief. "Your references are all in good order, and you may begin work tomorrow," she said kindly. "See Buxley and he will give you further instructions."

A smile broke over the girl's relieved face and she curtsied deeply. "Oh, thank ye, milady. I'll work 'ard, I will. I'll be the best maid ye ever 'ired!" Her eyes swimming with tears of gratitude, she backed away, then turned and hurried from the small room, her thick-soled soles clattering over the rough flooring.

Aunt Violet glanced down at Pell and touched her arm. "Well, you handled that very well, my dear, although for a while you seemed lost in thought."

Pell rose, a smile touching her lips. "I'm sorry. The girl just reminded me of myself in so many ways. A few months ago, that terrified girl was me."

Aunt Violet chuckled softly. "Oh, no, dear. I don't remember you being as docile as that poor girl! But I *do* remember something about a bath and fighting you for your hat."

Pell's lips twitched with amusement. "Yes, and how I ate. You must have thought me a savage!"

"No, no, just a bit hungry." A tender look glazed her eyes. "And you needed that spirit or you would never have survived Alex's regimen to turn you into a lady. When he returns from the solicitor's office, I'm going to tell him how well you did with the interview."

Pell gave her an impulsive hug. "Thank you for staying," she whispered. "Thank you for staying until I gain a little more confidence. Everything still seems so bewildering. I'm going so slowly."

"As slowly as a snail on crutches?" the old lady remarked laughingly. "Don't fret, my dear. Most of the hard work is done. You'll soon be an old hand at hiring servants and giving dinner parties . . . and then, someday, you may be blessed with an addition to your family."

Pell blushed, and, realizing she had touched upon a delicate subject, Aunt Violet smoothed back her hair and moved toward the door. "I think I'll go to my room and read until dinner, dear," she announced at the threshold. "I want to be well rested, because Mr. Peebles is taking me to a reception tonight."

Pell smiled at her, glad that the solicitor had added a bit of color and excitement to her bland life.

Aunt Violet put her hand on the doorknob, her face aglow with happiness. "He's such an interesting man, and so well educated too. It seems we never run out of subjects to discuss."

When she was gone, the smile faded from Pell's face, and she slowly paced about the pantry, thinking things over. Aunt Violet had mentioned children, which implied not only physical intimacy, but also a view toward the future—a future she and Alex had not discussed. Since getting back to London, he'd been tenderly affectionate, but he'd also vanished several times, not telling her his business, and she had been consumed with the need to know what was going on in his life. Today was a case in point. She knew he was at a solicitor's office, but had no idea why.

She constantly thought of the expression on his face the day they left Stanton Hall. And his words haunted her. *There are some business affairs that you should not concern yourself with.* Did he save his intimacy for the bedroom alone because he regretted being forced into a marriage beneath his station? In many ways, she thought her confrontation with him that day had been a mistake. Then again, she knew it was necessary if she was to remain true to herself. As she had realized today, she was a person in her own right now and Alex's equal, not someone he could ignore if he didn't feel like communicating.

She recalled that he'd actually locked the library doors when he left today, an action that had piqued her curiosity and stung her pride. Crossing her arms, she gave a weary sigh. Then, as she walked about, her gaze fell on a ring of keys hanging from a peg on the wall. She had seen Buxley using it, and knew that the ring contained a key for every room in the house. She stared at it for a moment, then snatched the ring off the peg and hurried from the butler's pantry.

After climbing the steps to the first floor, she went to the library and tried several keys, at last finding one that would fit the lock. Opening the doors, she looked about for something amiss; the sight of Alex's desk piled high with ledgers and papers drew her toward it. His chair was pulled back and the crumpled papers littering the floor gave the impression that he had departed hastily. What in the world had he been working on before he left this morning?

Pell placed the keys on his desk and picked up a piece of wrinkled correspondence. Her business knowledge was slight, but she surmised the paper was a bill. After scanning it carefully, she let it flutter to the desk, and as she picked up other pieces of correspondence, she realized that all the papers were bills! And many of them were scrawled with the words *Payment past due.*

Never in her wildest dreams could she have imagined finding such news. Instead of dissertations on politics as she thought they might be, the books were merely ledgers filled with boring rows of tiny numbers. As afternoon sunlight illuminated the inked pages, she riffled through them, hoping to find a clue to what might be troubling Alex.

As she continued poring over the ledgers and examining the bills, the full effect of what she had discovered hit her with crushing force. Feeling as if the breath had been knocked from her lungs, she eased herself into the leather desk chair. "Why, Alex is almost bankrupt—and he's living on credit, using his title to obtain more credit," she whispered to herself.

She sat stunned for a minute, trying to sort everything out. "No," she finally muttered, "that can't be true. Alex is an earl with a great fortune—a mansion in London and a fine estate in the Cotswolds. Perhaps he just forgot to pay the bills." Even as she spoke the words, the rational part of her mind refused to listen to her confused reasoning.

Frantically searching for answers to her questions, she remembered Aunt Violet. Of course, she thought as she rose from the chair and picked up a handful of the bills, Aunt Violet would probably know about Alex's business affairs. Pressing the much-folded papers against her bosom, she left the library and hurried up the staircase to the second floor.

A few moments later she knocked and entered the old lady's bedroom, which as always held the sweet scent of vanilla potpourri. As she expected, she found Aunt Violet seated in one of the winged-backed chairs placed on either side of the fireplace, reading another of her romance novels. Aunt Violet looked up, then, as Pell neared her with the bills, she paled and closed the book.

Silently, Pell placed the bills upon the cover of the closed book. "What can you tell me about all these?" she asked in a trembling voice. "I found them on Alex's desk."

Aunt Violet refused to meet her eyes. "Well, dear," she stammered, "I'm sure Alex just forgot to . . . to pay them." Pulling a silk handkerchief from her pocket, she twisted it in her hands, glancing at the carpet. "Yes, I'm sure that's what happened."

Pell thumbed through the papers. "If that's the case, why are the bills marked so far past due? And why are there so many of them?" she demanded, shaking the papers for emphasis. "I hired a maid less than an hour ago. It seems we're living on nothing but credit!"

"Well, I . . ." the old woman slowly began.

"Look at this one from a tailor," Pell interrupted, handing a weathered slip to her. "It's for services rendered over three years ago." Rustling through the invoices, she pulled out several more. "And these are at least two years old," she added.

The old lady let the bill from the tailor float to the carpet, then weakly clasped the handkerchief over her heaving bosom. "Oh, dear," she mumbled in a confused voice.

With a rustle of silk, Pell sank to the floor and met her troubled eyes. "Yes?" she gently prompted. "Please tell me what Alex is keeping from me. I've known something was wrong for weeks now, and after all I'm his wife now, not a boarder or an . . . *experiment* like I was when I first arrived." She clutched the old lady's arm and searched her face.

Grasping Pell's hand, Aunt Violet heaved a deep sigh and blinked back her tears. "All right, dear," she replied in a broken voice. "I suppose you should know what is going on. It's only right." She glanced about the opulent bedroom and gave another little sigh, then finally looked Pell in the eye. "It's true. Alex is in debt. Deeply in debt."

The confirmation rocked Pell, but before she could react, Aunt Violet blurted out, "But it isn't his fault. You must believe that. Alex's father and brother were . . ." She paused as she searched for the right words. "Well, they were such poor managers," she finished in an apologetic tone. "I'm sorry, dear. Along with a title, Alex has inherited a bundle of troubles and woes."

Pell appreciated the older woman's honesty and she squeezed her hand affectionately, realizing how painful the confession must have been. "How does he expect to pay for everything?" she asked quietly.

"There's a little household money left. And he's hoping to secure a high-ranking position in the conservative government. But the appointment is largely political, and he's still very uncertain of his possibilities."

Pell stood, turning over the situation in her mind. "Must he repay all the bills? Isn't there some way he could start fresh and forget the past?"

Aunt Violet gave a dry laugh. "Oh, dear, I see you

really haven't learned everything about Alex yet. He's so proud! He wants to pay back every penny of his family's debts and remove the stigma from the Chancery-Brown name," she explained with a flutter of her handkerchief.

"Restore the name?"

"Yes, dear. If truth be told," the old lady went on in a stronger voice, "Alex's father and brother were hardly better than reprobates. They spent their money wildly and incurred many gambling debts. Alex would like to move among society again without knowing every man there holds one of their promissory notes. Think how he must have felt the night of your coming-out ball."

Pell stared at her, taking in every word she said.

Aunt Violet slowly rose. "Don't worry, my dear. Alex is clever, and he will find some means of taking care of his financial difficulties."

"But . . . but what if he can't?"

"In that sad situation," the older woman said, "he would be forced to sell Stanton Hall and all his land in the Cotswolds. Of course, everything is heavily mortgaged already. In the worst of straits he would be forced to dispose of this mansion and take a few rooms somewhere. A duke or an earl rarely loses everything—but it is not unheard of. He is a fine solicitor, but he could never earn enough in a lifetime to pay back all the debts."

With a surge of panic, Pell went to the bedroom windows and pulled back the drapes, Aunt Violet's earlier statement ringing in her ears. *Alex is clever and he will find some means of taking care of his financial difficulties.* Trembling like the maid she had just hired, she leaned against the window casing and stared out at the passing carriages in the street.

When Alex took her virginity, she thought he had asked her to marry him out of duty. Then during their honeymoon she came to believe that he might actually love her as a man loves his wife. Now she had to face the likely possibility that he had married her for money.

Aunt Violet moved to her side and put a comforting hand on her shoulder.

"I understand everything perfectly now," Pell murmured, clutching the velvet drape in her hand. "No wonder the furnishings at Stanton Hall are in such a state of disrepair and valuable paintings are missing—anything that might fetch a price has been sold. Why, I'll bet Mr. Potterfield took paintings to an art dealer in Cheltenham to have them appraised while we were there! And now I understand why we returned to London so quickly," she added, remembering the letter with the ornate handwriting. "No doubt another financial crisis arose and Alex had to pacify an irate creditor. Yes," she went on, her voice trembling with emotion, "I'm sure he was scanning the bills this morning, and in his rush to meet with the solicitor, he locked the library against me, intending to work more when he returned."

She let the drape fall from her hand and turned about, looking into Aunt Violet's teary eyes. "Now I know why Alex condescended to marry me—he needed my inheritance!"

A pained look tightened the old lady's face. "No, dear, you cannot be sure of that," she said in a soothing tone. "True, Alex is in financial difficulties, but you must not accuse him of being a fortune hunter!"

"Then why does he always refuse to discuss business matters with me?" Pell asked with a dull ache in her heart. "Why does he always keep everything secret?"

Aunt Violet give a heartfelt sigh. "Perhaps he wants to protect you . . . or perhaps he is simply embarrassed. You must realize that you are basing all your doubts on supposition. You cannot let yourself fall into this dark mood when you have a chance at such a wonderful future."

Pell searched for hope in Aunt Violet's words, but she could find none. Why would Alex keep such a thing from her if he didn't want to deceive her? The fact that he was about to lose everything, that he had a crisis of the most pressing type, was something that a man should share with his bride before he married her—but Alex had never mentioned the difficulty whatsoever! The fact that he *did* have financial problems didn't disturb her, but the fact that he had hidden them bothered her tremendously.

Aunt Violet caressed her arm. "You must believe that Alex loves you and let it sustain you," she said pleadingly.

Pell touched her hand affectionately, but remained silent.

Her eyes moist with emotion, Aunt Violet gave her a long hug, then, murmuring something about speaking with the cook, left the room.

Pell moved from the window and picked up the bills with trembling hands. Trying to organize her whirling thoughts, she walked back to the library. Her better judgment told her it would be wisest not to confront Alex with her discovery and accuse him of the fear that lurked deep within her heart. She would arrange his desk as she had found it, and take the key ring and lock the library doors behind her. Whatever the reason, he *had* asked her to marry him, and she was now his wife. But the realization that he had concealed his financial situation from her stirred painful doubts about his love and integrity.

As she placed the bills upon his desk one thought occupied her mind. She had to be very careful not to reveal her past, either by foolishly telling someone about it as she had told Claude, or by her actions. Her talk with Aunt Violet had made her realize just how proud Alex was.

With a prickle of cold fear, she thought of Claude. When she first returned from the Cotswolds, she'd heard he had gone to Kent, but he could return to London and reveal her secret at any time. And when he did, the revelation that Alex had presented a guttersnipe as a real lady would crush his chances for a political appointment. The scandal might also send her to the country to live alone, or, worse yet, she thought as she moved to the library doors, he might divorce her.

The realization that she might be cut off from Alex and never see him again made her weak. No, she resolved, closing the library doors and locking them behind her, that tragedy must never happen. *Never.*

After attending a stuffy society luncheon the next day, Pell changed into a candy-striped day dress, then paced about the drawing room for the better part of the after-noon, worrying about Alex's financial problems and her own secret past. Plagued with jitters since her shocking discovery in the library, she sank down on the sofa and sighed with relief when the maid brought tea at four o'clock. After the girl poured the strong brew, Pell raised a cup to her lips with trembling fingers in the hope of calming her nerves and resting a bit, for she was to attend the opera that evening. She was just about to send away a tray of small sandwiches and iced cakes when Buxley en-tered the room and announced, "Lady Lilly Harrington is here to see you, milady."

The announcement disturbed her, for she desperately wanted to be alone, but before she could tell Buxley she wasn't receiving this afternoon, Lilly sailed into the room dressed in a burnt-orange dress that flattered neither her sallow face nor sticklike figure. Pell knew Lilly meant no harm, but as with so many debutantes, gossip was her only recreation. Realizing she was trapped like a fly on a pin, Pell smiled at the girl who swiftly claimed a seat next to her on the settee and launched into a stream of mindless chatter.

"Did you see what Lord Chettleham's daughter was wearing the other night at Lady Chanley's party?" Lilly asked, batting her eyes. "I loved the gown and asked her for the name of her dressmaker, but she wouldn't tell me!"

"No . . . we were still in the Cotswolds. Unfortunately I missed the party." Pell mumbled, expecting Lilly to rattle on for hours. At times Pell harbored pity for the girl, but now, when she had so much on her mind, she ached for her to be gone. In the East End, she would have asked her to leave, but as the Countess of Tavistock she must offend no one, even wearisome Lilly.

"Oh, my gracious . . . that's right. You *were* out of London, weren't you? You've missed so much," Lilly said, arching her colorless brows. "Things change so fast in society. Just yesterday I heard some interesting news about Claude."

Pell's heart lurched, then raced frantically. "Claude?" she echoed weakly.

"Yes, he's back in London now." Lilly leaned toward her, and her usually dull eyes held a spark of excitement. "You will never believe what has happened. Never!"

Pell could only sit there wondering if Claude had already revealed her past. "Yes . . . go on," she prompted in a wavering voice.

"Claude has married Sabrina Fairchild. They were wed two days ago. Can you believe it!"

Fear rocked through Pell and the cup and saucer clattered together in her hand. "Sabrina Fairchild?" she whispered, managing to place the china on the tea table. "I never expected that alliance."

"I know! There's *years* between them, but it seems while you were in the Cotswolds he started courting her."

Pell knew the news must have disappointed Lilly, though the girl now seemed more enthralled than upset.

Lilly crossed her arms and sighed heavily. "I'll never understand why Claude just disappeared from London so quickly," she whined. "And now that he's back why did he marry Sabrina Fairchild?"

Of course, Pell understood everything perfectly. She understood that Claude had decided that if he couldn't marry Pell for her fortune, he would marry Sabrina's. But she tried to make her face seem blank and disinterested. "I have no idea why they would wed. It does seem a bit strange, doesn't it?"

"Yes, it does. It's for money, I suppose. I hear Sabrina has sold some of her jewelry to buy Claude a studio and finance a great art show he's having soon. There will be a lavish reception and everyone of importance is invited." A puzzled look raced across the girl's face. "I wonder why she had to resort to selling jewelry. I understand that General Fairchild was very wealthy."

Pell held her tongue, knowing that Sabrina had to sell her jewelry because Mr. Peebles had her on a tight budget just like herself.

"You made a grand catch," Lilly said. "But where does that leave me? I always thought that Claude cared for me, then he suddenly marries Sabrina Fairchild of all people!"

Lilly's voice faded into the background as Pell realized that the worst thing that could possibly happen had actually taken place. From their encounter at the Duchess of Roxbury's, Sabrina already suspected that Pell was the general's by-blow, and since she had married Claude, she undoubtedly knew for sure. The picture of Claude sprawled on the platform in front of the Continental train, his face smeared with blood, his dazed eyes sick with hate, flashed into Pell's mind.

As Lilly babbled on in an inane manner, Pell sat quietly, trying to conceal her trembling hands. Thinking of the marriage of Claude and Sabrina almost made her physically ill: the two people who hated her and Alex the most had joined ranks to seek revenge. Drawing in a long, steadying breath, she told herself that their future looked treacherous indeed.

Chapter 21

That evening Pell glanced at her reflection in one of the gilt-framed mirrors in her bedroom, noticing her milk-white face and frightened eyes. As she tugged on long white gloves of the softest kidskin, she studied the gown she was going to wear to the opera. Cut by a master hand, the cream-colored creation glistened with heavy embroidery. The bustle was fashionably large and the neckline low, revealing the perfection of her throat and shoulders. A maid had artfully arranged her hair, and her silvery curls were sleekly drawn back to cascade over the nape of her neck and tumble down her back. Brilliants sparkled among her curls, making them even glossier. Draped over a chair, an opera cape gleamed softly in the lamplight.

Yes, thought Pell, as she moved to her vanity and sat down, Alex had provided her with a magnificent creation for the gala opera—but the costly ensemble could not hide the fact that she was miserable and terrified. Having him by her side would have made her feel better, but he had an important speech to write that he must present to the House of Lords tomorrow, and had insisted that Aunt Violet take his seat beside her in the Covent Garden Opera House.

Pell picked up her rouge brush and dabbed at her cheeks, trying to give herself a bit of color. She had just lived through the worst afternoon of her life. She wanted to share her concerns about Claude and Sabrina with Alex, but was afraid to do so, because she didn't want to reveal that she had been foolish enough to tell her secret to the artist. She guessed that financial problems plagued Alex's mind, for he had been quiet and moody when he returned home that evening. Lord, what a tangle everything was in, and how upset she was! How on earth could she go to the opera to face the elite of London society when she felt like this?

"Are you ready, dear?"

Aunt Violet was standing at the open bedroom door. She was wearing her blue-and-purple gown from the coming-out ball, and had added a purple opera cape for the occasion.

Giving a weary sigh, Pell hung her head. "I don't feel well tonight. I . . . I have a headache and feel the sniffles coming on." She turned about on the vanity chair and gave the older woman a tremulous smile. "Why don't you go on without me this evening?"

Aunt Violet placed her gloved hand on her shoulder. "Are you sure you aren't just depressed, dear?" She glanced down in embarrassment, then looked up again. "You've seemed out of sorts lately." She caressed Pell's shoulder. "If you get out, it might do you a bit of good. You know . . . cheer you up." With a thoughtful look, she tapped a gloved finger on her cheek. "Let's see now. I think they're doing *The Marriage of Figaro.*" She fluttered her eyelashes. "No, that isn't right. Maybe it's *Don Giovanni,* or *The Magic Flute.*"

"It's *Lucia di Lammermoor,*" Pell murmured.

"Oh, yes. Now I remember," Aunt Violet responded cheerfully. "You'll love that one, dear. It has brilliant arias for the coloratura singer!"

Pell sighed again. "I don't know. I'm just so tired."

Aunt Violet patted her shoulder. "Well, why don't you just think about it for a while? There's a little time before we have to leave."

After the old lady had gone, Pell looked at herself in the mirror again and then lowered her head into her hands.

Alex stood at the open bedroom door gazing at her as

she sat before the vanity. His first impression was how strikingly beautiful she was in the dramatic opera gown with the lamplight washing over it and the brilliants in her hair. But his next thought was how every curve of her body spoke of despair. When he moved toward her, she turned about, her eyes large with surprise.

"Aunt Violet tells me you have the vapors tonight," he said gently.

She straightened her back and raised her chin, but he felt she was holding her emotions together by sheer force of will.

"Yes," she said dully. "I'm afraid I really don't feel like going."

Lifting her dainty chin, he gazed into her troubled eyes. "I think something else is wrong. Don't you want to tell me about it?" he asked softly.

Pell bit her lip in indecision. She wanted to tell him that Claude and Sabrina were married, but as the sentence burned on her lips, she realized that it might bring up some embarrassing past history. And after what she had discovered in the locked library yesterday, she wondered if he would stand by her once the scandal broke, as she was sure it would. Still she was nauseous with worry, as she had been since Lilly's visit, and felt an overpowering urge to confide in him. Swallowing back her fear, she ventured, "Lilly came to visit this afternoon. She . . . she told me that Claude Dubois and Sabrina Fairchild were married two days ago." She remained motionless, her heart racing as she waited for his reaction.

Alex was quiet as he considered the potentially dangerous situation. Sabrina had said nothing about the marriage in her letter, and that surprised him. Still it didn't necessarily spell disaster. The widow was clever indeed, and he knew Claude wouldn't flinch at betrayal, but he felt confident that Pell had been discreet about her past. From the very beginning they had both understood that it was a matter of the utmost secrecy, and in a way, the secret itself had bonded them together. Pell would never break such a private trust.

At last he flicked a thoughtful gaze over her. "I can see why the news would surprise you, and even hurt you after your association with Claude, but I don't think it's anything you should be concerned about. General Fairchild's wealth was a legend in London, so it's easy to see why Claude would be determined to win Sabrina's hand. I suggest you take heart and go on about your business with confidence." He smiled at her. "After all, even though Claude tried to take you to Paris, he still thinks you're from the north. He knows nothing about your past."

Pell ached to clutch his hand and spill out the truth—but she just couldn't. "Can't you go to the opera?" she asked lamely.

Alex sighed, and began to pace the carpet, feeling a surge of guilt. The opera tonight was a big occasion, and he had intended to escort Pell, but an important bit of legislation had arisen that made it impossible. "No, I'm afraid I can't," he said at last. "I must finish my work. It's the first thing on the agenda tomorrow." He walked back to her and caressed her cheek. "For some reason, you seem unaccountably nervous tonight. Don't forget, Aunt Violet will be with you. Just relax and enjoy the opera."

Pell raised her eyebrows. "I'm afraid it's hard for me to relax at these great occasions. I'm afraid if people learn of my past, they'll send me back where I came from."

Alex chuckled softly. "Don't worry. They can't do that."

She looked up at him. "Maybe not physically, but they can do it mentally. People would be horrified if they knew about my mother and the circumstances of my birth."

Alex sighed again and ran his hands over her smooth arms, then took her hand and helped her to her feet. "And why should they ever know? I insist you go to Covent Garden and enjoy yourself."

Pell hung her head, and when she looked back at him, her eyes glistened with an emotion that touched his heart.

"Sometimes I wish I could just *resign* from society," she said miserably.

He looked down at her and chuckled. "Everyone has wished that at some time in their life, but I'm afraid it's impossible, love. In fact, in the military that kind of thing is called desertion, and society in general takes a dim view of deserters." He picked up her opera cape and gently placed it about her shoulders. Then he kissed her softly on the lips and escorted her to the bedroom door.

Outside the Covent Garden Opera House, the long line of carriages that extended in a westward direction down Long Acre slowly moved under the great portico. Alex's brougham was almost at the entrance, and as Pell looked from the carriage window she caught a glimpse of laughing faces and flashing satins as ladies and gentlemen stepped from their carriages. The police had kept a passage clear for the equipages, but she noticed a group of white-faced slum children crowded about the base of the opera steps, selling flowers and listlessly watching the proceedings.

When their carriage slowed and halted, the door was immediately opened, and a liveried attendant helped Pell and Aunt Violet alight to the paving stones. There was the sound of slamming carriage doors and the clatter of wheels over the cobbles behind them, and as the old lady and Pell walked toward the imposing steps, a ragged girl moved to her side and looked up with imploring eyes.

"Buy my violets, miss?" the girl asked, holding out a little twist of purple violets wrapped with colored paper. "They're very fresh, they are!" Pell's eyes misted with emotion as the last half year flashed through her mind. For a moment she was not the Countess of Tavistock, but the ragged child before her. It seemed utterly impossible that only a few months ago she had stood in front of the great theatre herself, selling fruit to the ladies after they left the opera.

To her, at that time, the women had seemed almost like

goddesses, and she had looked at them as the girl now looked at her, with worshipful eyes. Would she be unmasked tonight as what she really was, a person who belonged to the same class as the indigent waif, not the aristocrat she pretended to be?

While Aunt Violet patiently waited, Pell opened her reticule and pressed a pound note into the child's slender hand, knowing she had probably not eaten all day. The girl's face glowed with happiness as Pell smiled and took the proffered blooms. "Thank ye, miss. God bless ye, miss!" she cried with a little curtsy before she hurried away.

Aunt Violet gave Pell a tender smile. "That was nice, dear. You're very thoughtful that way."

As they moved ahead, Pell gazed about in astonishment at the throng moving up the steps beside them, and, despite her elegant evening ensemble, she felt her confidence ebbing away. Inside the great vestibule, which was supported by marble pillars and lit by glittering chandeliers, Pell saw diplomats, and rich Americans, and a throng of aristocrats, and she was almost overwhelmed by the magnificence that surrounded her. It seemed as if all of London had come to one great party to end the season and she knew she was witnessing one of the most brilliant social spectacles in Europe. There was the bustle and confusion of gentlemen taking off their top hats, and the floaty sweep of chiffon, as with an air of excitement couples gathered in groups and prepared to go to the stairs leading to their boxes.

As she and Aunt Violet walked up the stairs to Alex's box, Pell spoke to a lady she knew, and the woman turned her head the other way. Alarm rippled through her, but being in a social situation was always difficult, and she wondered if she had addressed the woman incorrectly.

Once in the box, she glanced down at the great auditorium, and as people exchanged pleasantries and gossiped, light laughter sparkled through the audience. Then as she moved to the front of the box, heads turned her way and a tense silence fell. The crowd began to rustle again only after Pell had seated herself.

Her heart beat a little faster as she glanced across the auditorium at the opposite boxes. Several of the ladies spread their fans, then, still looking at her, leaned their heads together in conversation, and the men who stood behind them gazed at her with strange looks in their eyes.

By now, the theatre was full and the orchestra was tuning up fitfully for the prelude to *Lucia di Lammermoor.* Nervousness rising within her, Pell clutched Aunt Violet's hand. "I know something is wrong," she whispered. "Something is very amiss. I can feel it in the air . . . and everyone is staring at me."

The old lady patted her hand. "Nonsense, dear. They're simply looking at you because you're breathtaking."

For the next few minutes Pell was hardly conscious of her actions, but she tried to answer Aunt Violet's questions about various people in the crowd, hoping her words were making sense. Then as she glanced about, nervously twisting the stem of the little violet bouquet in her fingers, she saw Claude and Sabrina sitting together, and her heart lurched painfully. At that moment all her strength and confidence drained away.

Dressed in his usual Bohemian style, Claude looked as dapper as ever, and as he smiled at her the soft houselights gleamed over his golden hair and twinkled from his diamond rings. Sabrina wore a gown of coral satin with a matching cape whose every seam bespoke elegance. With her dark hair, sophisticated features, and the emeralds about her neck, she stood out in the crowd like an exotic flower.

When Sabrina stood and locked eyes with her, a wild panic rose within Pell, but she found herself automatically giving her a polite nod. She looked at Claude as the widow passed in front of him, the same Claude who had given her the sentimental locket with his photograph and pledged his undying love. At that moment, she felt his betrayal again as strongly as she had the night she had read the detective's letter.

Pell stared in astonishment as the general's widow quickly moved down the aisle. Their eyes met again for a moment, but Sabrina's expression was too enigmatic to read. A feeling of dread flowed through Pell. Dropping her violets to the floor, she clutched the velvety armrest and glanced at Aunt Violet. "We must go!" she whispered in a strangled voice.

The old lady looked at her quizzically. "But why, dear? They'll be starting the prelude soon, and it's so beautiful."

Pell stood on trembling legs. *"Please,"* she said wretchedly.

By now the old lady looked quite alarmed, and began to rise slowly from her seat—but too late, for Pell heard footsteps in the hall outside the box, and a moment later, Sabrina pushed back the velvety drapes and made her entrance.

As their gazes locked, alarm raced through her, and Pell felt her heart fluttering in her breast like a trapped butterfly. Her hands as cold as ice, she tried to raise her chin a little higher, but the intense look in Sabrina's eyes made her gasp.

"So nice to see you again, Countess," Sabrina said smoothly, slowly running her gaze over her. "After your marriage you seemed to disappear, so I took the liberty of coming to your box because I wanted to offer my wishes for your happiness." Sabrina's eyes flickered over her in cool appraisal, and there was something about the expression on her beautiful face that made Pell feel sick.

Suddenly the widow drew something from the folds of her skirt. It was a magazine. Sabrina opened it and offered it to Pell. "I saw such an amusing cartoon in the *Tomahawk,* which just came out today. I thought you might be interested." Her voice sharpened as she went on, "The cartoonist is really quite clever. His work is the talk of London."

Pell knew the *Tomahawk,* which rivaled *Punch* for its

rapier wit and was popular with the smart set who spent their time around the Prince of Wales. Not knowing how to refuse, she took the magazine with trembling hands. Her thoughts were in such disarray that she could scarcely make sense of the print on the page, but the cartoon leaped out at her, and as she stared at it, her eyes filled with tears.

The piece pictured a newly married couple coming down the steps of a great cathedral, the handsome man in groom's finery, and the bride in tattered rags. The groom's face looked exactly like Alex's, and the blonde bride resembled her. The caption at the bottom of the cartoon said, *The earl takes a wife.*

With a shudder, Pell let the magazine drop to the box seat, and, covering her mouth with both hands, let out a soft sob.

A look of triumph suffused Sabrina's lovely face as she added, "As you know, Mr. Peebles will read Phillip's will in a few days. After everyone sees this cartoon and reads the accompanying article, their support will be entirely with me, and I suspect you will get nothing." Her eyes glittered like the emeralds at her throat. "You see," she said in cool tones, "we of the *true* aristocracy don't like those who try to hide their past and deceive us."

Pell wanted to challenge Sabrina, but the utter shock of it all caused the words to catch in her throat. No wonder the woman she had met on the stairs hadn't spoken to her, and everyone had looked at her so strangely. Everyone knew. *Absolutely everyone.* Claude and Sabrina had obviously gone to the magazine with the story, realizing that it would be the best way to destroy Alex and win popular opinion to their side.

She was sure the pair was even tonight busy broadcasting the details behind the cartoon. Soon all of Mayfair would know the whole story. She was now the laughingstock of the *ton*, and although he didn't realize it yet, so was Alex. To think of others mocking him was almost more than she could bear. And the worst of it all was that she had brought the scandal upon him, by telling Claude her secret.

Through a veil of tears, she saw Sabrina smile vindictively. The woman's meanness tore at her heart. To her consternation, she found that although she tried to speak, words would not come from her mouth, and the great theatre with its glittering patrons swam before her eyes. For a moment she thought she might faint, but with great concentration she managed to stand; she noticed, too, the expression of victory on Sabrina's face before she left. Pell clutched the back of the seat for support.

"Oh, love, you're as pale as a sheet," Aunt Violet said. "Don't worry, I'll take care of you."

For a moment Pell's breath caught in her lungs, and she stared at her, speechless. Then she finally managed to gather her cape and reticule. "We have . . . to go . . ." she whispered as she left the box. As Pell rushed down the stairs, Aunt Violet finally caught up with her and clutched her hand. Half-turning to clasp her plump arm, Pell cried, "Oh, Aunt Violet, they know! Everyone in London knows . . . My secret is out!"

Slamming the carriage door behind him, Alex stepped to the paving stones and made his way to the entrance of the Covent Garden Opera House. Dressed in dark evening clothes, he quickly walked up the marble steps that were now almost empty. After the ladies had left, he had gone to his desk to work, but found that thoughts of Pell's worried face so filled his mind that he couldn't think. Obviously she had been deeply troubled, and he wanted to help her, whatever her problem might be. What did it matter that he hadn't finished his work, he thought philosophically. Perhaps he could have the presentation rescheduled, or plead illness. This evening, his place was with Pell.

It was intermission, and ladies and gentlemen engaged in light conversation crowded the ornate vestibule. But as Alex walked among them, looking at the ladies' tightly corseted figures, smooth arms, and gleaming hair, he could

not find Pell. When a bell chimed, announcing that the
opera would soon be resuming, couples started making
their way to the auditorium. Some of the ladies gave him
strange looks, and he missed the gentlemen's bluff greetings, but his mind preoccupied with Pell, he lightly passed
off the social slights.

On his way up the cigar-scented stairs, Alex smiled,
thinking how surprised she would be to see him. He would
just quietly slip into the box, sit down beside her, and take
her hand. After the opera, he would take her and Aunt Violet to one of his favorite restaurants for a midnight meal
before they went back to Mayfair. Feeling much better
about the evening, he continued up the stairs with a feeling
of expectation, then smiled as he pushed back the drape to
enter his box.

He frowned when he saw that the box was empty, but
then, chuckling, told himself that he had probably missed
Pell and Aunt Violet in the packed vestibule. They would
be arriving at any moment. When he walked to the front
of the box, his gaze rested upon a little bouquet of violets
on the floor. Warmth stirring in his chest, he picked them
up, knowing Pell had bought them from one of the Cockney girls who sold flowers outside the opera house. How
he loved that part of her, he thought. That loving part of
her that always thought of the other person and how she
could help.

Sitting down, he noticed something in the seat next to
him that on first glance appeared to be an opera program.
He picked it up and turned it over, realizing that it was a
copy of the *Tomahawk,* a scandal sheet read by those
whose lives were so empty they lived through others vicar-
iously. He began to thumb idly through it, wondering what
the magazine was doing in his box.

Then he came upon the cartoon. The shock of discovery
hit him full force. He blinked, scarcely able to believe his
eyes. As he studied the cartoon and read the short article
beneath it, rage rose within him like a hot tide. How dare
the publisher print such a vile, damning piece of trash!

How dare he print something that could utterly ruin two lives!

His heart thudding in his chest, he thought of Pell, and, with a shaft of deep pain, knew exactly what had happened. Someone in the audience had presented her with the magazine. No doubt she and Aunt Violet had fled, leaving the thing behind them. Guilt flashed over him as he recalled that he had almost forced her to attend the spectacle tonight and had originally declined to go himself.

Outrage almost cutting off his breath, he scanned the audience, noticing that everyone was looking at him with interest. He had often thought how exposed a person appeared in a box—it was almost like being on the stage itself. And he now realized that many in the audience had been watching him as he looked through the magazine. With a surge of pain, he realized that Pell had undergone the same torture.

His gaze moved from face to face until he found the people he was looking for—Sabrina and Claude, sitting together, looking his way with a smile on their faces. When their gazes met, Claude's eyes gleamed with satisfaction, and Sabrina nodded formally, her smile widening. He knew *he* was really the target of Sabrina's malice, for without his assistance Pell could never have claimed a part of the general's fortune. How clever she was! She knew he didn't give a damn for society himself, but she had wounded him by humiliating Pell.

He met her eyes evenly until she had the grace to look downward, then he transferred his gaze to Claude, who after a few tense moments also looked away. Only then did Alex clutch the magazine in his hand and leave the box, his only thoughts of Pell.

Less than an hour later, Alex arrived home. As he laid his top hat on the table in the entry, he could hear both Aunt Violet's concerned voice and Hadji's agitated tones floating from the drawing room. Quickening his pace, he walked toward the chamber, wondering in what condition he would find Pell.

As he entered the room, three pairs of eyes fastened on him with surprise. Still dressed in her gorgeous opera gown, Pell half-reclined on a brocade sofa, sipping strong tea, while Aunt Violet sat beside her, patting her hand. His face distressed, Hadji stood nearby, holding a china pot, waiting to refill the cup. Quickly surveying Pell, Alex noticed that her face was ashen, and she looked very shaken.

When he neared the sofa, Aunt Violet rose and gazed at him with teary eyes. "Oh, Alex," she lamented in a broken voice as she twisted her lace handkerchief in her hands. "Buxley said you went to the opera. How I wish you could have arrived before . . ." Her voice trailed off, then, with a little sob, she added, "It was terrible. Absolutely terrible. I don't know how the woman could have done such a thing!"

With a sigh, he looked at her and nodded, then placed the magazine on the tea table, studying Pell's stricken face.

The old lady cleared her throat and glanced at Hadji, then darted a gaze at the open doors. Reading her signal, he set down the teapot and they both left the room.

Alex took Pell's cold hand and sat down beside her. "Are you all right?" he asked, tenderly brushing back a strand of her silky hair.

"Yes, I suppose so. Just a little shaken. It was all so sudden . . . and Sabrina seemed to take such joy in showing me the article." She glanced at the magazine on the table. "I see you found the *Tomahawk* in the box."

She watched his eyes darken with anger as he nodded. "Yes, I've seen it," he replied in a harsh tone. "I had no idea Sabrina would stoop to something like this."

"She said the aristocracy would be on her side now," Pell went on, remembering the look of triumph on Sabrina's face. "She said she would get all the inheritance."

Alex shook his head. "Some may favor her, but the will is binding. No amount of public opinion can change that."

As Alex stood and moved away from the sofa, deep lines furrowed his brow. "Damn Sabrina's impertinence anyway," he said roughly. "I knew she suspected you were the general's daughter, but I still don't know how she found out for sure ... where she got her information. That blasted article is full of personal things about you." He ran a questioning gaze over her. "Did the woman tell you who the informant was? Possibly one of your teachers or a servant?"

For a moment Pell felt an urge to escape the room, then she told herself she must tell Alex the truth. Drawing in a shuddering breath, she gathered up her courage and began speaking with quivering lips, wondering if he would divorce her when she was finished.

"One person knows the truth," she said in a soft voice, "because I told him."

Shock flashed on his face and his eyes looked hard for a moment. "Who, for God's sake?"

She trembled and her heart thudded under his gaze, but she knew she must answer. "Claude Dubois. I told him before ... we tried to elope in France."

Alex pulled in a sharp breath and gave her a look of utter disbelief. He stood frozen for a moment, then strode to the window and yanked back the drapes, staring at the darkness with crossed arms.

After a moment which seemed like an eternity, he slowly turned from the window, his gaze bold and overpowering. "I can't believe you would tell Claude about your past," he finally said.

Her heart ached as she gazed at him, but at the same time she felt a rush of relief that she had unburdened her conscience. "Yes ... I realize it was a terrible mistake," she admitted a little defensively. But then as she studied his angry eyes, her spirit bridled at the society that made such secrecy necessary in the first place. "But why does society have to be so cruel, so unjust, so unforgiving?" she asked in a broken voice.

He gave her a sardonic smile. "What did you expect?

Despite their genteel manners, the aristocracy has a simple code: loyalty to each other and old traditions, and a staggering hatred toward social bounders. Don't you see that we've mocked what they hold dearest, and made fools of the lot of them?"

Trembling with emotion, she could only stare at him, at a loss for words.

He moved from the window, passing an appraising gaze over her. "You'll now have to summon your courage and prepare to face everyone down. General Fairchild won several great victories for England, and in that regard was extremely popular. There is the possibility that if you fulfill your duty as a lady, people will forget your past."

Anger began to seethe within her. Even now, as everything was crashing down about them, he'd put on his imperturbable front. She knew he had to be furious with her. Why didn't he shake her or berate her?

Her pulse fluttering, she rose and walked toward him. "Is that all you ever think of?" she asked. "Fulfilling duties?" She crossed her arms. "I should never have tried to be a lady. I don't like tea parties and mindless balls. And every time I put on a silk dress I get my heel caught in the hem. I say the wrong things and do the wrong things." She swept a gaze over him. "And how do you think I feel, pretending to be what I'm not?"

He gave her a cool glance. "Everyone, no matter what their rank, must find their own purpose in life. The problem isn't confined to one class."

"You know what your problem is, Alex?" she said defiantly, gaining confidence as she spoke. "You know everything, but you *believe* nothing. You keep your emotions marching along in lockstep."

"What's that supposed to mean?" he asked smoothly.

A warning bell rang in the back of her mind, but she ignored it and went on, unable to stop herself. "I know about your secret. I know what you and Mr. Potterfield were discussing behind closed doors in the Cotswolds. I know that pictures were removed from the walls of

Stanton Hall while we were there and sold. And I know that the servants have not worn new liveries in years because there is no money in the family coffers!" She placed her hands on her hips, abandoning herself to her pent-up frustration. "You turned your self-control into an important advantage, didn't you? In fact, I'm sure it's the important quality that enabled you to marry a rich guttersnipe like me."

"Silence!" he commanded in a soft steely voice that was more intimidating than any harangue.

"Ah, I see I'm hitting close to the truth," she rushed on, now in too far to retrieve herself. "Yes, I know about your pressing creditors. And I know that you married me because you needed my inheritance."

He came close, passing an incredulous gaze over her. "How could you possibly think that? If I'm so honor-bound, as you suggest, how in God's name could you possibly come up with that idea?"

"Because you tried to hide your financial situation, and turned me aside every time I asked you a question about your personal business. Besides that, I've seen the mountain of bills on your desk."

He gazed at her with unbelieving eyes. "You actually searched the library?"

"Yes. You wouldn't have shown it to me any other way, would you?"

A dark look passed over his face that tore at her heart, and she wished that she hadn't confronted him with the accusation. But she had been so disturbed, the words just sprang from her lips.

He studied her for a long moment. "I'm going to stay at the Carlton tonight." His voice simmered with anger, and as he walked past her with cool dignity, she repressed an urge to call him back. Halfway across the room, he paused to gaze at her again, and for a moment, she thought he might speak. But then he walked to the drawing-room doors.

As she watched his large frame move over the threshold, she felt a sharp sense of loss spread through her body, and, when he was gone, regrets assailed her. Quivering inside, she sat down on the brocade sofa once more, and, closing her eyes, laid back her head, trying to control her surging emotions.

She hadn't meant to taunt Alex, but she was so filled with rage and frustration she couldn't help herself. "Why do I always say the wrong things to him?" she muttered in a broken voice. "Why don't I understand him better after all these months!"

A sinking tiredness rolling over her, she thought how much better off he would have been if he'd never met her—or her eccentric father who had the temerity to think that he could force society to accept his bastard daughter. *Oh, Alex,* she thought, forcing back her tears, *I've ruined your life forever.*

Then, with a stab of pain, she realized that perhaps she had not. If she were to disappear, perhaps he could eventually live down the scandal and in several years obtain an annulment or divorce and begin a new life. As long as he was married to her, he would never get a political appointment, and despite herself, she would keep on doing things to embarrass him.

True, it would take many years for society to forget the "Whitechapel Countess," but they eventually might . . . if she was not around to remind them of the scandal every time they saw her. Her heart constricting with anguish, she realized that to save Alex, she must do what she had dreaded most.

She must leave him.

Chapter 22

The scent of axle grease and densely packed human beings wafting about her, Pell jostled along on an omnibus as it made its way to the East End. Clutching a satchel in her lap that contained a blouse and skirt and a few personal belongings, she stared across the aisle of the horse-drawn vehicle, her mind in such turmoil, she hardly saw the other passengers.

She could scarcely believe that she had really left Mayfair. Once she decided to go, how simple it had all been! Feeling a bit devious for doing so, she had told Aunt Violet she needed to leave the house to divert her mind from the horrible evening, and would not be back until dinner. Knowing that Alex would not be home until that evening at the earliest, she had secretly packed a few things and simply walked to Hyde Park and waited for an omnibus, the same vehicle Rosie used when she came to visit her.

She thought of her old friend, knowing how surprised she would be to see her again. And she thought about the uproar her disappearance would cause when it was discovered. And Alex . . . Undoubtedly he would be upset. But would he truly miss her? Or would he heave a secret sigh of relief?

When the omnibus slowed and stopped at the corner of Martin Street and Cat and Wheel Alley, Pell stood, maneuvered her satchel between the passengers, and left the vehicle. A huge knot of emotion lodged in her throat as she watched the omnibus slowly move away, then slip into the noisy traffic. She had slept little the night before and the vanishing omnibus touched her emotions, vividly dramatizing the fact that she had chosen to turn her back on the West End and all that it represented.

Taking a deep breath and squaring her shoulders, she told herself she must control her weakening spirits. She hadn't been away from the East End so long that she had forgotten that living there required a certain emotional toughness.

With a resigned sigh, she hoisted up her satchel and started walking down Cat and Wheel Alley. As the inhabitants returned to their wretched homes for the midday meal, a host of almost forgotten sensations assaulted her eyes, and ears . . . and her heart. She looked at the tenements, knowing that inside each of them were families bound together in joy and pain, living on little more than hope alone.

The street crawled with humanity; beggars and sharpers crowded the entrance to the tall tenements. Used to the well-fed residents of Mayfair, the thin laborers reminded her of an army of gray ghosts. Thunder rumbled overhead as she trudged into the press of people, and a raindrop soon plopped down on her head, then another, and another, bringing with them the sweet scent of rain.

A rough-looking fellow with gin on his breath grunted and pushed her aside. "Watch where yer goin', girl. Are ye blind?"

Angry, she watched the man stride away. Then she told herself she had chosen to return to Whitechapel, and in doing so had traded away all those fine good manners she had once scoffed at, but now took as a matter of course.

The handle of the heavy satchel cutting into her hand, she walked ahead. In the low gray weather, the alley looked almost unbearably lonely.

Rain peppered down faster and plastered her hair to her scalp as she neared Rosie's tenement. Half its slate roof gone, the building's roof soared toward the smooth gray sky. In the yard that had been packed hard by hundreds of shuffling feet, a few weeds bravely struggled upward. An old woman sat on the stoop looking like a heavy sack of flour with a string tied in the middle. Lost to the world, she brought a bottle of gin to her lips.

Struggling with her cumbersome satchel, Pell entered the building's dark stairwell, knowing that Rosie wouldn't be home yet. As her feet creaked over the loose steps, she paused every now and then to catch her breath, noticing the familiar scents of dust and urine, both intensified by the heavy, moist air.

On the fifth-floor landing she dropped the satchel and pulled out a loose brick in the wall by Rosie's door. With trembling fingers, she searched the niche where she and Rosie used to hide the key; finding it, a sense of relief flooded over her and she opened the creaking door.

She surveyed the musty room, hoping against hope that it would look different than the last time she saw it—but, like the alley outside the broken window, it didn't. Paper hung from the wall in strips; a carpet made of mats covered the rotting floor; and an open trunk filled with cheap clothing sat in one corner of the room. Until Alex had taken her out of Holloway House of Detention, this had been Pell's home—a hovel furnished with a few rickety pieces of furniture, one sagging bed, and odd bits of pottery.

She closed the door behind her, placed the satchel on the floor, and plopped down into a threadbare chair. Her heart still thudding from the long walk and the climb up the stairs, she sat there for a while, listening to rain pour down the loose guttering and plunk into the jars Rosie always kept on the mantel to catch fresh water. When a drop splashed on her skirt, Pell looked up at the patched ceiling. Rain and smoke from the defective chimney stained the peeling mass. Lord, she had hardly noticed it when she lived here, she thought with a sigh.

Despair tugging at her heart, she laid back her head and felt a tear seep from the corner of her eye. Angrily rubbing it away, she told herself she couldn't be breaking down, for she had to put on a brave front for Rosie as well as herself. Trying to lift her spirits, she counted her assets: she was young and had her health and a fortune coming, and as soon as she was rested and stronger she would consider what to do with the rest of her life. Right now, she just needed a chance to heal.

Hearing brisk footsteps on the stairwell, Pell raised her head and stood. She smoothed down her damp, wrinkled shirtwaist dress, realizing that her friend had decided to come home after lunch. The door flew open and Rosie burst into the room. Seeing Pell, she dropped the basket of fruit she held in her hand, sending apples and peaches rolling over the floor. "Pell," she murmured in a hushed tone. "Bless my liver! Whot in the name of God are you doin' 'ere, girl?"

Pell moved toward her old friend. "I've left Alex," she said in a quiet voice, "and I didn't know where to go. Can I stay here for a while?"

Rosie stood frozen at the door for a moment, then, slamming it behind her, rushed to Pell, and started wiping moisture from the younger woman's face and hair with the end of her long white apron. "My poor little bird," she muttered, leading her to the table and plopping her down on a rickety chair. "'Ere, jest sit down and tell me all about it, luv." Rosie ceased blotting Pell's face for a moment, then, looking embarrassed said, "I'm sorry, luv, but I had to tell the professor about you and that Frenchie. I just couldn't let you ruin your life that way!"

Pell hadn't seen Rosie since the day they had said goodbye in Hyde Park, but she felt as if she had just spoken to her yesterday. She clasped her friend's rough hand. "Don't worry. You . . . you did the right thing. Claude turned out to be a cad," she said bitterly, remembering the night at Victoria Station. "He was a fraud. Charming and gay and fun to be with—but in the end he was a fraud and nothing more."

Tears glistened in Rosie's faded eyes. "You forgive me then?"

A smile trembled on Pell's lips. "There's nothing to forgive. We're mates . . . remember?"

A look of relief flooded Rosie's plain face, then, brightening up, she hurried to the small blackened fireplace and stacked up a small pile of kindling. "Since it's turned autumn, it's gone chilly and wet on us, ain't it? Why don't we just 'ave a nice cuppa and talk about whot's troublin' you?" she suggested as she found a match and lit the kindling, setting it ablaze.

"I knows you and the professor were married," she went on, filling a kettle with water and setting it on the grate above the crackling fire. "Someone whot lives on Cat and Wheel Alley read about it in the *Times* and told me. I was worried sick the professor would be too late, and I was real relieved when I found out 'e was marryin' you, instead of that Claude bloke." She gazed at Pell, then lowered her eyes. "I wanted to give you a little gift or somethin', but you bein' a countess, and me bein' whot I am, it didn't seem proper. And . . . I didn't know 'ow you felt about me tellin' the professor about you skippin' out on 'im."

Pell felt tears gather in the back of her throat and she held out her hand to Rosie.

The older woman took it and sat down beside her. "Now whot's this silliness about you leavin' the professor?" She ran her eyes over Pell. "Gaa, I can't believe it. You're a countess now. A bleedin' countess! Countesses don't disappear like flower girls. You can't leave 'im. You just can't."

Pell gazed at the wavering glow the fire cast over the wretched chamber. "It's over," she said dully, slipping away her hand.

Rosie frowned and raised her chin. "'Ow do you know it's over? 'As 'e told you so?"

Pell swallowed the lump in her throat. "No . . . but I know it is," she answered, her tremulous voice breaking with emotion.

The fruit-peddler stood and began pacing about the table, her eyes flashing. "'E loves you, bird. A blind man could see it!"

"*Loved* might be a better word," Pell suggested, her tone hardening with frustration. "And I'm not sure if even that is right. There is a possibility that he loved me before the scandal," she said sadly, remembering their heartrending discussion last night.

Rosie shot her an incredulous look. "Scandal? Whot are you talkin' about?"

Pell stared at the woman's confused face, then pulled a copy of the *Tomahawk* from her satchel. "Sabrina Fairchild gave this to me at the opera yesterday evening ... and Alex has seen it, too. I'm sure all of London is laughing about the cartoon," she explained, opening the magazine.

Her eyes glittering, Rosie took the magazine herself and read the caption under the cartoon, her lips moving silently. With a burst of anger, she threw it on the floor. "There oughts to be a law against printin' such trash!" she ground out. Her face softened and she took her friend's hand again. "Don't worry, luv. 'E'll stand by you."

Pell's shoulders slumped and she pressed her lips together. "I'm not sure if he will or not, and I don't want to hold my breath every day, wondering if I'll humiliate him." She drew in a long ragged breath. "I just can't stand the tension of facing society anymore. I'd be afraid that every time Alex looked at me, he'd see the woman who made him an outcast."

The kettle hissed and spouted white steam, prompting Rosie to return to the hearth and make tea for them. After placing a pot, two cups, sugar, and silverware on a battered tray, she brought it to the table and sat down again, waiting a moment for the brew to steep. Her eyes moist with emotion, she put out her hand and caressed Pell's arm. "I thinks you've made a great mistake, luv. The professor is mad in love with you. I saw it in 'is face the night we was 'avin' the party under the bridge."

Pell wanted to accept Rosie's judgment, but just

couldn't. "I made a mistake when I married him," she said, shaking her head. "I was so blinded by my feelings for him that I let him talk me into the marriage, but I shouldn't have. Even then I knew it was wrong."

"Wrong? 'Ow could it be wrong when 'e loved you and asked you to marry 'im?"

"The marriage was *inappropriate*, as he would say. There's just too much difference between us."

Rosie poured the tea, spooned some sugar into her cup, and stirred it. "'E took a great risk in marryin' you, all right . . . but 'e did. That just proves that 'e loves you!"

Tears welled in Pell's eyes. "That's just it, Rosie. You don't really know the professor. He always does his duty . . . it's like a religion to him." She swallowed back her emotions, wondering if she should continue. "You see," she said, looking down in embarrassment, "he took my virginity the night he saved me from Claude, so he felt he *had* to offer me marriage." She looked at her friend, blinking back her tears. "A few days ago, I found a pile of old bills, and discovered that his family left him bankrupt. Now I think he may have married me for my inheritance."

Surprise flashed on Rosie's face and for a moment she sat quietly, looking as if she were searching for comforting words. "I says you're wrong on both counts," she said lightly. "I says 'e married you 'cause 'e loves you. And 'e'll come after you, too. I'm sure of it!"

Pell finished her tea, then rose and walked to the rain-splattered window. Outside the sky had clouded to a dark gray, and cool air flowed through a crack where the pane was broken, washing over her. "I'm not sure he will," she finally said, her voice tight with defeat. She looked back over her shoulder. "Because of me and the scandal I've created, Alex stands in jeopardy of losing his political appointment. He'd be better off without me."

"Gaa, if you leaves the professor, whot will you do with the rest of your life?" Rosie blurted out.

Pell's eyelids fluttered and she rubbed her temples. "I really don't know right now. After I rest a bit, I'll think of something." She opened her eyes and looked at her friend with conviction. "I do know I want to be more than a socialite. I'd like to make my fortune count for something."

"'Ow can you even get your fortune from that solicitor if you ain't with the professor?"

Pell crossed her arms and thought of the day after tomorrow, when her father's will was to be read. "Mr. Peebles seems like a sensible man. I'm sure he'll understand the situation. I *did* become a lady and get married—even though the outcome was less than desirable."

Looking thoughtful, Rosie went to her trunk and rummaged through some clothing. Then, a smile on her face, she brought Pell the old hat with the bedraggled red plumes she had once worn and loved. Her eyes soft, she offered Pell the hat. "This was in with some of the clothin' you gave me, but I couldn't give it away. I ... I don't know why, but I thought you might like to see it ... maybe for old times' sake."

With trembling hands Pell took the hat and looked at it in the firelight. One of the plumes was now completely broken and the felt looked pathetically shabby. With some amazement Pell realized that the outlandish thing had once been her most prized possession. How she had fought Aunt Violet and the maids to keep it, she thought with sad amusement.

As Pell stood there without speaking, a worried look tightened Rosie's features. Then she moved about the room, lighting two small lamps to ward off the gloom and fluffing up the stained bed pillows. "I've got to see if I can sell some more fruit afore it gets dark, but when I'm done, I'm goin' to the bakeshop and get us somethin' wicked good for supper tonight," she said, anxiously glancing over her shoulder. "And we'll go to the pub tonight and see some of your old friends. We'll stay up late and talk, and you can tell me about life with the swells ... and ... and everythin' will be just like it used to be," she said in a desperately cheery voice.

Touched, Pell watched her gather up the fruit and arrange it in her basket, then bustle out the door and close it behind her. Poor Rosie. How her unexpected intrusion had upset her difficult, but well-ordered life. With a smile, she wondered if Rosie would tell the man at the bakeshop that she was having dinner with the Countess of Tavistock. Pell knew the rough ham-fisted man would never believe it, for she herself could scarcely believe she was a countess.

Clutching the old hat, she watched Rosie hurry away in the light rain. A few lights now illuminated Cat and Wheel Alley against the dreary weather. Piles of garbage dotted the cracked sidewalks and blocked the cellars. Water babbled down the gutters, flushing raw sewage over the broken pavement. All of this lay before her, when just this morning she had awakened in Mayfair between silken sheets.

Feeling a great sense of loss, Pell looked at the soft hat in her hand. How confident she had been when she wore it. How brave. How sure of life. In her bright cocky ignorance, the world had been hers!

Would Alex come for her as Rosie had suggested? Could he possibly love her? If he did, how could they overcome the seemingly impossible barrier between them? The tears that she had been holding back for so long stung her eyes. Caressing the plumes of her old hat, Pell stared at the misty street, fighting back her turbulent emotions.

Sadder—but much wiser—Pell Davis had returned home.

The next morning Pell placed a jack of spades on the table, then, after studying the rows of cards, heaved a sigh and threw down the rest of the deck. She had been playing solitaire by herself since Rosie left several hours ago and she was thoroughly tired of it. Feeling low and dispirited, she rose and walked to the window, staring at Cat and Wheel Alley.

Morning light washed over the dingy thoroughfare, which was filled with laborers dressed in shabby clothes and frayed caps. Most of them belonged to the working class and were employed to clean carriages, carry advertising signs, or do other menial tasks. Women in dark gowns and tattered aprons leaned against doorways; tots clung to their skirts, sucking their fingers. Somehow the people she had been raised with now had a strange, foreign look about them, she thought sadly, and things she was once hardened to now troubled her deeply. How much she had changed since she'd gone away from here!

With a sigh, she remembered the previous evening she had spent in the pub with Rosie. How awkward she had felt talking to her old friends. Their veiled looks and shy voices had told her what she already realized—like a cobble that had been removed from a street and couldn't be wedged back again, she didn't fit into Whitechapel life anymore. Of course, Rosie would always be Rosie, but, through no fault of their own, the others partly resented her. In fact, her presence seemed to embarrass them. Her old friends had said she looked *bleedin' fine,* but a shadow of something—suspicion or envy—shone in their eyes.

Deep in her heart, she knew she couldn't continue to live here, for she no longer belonged. She was an outsider now.

But if she was an outsider here, what of Mayfair? The fashionable section of London now seemed hundreds of miles and hundreds of years away. In Mayfair they had copper hip baths, and silver chamber pots, and ate three good meals a day, and slept between lace-trimmed sheets, and placed small white cards on silver trays . . . and Alex lived in Mayfair.

Alex, whose face haunted her constantly. She had sat quietly and read a book, or played solitaire, or looked from the window, or lay on the bed with her eyes open, staring at the wall—but she couldn't stop thinking of him. What had he done when he realized she wasn't coming home last night? What was he doing at this moment? What was he thinking? And what had he meant when he said that no matter what their rank, everyone must find their own purpose in life?

Just then, Pell heard brisk footsteps on the stairs, and as they became louder, she turned about. A few seconds later, Rosie entered the room, old garments heaped over her outstretched arms. With a deft movement, she kicked the door shut with her foot, then peeked over the pile of clothes at Pell. "Ding dong bell and bloody 'ell, whot are you doin' standin' at that window with a face as long as a cat's tail?" she asked crossly. "You spend 'alf your time lookin' out that bloody window, you does."

Pell gazed at her and shrugged.

"You needs to get out and stir about some," the older woman declared with a scowl. "I knows best on this, I does!"

"I suppose you're right," Pell replied dispiritedly, "but I just can't make myself leave the flat."

Shaking her head, Rosie walked to her trunk, and, after throwing the clothes on the floor, she knelt and opened the battered container. Pell watched her remove other garments from the trunk and add them to the pile on the floor. Her curiosity getting the best of her, she finally asked, "What are you doing with those old things?"

The older woman spread out a shawl, placed all the garments upon it, then tied everything into a lumpy bundle. "I'm takin' these things to Mrs. Marshall afore I goes back to Billingsgate, I am," she said as she stood and wiped her brow.

"Who's Mrs. Marshall?" Pell asked.

"She's a good woman whot's come to work in Whitechapel since you went away. She runs a little soup kitchen right off the alley about five blocks down. She's filled many an empty stomach, and folks 'as started bringin' 'er clothes when they 'ave 'em to give. I knocked on a few doors this mornin' and collected some things for 'er myself."

"Armed with a Bible and a breadbasket, is she?"

Rosie pursed her lips. "That's right. But she don't

preach about 'ell, then ride 'ome in a carriage to eat cake and drink champagne. If she tells some bloke 'es goin' to 'ell, she gives 'im a right proper dinner to take on the way! She even likes the big rough lads. Says they's *lackin' in opportunities.*"

"Where did she come from?" Pell asked with growing interest.

"Blest if I knows. But she ain't no proper swell. 'Er language ain't fine enough and she's real short on funds." Rosie raised her brows and blew out her breath. "That don't seem to stop 'er none, though. When she 'ears about a 'ungry babe, she goes into the filthiest cellars carryin' a cup of milk." She laughed with satisfaction. "And she collects the poor, like a pied piper. She 'as a big drum and a man who goes about Whitechapel banging' on it. The little ones 'as learned to follow 'em, knowin' they'll get food."

"Hasn't anyone tried to hurt her?" Pell asked softly.

"They 'asn't yet. All the blokes say she's too plucky. I thinks they secretly respects 'er, I does." Rosie hoisted the bundle of clothes over her back, then moved close and gripped Pell's arm. "Why don't you come with me, luv? Stayin' closed up like this ain't good for you."

"No . . . you go on. I'll have something here for you to eat when you return."

Rosie adjusted her burden and looked disappointed. "All right, if that's whot you wants," she said, walking to the door. "But you needs to get out, you really does," she advised in parting.

Pell listened to her walk down the creaking stairs, then heard the tenement door slam shut. As soon as her friend was gone, a host of troubling questions flooded back into her mind. Why had she left Mayfair and come here anyway? To protect Alex from her past and her mistakes, or because she was afraid and weak? And as Rosie had so plainly put it, what was she going to do with the rest of her life? She paced for a while, and, finding no answers, laid down to rest, finally falling into a fitful sleep.

About an hour later, the resounding *boom boom boom*

of a bass drum roused her from her slumbers. At first her mind drifted in drowsy thoughts, then the voices of shrieking children touched her ears and she remembered what Rosie had said. Pushing back her tousled hair, she sat up, then rose and slowly moved to the window. Through a bleary daze, she looked down and observed a man beating a big bass drum, with the words *Mrs. Marshall's Soup Kitchen* painted on the side. The additional words *No hungry child turned away* also appeared on the well-used instrument.

As the drummer marched on down the alley, a host of ragged children trailed after him. Pell watched, something stirring within her soul. She remembered when she had first arrived in Mayfair and how dazzled she had been with the abundance of material comforts there. And she remembered how she had often thought of the East Enders, wanting to help them but not knowing how to go about it.

After smoothing her simple blue cotton blouse into the waistband of her long skirt, she threw a shawl about her shoulders and left the flat. A little flicker of excitement leaped up within her as she left the tenement and scanned the street, cool air washing over her face.

Guided by the fading drumbeats, she followed the parade, her shoes clattering over the rough cobbles which she felt through her thin soles. As she hurried past the dark sooty buildings with their warped casings and broken windowpanes, she thought about this desperately poor section of London called the Rookery. Some worked here, some even had skills, but sickness and death always managed to keep the upper hand. And life in Cat and Wheel Alley tipped morality upside down. The rich were fair game, not authority figures; the police were enemies, not protectors; and phrases like *Cleanliness is next to godliness* and *A penny saved is a penny earned* were stinging mockeries, not comforting clichés. Still there was a rough comradeship and a toughness of the spirit that kept people living from one day to the next.

As she caught up with the last of the parade, the sound

of the drum boomed loud in her ears, and she saw the noisy children disappear into a dark court that emitted the scent of decay and rotting wood. Following, she entered a shadowy lane where ancient buildings towered above her, poles draped with tattered sheets protruding from their windows. In front of one dilapidated building, children ate quietly at long tables, served by a young girl of about eighteen. The parade dispersed, the new arrivals joining the other children at the tables and waving their hands; the girl gave them chunks of bread from a large wicker basket. At one point, she paused to wipe her brow, her face pale with exhaustion.

Hearing shrieks of laughter, Pell turned her attention to two boys of ten or eleven, who came rushing from the crumbling building. Clad in wretched rags, they sported about the tables, running and playing. They were thin and barefooted, but so merry it touched her to watch them.

Dressed in a modest cotton gown, a heavy older woman soon came from the same building with two pairs of boots under her arm and a stamp in her hand. Blessed with a kindly face and gentle smile, the matronly lady moved with purposefulness and quiet dignity. Sitting down on a bench, she stamped the insides of the boots, then gave them to the boys, who flopped down beside her and put them on. After the boys had put on the boots, they scrambled up, and, never looking back, raced away, their thick-soled footwear ringing over the cobbles.

Pell walked further into the court and drew close to the silver-haired woman, who looked up and smiled pleasantly at her. "Excuse me, ma'am, but might you be Mrs. Marshall?"

"Yes, dear. That is exactly who I am."

"Why did you stamp those boots before you gave them to the boys?" Pell asked, her voice edged with curiosity.

The older woman gave a dry chuckle. "I can tell by your voice that you aren't from this part of London, dear. Here in Whitechapel boots are a salable item."

Although Pell had been away for a while now, it surprised her that the woman thought her an outsider.

"I soon learned that the boots which I gave out ended up in pawnshops with the proceeds spent on drink," the woman continued. "I now lend them out with a stamp on each boot. If anyone tries to sell them, the mark will identify them as my property."

Pell scanned the children as they moved from the tables and began to leave. "Are these the only ones you'll be feeding today?"

"Oh, no! These are children with no parents—true ragamuffins. I make a habit of feeding them first, then families with children later."

As Mrs. Marshall spoke, the girl finished serving the bread, and now walked toward them, her shoulders slumping with weariness. "Pardon, ma'am," she sighed, wiping her brow on her sleeve again, "but I ain't feelin' too well. Could I go home now?" Bright spots blotched the girl's pale face and a pleading look veiled her tired eyes.

"All right, dear. I'll speak with you tomorrow."

After the girl had gone, the old lady's brow knitted with frustration. Brushing back a wisp of her straying hair, she nodded at the long line of adults now forming outside of the building, waiting for the signal to go in. "I'd best get busy," she said. "It will take me twice as long to serve the midday meal without help."

Something sparked in Pell. "My name is Pell Davis and I'm Rosie's friend ... you know, the same Rosie who brought a bundle a clothes today." She bit her lip. "Maybe I could give you a hand."

Looking surprised, Mrs. Marshall ran a gaze over her, then smiled. "Oh, so you're Rosie's friend. Well, come inside and I'll show you what to do."

Only minutes after Pell had put on an apron, she stood beside Mrs. Marshall, pouring out cups of milk as the older lady ladled up stew to a line of adults who filed past them, then took their food outside the building to sit at the table in the sunshine. There was a break in the line and Pell looked at Mrs. Marshall as she stirred the huge cauldron. "They all have such a vacant, listless look," she commented.

"Yes," the older woman said with a pained sigh. "We give them a small loaf of bread daily, a cup of milk, and an ounce of butter—if it is available. And three days a week they get a bit of meat cooked in a stew, or perhaps some beans. It's barely enough to keep body and soul together, but they have perhaps even greater problems. They need clothes and shelter and schooling. They need so much, and I have so little to give them."

The line had started moving again and Pell went back to work, but throughout the long midday meal she talked with Mrs. Marshall, drawing out information from her about her work in Whitechapel. After they had washed and cleaned the caldron and serving utensils, and scrubbed the outside tables, she stayed with her to mend clothes and stamp boots and give out bread to children who came to ask for it throughout the day. By the time the sun had started to set, her back ached with weariness, but her spirits were higher than they had been in a long time.

"Are you sure you don't want me to stay for the evening meal, Mrs. Marshall?" she asked as she took off her apron and laid it aside.

From her place at a worktable, now illuminated with a small lamp, the old lady put down a garment she was mending and looked up with a smile. "No, dear. I have another girl who comes about now. We only serve bread and cheese in the evening, you know."

Pell had attended many elegant Mayfair social functions, but this afternoon had meant more to her than any of the gala occasions. It gave her a feeling of satisfaction to think that she had helped someone instead of frittering away her time with gossip or shopping trips. It also warmed her heart that the woman had accepted her on face value without a thought of checking *Burke's Peerage* or asking her where she bought her clothes. "Thank you, Mrs. Marshall. Thank you for this afternoon," she said.

The woman scraped back her chair and stood, a puzzled look on her face. "Why should you be thanking me, dear? It is I who should thank you."

Pell drew in a thoughtful breath. "No, today has helped me straighten out some of my thinking."

Concern in her eyes, Mrs. Marshall took her hand. "You were a great help. If you have time, come back again someday."

Emotion flooded through Pell. "Yes, thank you. I will," she answered, slipping her hand from the woman's warm grasp and reaching for her shawl. Her mind full of thoughts and possibilities, she walked to the entrance of the building that was now shrouded with dark shadows. At the threshold, she looked back at the older lady, whose hair caught a shaft of lamplight, making it gleam like silver against the building's drab walls. "I'm not sure when it will be . . . but I'll return," she said in even tones.

After she left Mrs. Marshall's, Pell was so excited she almost forgot to stop at the bakeshop and buy something for supper that evening. By the time she returned to Cat and Wheel Alley with a paper-wrapped parcel under her arm, a coolness had moved over Whitechapel and gaslight streaked across the street, telling her that she was late. Her heart pounded with exhilaration as she climbed the five flights of stairs and turned the doorknob.

Carelessly flinging open the door, she saw Rosie standing just inside the threshold, a concerned look on her face. The gloominess of the chamber didn't surprise Pell, for a dull glow and the scent of burning wood told her that her friend had elected to build a fire, but had waited for her return to burn precious lamp oil. "Sorry, I'm late," she said brightly, taking Rosie's arm and stepping inside the room. As she studied her friend's face more closely, she realized that something was amiss—something more than her late arrival. "What's wrong?" she murmured, becoming more alarmed. "Has something happened?"

Rosie moved back a bit, and, clearing Pell's view, darted a worried glance at the fireplace. "'E just arrived," she whispered roughly. Following her gaze, Pell looked at the hearth and her breath caught in her throat, for Alex loomed before the crackling flames, his handsome face illuminated by the fire's glow.

Chapter 23

❧

Rosie awkwardly cleared her throat. "I thinks," she said, putting on her shawl and hat, "that I'll be goin' to the pub now. I suspects you two won't be needin' the likes of me 'angin' around."

Pell glanced at her and nodded. Rosie put her hand on the doorknob and winked broadly. "I told you the professor would come after you, didn't I? I told you 'e'd do it!"

After the door slammed, Alex walked to Pell and took her in his arms. The power and barely controlled passion seething within his large body made her heart nearly stop. "What in God's name possessed you to run away?" he asked in a rough voice. "I've been out of my mind with worry, and Aunt Violet is prostrate. Even Hadji won't eat." He pulled her against him, and she could smell his bay rum cologne and the beat of his thudding heart under his fine jacket.

A nervous pulse racing at the base of her throat, she dared a glance at his tense face. "Rosie took good care of me," she said softly.

He blew out his breath in pent-up frustration. "How in the devil was I supposed to know you were well cared for? You didn't even leave a note, just disappeared, like some Gypsy in the night."

She moistened her lips and swallowed the lump in her throat. "After I saw that horrible cartoon in the *Tomahawk*, I felt that I had ruined your life—that it would be best if

335

I just disappeared." Her eyelashes fluttered as she looked downward.

He lifted her chin and gazed at her with blazing eyes. "Good God," he muttered hoarsely. "Is that piece of despicable journalism what made you run away? I never imagined you would be so influenced by it."

"When we talked on the night of the opera, you seemed so angry."

A muscle flicking in his hard jaw, he heaved a great sigh and glanced at the little fire in Rosie's hearth. "I *was* angry," he admitted. Then he looked back at her, his eyes smoldering with emotion. "Angry at society for being so shallow, so cynical, so uncaring."

"You're not embarrassed over the cartoon?" she ventured quietly.

"No, I'm not embarrassed—I'm furious. Furious at the publisher of the *Tomahawk* and the insensitivity that prompted the cartoon to be printed in the first place."

Relief spread through her. *He came for me,* she thought joyously. *He came for me, just like Rosie said he would!* The realization left her stunned and a bit light-headed. "How did you know where I would be?" she asked, her heart beating a little faster as she studied his face.

He held her lightly in his arms. "For God's sake, where else would you go? I would have been here last night, but Aunt Violet convinced me to wait. She said you needed a little time on your own to sort things through. She said she'd make Hadji tie me down if I didn't agree to give it to you."

Pell laughed at the thought, then pushed back from him a bit, making an impulsive decision to tell him what was in her heart. Walking to the window, she crossed her arms, and gazed at the glimmering gaslights haloed in mist. "Before I left, you seemed so distant. I thought you were angry that I had told Claude about my past . . . and caused a great scandal."

"At the time," he said, "I confess I was mad as hell. The fact that you'd confided in Claude when we agreed on silence shook me deeply. Although I'd have preferred that you'd held your tongue, upon reflection I realized the secret had been weighing on your heart so heavily you had to tell someone." She turned about and saw a wry smile trace his lips. "As far as a *scandal* is concerned," he went on, "most of the aristocracy have numerous skeletons in their closets."

She looked at him and smiled, but concern about the *Tomahawk* still lingered in her mind. "But how can our lives be the same with that horrible magazine circulating all over London?"

"Actually, the things in the *Tomahawk* have worked against Sabrina. The night I went to the Carlton everyone was talking about it. It seems the result of the article turned out to be something of a backhanded tribute to the general. It got all his old friends thinking of him again . . . about all he had done for England. Of course, some of the philistines are shocked, but a lot of others are saying bully for him. They're glad he had some joy in his life. I think many of the men might have had suspicions that Sabrina was a cold wife, and anyone who ever met the general knows that he was not a womanizer—therefore his alliance with your mother must have been serious. And his decision to give you half his fortune was quite a noble thing. Manipulating public opinion can be quite tricky, and if Sabrina is expecting all of it to be on her side, she's mistaken."

Pell stared at him silently for a moment, thinking about how things often turn out very differently than expected. Then, trembling with relief and happiness, she walked back to him and took his outstretched hand.

"When I came home late last night and found that you had not returned when expected, and a satchel was missing from the attic," Alex went on in a strained voice, "I could scarcely believe it." His voice quickened with exasperation. "Why did you come back to the East End? You might have been assaulted or even kidnapped." He sighed. "What was going on in your crazy little head?"

His tone told her that he was still frustrated, but there was also concern in his voice, and she was wise enough to know that he truly cared for her. She studied his features in the wavering firelight, and noticed the deep worry lines etched into his face. "I don't understand everything myself," she said with a long shuddering sigh. She looked down again, nervously twisting the end of her shawl in her hand. "I suppose I thought you regretted your decision to marry me," she said at last, her voice trailing off.

"Why would you think such a thing?" he asked in an incredulous tone.

Her heart hammering, she looked up into his demanding eyes. "Don't you remember what you said at my coming-out ball? You told me that it seemed that love never lasts ... that so far the circumstances hadn't been right for you," she reminded him in a quavering voice. "Aunt Violet told me how much you loved Carolyn Ramsay ... and I knew there had been many women in your life after her. I felt that if none of them could take her place, a person like me would never have a chance of replacing her in your affections." She took a deep breath. "I thought that the pain of loving and losing her was so great you could never love anyone else."

A faint smile played over his lips. "I will not deny that since I've known you there have been days when I've wanted to throttle you. But even from the beginning when we were at loggerheads everyday, I wanted you. At first, I thought of my promise to your father and tried to carry out my duties as I always had ... but in the end I couldn't deny my feelings."

When she did not respond, he said, "I always knew I cared for you, but while you were gone, I realized that I valued you more than anything else in the world!" He brushed back a lock of her straying hair. "You know, you're not the only one who has changed in these last six months. I might have made a lady out of a guttersnipe, but you've also changed me. Before, I was a man who never

thought he could love again, and now . . ." His voice
trailed off as he touched his lips to her forehead.

They were talking, really talking now, and she couldn't
resist further unburdening her heart. "I was so angry when
I unlocked the library and discovered the mountain of bills
on your desk," she whispered. "I made poor Aunt Violet
tell me about your real financial condition." For a moment,
her gaze misted with tears. "I knew how desperate you
were, and since you had hidden everything from me, I
thought you had married me for my fortune."

Sadness gathered in Alex's eyes. "Yes, it's true," he
confessed tightly. "I'm near bankruptcy, and when we
were in the Cotswolds I swore Mr. Potterfield and Mrs.
Harris to secrecy. Perhaps it was wrong of me to keep it
from you, but I didn't want to burden you with the problem. And I hoped a political appointment was imminent,
so there would be no need to tell you. I also knew that
once you found out, you would naturally think that I married you for your money." A dark look crossed his face.
"Now I truly understand why you ran away. You wondered if I married you because I took your virginity, or because I wanted your fortune. Neither choice is that
appealing, is it?" His brows rose in sad amusement. "In
my attempt to protect you from my problems, I hurt you
terribly."

He sighed, then looked at her, his eyes full of deep
meaning. He put his arms around her. "That's especially
painful to me now, because I know that I love you more
than Carolyn Ramsay, or any woman on earth. I've always
been a military man and in control of things, but now I
have something that I can't control at all—and that's my
heart. Perhaps I did seal off my feelings for a while to prevent further hurt, but I'd never been involved with anyone
like you before . . . Your smile, your touch, your innocence, all melted my resistance. I love you very much."

As she relaxed in the warmth of his arms and laid her
head against him, her heart stirred with excitement. *He
loves me, really loves me,* she finally realized, the very

thought sending shivers of happiness through her whole being. It would have been so easy for him to have divorced her after the scandal broke, but he had come to this hovel to find her and take her home.

With a rush of euphoria, she looked at him and smiled. "I may never be a lady . . . a real lady, you know. I may always get my heel caught in my hem. And I'll laugh too loudly, and drop *h*'s, and say malaprops, and get everyone's titles mixed up . . . and embarrass you."

"Be careful now," he said with a chuckle, "you're talking about the woman I love." He brushed his long fingers over her cheek and his eyes softened with tenderness. "Do you think I care a damn about those things? I don't love Pell the lady. I love Pell the woman . . . and what a woman you are. I'll vow there's a fire in you that nothing can put out!" He held her tightly and kissed the top of her head.

Leaning back a bit, she ran her fingers over his lapel and murmured, "Because of the scandal your appointment probably won't come through . . . What will you do?"

He sighed and shrugged. "At this point I have no idea, but I do know the idea of bailing myself out with your fortune leaves a bitter taste on my tongue. It's something I refuse to do," he told her, caressing her back. "Whatever happens now, I have my priorities in order." He touched her raised face, and, smiling, grazed his thumb over her high cheekbone. "What have you been doing today?" he asked with amusement. "You're quite dirty, you know."

Looking at his dancing eyes, she led him to the rickety table, and as they sat down, she began recounting the events of her afternoon with Mrs. Marshall, telling him all her observations in detail. "I can't explain to you how exciting the day has been," she said, her voice alive. "I feel as if fate led me to her doorstep." She clasped both of his hands. "If my father's fortune is as large as you say, I'm sure there will be an amount that I can set aside for something special—and I know how I want it to be spent."

"Oh, you do, do you?"

"Yes," she replied decisively. "I want to do charitable work."

He raised a quizzical brow and studied her carefully.

"Working with Mrs. Marshall helped me to see that part of the reason I ran away was because I was tired of hiding my past from the aristocracy . . . tired of being ashamed," she explained, clutching his muscled forearm. "Now I know what you were talking about when you said everyone must find their own purpose in life."

Alex stared at her silently, but the look on his face told her he had weighed her every word. "You learned all that just this afternoon?" he asked with a chuckle.

Pell looked at his amused face. "Yes, and I learned that I can't retreat into the past . . . that I can't be a *deserter.* That's what I was trying to do, you know. I can't change my past either, but I can find a way to live with it." She took a deep breath, trying to steady her nerves. "Alex, I'm ready to stand up to the aristocracy and I want to do something worthwhile . . . something to give my life meaning. I want to open a soup kitchen in the East End, just like Mrs. Marshall. Rosie could run it—and I could pay her a salary. And I could visit often and see what was needed. Of course, I would do it quietly and no one would need to know I was involved."

He gazed at her reflectively and she held her breath, wondering if he would not like the idea. "No," he said at last.

Her heart sank at his refusal.

"I have a better idea," he went on thoughtfully. "I think we should let everyone know that you *are* involved."

She blinked her eyes in wonder. "But what about the Chancery-Brown name?" she blurted out. "Since that horrible magazine came out, everyone knows about my past. You wouldn't want them to also know I'm traipsing around the East End supervising the operations of a soup kitchen."

He stood and caught her gaze. "In that you are entirely wrong, my dear."

"But—"

"Silence, you little magpie," he ordered, bending to brush his lips over hers. "Didn't I just hear you say that you wanted to face up to society?" he added. A smile lifted the corners of his mouth as he looked at her. "I think we should both face up to society, and put your name *and* mine on the soup kitchen."

She sucked in her breath, thinking of his noble heritage, his great name, painted above the entrance of a crumbling building patronized by destitute East Enders. Her lips parted in amazement and she could scarcely believe her ears.

He laughed dryly and rubbed the back of his neck. "Actually it's a very good plan. Prime Minister Gladstone is presenting a bill right now that deals with the education of the poor. It seems that a new spirit of reform is sweeping over London."

Pell rose and moved to him, lightly holding his arms. "But all your associates in Parliament are very conservative. They always vote against that type of thing. You've told me so again and again. If you openly support a soup kitchen, you'll never get that appointment."

"True . . . but that might not be such a bad thing." Drawing in a long breath, he gazed at her with warm eyes. "You said we must find a way to live with the past. I think perhaps this is the way we can both handle the problem best. I've always wanted to help the poor, but I didn't know how to go about it. You've just provided an answer."

"I didn't realize you had such an interest in doing charitable work," she said in a surprised tone.

He gently clasped his hands at her waist. "Since I've known you, my interest has grown. Being your guardian has offered many interesting learning experiences that have helped me understand others better."

"Like what?" she asked in wonder.

He grinned, and he looked happier than she had ever seen him. "Like eating my first bowl of sheep-trotter stew."

They laughed together, and after he had brushed back strands of her tousled hair, he said, "I think *you* should follow your heart and *we* should sponsor a soup kitchen, and the critics be damned! It would show society that we aren't ashamed of your past. In effect we would be standing up to the snobs, looking them in the eye."

Suddenly Pell felt blissfully alive. If she had any lingering doubts that Alex might not love her, his suggestion had wiped them away. Tears moistened her eyes. Certainly he wouldn't stand behind her on this plan if he *didn't* love her.

Alex pulled her closer and lowered his head. "I have only one request," he said gravely. "I want my name to be emblazoned over the door of this soup kitchen in large, bold letters, so all the old death's-heads at the Carlton can read it without their spectacles."

Buoyant laughter filled the shabby little room. Then he tightened his arms about her, and took her lips in a slow, shivery kiss that sent ecstasy coursing through her body. A tender warmth fired the kiss, and joy flowed through her veins like heady wine. How she gloried in the moment! Although it was shadowy and chilly in Rosie's apartment, a rosy glow seemed to well up about them.

When Alex raised his head, Pell whispered, "Did you really miss me?"

As firelight washed over his rakish face, Alex lifted a brow and grinned crookedly. "Come home and I'll show you how much."

After Alex and Pell had eaten a light dinner, she walked upstairs to their bedroom, Aunt Violet and Hadji at her heels. When she paused at the second-story landing, the servant searched her face with troubled eyes. "Oh, missy, I am so relieved my glorious master is retrieving you from that den of vice and iniquity in the East End. Since you are now a countess, some disreputable person might have absconded with you!" he exclaimed, placing a spread hand over his spotless tunic. "Although I have never lived there myself, always being the servant of gentlemen of high position, I am hearing it is quite a dreadful place. And to my great consternation, after you vanished, it began raining rats and dogs!" His eyes widened. "I can assure you, I have been at the end of my leash worrying about you!"

As the servant babbled on about how happy he was to have Pell back where she belonged, Aunt Violet frowned and tapped his shoulder. "'Pon my word, Hadji, you haven't stopped running on since Alex and Pell returned. I think you are quite beside yourself. Go to bed now. You can talk to the girl tomorrow."

Hadji put his slim hands together, and, placing them before his face, bowed his head. "I am believing you are quite correct in that assumption, esteemed lady. I must give missy some time to recover from her exhausting ordeal." Smiling broadly, he bowed once more and descended the stairs.

"How that little man cares for you, child!" Aunt Violet said. "He was worried to distraction after we discovered you had gone. But we've *all* been worried sick about you, dear."

"I'm sorry I upset everyone," Pell murmured, flushing. "Can you forgive me?"

"Yes, of course, dear. We're all only too glad to have you back." She affectionately clasped her arm as they walked to the bedroom door together. "I've already ordered a bath sent to your room, for I'm sure you're utterly exhausted. Relaxing in a hot tub will do you a world of good."

At the door, Aunt Violet took Pell's hand in her own and pressed it warmly, a happy light shining in her eyes. "I may have a wonderful surprise for you soon," she announced breathlessly. With great curiosity, Pell studied her soft face, waiting for a further revelation, but the old lady smiled mysteriously and added, "I cannot tell you now, but in good time everyone will know." Caressing Pell with a last warm gaze, she turned and walked down the stairs.

Pell watched her go, thinking that she radiated a youthful glow. There was new life in her step. What is making her so happy? she wondered as she entered the bedroom and closed the door behind her. The puzzle of Aunt Violet's secret lingered in her mind for only a moment before the room's warm, familiar ambience wrapped about her like a soft blanket, easing away some of the stress of the last few days.

Glancing about the bedroom, she noticed a bath waiting for her before the fireplace which crackled with low flames. A black-and-gold Chinese screen, draped with several linen towels, partially concealed a huge copper hip tub that wafted steam and the scent of rose bath oil into the air.

Pell began to undress and was swiftly out of her simple skirt and blouse that had been so convenient for the East End. Flinging away the last of her undergarments, she gingerly stepped into the water, finding it to be hot, but just the right temperature to soothe away her tensions. With a long contented sigh, she sat down in the tub and felt the water caress her tired body. Leaning back to soak, she glanced at the room, noting familiar pieces of furniture and bric-a-brac that made her feel at home. The soft bed with its huge canopy looked so inviting, and the maid had thoughtfully turned down the top of the silken coverlet, exposing the lace-trimmed feather pillows. Yes, she was home. Home with Alex.

She picked up a bar of soap from a small table situated by the tub and lathered her body. Placing the bar aside and sliding down a bit, she rested the nape of her neck against the rim of the tub and closed her eyes. She relaxed this way for a few moments, then, hearing approaching footsteps, opened her eyes with a start to see Alex standing at the end of the tub, a broad smile on his face. A red paisley silk robe garbed his massive frame and a lock of black hair fell over his forehead.

With a gasp, she sat up straight and covered her bare breasts with her hands. "Alex, I didn't hear you. I thought you were still downstairs. I . . . I . . ."

He knelt by the tub and gently cupped her face in his large hands. "No one has ever been able to explain to me why women waste so much time talking," he remarked with a trace of humor in his voice. "One day we must go into the subject in more detail."

He swept her with a seductive gaze, making her heart race. For a moment, he looked at her as if he were trying to remember every curve of her face, then she felt him take the pins from her hair and heard them hit the carpet as he tossed them aside. The last pin removed, a silky cascade fell about her shoulders.

He assessed her boldly, and as he slowly lowered his head, a giddy sensation spiraled in the pit of her stomach. Then his mouth covered hers in a slow kiss. Excitement sped through her and she found her limp hands falling away from her breasts. Deepening the kiss with new urgency, he moved his hand over her neck and shoulders, and, tracing it lower, caressed her slippery globes, paying special attention to their sensitive tips. She felt her nipples rise and harden as his warm fingers worked over them, making them tingle with pleasure.

Her senses reveled in the long fiery kiss, then, as his lips seared a path to her breast and gently drew on her nipple, she gasped in delight. He twirled his tongue about the crest, making her head fell back. She groaned with desire, and grasped the side of the tub. A flush warmed her face and pleasure radiated outward from her breast as he continued to nuzzle and gently nip at her rosy peak. When he finally lifted his head, she sat forward, and, feeling thoroughly aroused, gazed into his eyes. "I'll bet you want to wash my back too, don't you?" she murmured huskily, tracing his jaw with her fingertips.

A small smile lifted his lips. "Excellent guess." His voice carried a casual, jesting tone. His smile widening, he rolled up the sleeves of his silken robe. Cupping his hands in the water, he poured it over her shoulders and let the warm liquid slide down her back. After repeating the procedure, he picked up the soap and lathered her back, massaging it with his strong fingers. As he continued, she felt his palms against her back and waist, and sweeping over the fullness of her buttocks.

Placing the soap aside and moving in front of her, he showered kisses over her face while he tweaked her rosy crests with his fingers, driving her to a frenzy of desire. Embarrassed by her own passion, she tried to distract him, chattering foolishly about topics like the weather and the rising price of bread while he kissed the pulse in her neck and continued lavishing attention on her sensitive nipples. At last, he raised his head and gazed at her with passion-heavy eyes. "I'm sorry," he apologized, his mouth quirking with mirth. "I've been a bit distracted. What were you saying?"

Feeling somewhat ridiculous even while she was saying it, she circled her arms about his shoulders and asked, "Why are you *talking* so much? Why don't you do something useful and kiss me again." Then she kissed him full on the mouth.

As the kiss progressed, he moved a hand to the junction of her legs, and, running two fingers into her wet curls, played with her most intimate flesh. The tantalizing massage rushed sexual hunger through her body and left her throbbing and weak with desire. A warm, drugging sensation rising up within her, she moaned with pleasure, then, moving away a bit, gazed at his rakish face which bore a lazy smile. "That's not fair," she murmured in a throaty voice, trying to collect her wits.

"I've been told all is fair in love and war," he replied.

As he moved closer, her gaze went to the robe that had become untied. She could see that he was nude beneath the silk, and the proof of his passion had already begun to harden and lengthen.

Regarding her with amusement, he raised his brows and sighed. "As you can see, I'm afraid we will have to shorten your bath this evening to make time for other activities." When she burst out giggling, he poured handfuls of water over her lathered body, then kissed her lightly on the mouth and put his hands under her arms.

She gazed up at him as he helped her from the tub. "Shame on you," she said playfully. "Taking advantage of me while I'm helpless. What a rogue you are."

"Yes, but you love me still, don't you," he said, amusement flickering in his eyes.

They stood together, and as they did so, he slipped off his silken robe and tossed it on the floor. A shudder passed through her and heat warmed her face as she swept her gaze over him. With his broad shoulders, well-defined muscles, flat stomach, and lean hips, he was a sight to quicken any woman's heart.

Lifting a towel from the screen, he gently dried her, and when he was almost finished her hand instinctively caressed his chest, and, trailing lower, found its way about his hardness, prompting him to pull her to him. He groaned, then took her mouth in a hungry kiss that roused a tender sweetness within her. Dropping the damp towel, he moved her hand to his muscled shoulder, then scooped her up in his arms and carried her across the room. Pell felt the cool silken coverlet against her bare back and buttocks as he lowered her onto the bed and she sank into the soft mattress.

As he stretched out beside her and took her in his arms, the images of the last few days flooded her mind, and she grew more serious. "I wish I hadn't run away," she murmured. "I've made so many mistakes since we met."

He gave her an irresistible grin. "It doesn't matter. People always learn from their mistakes."

She chuckled. "I'm afraid I haven't learned much until just recently."

He kissed the little curls around her hairline and whispered, "That's all that matters." He put a finger over her lips. "Now be quiet, and let me start making you happy."

He kissed her deeply again; one of his hands tweaked her aching nipple and the other worked between her legs. His fingers toyed with her pulsing bud until she wrapped her arms about his shoulders and trembled with desire. She was afire for him, and consumed with such a deep, lulling feeling of love that she thought she might faint with joy.

Tonight as she remembered their conversation at Rosie's, their warm, playful lovemaking glowed with a tender meaning that touched her deeply. As she ran a hand through his silky black hair, she could smell the musky scent of his seed, and feel the warmth of his body and the exciting thud of his heart against hers. "Please . . . now," she said, breaking the kiss to whisper against his lips.

"Just a little longer," he replied in a husky voice, disentangling himself from her arms and urging her onto her stomach. "I may have taught you everything you know, but not everything *I* know."

Moving away from her for a moment, he retrieved the pillows from the head of the bed and placed them under her so that her hips were slightly elevated. Spreading her legs, he knelt between them, then lovingly caressed her buttocks and rained kisses on the inside of her thighs; delicious thrills darted through her body.

Pell felt his warm fingers sweeping over the fullness of her hips, kneading her softness, then gently spreading her cheeks and working lower until they found her swollen bud. As he repeatedly skimmed over it, his expert touch fired her with raw sensation, and sent her into light-headed ecstasy. Speaking exciting words of love, he toyed with her this new way until she was moist and ached for entry. Delight shivered over her as he leaned forward and guided the tip of his steely hardness into her vagina. When he entered her fully and powerfully, she shuddered and a gasp of pleasure rushed from her throat.

Her senses whirled as he thrust inside her, flesh against flesh. Then he was still for a moment as he leaned forward and reached to find her nipple. As he rolled the tender crest between his fingers, he began to stroke her firmly and deeply in a manly, possessive rhythm that brought her close to climax. A hot flush rose on her bosom, and her heart fluttered as she became wetter still while he continued to thrust relentlessly into her.

She was gasping and quivering, and she writhed her buttocks against him, moaning with desire. He slowed his pace to prolong her pleasure, but as her cries of urgency increased, he thrust into her again, coming faster and faster as he worked them both toward their peak. Their bodies in perfect harmony, they throbbed in ecstasy, and for a precious moment, became one body and spirit as they both exploded in powerful orgasms.

After he had pulled himself from her, he moved to her side and held her in his arms, caressing her damp hair and fluttering kisses over her eyelids. As he cupped her breasts and swept his hand over the soft fullness of her hips, pulling her close against him, she sighed and felt herself already sliding into the dreamy state before sleep. Everything had been happening so fast lately that she had almost forgotten that tomorrow was the day she was supposed to go to Mr. Peebles's office to hear him read her father's will. Suddenly she wondered what it would have been like if she and Alex had not had the wherewithal to come back to Mayfair, if they had been as indigent as the people in the East End. "Alex?" she said drowsily.

He kissed her hair and pulled her tighter. "Mmmm?"

"Do you think we could be happy even if we were poor?"

He raised a brow. "Do you mean sheep-trotter-stew poor, or just average poor?"

"Any kind of poor."

He kissed the top of her head and chuckled; her heart warmed with satisfaction. "I was just teasing you. I could be happy with you and eat sheep-trotter stew every night. If two people are right for each other—the way we are—everything will fall into place, no matter what. They may have hard times, but they'll always have each other's love." He snuggled her against him. "How do you feel now that you're home?" he murmured sleepily.

His voice was warm and deep, and she reveled in the

peace and contentment flowing between them. How long she had wished for this moment of physical and emotional intimacy. "I feel safe and lucky . . . very lucky," she whispered. Everything was wonderful now, she thought as she floated into a mist of satisfied slumber. She and Alex had straightened out their problems, and, to make everything sweeter, she had thought of a way she could help her friends in the East End. All she had to do was go to Mr. Peebles's office tomorrow and get her fortune.

Yes, she thought as she snuggled into Alex's strong arms and fell into velvety blackness, her fortune at last.

Chapter 24

$\mathbf{F}$illed with leather chairs and lined with crowded book-shelves, Mr. Peebles's small Chelsea office smelled of dust and musty volumes, and the sound of rolling carriages filtered into the little room from the busy street below. Outside the office's arched windows, afternoon clouds hung low over London, necessitating the use of a green-shaded lamp that pooled light over the solicitor's littered desk. Dressed in a day gown of moss-green velvet trimmed in black braid, Pell sat next to Alex, while Sabrina Fairchild sat on the other side of him, her face stony. Ensembled in sea blue silk, she nervously smoothed kid gloves over her slender hands, trying to avoid Pell's gaze.

Pell knew she was angry because the *Tomahawk* article had not benefited her as she had expected. And she also knew that the reading of Phillip Fairchild's will was the only thing that could have lured the widow into the same room with her. In fact, her very presence here today was proof, as Alex had said, that the will was legal and binding. No amount of public opinion could change it. Pell wondered where Claude was, and could only assume that he had elected not to face her.

As a clock chimed four, the solicitor knelt to remove two large envelopes from his office safe. As its door slammed with a loud metallic *thunk,* Pell's heart lurched.

When Mr. Peebles stood and gazed at the envelopes, Sabrina leaned forward and raised her finely arched brows.

"Well?" she prompted. "Let's get on with it ... I've had to wait six months, you know."

With a weary sigh, the solicitor peered at the three of them over the top of his small half-spectacles, his face serious. Deep lines etched his brow and he pressed his lips together before he spoke. "I'm afraid I have a great shock for all of you," he announced tightly, placing one of the envelopes in Sabrina's outstretched hand. Upon receiving it, the widow sat back and began to rip open the envelope, her fingers trembling with eagerness. He handed the other letter, which bore the same almost illegible handwriting, to Pell.

Taking the creamy envelope between her fingers, she sat quietly for a moment, staring at the old gentleman. "Is there some problem? I don't understand."

Mr. Peebles raised his bushy brows and drew in a long, troubled breath. "I'm afraid that actually there is no fortune," he said in a broken voice.

Sabrina dropped the half-open letter in her lap and glared at him. *"What?"* she said incredulously. "But how can that possibly be true?"

Pell sank back limply, and reached for Alex's hand, noticing his own shocked expression. Too stunned to speak, she blinked, then searched the solicitor's countenance, looking for answers.

His face set in grim lines, he sighed and shook his head. "I'm afraid it's all true," he said, gazing at her with sad eyes. "Outside of the mansion Sabrina is presently living in, the estate of Phillip Fairchild hasn't an asset left."

"But there must be a mistake!" Sabrina raged, crossing her arms defensively. "Phillip was wealthy. When we were in India, I saw his stock certificates with my own eyes." Glancing at Pell, she gestured dramatically with her gloved hand. "Surely he didn't spend everything on this ragamuffin."

Mr. Peebles bent his head for a moment, then looked her in the eye. "A lot happened to the general after he became ill. He made some poor investments, lost money on business ventures . . . It's all in the letter," he explained, trying to calm her. "If you'll just read—"

"All he left me was the mansion on Park Lane?" Sabrina interrupted him in a desperate voice.

He frowned. "I'm afraid the home you're now living in will be sold," he said quietly, "and the money used to pay the last of the general's debts."

She stiffened, and, clutching the letter, slowly rose to her feet. *"He left me with nothing?"* The letter trembled in her hand as she glanced at Pell, then back at the solicitor. "He used the last of his money on *her,* and saved nothing for *me?"*

Mr. Peebles walked to her side and put his hand on her shoulder. "Madam, *please.* Calm yourself. I've dreaded bringing you this news, but the general mentioned that he gave you a considerable amount of jewelry during your years together. He felt sure that you would remarry. Until that time, he hoped that you could support yourself with the sale of your jewelry."

"But I've sold it all to fund Claude," Sabrina wailed, apparently too agitated to be discreet. "All I have left is the emeralds and he's selling them now!" Her eyes misted with tears. "He's lost it all, you know."

Alex stood and placed his hand on Pell's shoulder in a protective gesture. "Lost it all?" he echoed.

Sabrina gazed at him with desperate eyes. "Yes . . . he's lost it all at the gambling tables." Obviously distraught, she made a frantic gesture with her slender hands. "At the time it didn't matter . . . for we thought we had a fortune coming. What am I to do? I have nothing to fall back on . . . nothing but my clothing and the furnishings in my home."

Mr. Peebles cleared his throat. "The clothing you may keep, but I'm afraid the furnishings will be sold with the house."

She looked at him with parted lips. "You mean I'm to be turned out, utterly penniless? I ask you, sir, what shall I do?"

The solicitor hung his head, then sighed and met her gaze. "I'm afraid I cannot answer that question, but you'll have to think of something, because you must be out of the mansion by the end of the month."

With a cry of frustration, Sabrina whirled and went to the office door, still clutching her unread letter. As she placed her hand on the doorknob, she ran her gaze over Alex. "You knew him. What in God's name did Phillip want from me? I gave him my best years. I entertained for him. I lived away from London in all those dreadful military outposts. I gave him everything. *Everything.*"

Alex looked at her evenly for a moment, then he quietly said, "Yes, you gave him everything a man could want . . . except love."

A little gasp exploded from her lips, and then she yanked the door open. For a moment it looked as if she was on the verge of slapping Alex, but as the wind went out of her, she sagged. After a long frozen moment, she disappeared through the doorway.

As Sabrina left, Pell felt a surprising surge of pity for her. She herself had once been in her place and knew what it felt like to be betrayed by Claude. He could be so smooth and convincing, so lighthearted and charming, that when the betrayal came it made it that much more painful. It seemed the pair had been drawn together by their weaknesses—Claude for his love of money and luxury and Sabrina for her desire for revenge. Pell didn't harbor hate for either of them, only pity—for it seemed they both lacked the ability to really love another human being or give of themselves.

Sighing wearily, Mr. Peebles now looked at Pell. "Go ahead and open your letter, my dear," he advised kindly. "It's the last thing your father ever wrote in his life. Actually he dictated it to me, then scrawled your name on the envelope with his own hand."

Pell's fingers trembled as she studied the thick envelope, and unaccountably she found she could not open it.

With a brief glance at the solicitor, Alex took the envelope and ripped it open himself. "Go ahead, read it, love," he said, gazing at her tenderly. "Something tells me it should be quite interesting."

She unfolded the pages and began reading in a tense voice.

" 'My darling Pell,' " the letter began. " 'By this time, I am sure you have gone through many adventures and may, in fact, be quite cross with me. I only hope that with the assistance of Alex and Mr. Peebles, I have been a better father to you in death than I was while living. Please keep in mind that I have always loved you dearly and only wanted what was best for you. You may also rest assured that I did indeed love your mother and was quite distressed that our relationship should have ended as it did. On returning from India, where you were constantly in my thoughts, I became obsessed with finding you and securing your future before I died.' "

Pell paused to take a breath, and as she continued reading, her voice trembled a bit. " 'It has always been my firm opinion that fate is a rather fickle lady and needs as much assistance as she can obtain. On the day I heard that Alex had also returned to England, a plan began to form in my head. Some would call it foolish, even wicked, but in my condition, it seemed the only plan available.

" 'It is my sad duty to now inform you that, although I was once quite rich, I died in reduced circumstances. During the course of my lengthy illness, I made many bad financial decisions and lost the great fortune that I had accumulated during my years in India. To make a long story short, my dear, the coffers are empty . . . and I feel brokenhearted to tell you that I have manipulated your trust in me. You see, my darling, the bitter truth is that you have no inheritance . . . no inheritance whosoever.' "

Pell sat back and the sheets filled with Mr. Peebles's fine handwriting fluttered into her lap. She could scarcely credit it. For half a year she had considered herself an heiress, and now she found that she was as penniless as the day when Alex had taken her from Holloway House of

Detention. Wondering about his reaction, she stared at his taut face, realizing he was as shocked as she was.

She took a handkerchief from her reticule and pressed it against her damp forehead, then swallowed hard, feeling a bit light-headed. Totally baffled, she stared at the solicitor's concerned face.

His eyes warm, he walked to her chair and patted her arm. "There, there, my dear. I know it is a great shock— and how I've dreaded delivering the blow."

"It seems impossible," Alex said in a puzzled tone. "Utterly impossible."

"It's all in the letter," the old man said, giving him a worried look. "Everything is explained there."

Pell felt the weight of two expectant gazes, and, with shaking hands, she picked up the sheets, but emotion misted her eyes and the words ran together on the page. "Everything is so blurred . . ." She trailed off.

Still standing, Alex put a comforting arm about her shoulders, then took the pages himself and continued in his rich baritone voice.

" 'Please forgive me, my dear, but I could think of no other way to rescue you from your plight. I had just enough money left to see you through a coming-out ball and finance you for six months. I stipulated that you should take a husband before receiving your supposed fortune so that you would have the security of marriage. I could do this without fear, for I was sure Alex would guide you into a suitable alliance.

" 'Here I must chuckle a bit, as I know the prospect of a fortune hastened the courting procedure. From my experience in the military, I have learned that an imagined threat or reward often accomplishes the desired results as effectively as the real thing. Being acquainted with your beauty and spirit, I see no way that your husband could consider himself cheated. At any rate, you were innocent in the whole affair and all blame for the deceit must rest on my shoulders. I feel that your new husband will see the wisdom in remaining quiet about the whole situation, for

I'm sure he would not want the world to know he has been gulled by a dead man. And you yourself must understand that my deceit was necessary, for I doubt you would have submitted yourself to such a demanding transformation without great motivation.

" 'My common sense tells me that Alex will be present when you are given this letter. All I can say to you, my friend, is please forgive the desperate attempt of an old man to see his beloved daughter well-situated. I rest assured that you will take the whole affair as a great adventure. Knowing how you detest pomposity, I'm certain you had great fun passing off a fruit-vendor as a lady and pulling the wool over the eyes of every snob in London. If you are reproached by the stuffed shirts, simply blame everything on me—a crusty old general who spent too much time in the Indian sun. If you yourself have become entranced with Pell's charms and decided to take her as your bride, I would be very pleased with the situation and consider the whole operation a great success.

" 'I am certain you are now both feeling shocked, deceived, and manipulated—and quite rightly so. I only hope that the years will bring everything into focus, and that you may both find it in your hearts to forgive a foolish old man. I beg that you hold no animosity toward Mr. Peebles as I played on the good man's sympathy without mercy and swore him to utter silence until the six months were over.

" 'To you, Alex, my comrade in arms, many thanks for making a dying man's last wish come true.

" 'Again, my darling Pell, let me pledge my love to you. You were the joy of my youth and the hope of my last days. Devotedly, General Phillip Fairchild.' "

When Alex's resonant voice faded away, he slipped the pages into the envelope and handed it back to Pell. As if by tacit consent, they all remained respectfully quiet for a moment; then Alex crossed his arms and his mouth twitched almost imperceptibly. Gradually he began chuckling, and finally he laughed outright, his eyes glistening with humor.

Pell drew in her breath and looked up at him. Too shocked to speak, she could only stare, wondering what had possessed him.

At last, he managed to contain his mirth and glanced at her and Mr. Peebles. "The crafty old fox," he said softly, his voice tinged with admiration. "After he has totally re-arranged our lives for the last six months, he lies in the safety of his grave, protected from our rebukes. What a sly old man he really was—manipulating everything to his liking as he lay dying, making everyone swear that they would obey his orders after he was gone!"

"You're not angry at him?" Pell ventured quietly, astounded at his reaction.

Alex laughed again and shook his head. "Angry? How could I be angry? The situation is far too humorous. I can now see that he wanted *me* to marry you from the start. Realizing the alliance of an earl and a fruit-vendor was unthinkable, he devised this wild scheme which involved turning you into a lady, knowing I would be constantly exposed to your charms.

"The old fox was a wonderful tactician," he went on with a crooked smile. "According to his plan, he knew you would be transformed into a lady, and, in the unlikely event I *didn't* lose control of myself, necessitating me to do the gentlemanly thing, your looks and supposed fortune would ensure you would find another man. No wonder he gave me specific orders to find you a husband with his own money." He laughed a bit more. "And to think how I struggled with the thought of betraying him."

A hot blush leaped to Pell's cheeks and she glanced at Mr. Peebles to learn his reaction. Seemingly mesmerized by Alex's words, he stood quietly, an interested look on his face.

"He thought of everything," Alex went on. "If I didn't marry you, your *fortune* would ensure another husband. Once the poor devil, whoever he might be, realized you were penniless, the fear of being the laughingstock of London would make him accept the situation with good grace." Alex's smile broadened, and he nodded with satisfaction. "There was no way his plan could fail."

Mr. Peebles put a hand on Alex's arm. "I felt dreadful keeping everything from you, but there was nothing I could do. The general said we had to keep you in the dark. He made me swear, actually *swear* on the holy writ, that I would keep his secret. We were old school friends and it's true he played on my sympathy without mercy. He said he would die with deep regret, and Pell would be lost to a wasted life if I didn't cooperate with his scheme." He shook his silvery head. "He was old and feeble, but he could still be terribly persuasive."

Alex chuckled softly. "Yes, I know. On the day he died, he was drinking whiskey and issuing orders as if he meant for everyone to obey them immediately." He looked at Pell, smiling. "We've all been taken in royally by a stubborn old man who wanted to play God with our lives. But he was so clever about it that I cannot find it in my heart to dislike him."

Pell blinked at him, surprised that he had taken the bad news with such good grace, for she still felt numb with shock. What would they do now that their fortunes had been radically reversed? Without her inheritance they would lose Stanton Hall and eventually the mansion on Adam's Row.

Mr. Peebles adjusted his tie, and, swallowing nervously, looked at Alex. "Perhaps this isn't the time to speak of it, but I . . . I have something on my mind that we must discuss."

Alex tilted his brow inquiringly. "It seems this is a day for startling revelations. Go ahead. I doubt you can surprise me after what I've just heard."

The solicitor ran a finger around his tight collar. Pell wasn't sure, but she thought that he might have blushed.

"I need to ask you something of a delicate nature," he began in a hesitant voice. "Since you are the head of the

Chancery-Brown family, I felt it would be advisable to speak with you before implementing my plans." He smoothed back his hair. "I wish to marry your aunt. That is, if you would consider the alliance satisfactory."

Alex smiled slowly. "You want to marry Aunt Violet?" he asked with some amusement.

"Yes indeed," the older man replied quickly. "During my visits, we've become well acquainted and I find her a delightful lady. I've already spoken with her, and if it were agreeable with you, a quiet marriage could be arranged."

Alex shook hands with Mr. Peebles. "I would consider the alliance very favorable, sir," he replied amiably. "It gives me great pleasure to know that my aunt has found happiness."

So that was the wonderful news Aunt Violet had spoken about, Pell thought. No wonder she had such a glow about her lately. In her golden years she would capture the joy that had escaped her for so long. She pictured the old lady relaxing by the hearth, reading one of her romance novels, while Mr. Peebles sat at his desk working on a legal case—and despite the shock she had just received concerning her inheritance, happiness pulsed through her.

It seemed that a weight had been taken from Mr. Peebles's shoulders. He smiled broadly, looking ten years younger. After a moment of awkward silence, he cleared his throat and glanced at a grandfather clock that stood in the corner of his office. "Do you have other questions about the general's letter?" he asked, looking at Pell. "If so, I'm afraid we will have to hurry," he went on with a smile. "I have some other appointments."

With some surprise, Pell realized that he was signaling to her and Alex that the meeting was over. It was time to go. Time to go and decide what they would do now that their destiny had been totally altered. Feeling as if her legs would scarcely support her, she bade Mr. Peebles goodbye, then, clutching the general's letter in her hand, she let Alex escort her from the office.

Cool air wafted over her face and the noise of the street

rose up to meet her as they walked to the waiting carriage in the gathering twilight. What an interesting day this had turned out to be, she thought with an ironic smile. She and Sabrina had lost a fortune while Aunt Violet had gained happiness. At least she could be thankful that the fates had smiled on a kindly old lady. But her own concerns pulled at her whirling mind, dimming her joy for Aunt Violet.

Then, like a quick blow, another thought hit. She had been so busy worrying about their personal lives that she had temporarily forgotten about the soup kitchen she had dreamed of opening in the East End. When the full realization of that loss struck her, all her hopelessness and confusion mingled together and she had to fight back her trembling emotions with every ounce of strength she possessed.

After Alex had helped her into the carriage and closed the door behind them, the equipage rattled away from the curb. "Oh, Alex," she sighed. "What are we going to do? We've lost everything!"

He wrapped a strong arm about her. "You've only lost the promise of a fortune ... something you never had. Think what you've gained ... how far you've come ... all the way from Cat and Wheel Alley on your courage and pluck to be the most sought-after debutante of the season." He closed his hand over hers and gave it a reassuring squeeze. "You've set the whole of London society on its ear."

She gazed into his thoughtful eyes. "You enjoyed it all, didn't you?"

He tenderly cupped her chin. "Yes, every minute of it! It was one of the greatest adventures of my life." His eyes glinted with pride. "Remember how thrilled we were when you first learned to read? When you memorized your background speech?" He laughed a little. "Do you recall the moment I escorted you into your coming-out ball and Lord Mitford spilled his drink on his vest? And remember the triumphal welcome you received at Henley regatta?"

He hugged her close. "We've had a grand time ... the time of our lives!"

Pell felt her spirits lifting even as he spoke.

"Remember our little talk last night before we went to sleep?" he asked.

"Yes," she replied softly. "But I didn't know it would be so prophetic!"

He gave a rich laugh. "I think we should go home and open a bottle of champagne to celebrate."

"Celebrate?" she echoed with wide eyes.

"That's right," he said, kissing her forehead. "Let's celebrate our love tonight ... We can always worry tomorrow."

That evening, Pell sat on a leather sofa in the library, dressed in a comfortable day dress of pink silk, its skirt decorated with riots of ruffles. Holding the little picture of Alex, Major Hempstead, and her father in her hands, she studied the general's stern face, trying to understand how he could have devised a scheme that drastically altered so many lives. As she looked at the picture, Alex walked into the room, and, taking her hand, sat down by her side.

After they had left Chelsea, the weather had turned damp and chilly and a small fire now crackled in the marble fireplace, sending out the sweet aroma of burning wood. Outside of the servants, they were alone, for Mr. Peebles had arrived earlier to escort Aunt Violet to his brother's home to meet her future relations.

"Are you thinking about the general?" Alex asked as he took the picture from her hands and placed it on an end table.

"Yes," she responded softly. "During my childhood, a little dart of pain always pierced my heart when I thought of him. For years I both hated and loved him, but doubted he had any feelings for me at all. But today when I found out what desperate measures he had taken to better my life as he lay dying, I realized that he *did* love me."

Alex smiled and took her hand again. "Yes, I'm sure he

did." He caressed her fingers and chuckled. "Actually, for a dying man with no funds, few contacts, and a vindictive wife, he played his last hand with great flair." He rubbed his thumb over her wedding ring. "And quite successfully I might add."

Pell stared at the leaping flames, trying to weigh everything in her mind. "I've forgiven him, you know."

"Forgiven him?"

"Yes ... I've always borne some resentment against him, but after reading his letter, I believe he was as much a prisoner of his world as my mother and I were of ours."

Alex's fingers curved under her chin. "Exactly," he said in a quiet tone. He was dressed in the same fine suit he had worn to Mr. Peebles's office, and with his black hair, square determined jaw, and sensual eyes, the very sight of him made her heart beat a little faster.

"He brought us together," she continued in a stronger voice. "For that, I will always be grateful. But the sad fact remains that I have no inheritance."

Alex studied her with twinkling eyes. "That statement is utterly false," he said as his hand brushed her hair from her neck. Looking thoughtful, he stood and walked to a wine stand where an open bottle of chilled champagne waited. "What about your courage ... your spirit ... your quick mind? The general left you a fabulous legacy."

She smiled at him. "I'm not sure how that can get us out of our present situation." She studied Alex's amused face as he took the champagne from the slushy ice, then filled two glasses and returned to her side. "You're taking this all very calmly," she said, taking the bubbling wine from his hand.

A grin shot across his face, then Lord Tavistock, peer of the realm, member of Parliament, and honored recipient of the Victoria Cross, cocked a brow. "Well, luv, when we're totally done in, we can always pig in with Kid Glove Rosie, you knows. She ain't one to turn true friends aside." He gave her a reproachful look. "Your lack of faith is enough to make a saint swear on his blessed liver!"

Pell burst out laughing, and, placing the champagne aside, she laughed until tears moistened her eyes.

Chuckling himself, Alex reached inside his jacket and handed her his spotless white handkerchief. As she wiped away her tears, she realized how much he had changed. Could this warm man who teased her so lightly when they were in the depths of despair be the same disciplinarian she had met six months ago in Holloway House of Detention?

He sat down on the sofa once more, and, looking more serious, took the handkerchief and put it away. "You know," he remarked, sipping his champagne, "you weren't the only one who received a shock today, my darling. Sabrina is in a rather precarious position herself."

"Yes ... I realize that," Pell answered, picturing the look on Sabrina's face when she'd heard the bad news. "Do you think Claude will divorce her?"

Alex slid his warm fingers over her bare arm and regarded her thoughtfully. "I think it is more his style to simply desert her. With the stigma of the desertion, and no money to finance a new start somewhere else, Sabrina will find life among the English aristocracy very unpleasant indeed."

His gray eyes soft and contemplative, he set his glass aside, then rose and moved to the desk, where he opened his mother's music box. As the tinkling music floated over the library, he came back to the sofa, and, bowing his dark head, extended his hand. "May I have the pleasure of this dance, Countess?"

Pell rose and his strong fingers grasped hers, then, with quiet authority, he pulled her close to his hard chest. As they danced about the library, she felt his fingers pressing into her back, and, wrapped in his embrace, all her fears seemed to slip away. "I suppose we should start thinking about our future," she said quietly.

He gazed down at her with a hint of a smile. "Yes, I suggest a modest cottage in the Cotswolds where I'll be utterly happy with you. Perhaps I could set up a law practice in Cheltenham." As they glided about the library to the tinkling music, he held her closer. "Think of all those warm summer evenings filled with the scent of roses . . . or better yet, those chilly winter nights with a crackling fire and a cup of hot cider," he said with a little squeeze to her waist. "Since we won't be flitting from one Mayfair gala to the next anymore, we'll be forced to find other diversions to amuse us." He cocked a brow. "I'm sure we'll be able to think of *something,*" he said with a twinkle in his eyes.

They danced for a while longer, then she softly asked, "What about all those old bills you've wanted to pay back?"

Alex sighed heavily, then smiled. "All this has taught me something I'll never forget. If I'm ever able to, I'll take care of the debts. But I now know that it's more a matter of honor than obligation. Perhaps it was a bit proud of me to try to make up for my father's and brother's lives, when one life is enough for anyone to live." He kissed her forehead. "I've found what I want."

As the music box stopped playing, Pell nestled against him, and an idea suddenly popped into her head. "Alex," she said, searching his face, "why don't we go to India?" Before he could reply, she hurried on, "I know you love it there, and we could live cheaply."

A thoughtful expression filled his eyes. "Yes, that's a possibility," he said after a moment. "I do have contacts there and . . ."

Just then, there was a noise in the entrance hall, and Hadji walked into the library with Chi Chi perched on his shoulder. The servant's eyes held a look of rapture, and Alex put out a hand to steady his trembling arm. "Oh, sahib," Hadji said in a hushed voice. "You have a visitor . . . an Indian gentleman, and I am thinking he is very important indeed."

Alex ran a hand through his hair and narrowed his eyes. "An Indian gentleman, you say? That's strange. I haven't made the acquaintance of any Indian gentlemen since I returned to London."

The servant's large brown eyes became larger still. "Oh, sahib, he is saying he has a matter of utmost importance to bring to your attention. I am thinking it is imperative that you speak with him immediately."

Alex glanced at the library doors. "From where does our visitor hail?"

"Delhi, sir," Hadji explained, his voice quiet with wonder. "He's from Delhi, and he is being associated with Major Hempstead."

Alex smiled and hugged Pell to him. "Associated with Tom? Well, by all means, show him in then."

Hadji returned with a tall Indian gentleman dressed in a fine white suit and an elegant silk turban. The graceful, dark-skinned man carried himself with authority and Pell could tell that his clothes were of the best materials. Businesslike, yet warm in manner, he paused to formally bow his head. As if he were announcing royalty, Hadji extended his hand and proclaimed, "Sahib, may I be presenting Mr. Baijal, arrived in London only this morning."

When Chi Chi looked longingly at the gentleman's turban, Alex slid a warning gaze at Hadji, who removed the monkey from his shoulders and held him in his arms.

Alex met Mr. Baijal's hand with a warm clasp, and the foreigner bowed his head respectfully once again. "Sir," he said, with a forthright gaze, "I have the pleasant duty to bring you greetings from your friend Major Hempstead, with whom I spoke immediately before I sailed for England." His dark, liquid eyes glistened with anticipation. "I made his acquaintance after you left India, but he spoke of you often and bade me contact you as soon as I arrived in the city. I am a banker, and, like yourself, his trusted associate." The man's deep, rich voice was well modulated and his English perfect. Pell guessed that he came from one of the finest families in India, and had likely attended an English university in his youth.

His dark eyes swept over her dubiously, then locked

again on Alex's face. "Sir, I have come with good tidings, but I must speak to you privately."

Alex smiled at Pell. "May I present my wife, the Countess of Tavistock. You may speak freely in her presence."

Gazing in her direction, Mr. Baijal put his hands together and bowed low in a gesture of respect. "Forgive me, memsahib. I was not informed that the earl had taken a wife."

"Won't you have a seat, sir?" Alex offered, indicating an overstuffed chair.

Mr. Baijal moved a searching gaze over the library. "If it is all the same to you, sir, the convenience of a desk would be helpful."

Holding Chi Chi in the crook of his arm, Hadji rushed forward and pulled back Alex's desk chair, then positioned another chair near it for the mysterious guest.

When the Indian gentleman was comfortably seated, he reached inside his suit jacket and removed a soft velvet packet. His dark eyes lit with a happy glow as he said, "Major Hempstead was entirely too busy to sail for England, but since I have business in the financial district, he asked me to give you a bit of splendid news."

"I'm afraid I don't understand."

His white teeth flashing in a broad smile, Mr. Baijal flicked open the packet with his thumb and poured a glittering cascade of blood-red rubies onto Alex's desk. "It gives me great joy to inform you that you are now a very rich man indeed," he announced warmly.

Pell drew in her breath as the rubies gleamed in the light from the green-shaded desk lamp. For a moment her mind reeled with bewilderment and her heart hammered out of control, then, with trembling legs, she went to Alex's side, scarcely able to believe her eyes. A dazed expression suffused his face, as, with a crack of laughter, he bent over the desk and scooped up a handful of rubies, letting them slip between his fingers and clatter back to the desktop. With round eyes, Hadji stood frozen in amaze-

ment, a respectful distance behind Mr. Baijal, who beamed
with satisfaction.

"The jewels belong to you, sir, and there are many more
where these came from," the Indian remarked proudly. "Of
course, such a fabulous surprise had to be delivered personally. You see, after years of fruitless labor, Major
Hempstead hit a rich deposit. The vein is so rich, he has
employed extra labor to help him mine it. Great quantities
of rubies have already been extracted—enough to make
your half-interest in the mine worth millions."

Alex laughed with satisfaction. "So Tom's dream did
materialize after all," he said, holding one of the larger rubies in a shaft of lamplight.

Mr. Baijal stood and withdrew an envelope from his
jacket. "Yes, and yours too it seems." He handed the en
velope to Alex. "Major Hempstead has sent instructions
about the financial arrangements. Everything is in the letter. Let me simply say that an enormous sum of money
will be deposited in your account in the Bank of England.
Your faith in your friend has made you a wealthy man, sir.
An outrageously wealthy man." He stood and adjusted his
tunic. "I will be staying at the Dorchester while in London. If you will be so kind as to meet me there for lunch
tomorrow, I will furnish you with more details concerning
your good fortune."

With trembling hands, Pell trailed her fingers over the
pile of sparkling rubies, too stunned and confused to
speak. Conflicting emotions bombarded her bewildered
mind. How was this possible? How could this miracle
have happened when moments ago their future looked so
modest? Her eyes wide with amazement, she stared at Mr.
Baijal.

Smiling once more, he walked across the library, pre-
ceded by Hadji, who hurried to the doors, and, bowing
profusely, held them open for him.

As soon as he was gone, Alex swept Pell into his arms,
and, lifting her up, whirled her feet from the floor. "Did

you hear that? We're rich again. Rich as Croesus, it seems!"

Their sudden change of fortune had left her dizzied, but she laughed for joy as he swung her from the floor and settled her back down again.

His eyes wild with happiness, Hadji ran back into the room with Chi Chi clinging to his shoulder. Laughing himself, the servant whisked Alex's empty glass from the end table, quickly splashed more champagne into it, and rushed it back to his master. "On this blessed day, my illustrious master has risen from the ashes like a great turkey," he proclaimed triumphantly. "Eat, drink, and be merry! This is being a gold-letter day. Bottoms up. Down the hatch. And bumpers all around!"

Alex smiled and took a sip of the wine, then set it on the desk and pulled Pell against his chest.

Hadji danced about the library while Chi Chi shrieked and clung to his back. "Kismet has blessed our glorious master!" the Indian cried. "Once we were being poor, but now the mitten is on the other hand—and just in the pinch of time! I must tell everyone!"

Laughing and bouncing the monkey atop his shoulders, the servant scurried from the room, leaving the doors open behind him. Muted cries of "We are again being rich! We are again being rich!" filtered back into the library as his racing footsteps faded away.

The strength and warmth of Alex's arms now encircled Pell and she felt joy rising in her heart like the morning star. Their fate had been turned upside down yet again today, and as her emotions reeled from the sudden change, she fought feelings of disbelief. But from the corner of her eye, she saw the rubies glittering brightly on the desk, verifying that a miracle had happened. A sense of overpowering relief washed through her, leaving her shaken, but radiantly alive. Alex would be able to maintain his position as the Earl of Tavistock and they would have enough to keep them for the rest of their lives.

Lowering his head, Alex covered her mouth with his

own and stirred her senses with a delicious thrill of arousal. As he artfully traced her lips and grazed a finger over her breast, she flushed hotly. Aching desire washed through her body with the speed of quicksilver. It seemed that all they had experienced this afternoon had only drawn them closer. The deep kiss carried a special intensity and promised a night of glorious passion. At last he raised his head and gazed down at her, his face aglow with happiness. "What we've gone through today!" he whispered roughly. "From the depths of despair to the heights of joy. I can scarcely believe it has happened. We'll have enough money to visit India as often as we want, and we can open ten soup kitchens!"

As he caressed her hair and held her against him, she missed the pressure of his pocket watch, and, trailing her hand over his jacket, realized that it was missing. "Where's your watch?" she asked. "Have you lost it?"

A sheepish look came over his face as he checked his watch pocket and found that the timepiece was indeed gone. "Well, I'll be damned," he said thickly. "I *have* misplaced my watch."

A thrill of victory pricked Pell's heart, for to her this was the final manifestation of his transformation. Alex obey-the-rules Brown had lost his watch! She arched a brow. "Don't worry, guv'ner. Now that we's got enough money to singe an elephant, we can buy lots of watches. And I wants to buy lots of frilly gowns, too, I does. Great heaps of 'em, all bright red and purple—and I wants a hat with big red plumes, just like the one I 'ad when you brought me 'ere." She clutched his lapels. "And for supper tonight I wants some of those fat little birds with the frilly papers on their legs."

Alex chuckled and scooped her into his arms, then carried her from the library and started walking up the stairs to the second floor.

"Gaa . . . where are you a-takin' me, you blinkin' toff?" she teased, playfully pounding her fists against his back.

"If you thinks I'm loose as a bucket of soot, you're sadly mistaken. I gots my standards, I 'ave!"

"So have I. That's why I'm taking you to bed, you hot-blooded Cockney wench," he growled huskily. "You may have taken some of the starch out of my shirt, but I assure you that further south things remain as rock solid as the British Empire."

Pell laughed, then he kissed her again, making her heart flutter and her body thrill with delight. As he swung open the bedroom door, warmth glowed in her heart, for she had learned that there was something more important than a great inheritance, or protocol, or even the sacred honor of an English gentleman . . . something that could fill a gray London sky with dazzling sunshine. She had learned that the magic something was love.

Alex gazed down at her, his eyes shining with joy. "I love you, Pell Davis."

Tender emotion swelled in her heart as she replied, "The same to you with knobs on it, guv'ner!"

Avon Romances—
the best in exceptional authors and unforgettable novels!

THE LION'S DAUGHTER Loretta Chase
76647-7/$4.50 US/$5.50 Can

CAPTAIN OF MY HEART Danelle Harmon
76676-0/$4.50 US/$5.50 Can

BELOVED INTRUDER Joan Van Nuys
76476-8/$4.50 US/$5.50 Can

SURRENDER TO THE FURY Cara Miles
76452-0/$4.50 US/$5.50 Can

SCARLET KISSES Patricia Camden
76825-9/$4.50 US/$5.50 Can

WILDSTAR Nicole Jordan
76622-1/$4.50 US/$5.50 Can

HEART OF THE WILD Donna Stephens
77014-8/$4.50 US/$5.50 Can

TRAITOR'S KISS Joy Tucker
76446-6/$4.50 US/$5.50 Can

SILVER AND SAPPHIRES Shelly Thacker
77034-2/$4.50 US/$5.50 Can

SCOUNDREL'S DESIRE Joann DeLazzari
76421-0/$4.50 US/$5.50 Can

Avon Romantic Treasures

*Unforgettable, enthralling love stories,
sparkling with passion and adventure
from Romance's bestselling authors*

AWAKEN MY FIRE *by Jennifer Horsman*
76701-5/$4.50 US/$5.50 Can

ONLY BY YOUR TOUCH *by Stella Cameron*
76606-X/$4.50 US/$5.50 Can

FIRE AT MIDNIGHT *by Barbara Dawson Smith*
76275-7/$4.50 US/$5.50 Can

ONLY WITH YOUR LOVE *by Lisa Kleypas*
76151-3/$4.50 US/$5.50 Can

MY WILD ROSE *by Deborah Camp*
76738-4/$4.50 US/$5.50 Can

MIDNIGHT AND MAGNOLIAS *by Rebecca Paisley*
76566-7/$4.50 US/$5.50 Can

THE MASTER'S BRIDE *by Suzannah Davis*
76821-6/$4.50 US/$5.50 Can

A ROSE AT MIDNIGHT *by Anne Stuart*
76740-6/$4.50 US/$5.50 Can